God's Perfect Scar

by

Mike Johnson

authorHOUSE®

AuthorHouse™
1663 Liberty Drive, Suite 200
Bloomington, IN 47403
www.authorhouse.com
Phone: 1-800-839-8640

First published by AuthorHouse 9/1/08

ISBN: 978-1-4343-8817-9 (sc)
ISBN: 978-1-4343-8818-6 (hc)

Printed in the United States of America
Bloomington, Indiana

This book is printed on acid-free paper.

For Peter Bloomfield, Gene Johnson and Gene Johnson

Peter Bloomfield is a native of London. He is an alumnus of Christ Hospital School, a 1953 graduate of the Royal Military Academy at Sandhurst and a British Army veteran. We have been friends since 1979. For both *Warrior Priest* and *God's Perfect Scar*, he provided invaluable research assistance, including arranging a tour of Sandhurst for me. He now lives near Petworth, a village in West Sussex.

Gene Johnson graduated from Shelby, Ohio High School in 1944 and immediately enlisted in the United States Navy. He served on an LCS – Landing Craft Support – at Borneo, New Guinea and Okinawa. His vessel was designated LCS 23 and had a crew of some 60 men. He is my brother.

The second Gene Johnson, no relation but a dear friend, was born in 1931 in Manhattan and lived his entire life there – except for his Marine Corps service during the Korean War. Gene's two Marine jobs: jumping out of helicopters into the Yellow Sea to rescue downed jet pilots and conducting reconnaissance behind enemy lines. His base was a small, unnamed island off North Korea's coast. North Korean and Chinese forces knew he was there and often shelled his camp. I once held a large piece of shrapnel that nearly killed him. He died in 1992.

Also by Mike Johnson

Warrior Priest
Fate of the Warriors

CHAPTER 1

Auschwitz. A decorative black wrought iron gate, well-maintained red brick buildings, expansive and lovingly mowed and trimmed lawns. Today it looks eerily more like a manicured campus than a hellish death camp. It also is virtually silent. Visitors don't shout and seldom talk even at a conversational level. They whisper. They murmur. And they weep, softly, tears coursing down cheeks and onto hallowed ground.

To Kaz Majos late on the morning of October 5, 1944, Auschwitz looked and sounded precisely like its intended purpose. What he saw as he jumped down from a packed freight car at the Auschwitz train station was both horrifying and unutterably saddening, and the sounds were cacophonic. Black-booted red-faced German soldiers were stomping their feet and screaming, long whips were cracking, dogs with bared fangs were straining at leashes and growling furiously. Quivering children were clinging to parents, husbands and wives to each other. This malevolent greeting was at odds with what deportees had been told about conditions at so-called relocation camps. They were bewildered, shocked and terrified.

They had reason to be, Kaz was thinking. He had heard enough about this blot on humankind to know what was awaiting most arrivals. Kaz wasn't Jewish but Auschwitz, he knew, dealt death to more than Jews. Anyone regarded as subhuman, generally objectionable or an enemy of the state became a candidate for Auschwitz's gas chambers, gallows and crematoria. Kaz clearly qualified.

He drew a breath, semi-squatted, stood and then bent forward, hands reaching for his shoes, to unkink his legs and back. This is probably the only time I'll see this gate, he mused. Entering, not leaving. Arbeit macht frei. Work brings freedom. Those words, writ large, were atop the gate. The only freedom for me and my fellow Poles here will be freedom from fear and persecution. Lower the curtain of death. End the suffering. A one-eyed Polish Resistance leader can have no chance to survive Auschwitz. None. Not from what I've heard and not from what I'm seeing now. He sighed and closed his eyes.

Auschwitz and nearby Birkenau, also called Auschwitz II, didn't begin as death factories. In the spring of 1940 Heinrich Himmler, Hitler's

1

chief lieutenant, was looking for a location to build a new prison camp. In a remote corner of southwestern Poland near the town of Oswiecim, population 12,000, soon to be Germanized as Auschwitz, Himmler found abandoned Austrian artillery barracks. They included 20 single-story brick buildings. Nothing more. The setting was lovely. Meadows abloom with wild flowers. Foothills of the Carpathian Mountains looming close by. There also were daunting disadvantages – swamps, swarms of mosquitoes and polluted water. But one of Himmler's most dedicated subordinates, Major Rudolf Hoess, saw in Auschwitz two important advantages: it offered good railroad connections, and it was isolated from outside observation. "Hard work can transform this location into a valuable outpost for our Reich," wrote Hoess. And that was what Hoess and Himmler were visualizing – not a death camp but a detention center for thousands of Poles. "The need to establish law and order in the east is of paramount importance," Hoess reported to Berlin.

On September 1, 1939, when German forces invaded Poland, there were six major concentration camps in Germany, containing about 25,000 prisoners. At Auschwitz, Himmler told Hoess he was to build a camp for 10,000 prisoners, a camp that might expand to hold 50,000. They foresaw that those prisoners – Jews, Gypsies, political dissidents, captured enemy soldiers, intellectuals – would serve Germany's war effort, becoming armaments workers, producing munitions for Hitler's legions. In the nearby town of Dwory was a large I.G. Farben manufacturing plant. Many prisoners would work there – and slowly perish on starvation rations.

On May 20, 1940, 30 German criminals arrived at Auschwitz to begin transforming the former barracks into a sprawling camp. One of them, Bruno Brodniewicz, of Polish ancestry, was given the sad distinction of being given the number one. He was the first of perhaps four million hapless humans who would be shipped to Auschwitz.

Kaz Majos already was well acquainted with the sights and sounds of death. As a Resistance cell leader in Warsaw, he had risked his life often, had killed German soldiers and lost sight in his right eye to a German bullet on the opening day of the August 1944 Warsaw Uprising. The resulting scar ran from the outside edge of his right eye back across his temple. The disfigurement notwithstanding, Kaz, six feet tall, was handsome with

2

high cheekbones, blonde hair and a brilliant blue left eye. The right was clouded. Ironic, he reflected, I look like one of Hitler's sacred Ayrans. Kaz's shoulders were broad, his waist narrow, and he walked with athletic grace. Born in 1916, Kaz was 28. Not a long life, he thought. Eventful but short. I am not eager to die, but I am ready. Have been. Perhaps I can help ease the last moments of these people, say a few words outside the gas chamber, calm them.

Just ahead were two doctors. One of them was white-gloved Josef Mengele. He was whistling a Wagnerian opera and cursorily inspecting each arrival. A wave to the right meant a temporary reprieve, an assignment to hard labor on starvation rations. A wave to the left meant the gas chamber. Virtually all were waved left – most people older than 40, most women, almost all children under 15, families who asked to stay together. On average, only about ten percent of arrivals were waved to the right. Kaz was waved to the left.

My last hours. Was it worth it? Kaz asked himself. My life? I think so. Will there be anyone to remember me? To mourn me? Not if all my friends and family not already dead die in this madness. The Nazis will execute me and perhaps record my death in one of their infernal logbooks. They keep count of everything. Maybe their own farts. Kaz silently chortled. He heard – felt – a whip crack near his blind eye. Should I let them execute me without resisting? One more time? Should I punch a guard? Seize his machine pistol? Kill a guard or two? I would be shot immediately, no doubt, and that is the most merciful end I could hope for. But if I do something like that, the rest of these people will panic. Their terror will know no bounds. Some still have hope. False hope but I cannot destroy that. Gas me. I've heard that's the way most are murdered here. Choking on gas. I am ready. God knows that.

✝✝✝

In Shelby, Ohio the two babies were just beginning their lives. They were twins – a boy and girl – born three weeks earlier to Tom and Bridgett Brecker. Tom considered the babies his second miracle. The first had been surviving the sinking of the aircraft carrier USS Hornet at the battle of Santa Cruz Island on October 26-27, 1942. Tom had been a deck fireman and had lost his left foot to shrapnel in the fearsome Japanese attack that,

3

during a seven-minute span, included seven falling bombs, two crashing dive bombers and two torpedoes.

Bridgett was the younger sister of Theresa Hassler who was in Europe serving as an Army nurse. On October 1, 1944, Bridgett had written Theresa to tell her the news about the births. *We are so thrilled! Tom and I. Both our parents. The little darlings are just perfect!* Their names – Theresa in honor of Bridgett's sister and Jack – given name John – after Tom's oldest brother who was serving as a chaplain with the 82nd Airborne Division in Europe.

Tom and Bridgett had settled into a cozy three bedroom prewar ranch house on Mansfield Avenue near the city limit sign. On this October 5 little Jack was lying in a bassinet while little Theresa was at her mother's breast, sucking in the milk of life.

✝✝✝

At that same moment 15-year-old Michael Cornelius was celebrating life, sitting astride one of the four massive bronze lions in London's Trafalgar Square. He was a strapping boy at five feet ten inches, with black hair and gray eyes, the left one of which opened less than the right. Michael was oblivious to the pigeon droppings on the lion. He was exultant, arms thrust above his head, celebrating the Allies' progress in France. His baritone voice – he was a good singer in his school choir – carried his cry of "May the Jerries continue their not so jolly journey – back to Germany" across the square. Perched on another of the lions was Michael's pal Kendall Thorne who answered to K. He also was 15 and was two inches taller than Michael. Towering over both of them was Admiral Horatio Nelson atop his 185-foot column, surveying the horizons.

"K," Michael shouted, "look!" He was pointing to a mounted bobby entering the square from Whitehall Street. Michael slid off the lion and went loping toward the police officer. "Wonderful, isn't it, sir? We are really taking it to Hitler's Nazis. What a mad sop he is. My dad is a major."

"It's past due," the aging police officer smiled. "Well past due. And I'm certain your dad is doing his bit."

A thought popped into Michael's excited mind. "Sir? Would you let me ride with you? Around the square?"

The veteran bobby's surprise showed clearly in his widened eyes. The occasional parent had asked to have a child's picture taken with the bobby on his saddle. But a teenage boy, asking for himself. That was unprecedented and granting his request would be highly irregular. If seen, he'd no doubt be reprimanded, perhaps disciplined formally. Then he removed his left foot from its stirrup. "Put your foot in there, you fine son of a soldier, and swing up behind me."

Michael was spirited but hardly a frivolous lad. His youth notwithstanding, he possessed seriousness of understanding and intent. During the 1940 Battle of Britain, he was among thousands of London children evacuated to outlying towns and villages, in his case Petworth in West Sussex, a 90-minute train ride south of Waterloo Station. From the village's picturesque market square he had watched German bombers droning toward British targets – the Thames River docklands and the city itself – and he had craned his neck, observing numerous dogfights. He knew the sacrifices his Army father, who had gone ashore at Sword Beach on D-Day, was making. And now, back in London, he had seen the devastation wrought by German bombs and rockets. Michael was thinking he might one day join the British Army. Today, though, he was experiencing scarcely bridled teenage joy. The bobby's horse was stepping smartly around Trafalgar Square, and Michael waved happily at his friend K.

✝✝✝

Half a world away in Wellington, New Zealand another 15-year-old also was contemplating her future, but not as a soldier. Lucy Crispin was weeping. Not from sadness but acute, grinding pain. A rehabilitation specialist was urging Lucy to continue lifting iron weights with her left arm and hand, slightly withered and clawed by an attack of that twentieth century scourge – polio. Rehabilitation was something Lucy had undertaken willingly, but its rigorous demands induced suffering and tears. The draining session at last ended, Lucy now was reading a newspaper article on the war while listening to a radio account of the Allies' rapid progress. But she was feeling no joy. The article was reporting the number of New Zealanders wounded in fighting, and Lucy was beginning to dream about becoming a nurse. She was visualizing her crown of curly brown hair capping her white-uniformed five feet five inches. She put the paper down, stood, walked to her bedroom and studied herself in the dresser mirror. She smiled her slightly crooked smile – the left corner of her lips elevated above the right – and addressed her reflection: Yes, I could do that. I could treat the wounded and the sick. I could see the torn flesh, the scorched skin and not be squeamish. Lucy's voice was soft but her words were spoken as crisply as her surname might suggest. "I need to be involved," she said aloud. "It's in my being. I can feel it."

† † †

"Hitler sowed the wind. Now we will reap the whirlwind." Joseph Stalin was speaking to Vyacheslav Molotov, his minister of foreign affairs since 1939, and Laurenti Beria, deputy prime minister since 1941 and director of state security, an organization that included the deservedly dreaded secret police.

Stalin, five feet six inches, was standing beside the expansive desk in his birch-paneled Kremlin office. Despite his age, 65, Stalin regularly worked 16 to 18 hours a day. He had been born in 1879 in Gori, Georgia as Iosif Vissarionovich Dzhugashvili. His father was a shoemaker who died when Stalin was 11. After elementary schooling he attended Tiflis Theological Seminary where he was a good student but a radical one who preferred reading Karl Marx to religious tracts. Seminary staff grew weary of young Stalin's obstinacy and expelled him before graduation.

Now on this October day in 1944 he was quite satisfied with the military situation. "Let our army continue to rest. Keep them on the east bank of the Vistula while the Germans and Poles go about killing each other," he was saying to Molotov and Beria. "Save bullets, men too. The Poles' uprising in Warsaw ended with their surrender on October 2. But let the Germans do the dirty work of clearing out the survivors. And let them finish dynamiting the city before we cross the river. Typical of Hitler. The man has a vision, I'll give him that. But his judgments are often rash and now are proving ruinous. The Poles turned out to be tougher fighters than he or Himmler imagined. We could have warned them," Stalin chortled. He was alluding to the defeat the Poles had handed the Russians in 1919. "Now in his rage he is leveling what's left of Warsaw. Stupid. That will only make it easier for our troops to cross the Vistula."

"He knows we are coming," said Molotov. "You would think someone in his inner circle would caution him. Make him see that a razed city means less cover for his soldiers."

"Perhaps," Stalin said, fingering his bushy mustache, "they have tried. But not too hard." He chuckled coldly, and Molotov and Beria followed his lead with their own mirthless chortling. They were well schooled in taking cues from their ruthless boss.

"Once our army crosses the river," observed Molotov, pointing toward the wall map behind Stalin's desk, "we should make short work of the Wehrmacht. We have more men and weapons, and they are losing heart. I'm sure the more thoughtful of them know the war is lost. Lost since we captured Paulus and his Sixth Army and lost since the Americans and British invaded France. I've heard Hitler was actually foaming when the Allies liberated Paris. That little jig of joy he danced on the Champs Elysees in 1940 must seem like a distant memory."

"Agreed," said Stalin. "Let's adjourn for now and meet again in the morning." Molotov and Beria nodded and turned to leave. "Oh, by the way," Stalin added casually, picking up a sheet of paper from the right front corner of his desk, "these men are to be liquidated. They are not loyal – enough." He handed the sheet to Molotov. "You sign the death warrants."

Molotov showed no visible reaction. He looked at the names on the list. There were 31. They included a range of senior and midlevel military officers and Soviet government officials. "Yes, of course." Molotov in Russian means "of the hammer." But that translation didn't apply to his relationship with the pitiless Stalin. After all, he was the leader who had disowned his soldier son Jacob who died after being captured by the Germans. Molotov and Beria held onto their jobs and lives when so many hadn't, by virtue of competence and unquestioning acquiescence.

More than once Molotov had been ordered to sign death warrants for victims of Stalin's paranoia-fueled purges. More than once he expected to see his name on one of those lists. If that happened, he knew, there would be no appeal and perhaps not even a brief show trial. Just an arrest followed quickly by a bullet in his head. By this time estimates put the victims of

Stalin's purges – executions, forced starvations and exiles to Siberia – into the millions with the count escalating. Unlike the Nazis, Stalin preferred not to keep precise records.

Born in 1890 Molotov bore scant resemblance to his boss. In a show of fashion loyalty, he did sport a bushy mustache. But his round face and high hairline contrasted with Stalin's square features and low forehead. Molotov wore wire-rimmed glasses whereas Stalin's piercing eyes needed no assistance. He was the only Bolshevik who consistently wore a suit and necktie instead of a military tunic. Outwardly dull – some thought Molotov boring in the extreme – he was sharp-minded. Stalin valued Molotov for his combination of toughness and smoothness. It was Molotov, though not seeing combat during the Russian revolution or World War I, who had pushed for hostility toward the West. During the early years of World War II he also had traveled to London and Washington to press for more war materiel – and for faster shipments to his beleaguered country. He was sufficiently successful to retain Stalin's confidence.

"As soon as Comrade Molotov signs the death warrants," said Beria, age 45, "I will see that they are carried out immediately – if that is your wish, Comrade Leader."

"It is."

CHAPTER 2

"Down. Stay down," Kim Il Sung whispered to his fellow Korean guerillas. "How many do you see?" he asked Sergeant Kwon Oh Bum.

Kwon adjusted his binoculars. "At least one hundred." A pause. "We've never attacked this close to a city before."

"We are closing in for the kill," Kim replied. "Those men down there might not know it, but the Japanese have lost this war. Their leaders know it. I think some have known it since they attacked Pearl Harbor. That was madness. Utter stupidity. It woke the sleeping bear. Anyone who attacks America is a fool. Stalin would never do that. Neither would we."

Kwon and 50 of their guerilla force were hidden among rocks on a mountainside, some 300 feet above the narrow dirt road. They were near

Wonsan, a port on Korea's east coast. Below them came their quarry, a company of Japanese Army troops, about 150 men, marching two abreast toward the city.

"Pass the word to the men to hold their fire," Kim whispered to Kwon. "I will fire the first shot and only when all their men are right below us."

Kwon nodded and carried out his leader's order. Kwon was 22 years old and a veteran of combat against the occupying Japanese who had brutally colonized Korea in 1910. He had a family – parents and two younger sisters – in Pyongyang. Kwon had killed often and with increasing ease. He stood five feet eight inches with piercing black eyes, and he found it difficult to smile.

Kim Il Sung, a decade older than Kwon, was born in 1912 in a village near Pyongyang in western Korea. His father was a school teacher. When Japan invaded Manchuria in 1931, later considered by many the first step toward the coming global conflagration, the family emigrated to China where father and son joined the Communist Party. Kim began fighting with guerillas against the Japanese in the early 1930s and soon ascended to leadership. He was smart, energetic, handsome and grimly determined to do all in his power to drive the repressive and vilified Japanese from his homeland.

"I see the end of their column now," Kwon whispered to Kim, handing the binoculars to his leader.

Kim studied the advancing Japanese, walking briskly on this crisp October morning. Then he lowered the binoculars to the ground and readied his rifle. Kwon did likewise, and the other guerillas prepared to fire.

"Show no mercy," Kim whispered to Kwon. "Kill them all. Take no prisoners. It is the only message the Japanese understand. Their Samurai mentality has much to recommend it, but it makes killing them all an easier matter. If we didn't finish them off, they would kill themselves before surrendering. They cannot tolerate defeat. And they find it difficult to retreat and regroup. They are too self-absorbed."

Kim inhaled deeply and exhaled slowly. He squeezed the trigger and a second later a fusillade of rifle rounds began tearing into the Japanese. Blood was squirting and chunks of flesh were flying in all directions. Shouts to disperse and screams and moans of agony rose from the road up the mountainside. Within moments 40 Japanese lay on the dusty surface, many dead, some wounded and crawling toward the roadside seeking cover.

Kim raised his right hand and waved vigorously to the other half of his force, positioned on the opposite mountainside. Immediately a second volley of fire ripped into the Japanese.

Now Kim shouted a command. "Grenades!"

From both mountainsides, guerillas began pulling pins and lobbing grenades that exploded above and among the Japanese, sending jagged shards into the flesh of the despised occupiers.

"Move down! Close the trap!" Kim shouted, and his men began descending, firing as they moved. They knew the Japanese would not surrender. Some might try to escape, but Kim's well-trained and experienced guerillas would prevent that. Already five guerillas from each side of the mountain nearest Wonsan were moving quickly down to the road to seal off the only possible escape route.

It took another half hour of fierce combat before all the Japanese had been hit. The last to die were the wounded. Kim's guerillas walked among them, calmly firing rounds into any Japanese body that so much as twitched.

✝✝✝

That same morning 150 miles to the west near Korea's Yellow Sea coast, the Park brothers were in high spirits. Older brother Park Min Shik was galloping a chestnut gelding on a hard-packed earthen road. A westerly breeze was streaming the horse's mane toward Min whose coal black hair was whipping back and away from his face. He was 15. Behind him on the saddle was his 15-year-old girlfriend, Ahn Kyong Ae. The sea-stirred breeze was straightening her long black hair that ordinarily fell below her shoulders. Both Min and Kyong were laughing joyously, if not entirely carefree.

Standing in the middle of the road about a hundred yards ahead was Park Han Kil, Min's younger brother by a year. He was waving his arms high above his head, urging Min to push the gelding to racing speed.

Both Min and Han were handsome strapping boys, square-jawed with wide-set coal black eyes and matching hair. They were broad-shouldered and narrow-waisted. Min stood five feet eleven inches with Han an inch shorter. They were bigger than most of their countrymen but also reflected Koreans' standing as the largest of the Asian peoples.

Kyong stood five feet four inches. Her black eyes sparkled like a pair of polished onyx. She was in love with Min and he with her at a time when many Korean parents still preferred arranged pairings. Min and Kyong were unconcerned, not because they foresaw rebelling against parental wedding wishes but because both sets of parents thought well of each other's child. That was particularly true of Min's parents in nearby Kaesong. Min's father, Park Bong Suk , and his mother, Park Soon Im, owned a general store, and they were genuinely fond of Kyong.

As the handsome horse neared Han, arms now at his sides, Min pulled back firmly on the reins. The gelding snorted and threw back its head as though endorsing Min's horsemanship.

At the edge of a rice paddy beside the road a farmer stood watching. "I should tell Colonel Fukunaga how you exercise his horse," the farmer grumbled.

Min took on a look of patently false remorse. "I am shamed by my treatment of this poor Japanese brute. He deserves only the gentlest handling – like Colonel Fukunaga himself."

The farmer's hard visage softened. He began laughing and returned to his work, his head shaking at the boy's infectious good humor.

"Do you think Fukunaga has ever ridden his horse as fast as you do?" Han asked Min as he and Kyong slid from the saddle.

"With Fukunaga in the saddle this horse knows only strutting – like his master."

Colonel Takeo Fukunaga commanded the Japanese colonial garrison headquartered at Kaesong, about 15 miles inland from the Yellow Sea. Kaesong was a major railroad hub, connecting Pyongyang to the north with Seoul to the south. During his years in Kaesong, Fukunaga had deservedly earned a reputation for punitive treatment of his Korean subjects. He unrelentingly had implemented Japanese policy that required Koreans to adopt Japanese names and learn Japanese. He punished even the mildest resistance with lashings and beatings. Fukunaga meticulously fostered his image as grimly austere and militarily rigid. Maintaining control and thus his own security was his highest priority.

Min was right. Fukunaga wouldn't dream seriously of riding his horse faster than a distinguished canter. That's why he employed the Park brothers to exercise his mount on nearby country roads.

One thing went unspoken because it wasn't necessary. The boys were not to abuse the animal. They abidingly vilified Fukunaga but their hatred was not to extend to the horse. Any evidence of maltreatment and Fukunaga's response could well mean the offender's public execution, likely with a bullet to the back of the neck or with Fukunaga's sword separating head from shoulders.

That wasn't something Fukunaga longed for. He could easily be as tough as policy enforcement demanded. But he was educated and thoughtful and preferred to spend his time concentrating on how to survive the war he knew his beloved nation was losing. More than once he wished he were based in eastern Korea, nearer his Japanese homeland. Returning safely to Japan from Kaesong could be problematic. Fukunaga kept a short hara-kari sword in his office but hoped that it could remain permanently in its decorative leather case.

On this October morning he heard the clip-clop of his horse's shoes on the hard but unpaved street. He rose from his desk chair, smoothed his tunic, stepped outside and permitted himself a small smile. A handsome boy astride his mount, another boy and a pretty girl walking at its flanks. I'll be lucky to get back to Japan, Fukunaga reflected, but my horse will have no chance. None at all. In the war's final days – and they are coming soon enough – order will end. Chaos will break out and rule. My horse will become transportation for a Korean farmer – or food for Korean tables. There will be no escaping that fate.

Chapter 3

Aline Gartner looked furtively around the huge I.G. Farben munitions plant. Prisoner-workers were completing a long shift. A once striking woman, now gaunt, Aline breathed deeply, attempting to will away fatigue and hunger pangs. Her ultimate fate, she figured, had been sealed from the moment she had been shoved into a boxcar and begun the long journey to Auschwitz.

She was surprised to still be alive. The trip in the suffocating, filthy boxcar had killed many and sickened still more. Nothing to eat, no water, only an overflowing bucket an excuse for sanitation.

Most arriving women were gassed immediately. And then cremated. Aline hadn't become a prostitute in the camp brothel – known as "the puff" and available to prisoners favored for good behavior – nor had she been selected to play in Auschwitz's women's orchestra. Aline ascribed her survival to her size – she stood five feet six inches – and strong build. How ironic, she reflected, how richly and absurdly ironic. When I was a little girl, I didn't enjoy boys' play. I didn't climb trees or play soldier. I liked to sing - mother told me I had a sweet voice – and I liked to make clothes for my dolls. In the summer, I liked to sit under the apple tree and read. Good books about adventure and living in exotic places. The boys in the tree above used to tease me. They would drop little green apples and twigs on me. I did nothing in particular to build my body. Oh, I did enjoy swimming. I liked to float on my back too. The water was so nice. Well, enough of this daydreaming. I must concentrate on the here and now if my girls and I are going to survive.

At the Auschwitz train station Dr. Josef Mengele had eyed Aline briefly, noted her youth and impressive physique – suitable for enduring hard labor, the doctor concluded – and waved her to the right. She then had been marched to the women's barracks.

Within two days she had begun daily treks to the I.G. Farben plant. Women, she learned, were prized for their dexterity and delicacy in handling components for explosives and the finished products. I.G. Farben plant officials didn't want to see their magnificent factory blown to bits.

On this October evening Aline surveyed her surroundings thoroughly, her eyes sweeping back and forth, searching for any sign of Nazi overseers. She then reached beneath her black- and white-striped prisoner's uniform and stealthily removed a small sack she had fashioned from a piece of a dead inmate's uniform. Again she surveyed her work area. Three other women – "Aline's girls" she called them – were extracting similar sacks from under their uniforms.

For the past four months, since June, the women had been smuggling black powder and lengths of fuse into Auschwitz and handing off their contraband to sonderkommandos, the prisoners charged with operating the camp's gas chambers and crematoria. The sonderkommandos were rewarded for their degrading work with special rooms and treatment in the crematoria buildings. Their dining tables were covered with silk brocade cloths. They ate off porcelain dishes and, with silver place settings and fine glassware, they consumed good, plentiful food, drank fine cognac and slept on linen sheets. Simultaneously they learned to live with the nauseatingly sweet stench of burned human flesh.

They also saw the war's end coming and expected Auschwitz to be liberated soon. They anticipated that witnesses to the camp's horrors would be eliminated and concluded that their own turns in the gas chambers were imminent. Although thoroughly accustomed to shepherding others to their demise, the sonderkommandos were not ready to surrender to death.

Since June they had begun planning their escape and enlisted Aline Gartner's help – in return for additional food for her and her three "girls."

Escape attempts from Auschwitz were hardly unprecedented. They had been frequent since the camp's earliest days. On July 6, 1940, a prisoner named Tadeusz Wiejowski escaped. For three days SS troops hunted for but failed to find him. On June 24, 1944, Eden Galinski marched out of Auschwitz in an SS uniform. Using forged documents he had escorted his prisoner girlfriend, Mala Zimetbaum. Weeks later they were captured and returned to Auschwitz. Mala was clubbed to death and Eden hanged.

By October 1944 Nazi camp bureaucrats had recorded more than 600 escape attempts. About 200 were successful. Planning and implementing an escape attempt was stressful in the extreme. Unsuccessful escapists were tortured and hanged.

There were worse fates, Aline knew, not least of which was slow starvation or gassing. She finished filling her small sack, tied it off with a brown shoestring and tucked it beneath her uniform. The other three women did likewise.

As Aline turned to head toward the plant's nearest exit where she would form up for the march back to camp, a Nazi guard, Erwin Kressler, materialized in front of her. She felt a surge of terror chilling her torso and blood draining from her face.

The guard cocked an eyebrow and pointed menacingly to Aline's breast. Kressler wasn't certain of her intention but had been observing her daily sack-filling ritual from an overhead crane.

Aline could feel her knees on the verge of buckling. She struggled to regain her composure and whispered, "Tomorrow, during your break, in your washroom."

Kressler understood and let her pass.

CHAPTER 4

Kaz Majos was walking slowly with a throng of newly arrived prisoners who had been waved to the left. They had been warned to remain silent and for the most part were complying. A few dared to murmur assurances to spouses and children.

Arriving outside the gas chamber, Jacob Kuron, a sonderkommando leader, directed the prisoners to strip. He explained patiently that after delousing in the shower building they could retrieve their clothing. Many of the prisoners, men as well as women and children, were trembling. Nervously, awkwardly, they began to shed clothes. Virtually all men placed hands over their exposed penises while women cupped one hand over their genitals and an arm and the other hand over breasts. Children clung to parents' bare legs. Some believed the sonderkommandos, but Kaz wasn't alone in understanding the ruse. Abiding fear caused more than one victim to urinate.

Kaz saw that sonderkommando Kuron bore facial scars similar to his own and curiosity caused him to inquire, "Combat?"

Kuron looked at Kaz and found himself replying, "Where did you fight?"

"Warsaw," Kaz replied. "For five years. Lost this" – he pointed to his sightless eye – "on the first day of the uprising."

Other prisoners were watching and listening to this exchange.

"You kept fighting?"

"When I could. After I recovered."

"Where did you hide?" Kuron asked.

"St. Ann's. In the basement."

Kuron was astonished and it showed. "I grew up near St. Ann's. Just blocks down Cracowskie Przedmiescie."

"Nice street, nice neighborhood. Before the Nazis arrived."

Kuron pursed his lips and nodded pensively. "I got on well with you Catholics and they with my Jewish family. You are Catholic?" Kaz nodded. "We were shopkeepers. Dry goods."

"May you survive," Kaz murmured and began unbuttoning his shirt.

"Wait." Kaz looked up at Kuron who glanced furtively to his left and right. The other sonderkommandos seemed indifferent. "Step over here."

✝✝✝

Minutes later, standing beside Kuron, Kaz was shuddering at the screams of panic and wailings of agony and despair penetrating the gas chamber's walls. What he couldn't see were the death throes. When the Zyklon B was released from the overhead induction vents, it flowed down shafts to the floor and began diffusing. Some victims, especially those closest to the escaping gas, died almost instantly. Others began clawing their way on top of dead bodies, trying instinctively to stay above the rising gas. Soon there was silence. Kaz made no effort to choke back tears.

✝✝✝

It made no sense to Kaz, none at all. He saw it as the ultimate paradox. Why should a death camp have a hospital? Yet that's where he now was, and the Auschwitz hospital had expanded to include several barracks-like buildings staffed by some 60 doctors and 300 nurses. Moreover, he learned quickly that the camp's Polish underground had infiltrated the staff. It was true that thousands admitted to the hospital were murdered – most by phenol injections, with many succumbing to inhumane medical experiments conducted by Mengele and his adherents. But it was equally true that the underground helped save thousands more.

"I will get you into the hospital," Kuron had told Kaz after the gassing, "after we remove the corpses and move them to the crematorium. You need a night of rest and food. Then we will get you back here with us."

Kaz, numbed, nodded his gratitude and murmured, "The risk to you?"

"No guarantees," Kuron said. "The SS could turn on us at any moment. We half expect it. They see us as scum, but scum willing to do work they deem disgusting but necessary. They are right. We are scum. We do this to stay alive in a living hell, and that does not make us saints."

†††

The next morning, October 6, about 10:00, Aline Gartner was at her workbench inside the I.G. Farben plant. The air inside was chilly. She exhaled and could see her breath. She shivered and rubbed her hands together.

"Five minutes." Behind her she heard the voice of Erwin Kressler, the Nazi guard. "The washroom." He walked away.

Perhaps, thought Aline, I could surprise him there. Strangle him with fuse. He deserves death. But no, I am too weak. Even if I tried it, he would still rape me. Then kill me. The other girls too.

Aline wiped her hands on her coarse apron, removed it and began walking across the concrete floor to the guards' washroom. In a perverse way, she thought, I am glad he still finds me attractive.

†††

Self-preservation was foremost on Heinrich Himmler's mind. He knew the Reich's end was nearing and already was considering ways he might approach the Allies about negotiating a peace. First, though, he knew he had to take actions to lessen the likelihood of his being captured and treated as a war criminal. An arrest, a trial, conviction, execution. It could happen fast. Undoing what he had wrought would take time, and time was not his ally. The Russians were closing in on Warsaw, and the

Allies were advancing rapidly across France and north through Italy. In his Berlin office Himmler removed his thin wire-rimmed spectacles and rubbed his eyes. The stress was becoming unbearable.

In mid-September Himmler had ordered gassings to stop at all camps. In fact, though, the last Zyklon-B gassing of Jews at Auschwitz wouldn't take place until October 20 when 1,700 innocents would be herded into the chambers.

On November 26, 1944, Himmler would order the crematoria dismantled.

But on the morning of October 7 other news galvanized Jacob Kuron and his fellow sonderkommandos. Members of Auschwitz's gentile Polish underground working in the camp's administrative offices had learned that the sonderkommandos were to be liquidated. Himmler now regarded them as more of the damning evidence he felt compelled to destroy.

†††

"Aline," Jacob Kuron said, making the introduction, "this is Kaz Majos."

Kaz extended his right hand and Aline shook it. "Nice to meet you," he said. She remained silent, her face expressionless. She now distrusted all new arrivals. Who was to say they weren't informants?

They were standing outside the hospital near the sprawling camp's northwest perimeter.

"Kaz was a Resistance leader in Warsaw," Jacob explained. "He arrived two days ago."

Aline looked at Kaz's blind eye, scarred temple and his arms. "No tattoo."

Before Kaz could reply, Jacob spoke. "He was waved left. Outside the chamber I took a chance."

"Another one," Aline murmured, smiling ruefully.

Jacob acknowledged her compliment with a slight nod. "I got him into the hospital."

"You are very lucky, Majos," Aline said. "So to speak."

Kaz closed his eyes and pursed his lips, nodding his agreement with her assessment.

"Aline is the one who takes chances," Jacob said. "Big ones. Many of them."

"But not for much longer," she said. "One of the guards has found me out."

"When?"

"Two days ago."

"He has demanded compensation?"

"Yes. But even so I don't think you can rely on me for more deliveries." Aline reached beneath her uniform, extracted the small cloth bag and handed it to Jacob.

Kaz looked questioningly at the two of them.

"Explosives," Jacob whispered, tucking the sack inside his uniform. "This was your final delivery," he murmured.

"Oh?"

"The Polish underground has told us that we sonderkommandos are to be gassed."

That evening inside the crematorium some 20 sonderkommando ringleaders crowded close to Jacob. Kaz was with them. In the crematorium room set aside for the sonderkommandos' dining, they had finished their evening meal – salami, bread, small cakes and jellies.

"You all know the risks," Jacob said. "No one is forcing you. Prisoners were successful in rebelling at Majdanek, but their commandant was soft and controls were lax."

In fact, back on July 24, 1944, a Polish Resistance group had seized control of the Majdanek camp, far to the northeast of Auschwitz. They then turned it over to the advancing Russian Army. Majdanek's commandant had been Lieutenant Colonel Arthur Liebehenschel who from November 1943 to May 1944 had commanded Auschwitz while Rudolf Hoess had been away serving as chief inspector of all Nazi concentration camps. Liebehenschel was a short, pudgy man and while in charge at Auschwitz had eased some of the most draconian punitive measures. He even had canceled the rule decreeing an automatic death penalty for those caught trying to escape. Henceforth, such cases were to be judged individually.

Now, though, Hoess was back at Auschwitz. He had delegated direct control over the camp to Richard Baer and over nearby Birkenau to Josef Kramer who had demonstrated amply his ruthlessness while commanding Natzwiller-Struthof, the Nazis' only death camp in France. Kramer had been transferred to Auschwitz after Natzwiller-Struthof was abandoned following the Allies' liberation of Paris.

"We are ready," said one of the sonderkommandos, "but it would be wise to review the plan again. The details-"

One of the two heavy wooden doors to the crematorium began inching open, and the sonderkommandos froze. Jacob rose and moved stealthily behind the opening door, prepared to pounce. A moment later he exhaled audibly. It was Aline. "Come in," he whispered and closed the door.

"I had a feeling I would find you here," she said. "I felt a need to know."

"You deserve to," Jacob replied. "Sit down." Then he addressed Kaz. "You are new here. With the Russians heading this way, you might survive until liberation. Perhaps we could get you assigned to the hospital staff. Aline, could you help with that?"

"I can try. I know what to offer."

No one smiled at her little unfunny joke. Kaz cringed. That this woman would even consider sacrificing herself to save a man she had just met touched him deeply. It also reminded him of Bernadeta Gudek who had been both his Resistance cell colleague and soul mate in Warsaw. Kaz also was remembering counsel he had given to 20 elderly Jews after he, Bernadeta and three other partisans had rescued them from execution and mass burial in a Warsaw cemetery by slaying their Nazi captors. Stay in Warsaw and you have no chance at all, Kaz had told the men. Or come with us and at least you will have a chance and that seems better than no chance at all. The Jews had huddled briefly among themselves and decided that they wanted to live. They fled into the countryside where Kaz connected them with other partisans who took them into hiding. They survived.

"I don't like my chances in this hell," Kaz said. Nor, he was thinking, do I want Aline Gartner to further endanger her life for me. Or to sacrifice her body – her dignity. Then another thought: "Aline, do you want to go with us?"

She smiled and could see in Kaz a man of both courage and compassion. "Thank you but no. I would like to escape but I must stay with my girls." Her voice was flat, devoid of discernible emotion. "If I escape or even try to, they will have no chance of surviving. When do you go?"

"Tonight," Jacob said, "about nine."

Aline then stood to leave and return to the women's barracks. "I wish you well. Perhaps if we all survive…" She shrugged and a sonderkommando respectfully opened the crematorium door for her.

After she exited, Jacob turned to Kaz. "Aline was a mother."

"Her girls-"

"No, those girls are women, just a little younger than she. No, Aline had two children, a daughter and son."

"Here?"

"They arrived together."

† † †

Dusk was beginning to settle over Auschwitz and with it an eerie quiet. Jacob, Kaz and seven other ringleaders remained in the crematorium. The others had dispersed as planned to other parts of the camp, positioning themselves to lead other sonderkommandos in the breakout.

"How many are going tonight?" Kaz asked.

"Three hundred," Jacob replied. "The majority of us."

"Not all?"

"Some are too afraid or in denial. They think the SS actually needs them."

"Weapons?"

"Some, not many," and Jacob motioned to Kaz to follow him to a corner of the room. From under a cloth-draped dining table Jacob pulled out a wooden box. He lifted the top. "Courtesy of the Polish underground."

Kaz was looking at four lugers, five machine pistols, three grenades, two bayonets, a dagger and two pairs of wire cutters.

"Is that all?"

"No. More is hidden at other points."

"Experience?"

"Not really. Few of us have ever fired a weapon. But you…"

"Enough. May I?"

Jacob nodded his assent and Kaz reached into the box and picked up one of the lugers. It was well oiled and loaded.

"It would be good," said Jacob, "if you-"

One of the crematorium's doors was pushed open abruptly. In stepped Frederick Karlinski, one of the camp kapos, the prisoners who cruelly oversaw the barracks. There was no exchange of pleasantries. Sneering, Karlinski quickly took stock of the room, saw Kaz holding the luger, pursed his lips and nodded smugly. "I heard something was up. Idiotic. Just simply idiotic." Karlinski shrugged dismissively, underscoring his disdain for the sonderkommandos' plan. He turned to leave.

"Stop him," Jacob ordered, and two sonderkommandos – Tomasz Dolata and Michal Olinek – nearest Karlinski grabbed and pinned his arms behind him.

Jacob walked across the room, proceeding contemplatively. Kaz was following. Without turning, Jacob said, "Hand me the luger."

Kaz extended his right arm forward and Jacob, without shifting his eyes from Karlinski, reached down for the gun.

Karlinski struggled, trying futilely to free his arms. "Don't be stupid," he warned. "Hit me and you know your fate."

Jacob's jaws clenched. "We know what the Nazis have planned for us. It is not hard for us to imagine a more appealing alternative." He reversed the luger, gripping it by its barrel. He elevated it above his head. Karlinski's eyes followed the upraised arm and flinched. Jacob brought his arm down, slamming the gun's butt against Karlinski's forehead, opening a gash and sending blood streaming down his face. Karlinski's consciousness was fading.

"Hold him up," Jacob commanded. Then he struck again, hard against Karlinski's left temple. "Take him to the furnace room." Tomasz and Michal hesitated. Jacob's jaws clenched again. "Now."

The two sonderkommandos dragged Karlinski away. Jacob turned to face Kaz. "Necessary? I could gag and tie him," Jacob muttered. "That would be humane. This is more fitting."

Kaz breathed in slightly and exhaled but said nothing for a long moment. Briefly, he regretted the rough justice he was witnessing. Then his memory recalled all those waved to the left, all those who had died at the hands of the Nazis in Warsaw. "Agreed."

"Let's get to work," Jacob said to Kaz and his five other compatriots. He led the group to another corner and a second box. This one contained sacks of gunpowder, fuses, rags and a large can of gasoline and matches. To his men Jacob said, "There aren't enough fuses for all the sacks of powder. That's what the rags are for. Soak them in the gas and then tie them to the strings holding the sacks shut."

The men went to work and soon were joined by Tomasz and Michal who had disposed of Karlinski. "Soon he will be only ashes," Tomasz muttered, answering the question no one had yet asked.

After the sacks had been prepared, Jacob spoke. "Place the sacks in the center of the room. Not near walls. Then," he said, pointing to the other men, "each of you take a sack and matches to your assigned contact and then get back here."

Each man picked up a gasoline-soaked sack, tucked it beneath his uniform and left, hoping that the fuel odor wouldn't catch the attention of guards or kapos.

"What now?" Kaz asked.

"Are you certain you still want to stay with us? The Nazis aren't gentle with failed escapees."

"Like I said, what's next?"

A thin smile creased Jacob Kuron's face, aged beyond his years by the unrelenting stress of trying to survive Auschwitz. "What's next is relax for awhile. If you can. We wait for the men to return."

Kaz stepped to a wooden chair and sat. He was tired and his head shook slightly. He closed his eyes and let his head rock back. He could see Bernadeta Gudek walking sadly from St. Ann's church the night before the Warsaw Uprising ended. Incredibly, that was only five days ago. It seemed a lifetime. Kaz was hoping she had made it back to Zyrardow, to her family's farm, the one he was hoping someday to see. Kaz had wanted to leave Warsaw with Bernadeta – he had made that clear – but felt obligated as a cell leader to remain with his group for the formal surrender. He could envision her sneaking through sewers and alleys into the countryside and onto the road to Zyrardow, about 40 kilometers southwest of Warsaw. Then another image formed clearly – of the doomed naked victims, about to perish in a gaseous hell. Next came a vision of Aline Gartner, and he tried to imagine what she was doing. Kaz sucked in a deep breath, held it and then let it out slowly. I should be feeling some fear, he mused. But maybe I've gone beyond normal reactions to uncertainty. I can only hope that's good.

CHAPTER 5

Polska in the Polish language means the land of the plain. The country's flat expanses historically had furnished land rich for farming. They also had provided easy avenues for invaders from both the east and the west. During that first week of October in 1944 Bernadeta was nearing her family's farm near Zyrardow on the central plain. She was walking slowly, warily surveying the pastoral scene. Her years fighting with and taking risks for the Home Army – Poland's Resistance force – had taught her the value of blending boldness with caution. Mistakes could be – too often were – fatal.

In the distance, when she saw her younger sister Barbara exit the barn, Bernadeta drew in a sharp breath and quickened her pace.

A few moments later an excited shriek from Barbara startled all the farm's inhabitants, animals and humans alike, and Bernadeta found herself locked in a four-way embrace of ecstasy with her sister and her parents, Jszef and Tosia.

When they released each other, still holding hands, Jszef smilingly inspected his older daughter. "A little more weight lost since we last saw you, but your mother can remedy that soon enough."

"Oh my," Tosia said with genuine concern. "We weren't expecting you. I have nothing prepared."

"Not to worry, Mother. I am not starving." That was true but barely; only the joy of reuniting with her family was temporarily allaying hunger pangs.

"But you must be hungry. Such a very long walk from Warsaw. You did walk again?"

"Like before. I stayed the nights in barns. I had bread and a little wine." She placed her hand on her leather wine pouch, hanging from her cloth belt.

"Nevertheless," Tosia said, regaining her motherly command presence, "I will begin preparing an appropriate welcome home dinner. A feast."

The daughters and their father laughed, Tosia harrumphed, disengaged and moved smartly into the house. Tosia already was deciding on a menu: pork, boiled potatoes, sauerkraut, dark bread, carrot cake and ersatz coffee made from local grain.

Jszef stepped forward to hug Bernadeta once more and felt his right arm squeeze something hard. He stepped back and pointed to his daughter's waist where a small cloth bag hung.

Bernadeta removed the sack from her belt, opened it and lifted the content – a luger that she handed Jszef. "This time I didn't think I should leave it in Warsaw."

"Wise," said Jszef. "Soon we'll likely have company, either Germans or Russians. Not pleasant guests in either case."

Then Barbara spoke. "Your friend. Kaz Majos. Where is he?"

✝✝✝

Kaz was listening attentively and watching closely.

"We have only a little while to wait for darkness," Jacob said. The five sonderkommandos who had made deliveries of the powder-filled sacks to their fellow conspirators had returned, and now all nine men were gathered in the center of the crematorium room, standing near the pile of powder sacks. "Just a little more time."

In the next moment, time speeded up. Another sonderkommando shoved open one of the heavy wooden doors. "An informant!" He was excited but not breathless; running would have been unseemly and drawn unwanted attention. "Three SS are just a minute behind me. Or less. A captain and two men, one a sergeant."

Jacob didn't hesitate. He went running to the weapons cache, reached in and removed the two bayonets and the dagger.

"No," said Kaz. "Leave them. Bring the lugers." Jacob shot him a questioning look. "Just the lugers," Kaz repeated. "We don't want knife wounds or blood."

"Noise?" Jacob asked.

"There won't be any." Kaz tossed the luger he had been holding to one of the sonderkommandos. To Jacob, he said, "Give those to the men.

Good. Now, you men stand to the sides of the doors. The rest of you hide. You too, Jacob."

"And you?" Jacob said.

Kaz pointed to the pile of powder sacks on the floor in the center of the room. "I will focus their attention. When they come in," he said to the four sonderkommandos holding the lugers, "they will see me immediately. Club them. Hold them and disarm them." Kaz's directions were greeted by silence. He smiled self-deprecatingly. "You asked about my experience in these matters. Well…"

The men nodded and took their positions. Tension was building quickly but they didn't have long to wait. Seconds later both wooden doors flew open, followed immediately by the SS captain with luger drawn and the sergeant and private with their machine pistols at the ready. They saw Kaz standing, apparently calm, arms at his sides, and stopped.

An instant later the sonderkommandos attacked from behind, bludgeoning the three Germans who crumpled and stumbled toward Kaz. The remaining sonderkommandos emerged from hiding and came running to disarm and help subdue the Nazis. The sergeant and the private were moaning. The sergeant was rising to his hands and knees.

"Hit them again," Kaz directed. "Hard." Three more heavy blows and the moaning stopped.

"Strip them," said Kaz. There was a long pause before the sonderkommandos stooped to begin removing the SS uniforms. Kaz spoke again, "Then burn them." Jacob looked at him dubiously. "The SS," said Kaz, "not the uniforms."

"Should we kill them first?" asked one of the sonderkommandos.

"Why?"

"Your experience is showing," Jacob said with open admiration.

"Like I said, five years of fighting them. Five years of watching their depravity, slaughtering our people, ruining our country."

"Do you speak German?" Jacob asked Kaz.

"No. Do you?"

"Yes."

"Then you wear the captain's uniform. Do any of you other men speak German?"

"Yes," said several men.

"Give the other uniforms to two of them."

"No," said Jacob. "You wear one. The sergeant's. I think we will need your leadership, Sergeant Majos. But we need to get you a proper German eye patch so you look properly teutonic." The men laughed and Jacob grinned, the first time Kaz had seen a mischievous gleam in any eyes since arriving at Auschwitz.

Six sonderkommandos were roughly dragging the three unconscious, naked Nazis toward the furnace room. "Up the chimney with you bastards," one of the men muttered. "If ever there was justice administered justly, this is it. I will take pure joy in this roasting."

The Nazi private was beginning to regain consciousness as the sonderkommandos maneuvered him and the other two into the furnaces. He screamed and squirmed as heat met and began singeing his bare feet. The sonderkommandos continued their work and then slammed shut the furnace doors.

✝✝✝

Darkness had descended. "I think it is time," said Jacob. He breathed deeply and exhaled. "Let's get going."

Without a word the five sonderkommandos who earlier had delivered the gunpowder sacks and fuses to their contact points again departed to spread the word that the escape attempt was imminent.

Jacob, Kaz and Tomasz had removed their prisoner garb and donned the SS uniforms. The fits weren't perfect but in the darkness they would do.

"We'll give them a few minutes to reach their contacts," Jacob said, "and then we'll proceed." To Kaz, Tomasz and Michal, he added, "I wish you all luck. If you believe in God, may he be with you. Whatever you do, don't let yourself be captured alive. We can't take a chance that the Nazis will torture information out of one of us and jeopardize everyone else." The men nodded. "We all have killed to stay alive. Tonight if we have to kill any more, it will be for something more precious than life. It will be for freedom."

"And redemption," Michal added solemnly.

They stood silently for another three minutes.

Outside, elsewhere near the camp perimeter, other sonderkommandos were making final preparations while still others were watching for Nazi security patrols – armed guards with their dogs, always straining to pick up suspicious scents.

Jacob patted his holstered luger and Kaz did likewise. Tomasz and Michal squeezed the barrels of their machine pistols. Michal's palms were moist. He rubbed them against his pants.

"All right," Jacob said and knelt. The other three men followed his lead. They all struck matches and put the flames to the fuses. Then they extinguished the matches. "Outside," Jacob said. "Quickly, and move away from this building."

The men went hustling toward the two wooden doors, pulled them back, passed through, closed them and went walking away briskly.

They didn't have to wait long. The red tile roof exploded apocalyptically, lifting off the crematorium walls and sending a tower of flame soaring into the night sky.

"That will draw their attention," Kaz said. "Well planned and well done."

"I'm sure it was a pleasing sound to Aline and her girls."

In the next instant five more explosions, smaller ones, tore ragged gaps in the perimeter fencing.

"Faster than wire cutters, but we have those too," Jacob said, "just in case. Let's go," and he, Kaz and Tomasz in the SS uniforms, plus Michal, went dashing for one of the blown gaps in the fencing.

In the same moment, sirens started wailing, searchlight beams began slicing the darkness, scanning the camp's grounds, and gunfire erupted. Then came the most terrifying sound – some 50 angrily barking dogs all unleashed.

At the fence Jacob found the wire intact. "Shit," he muttered and then knelt and quickly went to work with the wire cutters.

Through the darkness, illuminated by the flaming crematorium, Kaz, Tomasz and Michal saw two dogs racing toward them. The men tensed. No one gave an order; none was necessary. The three men steadied their guns and fired into the faces of the onrushing dogs.

The flashes from their gun muzzles began drawing fire from arriving SS men and bullets began biting the earth around them and pinging on the fence wire.

Jacob pulled back hard on the cut fence and shouted, "Now, through, now!"

Tomasz and Michal ducked and squeezed through, followed by Kaz who then reached back to pull Jacob through. In the next sliver of time Jacob screamed and fell.

"You're hit," Kaz said grimly and he and Tomasz grabbed Jacob's upper arms and jerked him to his feet. "Come on."

Jacob groaned. "It's my knee," he said through the fiery pain. "Shattered. I can't go on."

"You will," Kaz commanded, continuing with Tomasz to pull Jacob farther away from the fence. Michal was providing covering fire against the SS men, some kneeling while others went scrambling for cover.

"No. Leave me," Jacob demanded. "This is my command. I will slow you down. You know that. Besides, you have something to be proud of. I don't."

"Enough," Kaz said roughly. "Sometimes men must disobey orders. You are coming with us."

"No. I am nothing but a sonderkommando. A traitor to my people." In self-loathing he pounded his right fist against the ground.

Michal ejected his empty clip and inserted his only extra one. He fired another covering burst.

"If you hadn't become one, the SS would have killed you immediately and found someone else."

"Precisely. I made a choice and died a little every day. At least my soul did."

"I don't think God is ready to take what's left of your soul. Come on," Kaz urged him. "Michal said it best, redemption. This is your second chance to choose."

Kaz and Tomasz hoisted Jacob to his feet and continued serving as his crutches.

"Let's get to the woods," Michal shouted above the din.

In the next moment Jacob wrenched free from Kaz and Tomasz and fell to the ground. Before the two men could react, Jacob unholstered the luger from his uniform belt, jammed the muzzle into his mouth and pulled the trigger.

In the forest all three – Kaz, Tomasz and Michal – were bent over, hands on knees, gasping for air and sweating in the cool October night.

"What now?" Tomasz asked, looking at Kaz on his left.

"Even in these uniforms we keep moving." They could hear SS dogs in the distance. "We keep to the forest and stay off the roads. And out of meadows and fields where we could be seen too easily. We try to put more ground between us and them. In the morning we'll try to find clothing so Michal can get out of that," Kaz said, pointing with his right forefinger to Michal's striped prisoner uniform. "Truth be told, I'd feel better if we got out of these SS uniforms and into civilian clothes. I think we would be less conspicuous and less likely to be asked questions. And we wouldn't have to worry about not speaking German."

"Jacob was right," Tomasz observed, "you have the benefit of experience."

Kaz shrugged self-deprecatingly. "We'll also look for food. Then if we make it through tomorrow, we'll have to find a place to rest at night."

"Ideas?" asked Michal.

"Yes, I think we should keep heading east. Toward Cracow. It's a big town, and I've heard it has largely escaped war damage. I'd like to think we could blend in there. Lose ourselves so to speak. On the way at night I think we should sleep in the open. It will be cold. Maybe we can find some blankets. But we should stay out of barns and sheds. That's where the SS will be searching for our fellow escapees."

"More experience speaking?" Michal smiled.

"Not really. In Warsaw we lived in church basements and sewers. Chilly, damp, smelly. The Nazis were squeamish about coming after us. Not so much because they had qualms about desecrating houses of worship but because they feared being shot in those close underground spaces. They knew if they were wounded we would kill them before help came. When they are searching for us Auschwitz escapees in barns, sheds or houses, I don't think they will have any such qualms. None at all."

✝✝✝

Kaz was right. On that first night SS dogs followed the scent of a group of 28 escapees west to a small barn near the village of Rajsko. But the SS troops didn't shoot their way into the barn. Instead, partly out of caution, partly for sport, they torched it. Then as the escapees fled the flames, the

SS cut them down. Still, many of the 300 made their way into hiding and eventually to freedom.

After the SS called off their search, 198 sonderkommandos remained in Auschwitz. Few of them had participated in the breakout and thus were hoping they would be spared the executions that had been visited on most recaptured prisoners. The SS didn't deviate from their original intent. On November 17, 1944, at about 2 p.m., they marched all remaining sonderkommandos to a gas chamber. They were told not to strip because there was no need for pretense. Devoid now of hope, many of the sonderkommandos let guilt seep into and rule their thoughts. They didn't protest. They were ordered inside where they stood silently, waiting for the cloud of death to descend.

CHAPTER 6

Inside the I.G. Farben plant, Erwin Kressler sat inside the cab of the overhead crane, high above the factory floor. He was looking down on Aline Gartner, busy at her workbench. Not ordinarily a meditative man, Kressler was nonetheless pondering possibilities. There were many.

On the night of October 7 the explosion that blew the roof off the crematorium and signaled the sonderkommandos' breakout had literally lifted Kressler off the mattress of his bed in the SS barracks at the east edge of the camp. Kressler didn't need much time or thought to make the connection between the explosion and Aline's smuggled sacks of black powder. What had him deep in thought this morning, two weeks after the escape, was another choice – between self-gratification and self-preservation.

The SS had begun its investigation and Kressler knew it would be comprehensive and probing. Eventually he knew he would be questioned. Everyone who worked at the plant – I.G. Farben staff, prisoners, SS guards – would be interrogated, some less gently than others.

Kressler's quandary was profound. What will I say – or not? Kressler asked himself. Gartner hasn't tried smuggling powder or anything else from the plant since the day I caught her. And her washroom visits have been very pleasant. She does whatever I ask. I really don't want to see them end. I like looking into her face. Sometimes I think I see traces of pleasure she'd never admit to. But lying to the SS? That's the quickest way I know to meet an early grave. That or being sent east to fight the Russians. A nasty prospect and another express ticket to the afterlife. What about being evasive? Could I answer their questions without revealing everything I know? That seems dangerous. Too dangerous. I can see myself sweating, and they would see the stains spreading on my uniform. But if I do inform, the SS would know I withheld.

Aline knew Kressler was watching her. By now she also felt she could accurately divine this thinking. For the first couple days after the explosion and escape she was surprised that Kressler hadn't reported her to his SS bosses. When he didn't, Aline knew the reason – those washroom visits. They are disgusting and degrading, she reflected, but they have been keeping me and my girls from SS torture and execution. What will Kressler say when he is questioned? He will be questioned. The SS is too thorough not to. But will he point to me? I don't think so. Not because he wants to keep fucking me but because he can't incriminate himself. If he does that, he knows he could be executed faster than I. Or worse, publicly tortured before being hanged or shot.

She glanced up and saw Kressler looking down. But what about my girls? No, he won't give them away either. Same reason. And I won't give them away either. Not under questioning. Under torture? In pain I don't even want to think about? I pray I could hold out. The girls themselves? I hope they are strong enough. I would like to think so.

✝ ✝ ✝

One wasn't. The SS spent nearly three months investigating, working to link the source of the explosives to the sonderkommandos. They did indeed question Kressler, and he did manage to lie convincingly. He could feel perspiration dripping from his armpits but concluded correctly that the SS was used to seeing its interrogation targets sweat and squirm. Worried that he would be watched closely, Kressler also halted his washroom rapes.

Aline lied too, even when questioning escalated to beatings, administered by leather-gloved SS fists. They struck her face, upper chest, breasts and midsection. Her face – lips swollen and left eye nearly closed – and torso became streaked with bruising. Her tormentors threatened her with death and to drive the point home strangled her to the verge of unconsciousness.

Two of Aline's girls were sisters. The younger sister was forced to watch her older sister endure the application of heated prods to her nipples. Her sister's screams foretold her own, and she screamed her own guilt.

Although the remaining crematoria at Auschwitz and those at nearby Birkenau had been dismantled by now, death continued daily visits. Prisoners continued to die from disease and starvation. And in early 1945 a special gallows was erected. On January 6 women prisoners, most emaciated, were assembled to watch a hanging.

Among SS guards in attendance was Erwin Kressler. He was wishing he could be somewhere else, anywhere else. But his job had been guarding women, so he wasn't surprised that duty had him here this morning.

Polish winters are raw, white and blustery. This morning was no exception. A thick carpet of snow covered the ground and had to be swept from the wooden steps leading up the gallows. A woman prisoner equipped with a straw broom was assigned that task.

Aline was shivering. She and the older of the two sisters were being marched to the gallows. Both were wearing ragged skirts and blouses but not their coats.

Earlier that morning the younger sister had suffered a nervous breakdown. Her primal screams could be heard clearly in the distance. Because the SS wanted orderly and not chaotic executions, the younger sister and a fourth girl were spared but not for long. They would be hanged that night.

Aline's hands and those of the older sister were bound behind them. Why tie our hands? She was thinking. Do they fear we will struggle? Or is it merely Nazis mindlessly following rigid Nazi protocol? How silly. Aline noticed that her shivering had subsided. Resignation? Spectators could see that her visage had become serene. Soon I will be free. From pain, from hunger, from fear, from watching my friends violated and murdered. From a world gone mad and lusting for blood. God, if you really do exist, I look forward to asking you just one question: Why? I want to speak with you. I want to hear your answer. You have much to explain.

Now on the gallows platform Aline and her girl were lifted up onto a table. Nooses were fitted around their necks. The executioner adjusted the nooses just so, wanting to avoid a decapitation. That would be too fast. He didn't mind if they strangled slowly. Aline's eyes were closed. Then they snapped open. She had found her earthly voice. In the next moment what she said wasn't profound, but it was spoken with iron resolve and would be remembered by an eyewitness, Judith Sternberg Newman. "You'll pay for this," Judith later recalled Aline calling out. "I shall die now, but your turn will come soon."

Erwin Kressler believed her. If I am taken by the Russians, my fate is sealed. Captured by the Americans and maybe I have a chance. Unless they try me as a war criminal. What would be my defense? That I was only following orders? Like any experienced, obedient soldier? Even if that was believed, would it be excused?

The table was pulled from beneath Aline and her girl. When the trap door dropped open, Kressler averted his eyes. The ropes went taught and the nooses tightened, choking life from their tired, wasted bodies.

"They hung there like two marionettes," Newman later recalled, "turning in the breeze. It was a horrible sight."

CHAPTER 7

On the same day that Aline Gartner was executed and freed from earthly torment, any possibility of postwar freedom for Poland and her people was beginning to be snatched away. Five days earlier on January 1, Poland had started experiencing the repression that Soviet Russia would eventually impose on virtually all of Central Europe. That was the day when Russian forces crossed the Vistula River and entered Warsaw. At first the Russian presence felt like the longed for liberation from Nazi cruelty. Days later, though, the Soviet hammer slammed down with news that would sicken millions pining for freedom and amount to a barometer of the coming Cold War.

In Belgium near Bastogne, when Chaplain Jack Brecker heard the news, he knew Thaddeus Metz, his Polish friend, would be deeply disappointed. Jack was keenly aware that Thaddeus had volunteered for the Polish Airborne Brigade because he was intent on returning as fast as possible to liberate his Polish homeland from the grip of the Nazis and lead to establishment of democracy. Today's news quashed that hope.

Thaddeus, the former lancer turned airborne trooper, was back in England after the disastrous Market Garden operation during which his brigade of 2,200 men lost half its members and the British 6th Airborne Division lost 80 percent of its 10,000 men to death, wounds and captivity. When Thaddeus heard the same news, his sense of loss was overwhelming. In coping with his distress, a parade of haunting images went quick-stepping through his mind. Among them:

- After Hitler's takeovers in Austria and Czechoslovakia, leaving Jagiellonian University where he had been studying history – along with French and English – and planning a career in law or government, joining the military and becoming a Polish lancer.
- Astride his charging white warhorse, bearing down on German infantry on September 1, 1939, the morning Hitler's legions came pouring across the border into Poland.
- His long lance spearing a young shrieking German.
- Captivity in a barn with 11 other soldiers, including General Stanislaw Sosabowski.
- In the cow pen inside the barn on the Gudek family's farm.
- Bernadeta Gudek smuggling a bread knife into the cow pen and then distracting two German guards so that he could slay them.
- Saying farewell to Bernadeta, searing into his memory the image of her face, creamy complexion and the thin scar running downward from the left corner of her mouth.
- Escaping to France, then again fighting the invading Bosche.
- Serving with fellow Poles as the rear guard at Dunkirk for British and French troops being evacuated across the channel to England.
- On the beach, German shrapnel slicing his shoulder, thigh and ankle.
- Being lifted onto a stretcher by fellow cow pen soldiers – that's how they took to referring to themselves – and being carried into the surf to a small boat that would take him to the Abderpool,

the last evacuation vessel to leave Dunkirk with 3,200 Polish soldiers.

- Still limping, being the first to volunteer for General Sosabowski's newly authorized First Independent Polish Airborne Brigade.
- The 1944 Easter Mass with Jack Brecker celebrating.
- The disastrous crossing of the Rhine during Operation Market Garden. Nearly 400 of the brigade killed or wounded, including Stephan, one of his fellow cow pen soldiers.

Thaddeus shook his head and smiled ruefully. So much had happened in, what, just a little more than five years? From serious student to combat veteran, from never having traveled to not setting foot in his homeland for five years. Now he stood outside General Sosabowski's command tent. "General, do you have a moment to spare?"

"Come in, Captain Metz."

Thaddeus pushed aside the tent flap. General Sosabowski's radio, tuned to the BBC, told Thaddeus that the general likely had learned the bad news. "You've heard?"

"It is disgusting." Sosabowski's gravelly bass voice bit off each word savagely. "The Russians push back the Germans. They supposedly liberate our country. Instead they are enslaving us. And what does Roosevelt do? Churchill? They talk with Stalin. Stalin." Sosabowski spat. "Stalin promises free elections. Stalin and free elections. There's a classic contradiction in terms."

"It's a complex situation, sir. With Hitler refusing to surrender and the war in the Pacific still not won," Thaddeus observed, trying to soothe the general who had become his friend and mentor, "there seems little more that Roosevelt and Churchill can do. Talk. Certainly they won't fight Stalin. Not in Poland. It's too far from their base. Even if they had the will – and I don't think they do at this time and won't for some time to come – they probably don't have the resources."

"So," Sosabowski said with resignation, "Stalin gets his way again."

✝ ✝ ✝

Joseph Stalin had been getting his way often and for a long time. What had Sosabowski verging on apoplexy and Thaddeus suffering deep disappointment was Stalin's pronouncement on January 1 that he had installed the Soviet-sponsored Polish Committee of National Liberation (also known as the Lublin Committee) and that he was recognizing Poland's new government. It was the first of what the West would come to regard as Soviet satellite governments. Stalin saw them as something else – buffer zones vital to protecting Mother Russia from any future western onslaught. And given invasions led by Napoleon, Kaiser Wilhelm and Hitler, Stalin saw his aims and gains as eminently reasonable.

In 1941 Stalin had miscalculated Hitler's territorial designs and military wherewithal, and his misjudgment had nearly cost him his country. Subsequently, ever since the Russian Army had stiffened and stopped the Germans at Moscow's gates, Stalin had been pushing hard to get his way. One major goal was to goad the Allies, chiefly the U.S. and Britain, to open a second front in Western Europe and divert some of Hitler's forces from the East. When in August 1942 Churchill flew to Moscow, words also took wing and they were lifted by fear and anger.

"We cannot invade France yet," Churchill had patiently explained in Stalin's Kremlin office. "We are still recovering from our losses in France, and America is only now ramping up wartime production."

"So you do nothing," Stalin had replied with cutting sarcasm, "nothing but wait while we fight for our very existence."

"Not at all," Churchill answered, trying to placate the ally he didn't trust. "We are going to join with America to drive Hitler out of North Africa."

"North Africa!" Stalin had erupted. "Of what earthly good is that to us? To Russia?"

"Hitler has tanks, planes and men in North Africa," Churchill had said, struggling to remain calm in the face of Stalin's furor. "If – when – we defeat Hitler there, he cannot use those resources against either you or us."

"You are cowards!" Stalin coiled both hands and slammed them on his desk.

Churchill's eyes widened, then quickly narrowed but didn't blink. "When are you going to start fighting? Are you going to let us do all the work?"

Stalin's inhospitable treatment notwithstanding, Churchill flew back to Moscow again in October 1944. This time he found Stalin less bombastic.

"Your Field Marshall Montgomery is a little too timid for my taste," Stalin teased Churchill. "Would you mind asking Roosevelt or Eisenhower if I could borrow General Patton? He seems to have a firm grasp on the concepts of speed and force. He understands the value of taking and holding real estate."

Churchill was tempted to say what he thought might now be worrying Stalin – that the Allies' rapid advance from the West could deprive Soviet Russia of eventual mastery over Germany. Instead Churchill replied, "I'm quite sure General Patton shares your high opinion of himself."

Stalin laughed heartily. "General Patton and modesty. Now there is a contradiction in terms."

✝✝✝

Joseph Stalin was embarrassed. It was the first week of February 1945, and he was preparing to host Churchill and Roosevelt at a conference at Yalta on the Black Sea shore in Crimea. The conference was due to begin on February 4.

"This is not acceptable," Stalin complained to his foreign minister, Vyachelsav Molotov.

"When the Germans vacated, they left a mess." Molotov agreed with his boss, as was his wont.

The two men were standing in one of Yalta's palaces, long used by the czars, their families and entourages. Stalin's plan was to install himself, Churchill and Roosevelt and their respective staffs in three of the palaces for the conference's duration, February 4-11.

"Fix it," Stalin said roughly.

"But the conference begins tomorrow," Molotov said and was already wishing he could recall his words. He knew what was coming next – his boss's rapidly rising ire.

"Call Moscow." The ice in Stalin's voice was freezing fast. "Call my offices. Tell them I want planes in the air tonight. Furniture, silverware, maids, waiters. Tell them to get the best from the best hotels. I want everything here by morning."

It was.

✝✝✝

During the historic conference Stalin knew precisely what he wanted to achieve and was determined to get it. Poland, crucial to Russian security, was at the top of his list. If possible he also was aiming to gain control over Germany, Czechoslovakia, Hungary, Albania, Bulgaria and Romania.

"We will lie if necessary," Stalin told Molotov. "Politely but resolutely. More than anything, Roosevelt wants the war in Europe finished so he and American forces can concentrate on defeating Japan – which would be nice to have in our portfolio. Churchill will oppose us, but he cannot stand alone. He will need Roosevelt. Who by the way does not look well at all. Pale. Drawn. I think he is seriously ill and might be dying."

"Let's hope not," said Molotov. "We know nothing about his vice president Truman, except that he speaks crudely and lacks leadership experience. Roosevelt is a known quantity, and we can work with him."

At the conference U.S. Secretary of State James Byrne articulated America's position. "Our objective is a government in Poland both friendly to the Soviet Union and representative of all the democratic elements of the country."

The climate in Crimea was milder than that of northern Russia. But the words coming off the Black Sea were unmistakably wintry. So was Stalin's reply. "For the Russian people, the question of Poland is not only a question of honor but also a question of security. Throughout history, Poland has been the corridor through which the enemy has passed into Russia. Poland is a question of life and death for the Soviet Union."

Stalin leaned back from the large round conference table and studied the faces examining him. I am winning, he concluded. Roosevelt is sick and weak. Churchill needs him, but he needs stronger support than Roosevelt's ghost can provide. Stalin glanced furtively at Molotov whose slight nod confirmed Stalin's thinking.

When no reply was forthcoming, Stalin continued. "Boundaries must be altered," he said calmly but firmly. "We insist that eastern Poland become part of Russia. Only that can assure our security." Then, hoping to appear reasonable and appease the objections he was anticipating, Stalin added, "We should let Poland expand its western border. Let it have Silesia, Pomerania and East Prussia. Poland would add valuable land. And of course we would evict Germans living there. Send them back to Germany. I think the number is between six and twelve million." Stalin looked at Molotov for confirmation and received it with a nod. "Let Germans live with Germans, not contaminating Poles."

"We understand your position," Byrne said sympathetically, "and what you propose has some merit."

"Propose?" Stalin replied darkly. "Let me be clear. I am talking about essentials, not luxuries. Now, here is what I propose. Even though the government in Lublin is correct and valid in every respect, I do agree to free and unfettered elections as soon as possible on the basis of universal suffrage and a secret ballot." Stalin was lying and most in the cavernous conference room knew or suspected as much. "Furthermore, with you as my witnesses, I pledge to reorganize the Polish government by bringing in Poles from the country's government-in-exile in London."

In Stalin's thinking, if one transparent lie was proving effective, two would be more so. Stalin got what he wanted from a weakening Roosevelt and an acquiescent Churchill. They all agreed that Soviet forces would remain in Eastern Europe until free elections were held and peoples, including Poles, chose their own forms of government.

At the conference's end the Big Three and their senior staffs gathered and sat for a ceremonial group photo. Afterward, as they were dispersing, Stalin whispered one word to Molotov: "Victory."

In Poland Stalin already was reneging, beginning to suppress freedom of speech, assembly, religion and the press. The Soviet hammer and sickle would continue striking and shredding freedoms. Stanislaw Sosabowski, Thaddeus Metz, Kaz Majos, Bernadeta Gudek and millions of other Poles saw that clear-eyed as the coming reality. For years to come, they sensed that their only freedoms would be of the mind and soul.

CHAPTER 8

Kaz Majos and the two sonderkommandos, Tomasz Dolata and Michal Olenik, hardly felt free. Yes, they were now removed from the hell of Auschwitz, but they knew their survival would depend on remaining ghost-like – silent and invisible.

With stealth that Kaz had honed during his years with the Resistance in Warsaw, the three escapees had successfully trekked east toward Cracow. They had slept on leafy forest floors, taking turns on watches. They had pilfered civilian clothing from backyard laundry lines. They had stolen eggs from hen houses and eaten them raw. They had taken freshly baked bread from kitchen windowsills. They also had learned something about each other.

"So, Kaz – short for Kazimir?" Tomasz asked one night as they settled in. Kaz, reclining with arms folded across his chest, nodded. "Tell us about yourself," said Tomasz. "We all have a story and I have a feeling that yours is more interesting than most."

"Not really." Unconsciously, Kaz unfolded his arms and lightly brushed his scarred right temple. "When war seemed a foregone conclusion, I joined the army. I mean, who could believe Hitler's promise of no more territorial gains after he waltzed into Austria and Czechoslovakia? I volunteered to become a lancer. I served with some excellent men. Brave. Great riders and fighters. I remember one in particular. He was a magnificent horseman. He and his mount seemed as one. I was riding to his right and saw him spear a German soldier. He inspired me and others."

"What was his name?" Michal asked.

"I don't remember."

"What happened to him?"

"After we engaged the Germans, we knew we couldn't stand and fight. There were more of them and they were better armed. Much better. Small arms, grenades, tanks, planes. We turned and rode off. The last I saw of him he cut to the south. I rode north for Warsaw – my hometown." Tomasz and Michal were listening raptly. "You, Tomasz?" Kaz asked.

"Hah. I was one of those rich Jews everyone loved to hate." He laughed heartily. "Just joking. Actually, I was working for my father in his clothing shop. A small one. Suits, shirts, accessories. It was a nice living, but it was boring. I know, I don't look like a shopkeeper. I shave in the morning and by afternoon I look like I'm starting a beard." Tomasz's beard and hair were black and thick. He stood nearly six feet, was thick-chested with slightly sloping shoulders. The overall effect of his appearance: a hulking malevolence. "Anyway, I kept thinking, what else can I do? Where can I go? I was thinking maybe go to the University of Warsaw, study engineering, then get a good job and travel. I was 17 then, 23 now. I know, I look older. I feel older."

"How about you, Michal," Kaz asked.

"I look like what I was – a farm boy. There's this" – he pointed to his hooked nose – "and these" – he pointed down to his large feet. Kaz and Tomasz laughed and all found the laughter therapeutic. A mop of unruly brown hair topped Michal's skinny frame that reached six feet one inch and made him the tallest of the three. If it is possible for someone to look perpetually sad, Michal met the standard; even when hugely amused his eyes seemed at odds with his gaiety. "I wanted to try city life. So I went to Warsaw. I had almost no money, just a few zlotys, but I was confident. That was 1938. I was 18. My timing wasn't so good, eh? I found work in a bearing factory. Good work with good pay. But it was one of the first factories the Nazis took over. When they asked who the Jews were, we were fingered right away. I thought I would be shot on the spot." A pause. "Sometimes I think that would have been best."

The next morning they were in Cracow, and Kaz saw rich irony in their situation. "Five years ago," he told Tomasz and Michal, "I had never been in a basement. My family lived in an apartment on the third floor. Not far from Old Town in Warsaw. Then after the war started and I joined the Home Army, we took to hiding in a church basement. The people in my cell, I came to think of them as family. Since then the only days I have lived above ground were my two nights in Auschwitz and our nights in the forest. Now I see us looking for another underground sanctuary."

"Maybe you have been reincarnated," Michal joked. "Maybe in an earlier life you were a mole – or a rat."

The men laughed and laughter felt rejuvenating. Tomasz and Michal felt themselves slowly regaining some of the humanness they had lost at Auschwitz.

Kaz saw more irony in their searching for refuge in Cracow. The lovely medieval city had been spared war's physical horrors. Not so its social and psychological nightmares. The city long had been home to a thriving Jewish community in a section called Kazimierz. Before the war it was home to some 65,000 Jews. Now, though, the Jewish quarter was barren, stripped of its population, families having been rounded up and dispatched to the camps. Only 6,000 of the 65,000 would survive the war and fewer than 200 would ever return to Cracow.

The night before, as the three men had neared Cracow, Kaz detailed the half-truths he would tell. He figured his sightless eye and scarred face would prove convincing. Their first look at Cracow's bustling central plaza – Rynek Glowny – was encouraging. Just maybe they could lose themselves here and elude the Nazis until war's end.

Rynek Glowny was the largest central plaza – measuring more than 200 yards by 200 yards – in any European city. Anchoring the plaza was St. Mary's church that stood on the northeast corner. The church was built in the 1220s and rebuilt after destructive Tatar raids. Flanking its main portal were two asymmetrical towers. The lower one, about 220 feet high, was topped by a small Renaissance dome and contained five bells. The taller tower soared about 250 feet, traditionally was the city's property and served as a watchtower. Just below and circling the spire was a gilded crown, about eight feet in diameter, which was added in 1666. At the spire's pinnacle was a gilded ball on which was inscribed Cracow's history.

St. Mary's would have dominated Rynek Glowny were it not for its sprawling expanse and the Town Hall Tower that rose more than 200 feet in the plaza's center. That tower, built in the 1400s, stood adjacent the Sukiennice or Cloth Hall, a market building constructed in the 1400s and rebuilt in Renaissance style after a 1555 fire started by an invading Swedish army. The Cloth Hall stretched more than 100 yards. The first floor contained rows of market stalls and the second housed a gallery displaying 19th century paintings. Thousands of Cracowians visited daily. On both sides of the Cloth Hall and at both ends were broad, stone-paved expanses dotted with trees, tables and chairs, a fountain and a larger-than-life statue of Adam Mickiewicz (1798-1855), Poland's most celebrated poet and a revered patriot who is buried in Cracow's Wawel Cathedral.

Rynek Glowny's perimeter included three-, four- and five-story homes, apartment blocks and office buildings. It was, thought Kaz, the perfect place to become invisible. Kaz led Tomasz and Michal into Polska Kopernika, a restaurant on the plaza's southwest corner. He saw a waiter. "May I please speak with the owner?"

The man smiled thinly at the strangers. "I wait tables but I am also the owner. Jacek Frantek." He was five feet six inches, stocky and bald with a black fringe. He was wearing black trousers, white shirt sans jacket and black bowtie. Frantek studied Kaz's scarred face and then peered past it to Tomasz and Michal. "What is your story? You must have one."

Frantek's abruptness was off-putting, momentarily startling Kaz but then comforting him. Perhaps, Kaz was thinking, my lies needn't be so big or so many. "Yes, I was with the lancers and then the Home Army in Warsaw. Until the last day of the uprising. My name is Kaz Majos. My friends, my fellow fighters, are Tomasz Dolata and Michal Olenik. We were shipped to Auschwitz, you've heard of it?" Frantek nodded. "Then I needn't tell you how lucky we are to be standing here."

Frantek continued to scrutinize these three men who had materialized with the suddenness of a winter storm sweeping across the Polish steppes. "Go on."

"We arrived at the camp just two days before the sonderkommando breakout." Frantek nodded his understanding. The Nazis hadn't permitted Polish radio to air news of the mass escape, but truck drivers making supply runs between Auschwitz and Cracow were eager to tell a riveting tale. "We have been on the run since. Sleeping in the forest. We need food and a hiding place." A pause followed during which Kaz pondered the possible merits of additional honesty. "Perhaps for a long time."

"Your clothes…"

"We stole them."

"The SS will keep hunting for you."

"Yes. Unless the Russians beat them here."

"Right, the Russians. Eternal barbarians. More the devil's creation than God's. Were I to help you, my risk would be great. Enormous. For me and my family. You know that."

"I know. It's asking a lot."

45

"And harboring Jews. That could get us shot. My entire family. I have no fondness for Jews."

Tomasz and Michal immediately felt stabs of fear. Would this man inform on them? Point them out to the SS?

Kaz considered briefly and dismissed lying about Tomasz and Michal's religion or ethnic origins. "These men saved my life. They killed three SS."

Kaz looked hard into Frantek's eyes for telling signals. They were easy to spot.

"SS," murmured Frantek, face and tone softening.

"They burned them alive," Kaz elaborated. "In the ovens."

A long moment of silence followed. Although Tomasz and Michal's initial rush of fear had subsided, a sizable measure of tension remained.

Frantek's eyes and the downward set of his lips and lower jaw reflected gestating respect. "I might be able to help...for awhile. If you are willing to stay in my basement. Our wine cellar. We have extra blankets and pillows."

The staircase descending to the basement of Polska Kopernika was wide and curving. The basement itself was vaulted with arches separating its three sections. It looked like nothing so much as the ancient catacombs of Rome. Stored there were restaurant supplies, two extra tables with chairs and hundreds of bottles of wine in the floor-to-ceiling racks.

The interior walls of the restaurant itself were red brick. The tables and chairs were dark brown as were the bar and stools. Overhead were three ceiling fans.

The staff was the Frantek family. In addition to serving as waiter, Jacek, age 40, tended bar and ran the business. His wife Maria, 39, was chef. She was a lovely woman, still shapely with light brown hair, hazel eyes and an unlined face. Their 15-year-old son Edward both waited and cleared tables. He was lanky and still growing, already nearing six feet. Their daughter Marzena, 17, did whatever was necessary, helping Maria in the kitchen, waitressing during peak periods, fetching supplies and wine from the basement. Marzena's hair was blonde, her eyes blue, cheekbones high, bust smallish. She was a beauty well along in the making.

Frantek assured Kaz, Tomasz and Michal that his family was something more: patriotic and discreet.

CHAPTER 9

Snow. Freshly fallen, is there anything whiter? Purer? Is there anything in nature that inspires more wonderment than winter's first snow? Is there anything more conducive to frolic? To meditation? Can anything better mask earth's scars and blemishes and those of man?

In early February 1945 fresh, unsullied snow was blanketing central and northern Korea, and it was fueling frolic for Park Min Shik and Ahn Kyong Ae. They were both seated on the saddle of Colonel Fukunaga's chestnut gelding, and the animal's galloping hoofs were kicking up sprays of white.

Min and Kyong, dressed warmly in heavy cloth coats and woolen caps with earflaps, were half-laughing and half-shouting and each exhalation emitted a cloud of vapor. The horse's exertions, too, had it expelling crystallized breaths. It was hard to judge who was luxuriating more in merriment, the two exultant teenagers or their proud, powerful mount.

Min pulled back on the reins and slowed the energized horse to a walk. The animal twice threw back his head and snorted loudly; clearly he wasn't ready for this interlude to end.

"I'm glad your brother isn't with us," Kyong smiled.

"It is nice to be alone for once."

"Is it the snow and the cold that kept Han at home?"

"Yes. The horse can't carry all three of us, and Han didn't want to have to walk. Not in deep snow on these country roads. Who can blame him? Besides, he wanted to check on a rumor."

"The one about the Americans?"

"Yes."

"I hear they are defeating the Japanese," said Kyong. "Everywhere. On all the Pacific islands, and they are bombing Japanese cities."

"We are hearing the same thing."

"I hope that is good news for us."

"Me too," said Min. "If Japan surrenders to America, I hope America forces Japan to leave Korea."

"Freedom. It was taken away from our country before we were born. I wonder what it feels like."

"I wonder what they are like," Min murmured, "the Americans."

"Do you think we'll ever see one?"

"I don't know."

"If we do, I hope we can be friends," said Kyong.

"We certainly don't need more enemies. The Japanese are more than enough."

"I hear Americans are ugly," Kyong said. "Big and hairy with scary round eyes."

"I hear their women are ugly too," said Min. "Bigger than our men."

"Do you think they are as brutal, as mean, as the Japanese?"

"I don't know, but they must be tough soldiers if they are defeating the Japanese."

"The Japanese have always told us they are the best soldiers. The bravest."

"They believe they are."

"But perhaps their heads have grown too big," Kyong posited thoughtfully. "They defeated the Russians at the start of the new century, and they conquered us. They destroyed the American fleet at Pearl Harbor and they defeated the American soldiers in the Philippines. Forced their leader to run away to Australia and captured many American soldiers. They also drove the British out of Singapore. They might see themselves as invincible."

"The almighty samurai."

"But perhaps the American giants are mightier. And kinder."

Without another word, Kyong slid off the saddle and, gathering up her ankle-length skirt, stepped delicately through six inches of undisturbed snow to the roadside.

"Do you need privacy?" Min asked.

Kyong didn't reply. She squatted, her back obscuring her hands' movements. Min wasn't sure whether he should keep watching or turn away. Curiosity won out. A few moments later Kyong straightened slowly – then whirled and hurled a snowball that struck Min's chest. Kyong squealed her mischievous delight.

"Hey!" Min shouted. He vaulted from the saddle and went lunging toward Kyong. She screamed and turned to escape but was too slow. Min tackled her none too gently, snow flying in all directions, and then grabbed a handful and crushed it against Kyong's crimson left cheek. Then the two youngsters were locked in a rollicking embrace.

Their zest for whimsy also carried over to other seasonal pursuits. Once on a sun-dappled summer afternoon they had fashioned a seesaw from materials at hand. First they rolled together tightly two sleeping mats. Then across the roll they centered and balanced a plank, about twelve inches wide and eight feet long. Next, about eight feet off the ground and parallel to the plank, they hung a long rope, anchoring its ends to a pair of stout trees. Kyong then stood on the end of the plank resting on the ground. Grinning broadly, Min leaped onto the other end, sending Kyong high into the air, shrieking and grabbing the rope with her left hand for stability. When she descended on the plank, her weight sent Min soaring, whooping delightedly and grabbing the rope. They continued this derring-do until both were exhausted, lying supine on the ground, side-by-side, sweating and laughing.

✝✝✝

Thousands of miles to the south there was no snow where Lucy Crispin was galloping her gray mare, Miss Kiwi, through the surf on the beach near Wellington. The salty sea breeze and spray was tangling Lucy's curly brown hair. Still, snow wasn't far away, and Lucy could envision the white crown of 12,349-foot Mt. Cook, about 300 miles down South Island. Majestic and endlessly varied landscapes were one of the things Lucy appreciated most about her native New Zealand. No spot on the 1,000-mile-long nation is more than 80 miles from a coast, and nowhere are mountains out of sight.

No European had seen New Zealand before 1642 when Dutch sailor Abel Tasman visited. He left his name for posterity – Tasmania, Tasman Sea, Tasmanian Devil. It was 1769 before British Captain James Cook paid a visit, and the last years of the 1700s before the first Europeans tried settling there. Greeting them were brown-skinned Maoris who had migrated from Polynesian islands northeast of New Zealand.

Like so many New Zealanders Lucy's ancestors had emigrated from Great Britain, in her case Scotland. They had prospered. Her father Morgan was a physician, working at Wellington Public Hospital. Her mother Clarissa was an elementary school teacher in a nation where education was prized; it was free for all youngsters up to age 19. Lucy's brother Gordon, older by four years, was attending Victoria University in Wellington and was intent on becoming a Presbyterian minister. Presbyterianism was the most common denomination among New Zealanders of Scottish extraction.

Lucy loved living in Wellington. The thriving capital city sat at the south tip of North Island. The surrounding terrain was rugged. Just across 16-mile-wide Cook Strait was 4,000-foot Mt. Stokes. It and other nearby peaks were all the more impressive because they sprouted and soared from sea level.

Across the strait Lucy could easily see South Island. The sea breezes continually brushing Wellington often escalated into gales that brought the rains that kept New Zealand perpetually emerald green and an agricultural powerhouse. The country's chief exports were butter, cheese, lamb and wool. The population of sheep and cattle – more than 25 million at the time – far outnumbered the nation's citizens.

Lucy also relished Wellington's beaches which she frequented year round. She swam in the warm water, rode Miss Kiwi up and down sandy stretches of coastline and from the bluffs behind them watched whales migrating north and south with the changing seasons. Most of the creatures were right whales, so named by whalers because they swim slowly, float when dead and yield large quantities of baleen. In other words they were just right for harvesting. Those same bluffs afforded Lucy views of seals, some cavorting in the water, others lounging and sunning on the rocks.

Lucy was enjoying her solitude, with only Miss Kiwi for company. She slowed the horse to a walk and reflected. I'm quite certain I want to be a nurse. I want to serve others as much as father with his doctoring, mother with her teaching and soon Gordon with his preaching. I love my family. They are wonderful. Couldn't ask for better. I like the idea of tending to the sick. I like people. But it's strange. I also like being alone. Treasure it, actually. All right, Miss Kiwi, so you would argue I'm not alone when I'm with you. Valid point, sort of. But solitude. It frees my mind for thinking, for dreaming. I think I could try living away from New Zealand. From friends and family. I think I would do just fine. I could live alone and be content. Just as long as I wasn't lonely. You do understand, don't you, Miss Kiwi?

Lucy laughed, noisily inhaled a gulp of salt air and patted Miss Kiwi's gray neck. Gordon is happy at Victoria, she mused. He has no plan but to spend his life here in Wellington. I could get good nurse training at Wellington Public, but I'm beginning to think I might like studying abroad. Perhaps Scotland or England.

"Come on, Miss Kiwi, let's pick up the pace again." Lucy flicked the reins, tapped her heels against the horse's flanks, and Miss Kiwi went galloping across the sand. "That's my girl!"

In London in his Notting Hill home Michael Cornelius looked outside at falling snow – not a frequent occurrence in London, warmed by Gulf Stream-powered winds, which made it all the more welcome. The family radio was tuned to BBC news, and Michael was far more interested in the report on the Yalta Conference than in the weather.

I don't understand, he was thinking. I am but a boy, but I can see bad things coming from Yalta. Can't they see it? Churchill. Roosevelt. Stalin wants to own Europe. Maybe Asia too. What will he try? How long will other nations abide it? If I were to join the army, I can see my uniform getting muddied or bloodied in some corner of the world where Stalin is trying his own form of Hitlerism. Bloody bastards. A pox on both of them.

†††

In the snow-clogged mountains west of Wonsan, Kim Il Sung and Sergeant Kwon Oh Bum had but one goal at the moment: staying warm. Biting Siberian winds were penetrating the uncaulked stone walls of their mountain hut. Kim and Kwon were squatting next to a small fire and blowing on their hands. They also were shivering.

"No fighting today," said Kwon, lips bluish. "Not until the weather warms up."

Kim smiled tightly. "The imperial Japanese have never gotten used to our winters. Their homeland is so much milder, or so they say. Here they don't come hunting for us. Maybe we could take a company of our guerillas, come down from the mountains, walk into one of their camps. Slaughter them all while they huddle around their stoves. Easy pickings."

Kwon looked through the flames at his leader, not sure of his seriousness and not wanting to say something witless. Kwon felt Kim trusted him but was uncertain how the renowned guerilla assessed his intelligence, judgment and capacity for providing effective senior leadership. "I will make tea."

"Yes, tea. Sipping tea is good for thinking. Good for dreaming and planning."

Kwon stood, reached for a pot and stepped outside to pack it tightly with snow. Back inside he slipped the pot's handle over his rifle's bayonet and held it over the fire until the snow melted and heated.

Minutes later both men were welcoming the liquid heat coursing into their stomachs and spreading warmth through their torsos.

Kim, still squatting, closed his eyes and let his head rock back. He sighed.

"Your thoughts?" Kwon ventured.

"Actually, my dreams."

"Will you share them?"

Eyes still closed, Kim replied, "I see myself as the leader of a strong nation. A free nation. From the Yalu River to Pusan. But I am also a realist. We need help to get the Japanese out, and those who help us might have their own dreams and demands. I wish my dreams were clearer."

CHAPTER 10

In Shelby Tom Brecker's alarm clock jarred him awake at 4 a.m. It was a Monday and snow had been falling since early the previous evening. He fumbled for the alarm pin and pushed it in. Bridgett stirred.

"Sorry, Bridg."

"Try not to wake the twins," she mumbled drowsily. Little Jack and Theresa both were in cribs in the adjoining bedroom in the small ranch-style house.

"Okay." Tom swung his legs off the bed and reached down for his prosthetic foot, fastened it in place and stood to dress. "But remember," he teased, "it was you who said I should run for mayor. Can I help it if I won?"

"You won't let me forget. Want some breakfast, Mr. Mayor?"

"Later."

"Do you really have to go out?"

"I know it's the superintendent's decision to close the schools, but he'll be looking to me for an assessment of road and street conditions. Plus I want to be sure our snowplow crews are out." C.G. Keck was superintendent of Shelby Schools.

"Be careful."

"I will."

"Ice on bridges."

"I'll take it easy."

Mayor Tom Brecker pulled on a brown stocking cap, red sweater, his thick blue wool Navy pea coat and lined leather gloves. He raised the garage door, started his 1939 blue Chevrolet – price: $689 new – and backed cautiously out of the driveway. He left the garage door raised, not worried about security at 4:15 a.m. in 1945 Shelby.

✝✝✝

Bridgett heard the garage door going up and the Chevy backing out. She had pulled a blanket tighter around her neck, hoping to go back to sleep. It's no use, she thought, as worry began setting in. In weather like this those country roads can be treacherous. Drive carefully, Tom, she pleaded silently, please drive carefully. She threw back the covers and swung her legs over the side of the bed. She slid her feet into pink, moccasin-style slippers, stood and pulled on a pink terrycloth robe. I'll check on the twins and go make coffee. Have it ready when Tom gets back. I hope the heater in the car is working. I'll be glad when the war's over and we can get a new car.

Production of new cars had stopped on February 9, 1942, as auto factories converted to making military vehicles.

In the kitchen Bridgett switched on the radio and tuned it to WMAN in Mansfield, 12 miles southeast from Shelby. She looked up at the clock over her stove. Almost 5 a.m. News should be on in a few minutes. She readied the coffee for perking.

A few minutes later, leaning against the formica-topped kitchen counter, her thoughts again turned to Tom. Sometimes I wish he didn't feel so responsible. But he's that way about everything. His work, the kids, me. She sighed audibly. That's a big part of why I love him so. But really, I shouldn't be worrying about him. If I'm going to worry – and what woman, what mother, doesn't? – I should be worrying about Theresa. And Paul and Jack. They're the ones still in a war. Tom's war is done. It ended when the Hornet went down. He lost a foot but so many of his friends lost everything. I have to agree with him; in a way, he's lucky.

The storm's been coming from the west, Tom was thinking, so I'll head west out of town and then circle around to the north. I'll finish up driving by the high school and then get back home and call Superintendent Keck.

Tom drove carefully through the driving snow north on Mansfield Avenue to Main Street. He turned left or west and crossed the Baltimore & Ohio railroad tracks. A few hundred yards ahead, as he started onto the Main Street bridge that crossed the Blackfork River, he brought the Chevy to a stop and looked down. Frozen, with this new layer of snow, about six inches so far, he was guessing.

The Blackfork is a stream that divides Main Street and the town into east and west but, except for occasional floods, hasn't been noteworthy and divides the community in no other appreciable respect. Despite its designation the Blackfork hardly qualifies as a river. The channel is seldom wider than 30 feet, although the section coursing through Shelby does have steep banks and runs deep after heavy rains and spring runoffs. Today below the ice it was nine feet deep.

Tom eased the car off the bridge and continued west up a grade on Main Street. He crossed a second set of railroad tracks – New York Central or Big Four as Shelbians called the double set of rails – continued cutting through town and headed into the countryside. He turned right or north on Funk Road. I think bus drivers are going to find this dicey, Tom was thinking. Those deep ditches could have some drop-in visitors. Tom's little joke tickled him and he chuckled. At Smiley Road he turned right again or east and drove back into Shelby until reaching North Gamble Street where he turned north and headed back into the countryside. If this snow keeps on coming down at this rate for the next hour, I'll recommend closing the schools. Too dangerous for kids to be standing on roadsides waiting for buses that could skid every time the driver touches the brakes. I'm sure Mr. Keck will agree.

At 5:30 Tom was back in Shelby and once again on Main Street. He turned south on High School Avenue and drove past the Shelby Salesbook Company where his older brother Paul, the middle of the three Brecker brothers, had worked before enlisting and eventually serving with the 101st Airborne Division in Europe. For Paul somewhere in Europe the day is already half over, Tom reflected. Then his thoughts turned briefly to older brother Jack and the snow he might be trudging through somewhere in eastern France or Belgium. Then it was back to more local matters. Even if the schools close, the Salesbook and other plants in town will be up and running.

Tom turned the Chevy west onto Park Avenue and drove slowly past the high school's main entrance. He smiled. He was remembering taking Latin with Dora Summer. Terrific teacher. She made learning fun. Doesn't seem so long since I was sitting in class there and itching to graduate and get on with life. He shook his head in mild self-reproach.

The grounds of the high school, built in 1924, and adjacent Central Elementary School, constructed in 1875, bordered a narrow driveway that paralleled the Blackfork. Both schools were three-story red brick structures. Where the driveway ended at Main Street stood the town's brick fire department station house, dating to the mid-1800s and one of the town's oldest buildings. All that separated the narrow driveway from the Blackfork was a thin strand of cable.

Past the high school Tom edged the Chevy into a sharp right turn onto the start of the driveway that dipped quickly into a sloping grade. Immediately Tom felt his tires sliding. Should have put chains on, he chided himself. He continued north on the driveway. At the point just before the slope began to flatten, the Chevy's tires again lost traction. This time the slide was more pronounced. Ice, Tom thought, and he felt the surge of adrenalin that accompanies the sudden onset of fear. The sliding car quickly picked up momentum and went careening into the strand of protective cable. It stretched and snapped and Tom's hands tightened their grip on the steering wheel as the car started over and down the steep, rock-lined embankment.

A second later the Chevy was on the ice. Tom heard it cracking and beginning to give under the weight of the car's 3,000 pounds. Tom's mind flashed back to the 1942 attack on the aircraft carrier USS Hornet and the unnerving sound of the wood flight deck cracking and splintering as seven falling bombs and two Japanese fighters crashed into the doomed ship. A piece of shrapnel that went slicing across the deck had cost Tom his foot.

Tom knew that seconds were precious. Without hesitating he pulled up on the door handle. It didn't budge. The car's front end was nosing down through the cracking ice and into the frigid stream. His mind was racing. I won't last long in that water, certainly not trapped under the ice. Tom pushed hard against the door.

† † †

Polish winters can be and often are brutal, and the winter of 1945 was proving no exception. As Tom struggled in the Blackfork, in Cracow at Polska Kopernika, Kaz, Tomasz and Michal ascended the staircase from the basement. It was noon – six hours later than in Shelby – and the restaurant was closed as it customarily was on Mondays, the day the Franteks relaxed. Jacek greeted the men warmly with a smile. "Maria has a nice meal ready for you. Chicken and dumplings and stewed tomatoes." Jacek then called for Marzena who emerged from the kitchen. "Go to the basement," Jacek instructed, "and bring up a nice bottle of riesling. Two bottles. It's German wine," Jacek smiled wryly, "perhaps the only good thing to come from Germany."

The men chuckled. Edward approached the table, holding one large plate in his left hand and a second in his right and balancing a third on his extended right arm. Artfully, he placed the first plate in front of Kaz.

The aroma of delicious food lovingly prepared caused Kaz to sigh. "We cannot begin to tell you how grateful we are," he said.

"Yes," added Michal, openly thankful, and glancing at Tomasz, "we as Jews have never experienced such kindness from gentiles."

"And I," Jacek acknowledged, "have never treated Jews so well. Never even thought to do so. Perhaps because you are special Jews – or perhaps because I've been a prisoner of my prejudice."

Edward positioned plates in front of Tomasz and Michal.

"Please sit with us," Kaz said and motioned Jacek and Edward to pull chairs from adjacent tables to theirs. "I have something to propose."

"Oh?"

"You and your family work very hard, and you harbor us and we do nothing in return."

"Pshaw," Jacek grumbled. "We are merely Poles helping Poles. Your gratitude is enough."

"No," Kaz said firmly, "it is not. We want to help you."

"How?"

"Cleaning up at night."

"I don't know. I-"

"Think about it," Kaz cut him off. "At night you are bone tired. All of you. It's all you can do to make it up the stairs to your apartment. My guess is that you get up there and collapse."

"Only every night," Jacek admitted.

"Here is my proposal. Ours. Tomasz and Michal firmly support it. After Maria has prepared the last supper for your guests, she leaves the kitchen and goes immediately up to your apartment. No staying late to clean up. Marzena can go up with her."

"What about your suppers?" Jacek asked.

"Leftovers. Just leave them on a counter or in the oven."

"I don't think Maria will approve."

Kaz smiled. "We are not totally helpless in a kitchen."

"Maria would no doubt disagree," Jacek said, his arched eyebrow underscoring his dubiousness.

"We can heat up food she leaves," Kaz insisted. "Anyway, immediately after your last guest has departed, you and Edward go upstairs. We three will clean up, wash and dry pots and pans and plates. Put them away. Reset tables for the next day."

Jacek's right hand rubbed his forehead. "A little more rest would be nice." Jacek looked at Edward who was grinning his agreement.

"Good," said Kaz. "That's settled."

Jacek laced together the fingers of his hands and rested his chin against them. "I've been thinking. You need something to do during the day besides reading our books. Do you play chess?"

Tomasz shot Jacek a look of mock dismay. "We are Poles."

"Of course. Wait. I'll be right back." He pushed away from the table and walked briskly to the steps leading up to the apartment.

Edward shrugged his shoulders, gesturing his puzzlement at his father's abrupt exit.

Moments later Jacek returned with a handsome wood case. Its lacquered sides bore the squares of a chessboard. He placed the case on the table and opened it. Inside were the two sets of pieces, carved from stone, one set white, the other black.

"It's beautiful," Tomasz said with undisguised admiration. "The most beautiful set I've ever seen."

"Yes," said Jacek, "it belonged to my father. I want you to take it to the basement. Keep it there."

Tomasz and Michal both felt their throats thickening with emotion. A prized family possession, belonging to a Catholic, offered to Jews. "Are you sure?" Michal asked quietly.

"Is Hitler the devil incarnate?" Jacek's reply lightened the mood and low chuckling followed.

"How well do you play?" Tomasz asked Jacek.

"Not nearly as beautifully as those pieces should be played. Edward beats me routinely." Edward blushed. "It's true," Jacek said proudly.

"Well then, we must have a tournament. We will all take turns playing each other," Tomasz said. "You, Michal, Kaz, Edward and me."

"Maybe we can improve our games," said Michal, "learn something from each other."

"I think we already are," said Jacek.

†††

Tom Brecker never had felt water so cold. Water that caused pain on first contact, that felt like ice picks stabbing every pore. He gasped. Gotta get out fast, he thought grimly. I won't last ten minutes in this water.

The car's front end was through the ice and below the water's surface. Then came a fleeting thought: I wonder if anyone heard the crash. He glanced up and looked at the houses on the other side of the Blackfork. No lights shining over there and the fire station is too far away.

Tom drew up his knees and maneuvered his legs onto the car seat. Water was rising quickly to seat level. With all the force Tom could muster, he propelled himself out through the open car door and onto the ice. Please hold, he thought, and spread his arms and legs as widely as possible to distribute his weight. He could hear – and feel beneath him – the ice still splintering. He knew the Chevy was continuing its slide beneath the surface but didn't turn to look. Slowly, as gingerly as possible, his torso flat against the ice, Tom began inching his way toward the embankment. He elevated his face to keep it above the deepening snow that continued falling unabated. Another minute and he was reaching out. A moment later he could feel the bottom of the embankment. Relief. I'm going to make it. He drew his legs forward and started to stand. With a decided absence of grace his body crumpled. Damn. My foot's gone. It still was in the car. The Chevy's plunge down the embankment and Tom's exertions had separated the prosthetic foot. He thought again about calling for help. No one's going to hear me at this hour, not in this snow. Not with the wind blowing from the west, away from those houses and toward the schools. And I need to get out of these wet clothes soon.

✝✝✝

"Stay tuned to WMAN, your official station for school closing announcements," the newscaster intoned gravely. He knew that mothers, especially mothers on farms whose high school-age kids relied on bus transportation, were already up and listening to weather reports. In 1945 many of their younger children still walked to nearby one-room red brick schools that dotted the Richland County countryside.

Bridgett peered through the kitchen window into the snow-blown darkness. Tom, I hope you're just about done with your inspection. Coffee's ready, honey. And Theresa, I wonder where you're at now, what you're doing. I hope you're safe.

Theresa was safe now and so were Tom's older brothers. Hitler's last offensive gasp, his Ardennes offensive, already dubbed the Battle of the

Bulge, had been blunted. But his forces had bulled their way through Allied lines for 60 miles before determined resistance at Bastogne and elsewhere, along with fuel shortages, had stopped the advance. Now it was Allied troops who were pushing forward toward the Rhine and across into Hitler's shrinking Reich.

During the worst of the battle Theresa's evacuation hospital had been shelled. Her commanding officer, Lieutenant Colonel Marilyn Carter, had been killed, and shrapnel had sliced Theresa's left hip, leaving her with a limp that would prove permanent.

Brothers Jack and Paul were out of harm's way; their units had been given temporary reprieves, rotated to the rear for a respite after the bludgeoning they had taken at Bastogne.

Tom had begun scaling the Blackfork's rock-lined embankment. His gloved hands kept probing upward for finger grips. Simultaneously he continued wedging the toe of his right shoe between rocks and using it to push himself higher. He was no longer shivering. Beneath his Navy pea coat he was beginning to sweat. His pants were water soaked and his legs were aching from the penetrating cold. Tom paused, for rest and for steadying himself on the steep slope. He breathed in slowly and deeply. His mind flashed back to the Hornet. Here I am, he thought, trying to climb up from freezing water. On the Hornet they were lowering me over the side and trying to keep me out of water that was oil-slicked and burning. My buddies wouldn't believe this, especially the ones who migrated to California and Florida.

Tom sucked in another deep breath of the cold morning air. Then he continued the torturous ascent. Minutes later his hands reached the top edge of the embankment. He spread his fingers and steadied his right foot on a rock below. Then he pushed upward hard with his foot and arms and heaved himself onto the roadway. In another moment he rolled onto his back, spitting snow from his lips and brushing it from his eyes. He lay there, breathing hard, eyes closed, falling snow melting against his upturned face. Then he rolled back onto his stomach, drew his knees forward and began crawling through the snow toward the fire station, still some 300 yards away. Through his awkward exertions, dragging a useless leg, a thought caused him to smile ruefully. *First I lose a foot, a real one, on the high seas. Then I lose its replacement in the Blackfork. The puny Blackfork. Maybe they'll find it when they pull the car out. Boy, would this make a picture and headline for* The Daily Globe? *Just imagine it:* Mayor Brecker Drives Car Into Drink; Loses Foot – Again.

CHAPTER 11

The pounding on the door to Polska Kopernica was loud and insistent. Jacek Frantek looked up at the clock above the bar. Nearly 10:00. The restaurant would not be opening until noon. He looked at his son Edward spreading a tablecloth, and he shrugged. *Can't be a regular customer*, Jacek was thinking. Maria was in the kitchen, organizing for lunch patrons. Marzena had descended to the basement to retrieve salt and spices for Maria.

Jacek stepped to the door and unbolted it. A Russian sergeant, Victor Yankov, reached out with his left hand and roughly shoved Jacek back away from the door. Four privates followed.

"You have food," Yankov growled, foregoing introductions. "We need some."

"We are not yet open for business," said Jacek, stumbling backward and trying to keep his balance while feeling anger beginning to boil.

"You are open for our business," Yankov replied brusquely in passable Polish.

"I am sorry but-"

"Where are your women?" Yankov asked, his question sounding much more like a demand. He and the four privates all were carrying a PPsh, the Russian submachine gun that was so common as to be virtually a badge for Soviet infantrymen. The gun held 71 rounds and fired at a rate of 800 rounds per minute, much faster than its British (500 rpm) and American (450 rpm) cousins.

With the mention of women, Jacek's anger was giving way to another emotion; he could almost smell his own fear and struggled to contain it. "My women...my wife-"

Yankov shoved the muzzle of his PPsh against Jacek's chest. "One lie and you are dead."

At that moment Maria was exiting the kitchen and, wiping her hands on a white apron, entered the dining room. A sudden surge of terror was rendering her speechless. These were the first Russian troops she had seen, but rumors of their savagery had been preceding them.

Yankov could see the panic in her hazel eyes; he had seen it often as he and vengeful troops made their way west across the steppes of Russia and Poland. Early in the war, the Russians had taken a terrible beating, almost lost the war at Moscow and Leningrad. Now they were winning, and they were taking spoils indiscriminately. He and his men were viewing Maria as prey, about to be caught and consumed.

In the basement Marzena froze. She couldn't make out all the intruder's words, spoken in fractured Polish, but there was no mistaking their criminal intent. Michal and Edward looked up from their chess game. Kaz and Tomasz, watching the match, slowly and quietly pushed back their chairs and rose. "Polish – with a Russian accent," Kaz whispered to Tomasz.

"What-" Tomasz began to ask.

"Shhh." Kaz motioned to Edward to stand. "Go upstairs," he whispered close to Edward's left ear. "Don't do anything rash and don't lie about your sister. Lie about us. Call out to your father on the way up. Let the Russians know you're coming."

Edward, eyes widened, nodded fearfully and stepped away from the table. Nervously, knees shaky, the lanky youth started up the stairs. "Father, what is it?" He wondered frantically whether the Russians could detect the tremor in his voice. "Is everything all right?"

"Who is that?" Yankov asked.

"My son."

"Tell him to get up here."

"Edward," Jacek called, "come up."

"What do we do?" Michal whispered to Kaz.

"For the moment, nothing. Be quiet. Be still. Listen." Kaz then tip-toed across the stone-paved floor to the base of the stairs.

† † †

"Who else is here?" Yankov asked Edward.

"Only my sister."

Jacek and Maria immediately found themselves wondering whether Kaz had coached Edward to lie. They both sensed approaching disaster, with Maria beginning to quiver at the mention of Marzena. The Russians' reputation for mass rapes was deserved.

Yankov stepped toward Jacek and took his right arm. "To the basement." Then, still holding the PPsh in his right hand, gestured with the weapon and said in Russian to one of the privates, "Stay here with the woman and the boy. If they try anything, kill them." Then, looking at his other men, Yankov said, "Come with me."

† † †

"They are coming down," Tomasz whispered.

Kaz stepped toward Marzena. Terror was paralyzing her. Kaz grasped her shoulders and shook her twice. "They must see you. Don't hide. Don't resist." Kaz's one good eye looked hard into hers. "If they don't see you, they will hunt for you and find us and we will be of no use. Do you understand?"

Almost imperceptibly, she nodded.

Kaz released his grip. "Tomasz, Michal, each of you take two bottles of wine, one in each hand. I'll do the same."

"Weapons?" Michal asked.

"If necessary," Kaz replied.

The Russians had not yet reached the sharp turn in the staircase.

"There is no gas here," Michal whispered through clenched teeth, "but this will be a death chamber. This time we will not help them kill."

"You could die," Kaz whispered.

"It would be past due."

Kaz nodded his understanding. "Tomasz, hide back in that corner." Kaz pointed to a distant, dark corner. "Do nothing until you see me move."

63

"All right." Tomasz, his hulking frame gliding with unexpected grace, moved away from the center of the room. Once in the corner, he looked for his shadow, saw none and was satisfied with the concealment.

"Michal, you and I over there. Now." Then to Marzena he said, "Do not look in our direction. Not even a glance. No matter what." Again, she nodded, her head the only part of her body capable of movement.

✝✝✝

At the bottom of the staircase Sergeant Yankov saw Marzena standing by the table. Then he saw the chess set. "How nice," he said derisively, "sister and brother playing chess together. So Russian. Who was winning?"

Marzena could barely find her voice. She managed to squeak, "Edward."

"Ah, the boy," said Yonkov. Upstairs the mother was terror-stricken, but the daughter, he could see, was petrified, literally. "Perhaps a future Polish master." A pause and then a smirk. "Fat chance of that. Polish master – a classic contradiction in terms." Yankov then shoved Jacek away from his side and in Russian told one of the privates, "Put your gun on him." Then to the other two privates, he ordered, "Put your guns down and put the girl on the floor."

They had the look of children at their own birthday party, just handed gaily wrapped presents to open. They grabbed Marzena's arms and shoulders and forced her down. She would have blanched had the color not already drained from her face.

Jacek protested, "No, please. She is young and innocent."

"All the better," Yonkov replied, smirking again. "Say one more word – just one – and you are dead. Just watch."

"We are Poles," Jacek pleaded. "Your allies."

"Kill him," Yankov ordered one of the privates.

"No!" Marzena cried out. "Please, no."

Yankov gestured to the private to lower his PPsh. Then to Jacek, "You will not receive another reprieve. Trust me on that. You call us allies. You are filth." Yankov spat on the stone floor. "You fought us in the Great War. You tolerate us now only because we are driving out the Nazis. But allies, no."

Yankov was alluding to World War I when Poland, allied with Austria, had in fact attacked and defeated Russian troops when it sensed an opportunity for independence, something that Poland had experienced only sporadically over the centuries.

The two privates pinned Marzena on her back. Her blonde hair spread on the cold paving stones, tears were seeping from her closed eyes and her chin was quivering. Yankov stood over her. "Pull back her dress," he ordered one of the privates who quickly grabbed the hem and jerked it toward him. "Cover her face with it. I'll do it first, then you."

Jacek gulped, gritted his teeth and pivoted his head to avert his eyes. If anything could be worse than being murdered, he knew it was about to take place.

Kaz was bending slightly, peering between wine bottles stacked in one of the racks. He could see Marzena's exposed legs and struggled to contain his mounting anger and disgust. So could Michal who felt instant loathing for the Russian sergeant. Swine, he was seething. Barbarian swine.

Yankov squatted, laid his gun on the floor and separated Marzena's legs. She whimpered. Then Yankov pulled roughly on her underpants. She drew up her knees, blindly trying to resist. He pushed them down and removed the pants. Instinctively she tried to close her thighs, but Yankov wedged his left knee between them.

Michal, aching to act, tossed his mop of brown hair back and glanced at Kaz who nodded. Stealthily, both holding full bottles of wine in each hand, they moved from behind the wine rack. Tomasz saw them and moved from his dark corner and closed athletically on the private guarding Jacek who saw Tomasz moving toward him.

The Russians, grimly intent on proceeding with the rape, neither saw nor heard the Poles coming.

Kaz swung first, slamming a bottle against Yankov's right temple, sending him sprawling with shards of broken glass and red wine going down with him. An instant later Michal and Tomasz were swinging their bottles-as-clubs against the heads of two Russian privates. More shattered glass and wine went flying around the room. The fourth Russian, startled, looked around in disbelief. Then seeing Kaz regaining his balance, the soldier reached for his PPsh and pointed it toward Kaz. Michal reacted instantly. He threw his second bottle at the Russian. His aim was good, the bottle bouncing off the soldier's left shoulder and diverting his attention from Kaz. The soldier jerked his gun toward Michal and fired. A spray of rounds sent Michal stumbling backward onto the chess table, scattering the pieces and toppling one of the chairs. Slowly he slid off the table onto the floor. Lying on his back, his chest heaved spasmodically.

Tomasz, putting his powerful shoulders behind the effort, swung with his second bottle and struck the Russian on the rear of his neck at the base of his skull. Using the jagged edge of the part of the bottle still in his hand, he sliced the Russian's throat.

✝✝✝

Upstairs the soldier guarding Maria and Edward was growing uneasy. "What is happening?" he shouted. No answer. Again he called out, "Sergeant Yankov, can you hear me?"

The sounds of breaking bottles and gunfire had Maria and Edward looking at each other, stunned, with Maria verging on collapse.

✝✝✝

Kaz bent low over Michal. Blood was staining his torso and seeping from his mouth. "No gas," he murmured, coughing and choking on his blood. Then, through his agony, he managed a slight smile. "But no help killing."

"Take it easy, Michal," said Kaz, one hand cradling his head.

"It is all right," Michal said in a choked whisper. "I am about to be free."

Kaz saw Marzena sitting up, pushing her dress back down over her legs, retrieving her underpants and struggling to stand. She moved behind a rack of bottles and stepped back into her pants.

"Michal-" Kaz whispered.

Marzena reappeared and Jacek quickly moved to his daughter's side, wrapping his right arm around her shoulders and drawing her close. The two of them stepped near Michal and Kaz.

"You saved me," Michal murmured.

"No. You have it wrong," Kaz smiled tenderly. "You and Tomasz and Jacob Kuron saved me."

"Save this family," Michal urged Kaz and coughed up more blood.

66

"We will try." He gently removed his hand from underneath Michal's head and stood. "Tomasz, Jacek. Help me drag these bastards over there," he said, pointing to the corner where Tomasz had been hiding. They did so and Kaz handed Jacek a PPsh. "Can you use this?"

"Yes."

"If they try to stand or even crawl to you, shoot. Immediately."

"I can do that," Jacek said grimly.

"Good." Then to Marzena, Kaz said, "Sit" and guided her to a chair. "No matter what you hear, sit here." A pause. "You are very brave."

"May I kneel with Michal?"

Kaz paused before answering. "Yes, that would be better."

Then Kaz picked up one of the submachine guns and Tomasz did likewise. They checked the fourth Russian, already dead, blood still seeping from the deep gash in his neck and pooling on the floor.

"Let's stay as far apart as we can on the staircase," Kaz whispered. "I'm not sure what we'll find upstairs."

Tomasz nodded and they began moving silently upward, a shoulder of each man brushing against a staircase wall. At the top, their guns at the ready, they stepped into the dining room and farther apart from each other.

At the sight of the two armed Poles, the Russian's head shook. Who are these men? What have they done? He now was feeling his own sense of rising panic. His left hand was gripping Maria's dress at the neck, his right the PPsh.

Kaz nodded to Tomasz and they put more distance between each other.

"Stop!" cried the Russian in accented Polish.

"No," said Kaz, and he and Tomasz stepped farther apart.

"I will kill the woman and the boy."

"I don't think so," Kaz said calmly, peering intently into the Russian private's widened eyes. "Maybe one but not both and then we will kill you."

"I'll shoot you first."

Kaz took the threat seriously, but the tremor in the private's voice gave him the confidence to keep speaking evenly. "Not both of us, though," said Kaz, sliding another step away from Tomasz. "You have several choices but they are all bad. Put your gun down."

"Sergeant Yankov-"

"He is alive, under guard."

"You will shoot me."

"Not if you put your gun down now."

"I don't believe you. You would-"

Before the Russian could finish the sentence, Edward swung his right arm upward and hard, separating the private's grip from his mother's dress. In a fluid motion Edward then pulled hard on his mother's left arm and they both went falling to the floor.

Reflexively the soldier turned his PPsh on them, but before he could squeeze the trigger, fire erupted from Kaz and Tomasz's guns, sending the private screaming and flying backward, mortally wounded. Kaz walked to the fallen soldier and hovered over him. "He is bleeding to death." One bullet had severed his spinal cord, rendering him motionless.

Kaz and Tomasz then moved to Maria and Edward and knelt. Maria was first to speak. "Marzena, Jacek, are they?"

"They're going to be all right," said Kaz, cupping her left elbow and beginning to help her up. "Marzena was shaken up but she will be all right."

"She wasn't-"

"No," Kaz interrupted. "There wasn't time. We stopped them."

"Thank God."

"I need to get back to the basement," said Kaz. "Tomasz, you stay here."

"No," said Maria. "Both of you go. Edward and I are fine." She hugged her son, shaking her head in gratitude for his quick thinking and bravery. They both looked down at the dying Russian; their eyes showed no sympathy.

Kaz and Tomasz went hustling down the stairs, Kaz calling out, "Jacek, it's us! Maria and Edward are all right."

At the foot of the steps Kaz motioned Tomasz to join Jacek while Kaz went to Michal. Marzena was on her knees, cradling Michal's head and shoulders against her thighs. Kaz squatted beside her.

"He is gone," Marzena murmured, fresh tears of grief trickling down her face. "He saved us. It is so sad."

Kaz sighed. "Yes, but for him this was the best way. He made amends. He knew that. Let's get you up."

"Not yet," Marzena said. "I want to stay with him a little longer. Say a prayer for him. Do you think God will hear a Catholic prayer for a Jew?"

Kaz smiled. "For this particular Jew, I have no doubt."

He stood and walked toward Tomasz and Jacek. Sergeant Yankov and one of the privates were fully conscious, and the other soldier was moaning, gradually regaining his senses.

"You Polish pigs," Yankov growled. "You're not fit to eat shit. Never have been."

"He has a rather warped view of history, doesn't he?" Tomasz quipped, his sarcasm heavy.

"Jewish reptile," Yankov snarled. "Hitler should have finished you all off. Stalin will finish the job. It won't be long now."

Tomasz shook his head. "What do we do with them?"

"We can't keep them here," said Jacek.

"And we can't chance taking them outside," Kaz said. "There probably are other Russian soldiers nearby. Or soon will be."

"That's right," Yankov said condescendingly. "You have boxed yourself in and have no way out."

"I don't think the sergeant is giving us enough credit for creative thinking," Tomasz said not unpleasantly. "He is not familiar enough with our body of experience."

"Or with our local geography," Jacek observed amiably.

"What geography? What experience?" Yankov mocked. "A restaurant keeper and runaway prisoners. At least one of you a Jew. Pathetic."

"Under the right circumstance," said Jacek, thinking more creatively by the second, "I think we could remove them."

"Not the present circumstance," said Kaz.

"Oh no."

"Noise? Too much?" Kaz asked.

"No one came into the restaurant when shots were fired upstairs. Here we are below ground. And look at these walls. Stone. And the ceiling. Thick beams and hardwood floor above."

"Tomasz," Kaz said calmly, "tell Marzena to go upstairs. You go with her."

Yankov's ego-fed, anti-Polish condescension was beginning to give way to puzzlement. Kaz could see the unmistakable change in his eyes.

Tomasz helped Marzena lower Michal's head and shoulders to the floor. Then he gently grasped her shoulders as she rose slowly and guided her to the stairs.

"I have friends," Jacek said pensively. "They can get a horse and wagon. A delivery wagon. One that brings food here daily. Nothing out of the ordinary. Just business as usual. The Vistula is not far. Only a dozen blocks. The water runs fast and deep. After dark…" He shrugged. "We should be safe."

Kaz nodded. "All right." A pause. "What about Michal?"

"I think we can arrange a burial. A proper one."

"I think he might prefer to be cremated."

"We can arrange that. Spread or store his ashes as you like."

Then without hesitation he and Jacek turned away from each other and leveled their guns at Yankov.

"You wouldn't-"

Two eruptions, one from each gun, ended Yankov's coming dare.

The other two privates, seated and cringing, scooted back the remaining inches to the wall. One raised his hand to shield his face. "Don't, please."

Two simultaneous muzzle flashes and his hands fell to his lap, blood immediately staining his uniform tunic.

The third Russian cowered, twisting his head and torso away from coming death. Kaz and Jacek squeezed their triggers. Seconds later the last echoes faded.

CHAPTER 12

V-E Day. May 8, 1945. War still was raging in the Pacific and Asia, with V-J Day still more than three months away. But that reality did little if anything to cast a pall over explosions of emotion throughout Europe, North and South America and Russia. In Moscow in his Kremlin office Stalin was celebrating with Molotov and Beria. They clinked glasses and knocked back numerous shots of vodka, swallowing as fast as they could pour. Stalin spilled some on his uniform and roared with laughter. Molotov and Beria never before had seen their boss so genuinely happy. Outside in Red Square a Russian officer, laughing and waving, was held aloft by an adoring crowd.

Nearly half a world away in Shelby, Tom Brecker, standing in front of his house, saluted the American flag and pumped his fists above his head. Bridgett was standing at his side, giddily wrapping her arms around his middle. She could scarcely believe her good fortune; her loving husband had survived two sinkings – the Hornet's and the Chevy's. In front of them the twins, in a pair of blue and white strollers decorated with red ribbons, gurgled happily.

Celebrants elsewhere were equally delirious. On the Gudek family farm near Zyrardow, Bernadeta, Barbara, Tosia and Jszef were holding hands, dancing uninhibitedly in endless circles, happily singing repeatedly the only song that came to mind. It was a merry ode to the splendors of summer.

In an evacuation hospital tent in Germany, Theresa Hassler sank to her knees, sobbing in cathartic relief; a wounded soldier rose shakily from his cot to comfort her.

Not far away Chaplain Jack Brecker offered a prayer of gratitude, asking God to show mercy on all those killed and wounded during the Nazis' years of hate-fueled frenzy. Then Jack accepted a fresh cigar and a foaming beer from an 82nd Airborne trooper.

At Hitler's Berchtesgaden retreat Paul Brecker stood on an Alpine mountaintop, looking westward toward the Alsacian village of Ribeauville and thinking about the young Resistance fighter, Lea Peiffer, whom he had met there and with whom he had fallen in love. Would he see her again?

When? How would she react? Could they have a future together? If yes, where? Meanwhile in Ribeauville's town hall plaza, Lea, her fellow partisans and two Jewish families they had hidden, saving them from arrest and the gas chambers, were quaffing champagne and new wine in decidedly indecorous fashion.

In England, Thaddeus Metz, the Polish lancer turned parachutist, moved solemnly from one airborne comrade to another, shaking hands, kissing their cheeks, weeping softly. They were like-minded, joyful that the war was over, sad that their country's independence remained uncertain.

In a restaurant basement in Cracow a family and their two guests, one Jewish the other Catholic, were uncorking rieslings and drinking straight from the bottles, decanting be damned. The future for all of them and their Polish friends was indeed uncertain, but today they were living only in the moment.

There were quiet interludes too. After their initial spontaneous revelry, that same Cracow family and their friends reverentially toasted Michal Olenik, the young ex-sonderkommando who had entered their lives so unexpectedly and who, a Jew, had given his life to spare theirs.

In New Zealand, Lucy Crispin led Miss Kiwi onto a beach and mounted her. Happy though she was that the war in Europe was over, the young curly-haired nurse-to-be sat looking at the sunset, uttering a prayer for all the wounded millions who never again would be whole – in body or mind.

Millions more in Europe would never savor the fruits of their sacrifices. The death tolls there: Soviet Russia – 26 million. Germany – 7 million. Poland – 6.8 million. Yugoslavia – 1 to 1.7 million; no one would ever be sure. Romania – 985,000. France – 810,000. Hungary – 750,000. Austria – 525,000. Greece – 520,000. Italy – 410,000. Czechoslovakia – 400,000. United Kingdom – 388,000. Netherlands – 250,000. Belgium – 88,000. Finland – 84,000. Spain, a neutral nation – 22,000. Bulgaria – 21,000. Norway – 10,000. Denmark – 4,000. In all, some 46 million Europeans perished.

The heady news of May 8 was slow to reach other corners of the war-torn planet. For the Park brothers Min and Han, early May passed uneventfully. They continued to exercise the horse belonging to Colonel Fukunaga, the Kaesong garrison's commanding officer. For their Japanese masters, responsible for uncounted millions of deaths in their Asian conquests and occupations, the news of the Allies' victory in Europe heightened concerns. When the news reached Kim Il Sung and his guerillas, he immediately absorbed and articulated its implications to Sergeant Kwon and his men. Atop a ridge commanding a stunning vista of surrounding terrain, Kim told them, "America is free now to concentrate its resources against the Japanese. Soon they will begin sending more ships, more equipment, weapons and men to the Pacific. This can only help our cause and free us from the Japanese yoke. And Stalin, he will be turning his eyes to the East and probably already has done so. Believe me, he has not forgotten Russia's humiliation in losing the Russian-Japanese War. In his fevered mind, 1905 is like yesterday, and he will want to gain a large measure of revenge. At the least, I expect him to make claims on Japanese territory, including Korea."

Kim Il Sung knew his Asian history. He was referring to the 1904-05 conflict which led to Russia recognizing Japanese supremacy in Korea and giving Japan the Liaotung Peninsula that Russia had leased from China. In addition Japan received the southern half of Sakhalin Island. Kim also would prove remarkably prophetic with regard to Stalin's intentions and actions. "Stalin will want to control Korea," Kim explained to his men. "He will regard our homeland as a buffer between Russia and any future Japanese aggression."

"What about the Americans?" Kwon asked. "What will they want?"

"If they are smart," Kim replied, "after defeating Japan, they will remain to occupy her. Pacify her, completely. Purge her of all militaristic aspirations and push their dreams of conquest into the shadows of democracy."

Kim chuckled, something he rarely did in the company of his fellow guerillas. Usually he was purposely dour, believing it strengthened his image as a leader. "If Stalin sends troops into Korea, I would expect America to do the same. The Japanese don't trust Stalin. The Americans don't. Should anyone? We might have to make the most of a very bad situation."

"Play the two countries against each other?"

"Perhaps. Or pick the right side and get them to help drive the other side out. Korea is our homeland," Kim said with rising intensity. "The Land of the Morning Calm. We should rule it, all if it."

"Democracy?"

"Democracy is messy. Badly organized. Korea will need a strong leader to survive. Not one shackled by the whims of ignorant voters and parliamentary niceties."

✝✝✝

"Check!" Marzena said excitedly.

Tomasz Dolata leaned back in his chair and studied the board. His hands ran back through his black hair. He rubbed his rough stubble. "It seems your knight and bishop have my king in a very uncomfortable pincer. You are really improving your game."

"Not every girl has her own private master," she replied impishly.

Tomasz leaned forward, hunching over the table. He reached out, fingered a pawn and eased it forward, blocking the check and threatening Marzena's bishop. "And," he grinned, "there are still lessons to be learned."

"You are a-" she began to reproach him teasingly, but couldn't sustain the charade and began giggling.

"Me? What about me? I know, it's my beard and my build. I look like a bear. They offend your fragile female sensibilities." Tomasz too tried to keep a straight face but failed, and he began giggling – which was infectious, causing Marzena to double over in glee.

These daily matches in the restaurant basement were leading to more than improved chess play. Kaz saw it happening and pondered for weeks whether to say something to either Tomasz or Marzena.

One night in July after restaurant closing hours, Kaz and Tomasz were in the kitchen. Kaz, hands immersed in soapy water, was washing pots, pans, plates, utensils and tableware. Tomasz was drying.

"How much do you love her?" Kaz asked.

The question startled Tomasz who quickly regained his composure. "Of course, I love her. I love the entire family."

"Ahem." Kaz shook his head and smiled. "Let me rephrase the question, my friend. Are you in love with her?"

The silence that ensued stretched to a full minute. "A Jew and a Catholic. In Poland." Tomasz sighed audibly. "I am not naïve."

"I think we should begin looking for another haven," said Kaz. "One with not so many complications."

"It's ironic, isn't it?" Tomasz murmured. "You are a Catholic and so is she, but she falls in love with a Jew. Not a particularly handsome one at that. And a Jew who has helped kill some Catholics, never mind Jews too many to count."

"She knows only the Jew who helped save her and her family. I don't think she has thought much about your time at Auschwitz. She can't imagine the horror. And if you asked her, I think she would tell you she has forgiven you your work at the camp."

Tomasz slowly ran a cloth over a newly washed plate. "She has been good for me."

"No doubt. And you for her. And," Kaz gently teased his friend, "not just her chess game."

"Still, forgiveness isn't enough, is it?"

✝✝✝

Battered though Warsaw was, President Truman and his military and State Department advisors knew that a strong United States presence was needed in Poland. And soon. They very much were worried about Stalin's apparent intent to bring Poland under his sphere of control. Permanently.

On July 5, 1945, the United States established an embassy on Koscielna Street, just a few blocks north of Warsaw's destroyed Old Town. The street was paved with bricks for its two long blocks that sloped gently downward to the Vistula River. The embassy occupied one of the few buildings – all three and four floors – that was not destroyed by the Nazis after the 1944 uprising.

Presenting his credentials to Stalin's puppet government was Arthur Bliss Lane. He was succeeding Anthony Drexel Biddle who had been U.S. ambassador to Warsaw in 1939 when Germany invaded. Biddle had followed Poland's government-in-exile, first to France and then to England.

In the ensuing years Biddle had been a busy envoy. From his office in London he also had represented United States interests with the governments-in-exile of Belgium, Czechoslovakia, Greece, Luxembourg, Netherlands, Norway and Yugoslavia.

Lane was a career diplomat, and his experience and skills would be severely tested. On arrival in Warsaw he found Poland being run by a pair of intelligent and unscrupulous Kremlin agents – Hilary Mine and Jakub Berman. They were Poles by birth but openly acknowledged Stalin as their leader and Moscow as their capital. Lane's chief mission: do his part to see that free elections would decide Poland's form of government. Months earlier he had told Franklin Roosevelt, and later Truman, that strong actions would be needed to preserve Poland's independence. Roosevelt's cool reply was a rhetorical question: "Do you want me to go to war with Russia?"

Lane was suffering no illusions about his challenges.

Chapter 13

It was mid-afternoon on a Tuesday, a quiet time in Polska Kopernika. Jacek and Maria were relaxing, sitting at a round table in the expansive dining room, when Kaz emerged from the basement staircase.

"Hello, Kaz," Maria said. "Please join us." The restaurant's red brick and brown interior was warm and inviting.

"Thank you." Kaz settled onto a chair. "Where's Edward?"

"Out," Marie replied, "with friends."

Family members had largely recovered from the trauma of the Russian incident. Bloodstains had been cleaned and spirits healed, perhaps strengthened. All had learned more about themselves, and the lessons had proved heartening.

"I thought you would want to be watching the daily chess match" said Jacek.

"Not today." A pause. "Marzena and Tomasz need some time alone."

"Oh? To concentrate on a close match?"

"Not exactly."

"I think I know what Kaz is referring to," Maria said.

Jacek eyed his wife questioningly. Then, smiling dubiously, he said to Kaz, "She is always seeing things that I don't."

"They are in love," Kaz said, sighing.

"Oh."

"You're not surprised?"

"I'm not sure," said Jacek. "I guess not."

"You guess? You would have to be blind – or a typical man – not to see it," Maria teased him. "And you are many things, Mr. Frantek, but not blind."

"It is not a funny matter," Jacek said defensively.

"Did I say it was? You are what's funny, my dear husband."

"No, it's not funny," Kaz agreed. "And Tomasz knows that. Tonight he is telling Marzena that – in so many words – we need to move on."

"Wait," said Jacek. "Don't be rash. There is no hurry."

"What are you saying?"

At the basement chess table something unusual was unfolding. Marzena was clearly taking the measure of Tomasz. That she was winning wasn't unprecedented, if not a frequent occurrence. She might have ascribed her coming victory to continued improvement, but the ease with which she was winning was inexplicable. She studied Tomasz's brooding countenance, his thick black stubble darkening his demeanor. His eyes were focused on the board, but his concentration seemed elsewhere.

"Are you letting me win?"

"What? No. I mean-"

"Your mind is not on the match. You look troubled. Is something wrong?"

†††

"I am saying I have become very fond of Tomasz," Jacek explained. "I would not like to see him leave. Not yet. You either. I agree it is safer now, but there are still rumors that Stalin is purging Polish Army officers and Resistance fighters, especially leaders."

"I won't debate you on that," Kaz replied. "I've heard the same rumors and given what we know about Stalin, they could well be true. But if we stay…if we stay, I think you can expect Tomasz and Marzena to lose themselves with each other. Completely. A Jew and a Catholic."

"Do you think Tomasz looks like a Jew?" Jacek blurted, a touch of plaintiveness thinning his voice. His exposed upper teeth were scraping his lower lip.

"What?" The question took Kaz aback. Maria too.

"Some Jews look like Jews. Some don't. It's true. You know that."

"Have you really looked at Tomasz's nose?" Kaz asked. "It bends like a fishhook."

"You exaggerate," Jacek said defensively. In fact, Kaz had exaggerated, but not wildly. His reaction was partly a reflex and partly to make a point.

Maria's eyes widened at hearing words she never had expected to emerge from her husband's mouth. This is – was? – the man with no fondness for Jews if not outright anti-Semitic.

"Where are you going with this?" Kaz asked.

✝✝✝

"That's not the real reason you're leaving, is it?" Marzena asked heatedly. "I am not yet the woman my mother is, but I am not a child. Nor a dunce."

"No, you are most certainly not a child. Not anymore. Not after what you've been through. That's..."

"That's what?" Marzena challenged him. "Talk to me honestly, Tomasz Dolata. This is not like you. Not like you at all. You played today's chess match as though you were in one of the dense fogs that hangs over the Vistula. Then you tell me you are leaving because it is safer now. I think it's because you think you have been here too long. Because you think you are imposing." Her tone was rising with her emotions. "Well?" she demanded, "am I right?"

"You are wrong."

"What?"

"I love you."

✝✝✝

"You're not suggesting that a Jew and a Catholic could have a future together," Kaz said to Jacek. "Not as husband and wife. Not in Poland. Not in Cracow."

"I'm not sure," Jacek admitted. "I do know that I have come to like and respect Tomasz very much. He has shown himself to be a man of courage and caring. And I certainly love our daughter and want her to be happy."

Now, Maria's shock at his words notwithstanding, she was looking at her husband with hooded admiration. She began to say Kaz is right but stopped the words before speaking them, deciding to let the conversation run its course.

✝✝✝

Marzena pushed her chair away from the table and stood. Her right hand pushed her blonde hair away from her forehead. She stepped around to the opposite side and hovered over Tomasz who was peering up at her. "Stand," she said puckishly.

Tomasz pushed back his chair and rose. They stood, mere inches apart, her blue eyes just above the level of his chin. She edged closer.

✝✝✝

"This discussion...I'm glad you think so well of Tomasz," said Kaz, "but Tomasz is telling Marzena that we will be leaving."

"Poland is a big country," Jacek observed thoughtfully, right thumb and forefinger stroking his chin. "It is a long distance to Warsaw."

"About 230 kilometers."

"And some rough terrain. Hills. Mountains."

"Yes."

"And you will be walking."

"Yes. Allied bombs destroyed the railroad lines, and money is short so it will probably be a long time before they are rebuilt. And," he smiled wryly, "it wouldn't seem terribly wise to try to catch a ride with Russians. If we're lucky, maybe we can ride part way with local Polish delivery trucks or wagons."

"Either way," Jacek said, "it will take many days."

"No doubt."

"I hear the roads are crowded with refugees. Displaced persons is the new term I'm hearing."

"We – Tomasz and I – qualify."

"Money?"

79

"We have none, as you know."

"We can help. You've earned it. Indeed, we owe you a huge debt."

"You have given us refuge. You have fed us. I think our accounts are settled."

"Perhaps," said Jacek. "Look. Stay here a little longer. Eat more of Maria's cooking. Get stronger."

Kaz smiled. "And give us all a little more time to think things over?"

"That too, my friend."

"Marzena and Tomasz?"

"Well, I suppose Tomasz can leave anytime, but I think he will wait for you."

"You know," Maria said, "I agree with my husband." She reached across and lovingly patted Jacek's bald head. "Give everything a little more time. It can't hurt. Warsaw will wait."

And, Kaz was thinking, Warsaw would be only a temporary destination. See my hometown. Or what's left of it. Has any European city suffered more than Warsaw? Moscow? Leningrad? Dresden? See what the Soviets are doing to it. Learn if any of my family and fellow Home Army members have survived and returned. I would need to take precautions…take care to appear harmless. Try to avoid suspicion and arrest. With my bad eye and scar that might not be easy. Then make my way to Zyrardow. To find Bernadeta…if she survived. He sighed. "Maybe you are right. Maybe we should stay. For a while longer anyway."

CHAPTER 14

Inside the barn Bernadeta and Barbara were preparing to milk the two cows. It seemed like old times. The sisters picked up two wooden pails and a pair of low, three-legged milking stools. They stepped toward the cow pen.

"I'm glad our cows survived the war," said Bernadeta. "I was afraid the Germans might slaughter them for beef."

"Me too," said Barbara. "The cows filled our needs for milk and cheese and helped us earn a little money – or eggs in trade. Father says it will be awhile before we can replace the chickens we killed." A pause, and her next words were spoken quietly, barely above a whisper. "Do you think Kaz Majos survived? Or Thaddeus Metz?"

Before answering, Bernadeta looked around the barn – at the cow pen where Thaddeus and his fellow soldiers had been held as prisoners in the days following Germany's invasion and where she had smuggled to him the bread knife he had used to kill the young German guard. Then Bernadeta looked up at the loft where she had climbed to distract the guard. "I can only hope," Bernadeta said wistfully.

"And pray?"

"At one time I did. Now it's too late for prayer."

"Do you think God answers our prayers?"

"If he does, not many."

Barbara nodded. "I think you are right. But I would never tell Mama that. You can imagine her reaction."

Bernadeta's soft chuckle was her only reply. She easily could visualize their mother picking up her rosary and fingering it as she prayed for Barbara to have stronger faith.

The sisters positioned their stools and pails between the cows and began squeezing their teats in a familiar and comforting rhythm.

"Now that the war is over," Barbara said without removing her eyes from her work, "if Kaz or Thaddeus survived, maybe they will try writing to you."

"Kaz, I don't know. He is many things but a letter writer, I don't know. And if he did write, who would deliver it? Our postal service was ruined. Thaddeus, I don't think we thought to tell him our family name. Everything happened so fast that day. The escape. Killing the guards, burying their bodies. And then Thaddeus and the other men were on their way south."

"You gave yourself to Kaz?"

"Yes," said Bernadeta, "in the basement of St. Ann's. Not a particularly romantic place to lose one's virginity." She looked back over her shoulder at her sister and smiled, shrugging with her eyebrows. "A hard clay floor. But still it was nice – and certainly memorable. I wonder what St. Ann thought."

"I want to lose mine too. I'm ready."

"It will happen. Just be sure it's with a good man."

"The right man."

"A good man. There might be more than one right man."

Their labor finished, the sisters stood and picked up their pails.

"Bernadeta."

"Yes?" she replied, turning to look at her younger sister. Her glance was met with Barbara's flicking fingers sending a small spray of milk in her face.

Barbara giggled. "Just the way I used to do it."

"I will get you back," Bernadeta laughed, dipping the fingers of her right hand into her pail. "There's no place to run in this pen."

Barbara shrieked.

✝✝✝

Thaddeus Metz had heard the rumors and now they had been confirmed. He would not be returning to Poland anytime soon. He went to see General Sosabowski. "You were right, sir," he said. "They are sending our brigade to Germany for occupation duty. Our men are not looking forward to it."

"How long will you be there?" the general asked.

"One year, they tell us, maybe two. No one seems sure now. Actually, the men are angry – and very disappointed. They were hoping to be discharged and get on with their lives."

"At least they will be closer to home. You too."

"And you?"

"I've made my choice. I'm staying in England…Making a new life… Putting all things military behind me."

"I look forward to that day myself," Thaddeus said longingly.

"You are returning to Poland?"

"Yes. I feel I must."

"If I may, I'd like to give you one final order."

"Of course, sir."

"Find that farm girl."

✝✝✝

The train was easing from Waterloo Station, near the houses of Parliament, and heading south to Portsmouth. Without stopping it passed through Clapham Junction, Wimbledon and Surbiton. Aboard were Michael Cornelius and his mother, Florence. Both were excited and had good reason to be.

"How long is the ride, Mother?"

"About one and a half hours. Perhaps closer to two."

"I know that's a short time, but today it seems so long."

"It's been a long time since you've seen your father."

"Fifteen months."

"Thank goodness he sent the wire so we could meet his ship."

"It had been so long since his last letter. I was beginning to worry."

"As was I."

"I wonder why he took so long."

"I'm sure there is a good reason and we'll soon learn of it."

The train was picking up speed, soon passing through Wimbledon and into the lush English countryside.

"How many stops enroute to Portsmouth?" Michael asked.

"Just a few on this fast train. Woking. Godalming. Haslemere. A couple more perhaps."

Soon the train was gliding through West Sussex, dense fog hanging languidly over its green hills.

"It's lovely here, isn't it?" said Florence. "Does it look familiar?"

"Very." As it should have. In 1940 as the Battle of Britain began bringing deadly rains of German bombs pouring down daily on London, first on the Thames docks of East London and then on the city center, Michael had been one of thousands of children evacuated to outlying towns and villages. He had taken up residence with an uncle and aunt and cousins in Petworth, a thousand-year-old market village of 3,000 people just a few miles east of the Haslemere station. The bombs had been fewer in that area, but Michael had watched dogfights in the skies above the village. In one memorable encounter he had watched in awe as a British Hurricane pursued a German ME-109. The two dueling planes seemed to be diving straight down on him. He stood still, transfixed. The ME-109 kept plummeting, finally pulling out of its screaming dive at treetop level, wings still fluttering from the stress. The Hurricane was close behind. Then the planes went speeding toward the Channel, hedgehopping over trees and houses.

Now the skies were clear of aircraft and the countryside devoid of the countless thousands of trucks, jeeps, tanks and other vehicles that had been collected while waiting transport to France on D-Day and the days following.

✝✝✝

"Mussolini would be pleased," Florence said dryly. "The train is on time." She tittered softly at her own small joke.

Michael, amused by his mother's excited nervousness, chuckled, his gray eyes twinkling. He patted her on the shoulder, at the moment feeling as much paternal as filial.

At Portsmouth they stepped from the train onto the platform that quickly became packed with others on the same mission.

"Come, Mother, let's hurry." And they did, scurrying through crowded streets as would a pair of youngsters excitedly skipping to the neighborhood sweetshop.

Minutes later they were dockside, part of a large throng gathered to greet returning British soldiers. Union Jacks were flying from every light pole and from most neighborhood buildings. Red, white and blue bunting was draped from nearly every windowsill, railing and the heavy chain at dock's edge. An army band was tuning its instruments. The breeze stiffened and a light, wind-driven mist began to fall. Faces, clothing, flags and bunting soon were dampened but not spirits.

Then the gangway was lowered, angling down sharply from the vessel's main deck.

"I wonder how long we'll have to wait to see him," said Florence, bouncing on her toes, barely able to contain herself. "There are so many soldiers onboard. Look at them lining the railing. I can't see your father."

"They will bring the wounded down first," Michael said.

"You sound very certain."

"It's been in *The Daily Telegraph*. *The Times*, too. The government wants them saluted and applauded, not brought down to just their families."

"Seems the right thing." Florence smiled at her son who now rose six inches above her five feet four. She pivoted back toward the ship and looked up. In another instant her head snapped in an involuntary double take. Near the front of the line starting down the gangway was her husband, Major Roger Cornelius.

"Michael! Oh, my God! It's your father."

Michael looked up. "I don't understand."

"You said the wounded would debark first."

"That's the planned procedure – according to the papers." Michael was puzzled, given the reputation of *The Telegraph* and *The Times* for getting these matters right.

The army band struck up *Rule Britannia*. People began applauding and cheering.

Florence began waving and Michael did likewise. Roger!" she cried out.

"Father!" Michael shouted.

A few more steps down the gangway, and their waves and shouts caught Roger's attention. His eyes beamed and a huge smile creased his face. Then he waved in return – with his left arm.

Florence's heart sank as fast and as far as her spirits had been soaring only seconds before. "Oh, my Lord," she groaned. "Roger, poor Roger."

Michael's reaction to his father's left-handed wave was the polar opposite of his mother's. He felt an almost overwhelming surge of pride. His father had given his right arm to defeat Hitler.

Now the band was playing *Land Of Hope And Glory*, and the crowd was exuberantly greeting the descent of every returning soldier.

"Mother, it will be all right. Come on." He grasped Florence's left arm, tugged gently and began guiding her through the throng, foot by slow foot. "I want us to be there when he reaches the bottom."

And they were. Roger's balance began to waver and he nearly fell into Florence's arms. She hugged him tightly, groans of ecstasy escaping through cascading tears. Michael squeezed them both. He knew then that this moment would never fade from memory, theirs or his. Nor, he knew, would he ever forget the significance of this father's sacrifices.

CHAPTER 15

The chess pieces were on the checkered board but no match was underway. Marzena and Tomasz were standing beside the table, locked in an embrace.

"My father is right and I wish he was wrong. With all of my heart I wish he was wrong." She was crushing her cheek against Tomasz's thick chest.

✝✝✝

It was the night before Tomasz and Kaz were setting out for distant Warsaw, and the last patrons had left Polska Kopernika. Kaz was sitting at a dining room table with Jacek, Maria and Edward. Their mood was subdued.

"You go up to your apartment," Kaz said. "I'll wait here until Marzena and Tomasz have said their farewells. It might take a while" – with "a while," they all knew, likely to be a painfully long parting.

"Come up with us," Maria said. "We'll have a toast."

"Wonderful idea!" Jacek said, not feeling nearly as jolly as his words might have suggested. "I'll open my best bottle of vodka and we'll toast each other."

"Me too?" Edward grinned.

"Tonight, yes, you too," Jacek laughed and cuffed his son on his left shoulder. "You've as much right as anyone to join in these toasts."

✝✝✝

"I would like nothing more than marrying you," Tomasz murmured. "Nothing at all. But we both know as well as your father and mother that a Jew-Catholic marriage won't work. Not here. Not now. We would be ostracized and so would your parents for not forbidding it if not approving it. There could be violence. You could be hurt. I will not risk that."

Marzena tightened her grip on Tomasz. "Oh, I love you so." Her groan said so as clearly as her words. "I always will. Maybe with time…"

86

"Perhaps," Tomasz said, not believing his own word. Not in Poland. Not among Catholics so many of whom loathed Jews and had done nothing to protect them from the Nazis' grasp. In truth, Tomasz reminded himself, some Catholics, Kaz among them, had risked all to spare Jews. Rescue them from the Nazis' clutches with fake identities and hiding places. But those Catholics were a tiny minority. Too many had remained too passive, if not overtly helpful to the Nazis.

"Tomasz?" Marzena still had not released her arms from around his midsection.

"Yes?"

She pulled back a little, enough to look up into his eyes. "I want to make love with you."

Tomasz looked into her unblinking eyes. They were glistening with hope. His owned closed for a moment. He shared her desire for intimacy, but his mind pictured complications.

"What if you became pregnant? Have you thought about that?"

"No."

"You should."

"You are right," she conceded.

"Good."

"I want us to make love anyway."

A long pause ensued. Then Tomasz sighed heavily through pursed lips and spoke. "I will spread the blankets."

CHAPTER 16

Kim Il Sung and Sergeant Kwon Oh Bum were leaning against the starboard railing of the Soviet warship Pukachev. The vessel was steaming south to the port of Wonsan on Korea's northeast coast. With them were 40 members of Kim's guerilla force. It was September 19, 1945.

"After all the walking we've done in recent years, it feels good to be moving while standing still," Kim observed dryly.

"We owe it all to you," Kwon said sincerely but with little trace of fawning. "Your success against the Japanese earned Russia's respect."

"But let's keep in mind that this ship is meant to be an expedient – much more than seeing to our comfort. Stalin sees the United States moving into southern Korea, and he can't abide the thought of America occupying Korea, or any part of it."

Kim Il Sung's assessment, born of becoming a student of Stalin's thinking and actions, was spot on. "The Boss" was pleased by how he was gaining control in central and eastern Europe. But he was fuming that his gains in Asia were far less impressive and considerably more tenuous. He was determined to establish a foothold there and rapidly.

"I have plans for Korea," Stalin had told Molotov and Beria. "They need to be implemented immediately." Molotov and Beria both nodded. "Beria, you and your secret police have recommended that Kim Il Sung lead our presence there."

"We believe he is the best qualified, Comrade Leader. He showed himself to be smart and bold and ruthless. He kept up the pressure on the Japanese for years. I'm told he can even be charming when it suits his purpose."

Stalin chortled. "That is promising, but now he will need to show the same qualities against our new enemy, the United States. We aren't calling them our enemy publicly, and neither they nor we are going to declare war anytime soon. But mark my words, we will be at odds with America for decades. It is inevitable. The Americans might not have designs on world domination, but they are now the greatest power, and their might is likely to keep growing and their presence expanding. That can only add to our vulnerability. That is unacceptable and I will not tolerate it. I want Kim and your secret police to set up a provisional government in North Korea. Start building a North Korean Army. I will promise free elections to keep America at bay but drag our heels on permitting a vote. I have already dispatched our troops to occupy the north. As allies in the war against Japan, that is our right." Technically, Stalin was correct. But Soviet Russia's aggression against Japan came late in the war and with little military effect. "Truman doesn't like it. He wants a unified Korea and so do I – but on our terms, not his. Move fast, Comrade Beria."

Beria did. Three weeks later on October 10, Kim Il Sung was installed in Pyongyang as the provisional government's leader. It formed the Korean Workers Party. The absence of the word Communist was purposeful, part

China (Manchuria)

Korea

Wonsan

Sea of Japan/East Sea

Pyongyang

DMZ

Yellow Sea

Kaesong

Panmunjom

Munsan

Kimpo Airport

Seoul

Inchon

Osan

Pusan

of Stalin's design to forestall Truman using force to unify Korea before the promised free elections. At that time, using force anywhere on the planet was the last thing Truman wanted, but the paranoid Stalin would risk no chance.

Kim's Workers Party initially listed 4,530 members. The new government instituted an eight-hour workday and equality of the sexes. It also began to nationalize industries, confiscate and redistribute land, suppress religion and initiate Soviet-style central economic planning.

Truman, new to the presidency, nonetheless moved decisively too, sending troops to occupy the southern half of the Korean peninsula.

"We need a provisional government in the south, just like Stalin has in the north," Truman said firmly to Secretary of State Dean Acheson. "But it has to have a leader, a strong one and politically savvy, and I have no idea who that might be. Do you?" Truman asked in his Missouri twang.

"No," the veteran Acheson admitted, "but I think I might know where to go to find one."

After the meeting Acheson cabled General Douglas MacArthur, already overseeing the occupation and rebuilding in Japan. But in pondering President Truman's need in his Dai Ichi Building office in Tokyo, neither could MacArthur think of a viable candidate. So he initiated contact with his own valued source.

"The man has to be strong-willed and tough," MacArthur told Chiang Kai Shek, China's leader, embroiled in a long-running joust for power with Mao Tse Tung. "He has to be someone I can count on to resist any expansion urges by Joe Stalin and Kim Il Sung. Do you have a recommendation?"

"I do," Chiang replied. "In addition to meeting your requirements, he speaks English and has university degrees from America. In fact, he is living in the United States, near your White House."

On October 12, 1945, MacArthur ordered Syngman Rhee fetched from Washington, D.C. for delivery to Seoul.

For Rhee it was the continuation of a remarkable political odyssey that already had spanned nearly 50 years. He was born on March 26, 1875, in Kaesong, home of Park Min and his brother Han. Rhee was ambitious and long had been an agitator. In 1897 he was arrested and incarcerated for leading protests against the Yi Dynasty monarchy. In 1904 Rhee, a strikingly handsome man capable of great charm, was released from prison. He emigrated to the United States and wrote a book, *The Spirit of Independence.*

Young though he was, Rhee didn't hesitate to seek help in high places. In November 1905 he pleaded – in vain – with President Theodore Roosevelt for American support in establishing a democratically independent Korea. He then resumed his formal education, earning a bachelor's degree in 1907 from George Washington University, a master's in 1909 from Harvard and in 1910 a Ph. D. from Princeton.

While at Princeton, Rhee was penniless. The university waived his tuition, and Princeton Theological Seminary offered him free room and board – he lived in Hodge Hall, room 111 – on his promise to return to Korea to spread Christianity. The deal appealed to Rhee.

His return to Korea in 1910 to teach at the Seoul YMCA was classically ill-timed. That was the year that expansion-minded Japan began its colonization and brutal 35-year occupation of Korea. Rhee resumed his anti-autocratic activism, angering his Japanese masters, and in 1912 he saw fit to move to a less threatening base – China.

Later that year he moved to Hawaii to become headmaster at a Methodist school – the Korean Christian Institute.

Still later he returned to China – Shanghai – and when Korean dissidents formed a provisional government in exile, its parliament elected Rhee president in 1919. His tenure foreshadowed his future. He proved bombastic, stubborn and corrupt. He managed to hold on to the presidency until 1925 when he was impeached. The charge: massive embezzlement for personal gain.

Once again Rhee headed to Hawaii. Subsequently he moved to New York and Washington, D.C., using his good looks and charm and passing himself off as "Washington Representative" of the Provisional Government of Korea in Exile-China. Rhee lived off donations from sympathetic Korean expatriates.

In 1934 Rhee again demonstrated his audacity. He traveled to Europe with the intent of seeking help from Joseph Stalin to free Korea from Japan's yoke. Rhee was stopped at Russia's border. The journey, however, was not a total loss. On another train trip that year in Europe, he met an Austrian woman, Francisca Donner. They soon married and returned to

Washington where they continued living on gifts from Koreans. In 1940 they were living at 1766 Hobart Street.

MacArthur took a quick and strong liking to the charismatic Rhee. But soon enough he would be showing proclivities that would have some U.S. leaders reassessing his status as an American darling.

✝✝✝

Colonel Takeo Fukunaga was sitting at his desk in Kaesong. Although the expression on his unlined face was inscrutable, his thinking was tormented. Events were overtaking him, and it was unsettling in the extreme. He was losing control over his situation and his emotions. I am a Japanese Imperial Army officer, he reminded himself sternly, and I must not let that happen. I have been in control, and I must remain in control of my personal situation. The war is lost – I knew we would lose from the day General Doolittle bombed Tokyo. In April 1942. Only four months after our great triumph at Pearl Harbor. I knew we could be no match for America's great industrial strength. We simply did not have the equal of America's resources – her oil, her steel, her factories, her population. What were our leaders thinking? Delusional. That is what they were. Still prisoners of the Samurai mystique. Their bushido code governs everything. Our national dreams and aspirations, our thinking and decisions. And our end. This is my end. I cannot control future events, but I can control my end.

Fukunaga stood and reached for the decorative leather case that sat on the far left corner of his desk. He opened it and removed the ceremonial hara-kiri sword. Seppuku – ceremonial suicide. It was part of bushido – the way of the warrior – a code that embraced child rearing, appearance, grooming and, most of all, preparing for death. Japanese commanders began giving up this rite in the late 1860s after the last Samurai were defeated and a modern army and navy established. But the practice never died out completely.

The hara-kiri blade was short, slightly curved and sharp enough to shave paper. It was designed to penetrate deeply and slice through abdominal muscles and the intestinal tract. Sometimes a commander committing seppuku would have an aide standing by to cut an artery in his neck or behead him to speed death after the hara-kiri thrust.

Fukunaga fingered the gleaming blade. Such fine craftsmanship, he reflected. *It is such a shame that it is meant to be used only once.*

"Corporal. Come here," Fukunaga called to his aide. The corporal stepped smartly into Fukunaga's spotless, spartan office where the only visible personal touch was a small framed photo of his pretty wife. The corporal crisply saluted his commanding officer. "Get the Park brothers. Bring them here at once."

"Yes, sir." V-J Day had come and gone but the corporal would obey unhesitatingly until American – or Russian – forces arrived to evict the Japanese and incarcerate or send them packing back to Japan.

The blade Lucy Crispin was holding reverentially in her right hand was every bit as sharp as Colonel Fukunaga's hara-kiri sword. Like the colonel's blade it was designed to slice cleanly through human flesh and muscle. The difference: the blade in Lucy's hand was meant to prolong, not end, life.

She was visiting her father Morgan, a physician, in his Wellington Public Hospital office.

"Dad, I'm more certain than ever that I am meant to be a nurse. Yes, the war is over, but I needn't tell you that peacetime doesn't necessarily mean a lighter load for doctors and nurses."

"Why not a doctor?"

"I've thought about it. But you know how dreadfully difficult it is for a woman to gain entrance to medical college. Even for ones with fathers as physicians."

"Admittedly, the hurdles are many and high."

"And then there's this," Lucy said, holding up her slightly withered and clawed left arm and hand. It rendered her unable to work as a surgeon but precluded little else. She had undergone long, strenuous and painful rehabilitation to increase use of the damaged limb. "I can do most things with it, but I don't think I would inspire confidence in surgical patients."

Morgan laughed. "It certainly hasn't dulled your wit or kept you out of a saddle."

"And no offense, Dad, but," and she raised the scalpel she was holding to eye level, "you perform a surgery and do your post-operative checks and-"

"I know," Morgan cut her off, smiling benignly. "I leave care and nurturing to the nursing staff. For whom, as you know, dear daughter, I have utmost respect."

Lucy smiled her slightly crooked smile. "Which I am sad to say is not the universal perspective of your brothers in the physicians' lodge."

"Touche. If I must be in a minority, I feel certain you will do your part to keep me there."

"Touche to you, Dad."

✝✝✝

Park Min and Han followed the corporal into Colonel Fukunaga's office. Though the war was over and Fukunaga soon would be departing, they still felt ill at ease in the colonel's presence. They couldn't be certain that he wouldn't lash out one more time. If he did, they harbored no doubt that his minions would swiftly carry out his will. They stood before him rigidly, arms straight at their sides.

Fukunaga's jaws clenched and he rose slowly from his cushionless chair. He sighed and swallowed. "As you know, my men soon will be leaving. You have done a good job of helping care for my horse. I sense you are genuinely fond of him. I..." Fukunaga's left hand rose and pinched his forehead. "I won't be taking him with me. The victors won't permit that. I do not want him to be slaughtered for food. Or mistreated." Min and Han remained silent, sensing no invitation to speak and not wanting to risk offending a man they still saw as powerful and willful. "I want you to have the horse." The boys were stunned, their widened eyes the evidence. "I know you don't have much money, and it costs money to feed a horse properly." Fukunaga stooped and opened the left side desk drawer. He lifted his revolver – pearl grips and a gleaming barrel. He extended his right arm. "Take it. You can get a good price for it. Especially from Russians or Americans."

Min edged forward carefully. He accepted the proffered gun. "Colonel, sir, we, yes, we will take the gift of your horse. You are correct. We like him very much."

Fukunaga swallowed. "Good. Thank you. Now, should there be any question of legal ownership..." Fukunaga opened the thin center desk drawer, removed a sheet of paper and handed it to Min. "This letter is very clear. I have given you the horse without conditions."

"Yes, sir."

"That is all. Your are dismissed."

As Min was turning to leave, he saw the hara-kiri sword. He paused and Fukunaga followed the line of his sight.

"You may have that as well," the colonel said, "after I am finished with it. It should bring an excellent price."

Min nodded and turned away. Then he stopped and pivoted to face Fukunaga. Min was experiencing unprecedented calm and courage in the colonel's presence. "Sir."

"Yes?"

"I agree your sword will bring a very high price. But I would prefer not having to clean blood from it before selling it."

CHAPTER 17

"This is hard. In a way," Tomasz murmured, "it is harder than being a sonderkommando. I know how that sounds...shallow, unfeeling and incredible." He shook his head in dismay.

Tomasz and Kaz were hours along the first day of walking north from Cracow to Warsaw. They weren't alone. Trafficking the dry, dusty road were units of marching Russian soldiers and numerous Soviet military vehicles that raised seemingly endless clouds of choking dust. Most of all there were thousands of shuffling, displaced Poles. They were trudging in both directions, yearning to return to homes that often no longer existed and to families decimated or obliterated.

"Some of these people are half-starved," Kaz observed. "Survivors from the camps. Some returning Polish soldiers, likely ones who fought in Italy. Wherever they are going, too many won't make it."

"At least I didn't murder them," Tomasz muttered in self-disgust, "but maybe their families."

Kaz knew there was no use arguing further that Tomasz should put that dreadful experience behind him and move on, so he tried changing the subject. "If we had taken all the food Maria wanted us to, we could feed the multitudes."

"That's your Christian new testament, isn't it?" Tomasz said, trying to smile. He shook his head sadly. "Look at all these refugees. They are everywhere. But I'm not sure I've ever felt lonelier. I never imagined that leaving one person, just one, could be so hard. So painful."

"Were you ever in love before?"

"No." A pause. "But you were and Bernadeta walked away from you. That had to be very hard – for both of you." He turned toward Kaz, not breaking their slow stride, looking for confirmation. He got it with a slight nod. "But now you have her to walk back to."

"Eventually, if she's still alive. If she and her family survived."

The slow pace continued. They really had no other choice; the long distance to Warsaw and the road congestion ruled out hurrying. They needed to conserve energy and food.

"The Franteks were so generous," Tomasz said. "All this food. Jacek having a cobbler friend repair our shoes. Almost like new. Maria giving us extra socks. Coats."

The large cloth bag that Kaz and Tomasz were taking turns carrying over their shoulders was heavier that it would have been had it contained only food, socks and coats. It also held two Russian soldiers' PPsh's and ammunition as well as a long-bladed carving knife that the Franteks had given them.

"Why the guns?" Kaz had asked Jacek when they were setting out on their long walk.

"Protection" the restaurant owner had told them. "You might need it. Silent protection."

Now, walking slowly, Kaz said, "I almost didn't take the weapons."

"I know. I saw your hesitation. We have seen so much death. Caused so much. I am so tired of it. Right now I think I envy Michal a little. No more loneliness. No more pain. He died in the arms of a woman who cared."

Kaz decided to make another conversational gambit. "Tomasz, look at the sky. What do you see?"

"A few clouds. The sun. Nothing else."

"That's right. You can make of it what you want." Tomasz shifted his gaze downward to Kaz. "Try thinking about that. It won't be easy but try."

"Is that what you are doing?" Tomasz asked plaintively.

"I am trying."

CHAPTER 18

"I think this is enough money to feed our horse for a long time," Han said. "I'm glad we didn't have to wipe blood from Colonel Fukunaga's sword before selling it. Although some of our neighbors wouldn't have minded." The brothers were standing on either side of the chestnut gelding in a dusty fenced enclosure not far from Colonel Fukunaga's former office. Min was patting the horse's neck.

"We should give it a new name, a proper Korean name," said Min. "His Japanese name is so – Japanese." Fukunaga had named his horse Empire.

"How about Kaesong, after our hometown?" Han suggested.

Min wrinkled his nose. "Not very creative." A pause. "Or Morning Calm, in honor of our nation's nickname?"

"Umm. Too long," replied Han.

"Then what do you think of Admiral Yi?" In the late 1500s Yi had developed ironclad warships called "turtles" that, combined with the admiral's renowned strategic and tactical leadership, defeated the Japanese navy in a series of battles. Yi's victories offset Japanese army wins in Korea land battles. A truce – a victory in the eyes of the smaller Korean nation – was declared in 1598.

"Fukunaga would probably object," Han laughed. "Admiral Yi is tempting, but I would like something less military."

"I agree. We don't need more reminders of the military. What do you think of Sejong?"

"Perfect!" Han replied with genuine enthusiasm. "It is short, the horse can learn it quickly, and it has true Korean meaning."

That it did. Sejong the Great (1397-1450) was a particularly enlightened national leader. In English his name is pronounced Sayjong. One of his greatest achievements was developing a phonetic alphabet consisting of only 24 symbols. The alphabet, called Han-gul, is widely regarded as one of the most successful writing systems. Sejong also initiated important advances in science, technology and music.

Min patted the horse's nose. "So, Empire, how do you like your new name, Sejong? Much better than Empire, eh? Sejong was a renaissance king, and you can be our renaissance horse. You can be our transportation, our companion, our means of exercise and entertainment." Min turned to his younger brother. "Let's saddle him up."

Moments later, Min swung gracefully onto the saddle. "Open the gate. Come on, Sejong, it's time for your first ride under new ownership." Min tapped his heels against Sejong's flanks, and the horse went galloping toward the countryside.

†††

Marzena Frantek would have seized an opportunity to be in the countryside or anywhere but where she was at this moment. She was kneeling on the floor, bent double, arms crossing her abdomen.

Her father, Jacek, heard her groaning in the bathroom and looked with concern at Maria. They both had been preparing to descend to the restaurant to begin their workday when they heard their daughter's distress.

Maria sighed. Her lovely countenance was reflecting both concern and motherly understanding. Jacek's visage was showing worry and puzzlement.

Edward entered the living room and, as younger brothers are wont to do, asked bluntly, "What's wrong with her?" It was the question Jacek was preparing to ask, albeit more gently.

Maria sighed again, more heavily. "I think your sister is pregnant."

Edward's sleepy 15-year-old eyes snapped open. Jacek's narrowed. "Are you sure? How-" he stopped himself.

"She told me she missed her last period."

Edward reddened. Color drained from Jacek's face. Thoughts went tumbling through his mind and none was pleasant to contemplate.

Maria stood expectantly, waiting for an explosion of emotion. It didn't erupt. Instead, Jacek blinked and blew out a breath. "This will be complicated."

Maria smiled thinly. "There is no denying that."

Edward found his voice and his words emerged in an unintended whisper. "She's going to have a baby…a half-Jewish baby."

Maria nodded. "You two go downstairs. I'll go see how she's doing."

✝✝✝

"Will you send me away?"

Maria reached out and brushed her daughter's cheek. The two were sitting with Jacek at a small table in their apartment's living room. Just a single lamp, its shade a pale blue, provided illumination. Edward had left when told the nature of the pending discussion. He was curious to be sure, but the topic embarrassed him, and he sensed correctly that his presence wasn't desired.

"There is nowhere to send you, not in Poland, not now," Jacek said. "A convent? They have been destroyed, nuns scattered if they are still alive. Yes, I admit the thought crossed my mind. I won't pretend that this isn't upsetting," he said, head shaking in deep disappointment. "It's the last thing we wanted for you or us. Jewish blood-"

"Jacek!" Maria began to scold as she saw Marzena's eyes brimming with fresh tears.

"This," Jacek replied grimly, "is no time for hiding our feelings. No, I am not going to disown our only daughter or turn her out. But she should know the truth."

Tears were streaming down Marzena's cheeks. "There will be suspicions," she said forlornly, voice wavering. "People will ask questions."

"I'm afraid so," Maria murmured, "many of them."

"Father's friends who helped remove the bodies…" Marzena was alluding to the Russian soldiers' corpses.

"They will have their opinions," Jacek said. "I'm not sure they will voice them, not to me."

"What if they do? What will you tell them?"

"I'm not sure."

"I am," Maria said, voice gaining strength. "We will tell them – anyone who asks – that you were not raped by a Russian. We will tell them that you fell in love with a hero. With a man who saved our lives. These things happen."

99

Jacek's surprised face showed clearly his respect for Maria and her position.

"Father?"

He nodded. "Your mother is right."

"I...I am so sorry for bringing shame to our family." A pause. "What if someone asks if we are going to look for Tomasz? How will we explain his absence?"

"With the truth. Part of it anyway. That he felt the need to go searching for his family. People certainly will be sympathetic to that."

"What if they ask if he's Jewish?"

"I could be wrong," Maria replied evenly, "but I doubt if anyone will ask. They might think it, but I don't think they will ask, not if we describe him as a hero. Besides, as your father once said, he doesn't look all that Jewish." A lie but this seemed the perfect occasion to tell one. "And there are hardly any Jews remaining in Cracow, not more than a few dozen. And how many people actually saw Tomasz? Us. Your brother. Your father's friends. That's all."

"Will we look for him? To let him know."

"Yes," Maria said firmly.

Marzena's relief was palpable but not complete. "If we can't find him, after the baby is born-"

"We will care for it – and you," Maria said softly. "And love you both."

✝✝✝

"In a way," Jacek said to Maria that night after Marzena and Edward were in bed, "it might be better if we don't find him. Can't find him."

"I don't disagree," she replied. "But we will be true to our word. In time we will search for him. And, yes, if we find him, there will be complications."

"You are a good woman."

✝✝✝

The next morning in the restaurant Jacek took his son aside. "Edward," Jacek said, "do you know what discreet means?"

"I can keep a secret."

"One in particular."

"Yes, that one."

CHAPTER 19

It was around midnight on August 10, 1945, in Seoul. Two highly regarded American colonels, Charles Bonesteel and Dean Rusk, were in a musty tent, huddled over a map of Korea. One 60-watt bulb dangling from the ridgepole was providing the only illumination.

Both North and South Korea now had their provisional governments in place under Kim Il Sung and Syngman Rhee. What hadn't been decided yet was where precisely to divide the peninsula, establishing a legal boundary between the pair of newly created states. This had become a matter of considerable urgency, and John McCloy of the State-War-Navy Coordinating Committee assigned Bonesteel and Rusk to recommend a demarcation line – and incredibly gave them only 30 minutes to do so.

The colonels studied the map. Rusk was rubbing his eyes.

"You see what I see, don't you?" Bonesteel said to Rusk.

"There seems one obvious – and very practical – reason for recommending the 38th Parallel. Agreed?"

"Agreed," Bonesteel replied. "It would place the capital city, Seoul, securely in our American zone."

"If we didn't, Rhee might keel over from apoplexy. Of course, Kim might come here from Pyongyang to bow down and lick our dusty boots." The colonels shared a brief chuckle.

"Rhee is already regarding Seoul as his capital," Bonesteel observed soberly. "Placing Seoul in North Korea would be a devastating loss of face."

"Do you think we should consult Rhee or any South Korean military leaders before making this recommendation?"

"It would be the prudent thing to do," Bonesteel replied. "Certainly the diplomatically correct thing. But the time McCloy gave us is nearly up, and I don't think he would look kindly on us going to wake up Rhee and his generals before reporting to him."

"I wonder if the Soviets will object."

To their surprise, they didn't.

Their proposal was accepted, and their work would lead to unforeseen career developments. Among them: More than 20 years later Bonesteel, wearing a black eye-patch, would be in Yongsan Compound near Seoul as a general, commanding all United Nations forces in Korea. Just 16 years later Rusk would become Secretary of State under President John F. Kennedy. Nearer term the proposed demarcation line would exert a major impact on the Park brothers and Ahn Kyone Ae and their families, friends and neighbors; Kaesong, their hometown, would be in North Korea, just north of the 38th Parallel.

CHAPTER 20

British Army Major Roger Cornelius, retired, was holding his favorite newspaper, *The Daily Telegraph*, revered bastion of conservative thinking, in his left hand. Beside his chair on a lamp table sat an ashtray holding a meerschaum black briar pipe.

"Still reading *The Telegraph*?" Michael said, entering his father's small book-lined study with a globe resting on a small side table.

"About the only respectable national paper we have," Roger grumbled. "You read *The Times* and you'd think we were going Commie – or should." Using his army contacts, Roger had secured a job in an export-import firm on Haymarket Street, just off Piccadilly Circus.

"The country does seem to be leaning more to the left," Michael teased his father.

"Voting Churchill out. A bloody disgrace."

Michael chuckled. "You won't change, Father."

"Would you prefer that I did?" Roger laid the paper on his lap.

"Assuredly not. In fact, I'm relying on your steadfastness."

"Do I detect something coming fast?"

Michael smiled. "Perhaps you should have been in intelligence."

"I might still have the other one," Roger smiled wryly, raising his handless right arm, now outfitted with a two-pronged hook. Roger had lost the hand to shrapnel and might have bled to death had it not been for a combat medic's quick, skilled work.

"Would it surprise you if I said I would like to follow your path? Your career path."

Roger sighed. He paused to re-light his pipe. "Truthfully, yes. Especially now that you can see this daily reminder of its dangers – and lasting consequences. Have you thought about your mother's wishes?"

"We both know she won't be terribly enthused about my choice."

"She'd rather you go into accounting or banking. Work in The City." The City was London's central financial district. "Or perhaps diplomatic service."

"That's not me."

"I can't disagree. I can see you riding a horse or a tank more comfortably than a desk chair."

"Will you side with me or her?"

Roger smiled. "That's putting it rather bluntly. No dillydallying. I like it. Look, I will sympathize with her – but respect your wishes and encourage her to do likewise. I trust-"

At that moment Florence materialized in the study's doorway. She smiled knowingly. "Is this one of those private male-only summits?"

"Not at all, dear," Roger smiled. "Enter and join the fun."

"Is it fun you are having?"

"You are your usual perceptive self, dear wife. No, not exactly fun. Michael was just discussing his next phase of life. You know," Roger winked conspiratorially at his son, "just a trivial matter."

Florence directed her gaze at Michael. "And my one and only son, what pray tell is it about your proposed next phase that has you confiding in dear old dad but not dear old mum?"

Roger's rumbling chuckle delayed Michael's reply. "Sarcasm well-honed," Roger observed admiringly. "One of your mother's more endearing qualities. Saves time if not stomping on sensibilities. She would have made a dandy sergeant major."

"We of the fairer gender weren't all brought up on a diet of bland niceties."

"Yours must have included the occasional tart berry." Roger chortled anew.

"Might I?" Michael asked dryly if not supplicatingly.

"By all means," said Florence. "Your father's drollery is generally tasty but smaller portions are more appetizing."

"Mother, I know what you'd rather I do."

"That being?"

"Enter university. Read economics. A career in finance. Perhaps in law or government."

"No dishonor in that. The City teems with gentlemen of means who also happen to be men of good character."

"No doubt."

"But?"

"I'm thinking the Royal Military Academy at Sandhurst might play more to my inclinations and aptitudes." Michael was prepared to hold his breath but there wasn't time or need.

"I quite agree," Florence replied unhesitatingly.

Michael's eyes widened in surprise. So did Roger's. Michael's then quickly narrowed in suspicion. "That's truly your position?"

"Sarcasm may be my forte but so is sincerity. This seems a proper moment for the latter."

"Actually, son," said Roger, his chest swelling with pride, "as a Sandhurst graduate, I've some contacts that might prove useful in helping you gain admission. Pull a few strings as it were and gladly so. Sandhurst offers a solid mix of military arts and academics."

"To be perfectly honest, Mother, I'm more than a little surprised you aren't objecting."

"I love you, Michael. And no doubt I would protest strongly but for one reason. World War II has just now ended. I can't believe this occasionally insane world could again be drawn into another war, not anytime soon. If there are dangers ahead for you, I would rather you find them happily in a tank or on horseback, not unhappily shackled to a Bond Street desk or in court wearing a powdered wig."

CHAPTER 21

The brown stallion traversing the central Polish steppes was walking easily in the new dawn, the facing sun barely peeping above the eastern horizon. The crunch of crusted snow beneath his hoofs seemingly was putting more lift into the horse's gait. His rider breathed deeply the fresh morning air – and then shivered.

"Brr. Another cold one, General," the rider said. "A warm stall and a cozy bed would feel good, wouldn't it? But billeting last night in Bolimow, I know we are getting close." He reached forward with his left hand and patted his mount's neck.

†††

"Time to rise if not shine, younger sister. The cows await us."

Barbara groaned and yawned widely but already was pushing back the heavy blue woolen blanket. "Do you know what I sometimes dream? That our cows might like a day or two off from milk production."

Bernadeta smiled. "You know what else they might like? A break from tugging at their teats twice a day."

†††

With each exhalation, General's breath crystallized in the sub-freezing air.

"You are looking better each day," the rider observed. "And feeling stronger too, I can tell."

General had been a surprise gift from General Stanislaw Sosabowski, founder and former commanding officer of the First Independent Polish Parachute Brigade, at war's end to his favorite aide, Captain Thaddeus Metz. From the day the two had met six years before – in September 1939 – while imprisoned by the Germans in a cow pen on the Gudek's farm, Sosabowski had reserved a special corner in his heart for the younger man.

After V-E Day Sosabowski had decided to remain in England, thinking the Soviets might well banish to the gulag or execute a returning Polish general – a man accustomed to voicing strong opinions and exercising bold leadership, the kind of man anathema to Stalin and his minions.

105

Sosabowski's airborne brigade had been assigned occupation duty in Germany.

Unbeknownst to Thaddeus, Sosabowski had given money to his second-in-command, Lieutenant Colonel Stanislaw Jachnik, to buy a horse to give as a gift to the former lancer turned airborne trooper. The money also had been sufficient to buy food for the horse for several months. For weeks Jachnik had searched for a suitable mount. When at last he found one that was somewhat gaunt but not emaciated, he paid for the stallion and drove Thaddeus from their occupation billet in an American jeep to a nearby pasture to see the animal. There, Jachnik read the letter Sosabowski had written earlier and given Jachnik to hold until this moment. In part the letter read:

Dear Thaddeus,

It has been more than six years since a Polish lancer and an infantry general found themselves together in a cow pen...I know that you are preparing to return to our precious homeland. If you do, to me it seems only appropriate that a Polish lancer should make his return astride a mount. You became a paratrooper, but I know your heart remains that of a lancer.

Even if you return as a merchant, well, it is not uncommon for merchants to ride horses...

Yours very truly,

Stanislaw Sosabowski, General, Retired, Polish First Independent Parachute Brigade

Immediately Thaddeus had begun helping the horse regain lost weight and strength. He exercised him daily. And he gave the animal a new name that he deemed fitting – General.

✝✝✝

"Do you see yourself staying on the farm?" Barbara asked her sister.

The two of them were sitting on their milking stools, relieving the two cows of their overnight production.

"So much of Warsaw is destroyed. There isn't much to go back to. I've heard that Cracow didn't suffer much damage."

"Does that mean you might become a city girl again?"

"I'm not sure. It would take the right circumstances."

"You mean the right man," Barbara teased.

"Am I being foolish?" Thaddeus asked General. "I know General Sosabowski told me to find the farm girl. But I don't even know her last name. And it's been so long. If she survived the war, she's probably married with children." The horse continued stepping spiritedly through the crusted snow. "I am fairly certain I can find the farm. On the east side of Zyrardow on the road to Warsaw."

The sisters completed the milking, stood, picked up the full pails and their stools, exited the cow pen and closed the gate.

"It's going to be another cold day and not much sun," Bernadeta commented as she set her milking stool on the barn's dirt floor. "I think I'll stay inside. Crochet. Read. Help Mama with the meals. Sounds so very rural, doesn't it?" she smiled.

"I'm thinking of walking into Zyrardow to visit friends," said Barbara. "Maybe play cards or chess."

"And drink beer?"

"Maybe one or two," Barbara smiled. "The beer is warm and perhaps a young man would like to buy me one."

"The last thing Poland needs now is another starry-eyed romantic," Thaddeus chided himself. "A poet in a saddle. The demand for such skill is rather low." A pause and he chuckled. "You make a good listener, General. Perhaps I should buy a few pots and skillets and become the itinerant merchant I'm supposed to be. Keep the Soviets from looking too closely at us, right, my friend?"

Bernadeta and Barbara exited the barn, carrying the full pails in their right hands. Barbara stopped and pivoted to push shut the barn door. As she did so, she saw movement to the west.

"Look," she said to her sister, "in the distance. It's still too dark to see clearly, but I think it's moving. Slowly, through the snow. A horse."

"Maybe it's a Soviet officer inspecting his new domain," Bernadeta said disdainfully. "They strut as arrogantly as the Germans. Come on, let's get this milk inside."

"You go ahead. I'm curious."

Bernadeta shrugged and went walking toward the house.

✝✝✝

Minutes later Thaddeus pulled gently on the reins, bringing General to a halt. "That could be it, boy. A farm is a farm, but that one seems to be about the right distance from Zyrardow – as best I can recall." Thaddeus pressed his heels gently against the horse's flanks and he resumed walking.

✝✝✝

"Huhh!" came the sharp intake of breath. Then "Aaiiee!"

Bernadeta had just closed the house's front door behind her when she heard the shriek. Anxiety surged instantly. That Soviet officer, her mind raced, he's assaulting Barbara. She lowered the pail to the floor, jerked open the door and stepped back outside into the snow.

Barbara's pail lay on its side, its white contents now indistinguishable from the snow. Barbara's hands were covering her mouth, as though trying to hold back a second shriek.

"What's wrong?" Bernadeta called.

Barbara didn't answer. Instead, she straightened her right arm, pointing to the west.

Bernadeta followed the line of Barbara's extended hand. "I-" she cut herself off. "Oh, my God," she whispered, "Oh, my Lord Christ."

✝✝✝

Nearing the barn Thaddeus stared hard at the two young women, now standing side by side. He began to apologize for frightening the one who had screamed, but something caught and held his attention.

It was the scar. The scar on the girl who had been walking from the front of the house – the thin scar that ran from the left corner of her mouth for an inch to the left and downward.

Bernadeta stood transfixed, arms at her sides. Her chest expanded with a sharp intake of breath. Barbara's extended right hand had retreated and was again covering her mouth.

The horseman dismounted.

✝✝✝

Forty kilometers northwest of the Gudek's farm Kaz Majos and Tomasz Dolata stood silently, shaking their heads sadly. A tear trickled down Tomasz's left cheek. They were standing on Warsaw's Cracowskie Przedmiesce, once an avenue lined with many of the city's handsomest structures and finest shops, now mostly reduced to rubble. St. Ann's church was an exception. Although most of its roof had collapsed, its walls still were standing.

"My hometown," Tomasz murmured. "Why?"

"In a way," Kaz replied softly, "you have me to thank."

"What?"

"We fought the Germans so hard Hitler felt compelled – teutonically compelled – to take revenge on our town as well as our people."

"Bastard," Tomasz muttered. "At least the river still flows." He nodded to his right toward the Vistula. "It's a wonder they didn't poison the water."

✝✝✝

"Are you all right?" Thaddeus asked Barbara. She nodded mutely.

Bernadeta was recovering her poise, so often tested during her years in the Home Army. "Usually you can't keep my sister quiet," she said softly, smiling warmly.

Thaddeus turned toward the voice. "Bernadeta, I remember. I'm afraid I never caught your last name."

"You had other matters more pressing." He nodded and smiled. "It is Gudek."

109

Thaddeus extended his right hand and Bernadeta took it. "It is nice to see you again, Bernadeta Gudek."

"It's nice to see you too, Thaddeus Metz."

✝✝✝

"I was thinking I might find our family's clothing shop and try to start the business again," said Tomasz.

"Where was it?" Kaz asked.

"Just ahead – on a small street near the Old Town plaza."

"Near the Jewish ghetto?"

"Yes, not far." That quarter of Warsaw, completely walled in by the Nazis, had been leveled.

"Let's check it out."

Tomasz shrugged. "Even if it's still standing, I wouldn't have customers, not nearly enough to make a go of it."

"What will you do?"

"I was going to ask you the same thing."

"I've been thinking too," said Kaz. "What do these Russian soldiers want most?"

"Polish women."

Kaz sighed. "I know. But what else?" Tomasz shrugged. "Beer. Polish beer."

"You plan to open a bistro?"

"Perhaps later but not now. We don't have the money for that. But I used to have friends in the countryside who made their own beer. In small quantities. I'm thinking if they survived they could resume brewing. Maybe on a little larger scale. We could offer to use one of their wagons to bring it into Warsaw to sell to thirsty Russian soldiers."

Tomasz was smiling in open admiration. "You should emigrate to America. I hear it has so many men like you. Big dreamers. Creative thinkers."

✝✝✝

While the Gudeks and Thaddeus were seated around the kitchen table and were happily consuming the mammoth breakfast Tosia prepared that winter morning, torrents of words were spoken. Not loudly. Not hurriedly. Unlike that day more than six years before, this morning provided the luxury of time. Tosia, Jszef, Barbara, Bernadeta and Thaddeus all spoke poignantly about events of the war and the months following its end. Thaddeus told them of his flight from the farm with General Sosabowski and the other cow pen soldiers, first to France. He described the fighting there and the action at Dunkirk – exploding German shells spraying sand, shrapnel and boardwalk splinters; shards and a splinter slicing his body in three places; fellow cow pen soldiers holding him aloft on a stretcher while they waded into the surf to an evacuation vessel. The Gudek family was listening raptly, with Barbara on the verge of swooning. Thaddeus described the formation in England of the Polish airborne brigade, and he spoke warmly of a name that was new to the Gudeks: Father Jack Brecker. Thaddeus described the Easter Mass Jack had said for the Polish troops and the small cross they had given him. He told them about the disastrous river crossings during Operation Market Garden and how Jack, who already had crossed the Rhine with American troops, had volunteered to cross with the Poles.

"Do you know where he is now?" Bernadeta asked.

"No. I made inquiries during occupation duty in Germany but no one knew. I did hear that more than fifty American chaplains were killed during the war."

"Let us pray he made it home safely," said Tosia.

"He seems like a warrior himself," Jszef said admiringly.

"He was a good man," Thaddeus said, his respect obvious, "and from a good family. His parents sent a package of special foods, cigars and money to buy spirits to us cow pen soldiers."

Jszef, though anticipating the answer, still went ahead and asked the obvious question: "What brought you back here?"

"Curiosity," Thaddeus replied unhesitatingly, knowing this was no occasion for half-truths. "I wanted to see the girl – the woman – who saved our lives."

His words again had Barbara close to fainting, and even Bernadeta felt goosebumps sprouting on her arms from the chills traversing her spine.

Jszef cleared his throat. "Clearly you never forgot."

"Neither did Bernadeta." The words escaped Barbara's mouth before she thought about them or their impact. But Bernadeta's blush confirmed the accuracy of her sister's disclosure.

An ensuing awkward silence seemed to have quick-frozen tongues and jaws much as would walking into a relentless winter wind. Jszef decided at last to break it.

"I have a suggestion," he said. "Have we all eaten enough?"

"More than enough," Thaddeus smiled, eyes shining brightly.

"Good. Now, let's give Bernadeta and Thaddeus a little time alone, in the living room. We'll stay in the kitchen, clean up." A brief pause, followed by a smile. "And one other thing, young man."

"Yes, sir?"

"Don't be in such a hurry to leave us this time."

Chapter 22

Winston Churchill stood behind the podium and cleared his voice. It was March 5, 1946, and Churchill was in Fulton, Missouri. He was 71 but his stocky body still radiated resolve and his voice still commanded attention.

Churchill had lost his post as prime minister within weeks after V-E Day. British voters, weary of war's deprivations, had resonated to promises by the Labour Party to introduce cradle-to-grave socialism. Moreover, the majority still blamed Churchill's Conservative Party for having failed to adequately prepare Britain for the war. The election outcome stung Churchill who retained his seat in the House of Commons and took his place as leader of the Conservative Party opposition.

Churchill was glad to be in the United States, a nation for which he had a naturally warm regard. His mother, Jennie Jerome Churchill, a woman of beauty and wit, was an American who had died in 1921 at age 67. Her father, Leonard Jerome, had made and lost fortunes in business, and Winston had enjoyed hearing tales of the man's enduring pluck. More than once he had wondered whether his own grit in the face of unrelenting adversity was a product of his bloodline. Now, although he had successfully led Britain through its bleakest hours and peace was at hand, Churchill was feeling deep concerns about threats emanating from Soviet Russia, a former ally he had never trusted.

After being introduced as a savior of mankind, Churchill again cleared his throat, projected his richly sonorous voice and spoke words that would be heard around the world and long remembered. "Beware," he cautioned, "time may be short. From Stettin in the Baltic to Trieste in the Adriatic, an iron curtain has descended across the continent."

Nowhere was that curtain hanging more threateningly than in Poland. It was a frequent topic of conversation around the table in the Gudek's kitchen. Would Stalin open his fist and permit a democratic Poland? Or would he keep tightening his grip, choking off any hopes of freedom?

On the evening of March 5, though, another kind of conversation was taking place. Supper was finished and Jszef and Barbara were seated in the living room, listening to radio news.

Tosia entered from the kitchen. "Where are Bernadeta and Thaddeus? I thought I would make tea for all of us."

"They wanted some time alone," Barbara said, eyes still focused on the radio, housed in a small, gray metal box.

"Where are they?"

"In the barn, I think."

"Will you tell them I am making tea?"

Barbara looked away from the radio to her mother. "I don't think they want to be interrupted for tea."

Tosia was baffled momentarily, then reddened. "Oh."

✝✝✝

In the barn's loft Bernadeta and Thaddeus lay side by side on straw. Below them General now had his own small stall, created by dividing the ox's pen. Neither animal seemed to object to its new neighbor.

"I've been here a month," murmured Thaddeus.

"That's why I decided we should come up here." A pause. "I love you. There, I said it. I know it sounds silly, but I think I fell in love with you during those first minutes in the cow pen."

Thaddeus chuckled softly and rolled a length of straw between his fingers and thumb. "You certainly made it difficult to forget you. Impossible actually. Coming into the cow pen. Sitting on the stool. Hiking up your skirt to reveal the knife. I'd not seen a girl's thigh before."

"And now?"

"I don't know that I fell in love with you back then. But I needed to find you. That says something. And since I've been here this past month...I love you."

Bernadeta's left hand brushed Thaddeus' cheek and forehead. "There was another man."

"Kaz Majos?"

"Yes."

"I've heard his name mentioned a couple times. Barbara, your mother."

"We grew very fond of each other. It was very intense in the Resistance. Danger. Constant stress. Living in the church basement. I think he probably saved my life once. At least from interrogation, torture and maybe rape. He is a brave man. He risked his own life. A good man."

"Have you heard from him?"

"No. Not since that last night in St. Ann's. He might have perished at Auschwitz or some other camp. The Nazis were supposed to treat Uprising survivors as prisoners of war, but we know the fate of many such prisoners." Bernadeta's eyes were scant inches from Thaddeus'. "I loved him, but I don't think we were in love. We were...we were good for each other. I couldn't bring myself to stay with him in Warsaw to die, and he couldn't leave with me to come here."

Thaddeus leaned still closer and lightly kissed Bernadeta's scar, then her lips. "I think if God likes a scar, it's yours."

She responded, tenderly and then with more force. "I never saw my scar as a beauty mark."

"Perhaps no one ever saw it the way I do." A pause. "How much time do we have here? Before someone comes looking for us?"

"No one will," she smiled conspiratorially. "I told Barbara we needed some privacy. She understood."

"Does that mean I might see your thigh again?" Thaddeus smiled.

"Both of them this time."

✝ ✝ ✝

Twenty minutes later, despite the cold air, Bernadeta and Thaddeus were sweating.

"Get on top of me," he murmured.

"Oh? Am I to be your blanket now that you've bared your behind?"

"You are a woman of uncommonly keen perception."

"You can compare me with others?"

"Hush."

"You know what this means, don't you?"

"Something more permanent than this bed of straw? Something less prickly?"

Bernadeta eased herself atop Thaddeus. "Wedding plans." She smiled brightly, eyes glistening.

"Your parents will approve?"

"They love you. They respect you. Father sees you as a son."

"Even after this?"

"They both know what we've been through. I'm not saying they...The war changed things. They know that."

"Your family is special. They are very warm people."

Bernadeta squirmed, edging side to side. "Let's see if this blanket can make you a little warmer."

CHAPTER 23

In Shelby it was 10 a.m., and the big bell in the red brick tower on the south side of Most Pure Heart of Mary church – referred to commonly as St. Mary's – was signaling the start of a wedding. The coming nuptials had been a source of chatter for weeks, since the wedding announcement had appeared in *The Daily Globe*.

The bride and her personal history were well known to Shelbians. Little was known about the groom, a former Army captain, which made the wedding all the more intriguing. Theresa Hassler was born in Shelby in 1917. After graduating from high school, she had gone to Mt. Sinai Hospital School of Nursing in Cleveland. There – at a dance – she had met and fallen in love with Hal Walker, an American Airlines pilot. When Walker decided to volunteer for the Royal Air Force and help defend England during the Battle of Britain, Theresa showed pluck and determination by accompanying him. In short order she had found work in London at St. Thomas Hospital near the houses of Parliament and Waterloo Station on the south side of the Thames River. Her regimen had been demanding, given the large number of civilian bombing casualties along with RAF crew injuries.

The head nurse had helped Theresa find lodgings – in a room above Ronald Turner's bicycle sales and service shop in nearby Carlisle Lane.

Hal Walker had proved a fast learner. His airline piloting experience provided a sturdy foundation. Within two weeks after arriving, he felt comfortable at the controls of nimble British Hurricanes. Hal proceeded to fly several combat missions from his Squadron 43 base at Tangmere, an aerodrome near Chichester and England's south coast and widely regarded as the nation's first line of defense against Luftwaffe air raids. Such duty was exhausting and hazardous in the extreme. On August 18, 1940, Hal suffered a close call when his Hurricane was hit, forcing him to parachute from his plunging craft. Three weeks later on September 7, following an aerial duel with an ME-109 over the English Channel, he was declared missing in action and never seen again.

Theresa, grief stricken, chose to remain in England and in the embrace of St. Thomas and its staff. Later, after Japan's attack on Pearl Harbor and Germany's declaration of war against the United States, she volunteered for military service, becoming the first U.S. Army nurse in Europe.

After the war Theresa returned to America. In the spring of 1946 came an unexpected, brief reunion with Father Jack Brecker, a friend since elementary school at St. Mary's. Theresa and Jack had been 8th grade dance partners, and she had grown to love him. When in 1932 Jack had departed from Shelby for a seminary, Theresa gave him a St. Christopher medal. After his ordination and America's entry into the war, the young priest volunteered first for the Chaplains Corps and then airborne duty. He was assigned to the 82nd Airborne Division. On June 6, 1944, shortly after midnight, Jack jumped into France with the pathfinders. In September he jumped again at the start of Operation Market Garden in Belgium, participated in Major Julian Cook's perilous crossing of the Rhine and then volunteered to cross the Rhine again with Thaddeus Metz's cow pen soldiers.

In December 1944 near Bastogne during the Battle of the Bulge at an evacuation hospital, an exploding artillery shell sliced Theresa's right hip, leaving her with a permanent limp. Days later, Jack showed up at the hospital. Surrendering to a rush of emotion amidst the carnage, they made love in the nurses' tent. Soon after V-E Day Theresa mustered out while Jack stayed with the 82nd Airborne for occupation duty in Germany. In late 1945 he returned to Arizona where he resumed ministering to his parishioners in Ajo and to Indians on their reservations.

He also took up flying. His plane, a Luscombe two-seater, was a gift from Elgin Hunter, the wealthy copper mine-owning father of Jack's army friend, Captain Walt Hunter. Once while in Europe, Jack had mentioned casually that he thought he'd enjoy having his own plane. His thinking: by flying his own plane he could better serve the people of his parish in Ajo and the Indians on their far-flung reservations.

Walt Hunter didn't forget. Soon after returning to Arizona, Walt told his dad about his friend, and Elgin's wallet opened quickly.

Jack proved an apt student and in April of 1946 had flown to Cleveland. He had surprised Theresa by phoning and asking to meet with her at the Cleveland Museum of Art near Mt. Sinai where she had resumed working as a nurse. It was there, during a walk around the museum's lagoon, he confirmed what she had expected; he would remain in the priesthood. Theresa had anticipated his choice, but it stung and she let Jack know it. Somehow, though, she felt sure they would remain friends, ready to help if ever help was needed.

For Theresa, her next move seemed natural; she returned to the town she had come to regard as home – London. She also returned to nursing at St. Thomas and her room above Ronald Turner's bicycle shop.

Enter Dean Morton. Or more accurately, re-enter. Back on July 10, 1943, during the Allies' landing on Sicily, Captain Morton had been grievously wounded. A German bullet had torn into his upper right chest that was gushing blood like a newly drilled oil well. Lying in a hospital tent, his back arching spasmodically and tasting his own salty blood, he felt death's grip squeezing hard. Enter Theresa Hassler. Her decisive and compassionate work – she had plunged her hand into the gaping wound – staunched the bleeding. Through his pain and blood-crusted lips, Dean had asked for a kiss. Theresa brushed his lips with hers, a kiss that Dean had come to regard as having the power of magic, of life.

During the early days of Morton's recovery and before being evacuated to the U.S., he had learned Theresa's name and hometown. After the war he showed resourcefulness and resolve. Using his congressman father's Washington connections – Raymond Morton was a Republican from Belvidere, Illinois – Dean had tracked down Theresa's whereabouts, sailed to England and waited for her on the sidewalk outside St. Thomas. He proved as persuasive as he had been resourceful and resolute, and the result was a late July 1946 wedding date.

For Theresa, wedding preparations also were proving to be a joyous homecoming, much happier than her first return in 1945. She was feeling a heightened sense of freedom. Perhaps, she reflected, it was because she had at last succeeded in closing past chapters and was concentrating on a future with a man who loved her unconditionally – limp and all – and whom she saw as the ideal father for the children she was hoping to bear. She also was taking particular joy in spending time with her niece and nephew, Bridgett and Tom Brecker's twins. Bridgett would serve as her matron of honor.

✝✝✝

On the day before the wedding two planes, both Luscombe two-seaters, were in the air, converging on Shelby's small grass-strip airport on Route 96, just west of town. Raymond Morton was piloting one of the planes with wife Jane as his passenger. Jack Brecker was flying the other.

A month earlier, back in Shelby after Dean Morton proposed, Theresa acted on impulse. She sat next to her parents' phone and dialed.

"Hello," Jack said, picking up the black rotary phone on his desk in the rectory next to Immaculate Conception church in Ajo. "Father Brecker here."

"Hello, Jack."

"Theresa?"

"Will we ever forget each other's voice?"

"Only in our dotage, if then." Jack was smiling widely.

"I have something to tell you – and to ask."

"I'm all ears."

"I'm getting married."

"Oh, well, that's – Sorry, I started to say that's fast, but-"

Theresa's laughter cut him off. "It is fast. But he's right for me. I know that. And, well, he didn't want to waste time and neither do I. I'm almost thirty. I think you'd like him, Jack."

"How did you meet?"

"He was wounded at Sicily. After the war he looked me up in London."

"I'm happy for you, Theresa. Truly. You deserve a good man. And he's a lucky guy. I mean that."

"I know you do, Jack. Thank you."

"You said you had something to ask."

"I do, but I think I'm getting cold feet."

"Not about the wedding."

"No. I...I have a favor to ask. Would you be willing to fly back to Ohio again? To marry us?"

✝✝✝

In the Gudek's barn it was difficult to excite the two cows, but this afternoon they were lowing loudly. The two docile creatures hadn't seen so many people since that September afternoon in 1939 when they had had as company the 12 Polish soldiers, their German guard and Bernadeta. Today the crowd was larger and noisier.

"This isn't what your mother would have planned," Jszef whispered, "or preferred."

"And you?" Bernadeta replied, her lips close to her father's left ear. They were standing at the barn's entrance, the double doors having been pulled open.

He eyed his daughter. "I admit, it does seem appropriate. And creative. It fits your personality."

"So you approve?"

"I do."

"Good." And Bernadeta squeezed her father's arm. "I'm happy."

In addition to Bernadeta and Jszef, the two cows, the ox and General, the barn's occupants included Tosia, Barbara, 22 of the family's friends, Thaddeus and his parents, and Father Waldemar Kowalski, an assistant pastor from St. Mattia's parish in Zyrardow.

It hadn't been easy to persuade Father Kowalski to come to the barn, not on this Saturday and not for this occasion. But Jszef, arguing on Bernadeta's behalf, had prevailed, not least because he had promised Father Kowalski a first-rate feast, a cake of his own to take back to the rectory and a gallon of fresh milk to be delivered on the last Sunday of each month for the next six months.

To Bernadeta, the family-barn-as-church made perfect sense. Yes, it had been the scene of a gruesome death when Thaddeus had plunged her bread knife into the German guard's back. Yes, a second such death had taken place moments later just outside the barn's door. But to Bernadeta, trying to peer into an uncertain future, this barn seemed the ideal launch point. This is where Thaddeus walked into my life and I into his. It is where memories were formed that refused to fade. This is where a bond took hold and where hope – lasting hope – was born. And more than that, if missing my period is the sign I think it is.

"We should get started," Jszef said to Father Kowalski. "Soon the cows will want to be milked."

"Of course," he replied. "Let me welcome all of you to this unconventional house of our Lord." He paused for effect and smiled. "At first I was opposed to performing a wedding – one of the holy sacraments – in a barn. But now that I'm here, among these creatures, and with you happy people, I am reminded that Jesus was born in a manger. So, yes, I think he is finding favor with his new house of worship, temporary as it is."

Well said, Jszef was thinking as he listened to Father Kowalski's comments. But I'm also thinking about the collection of incentives I presented you. They made it easier for you to sense the Lord's approval, didn't they?

"Would the bride and her father please step forward?"

Jszef and Bernadeta walked slowly on the earthen floor toward Father Kowalski. Thaddeus was standing off to the side by the cow pen gate.

Jszef removed his hand from Bernadeta's arm and stepped back. Thaddeus took his place. Discreetly, Jacek removed his watch from his small vest pocket. 5 p.m. Simultaneously, but seven hours earlier – 10:00 in the morning in Shelby on that same Saturday – Father Jack Brecker welcomed Theresa Hassler and Dean Morton into the sanctuary of Most Pure Heart of Mary.

CHAPTER 24

For many people 1946 is a forgotten year. It was the year after World War II ended. What's to remember? Yet looking back on the summer of 1946, if World War II had not ended a scant 12 months earlier, trigger points aplenty could understandably have been fueling widespread speculation of another imminent global conflagration.

Consider:

- United States scientists with encouragement from President Harry Truman were rushing to develop a hydrogen bomb, many times more powerful than the atom bombs that had leveled Hiroshima and Nagasaki and incinerated thousands of their residents.
- As Winston Churchill had warned, Joseph Stalin was, in fact, drawing down his iron curtain.
- That summer in China, Mao Tse Tung was igniting his communist crusade against Chiang Kai Shek and his nationalists.
- The French were struggling to maintain their hold on South Vietnam while Ho Chi Min, who had arrived in Hanoi from China a few days after Japan's defeat, was rallying support and rapidly establishing control over most of North Vietnam. On December 19 Ho's forces would attack the French throughout Vietnam, and the Indochina War would be on.
- Jews in Palestine were pushing for statehood – a prospect anathema to Arab aims.
- Kim Il Sung and Syngman Rhee both were beginning to make cases with their Soviet, Chinese and American sponsors for pre-emptive strikes to unify the two Koreas.

Denial can be decidedly dangerous, often causing problems to fester and erupt as crises. But in the summer of 1946 denial might have helped preserve a fragile peace. After all, none of those ambitious nations and their strong-minded leaders wanted to imagine seriously that their actions might trigger a third world war. Not yet. They persuaded themselves that no rational leader would countenance taking his country into another far-flung conflict that would extinguish millions more lives. If any did imagine that, they stopped short of trumpeting their forebodings.

Numerous private citizens, though, were not in denial. Clear-eyed, they did foresee more bloodletting, nationally or regionally if not globally.

"Someone, some nation, will test Stalin," Thaddeus said to Jszef. The men were in the barn, Thaddeus leisurely brushing General.

"You really think so?"

"I'm not smart enough to know when, but yes."

"Poland?"

"I don't think we would be first. Our top government officials are too beholden to Moscow. I think it will be one of Stalin's satellites with strong leaders yearning for independence."

"Yugoslavia?"

"Perhaps. Or maybe Hungary."

"Many will die…"

"Stalin isn't likely to show leniency. He's paranoid to begin with and sees threats in every nook and cranny to his power and control. That's what is behind his purges. That and an utter disregard for the sanctity of life."

"Whichever country it is, may God be on their side."

"So far," Thaddeus said dryly, "he's been on the wrong side as often as not."

✝✝✝

"I guess we'll have to be careful about riding Sejong south," Park Han said to his older brother Min. "At least until we see how dangerous it is to cross the 38th Parallel."

Min's chuckle was one of disgust. "Going to visit our friends in Munsan could wind up getting us shot as spies – by soldiers of either side."

"The 38th Parallel isn't closed yet. Not entirely."

"It's only a matter of time – and more dirty politics."

"Do you feel like a North Korean?" Han asked.

"I feel like a Korean but one who is losing something precious – our freedom."

"What do you think of Kim Il Sung?"

"The same that I think of Syngman Rhee. Neither man is worthy of our trust. You've heard the rumors about Rhee. A long history of corruption. And Kim, he fought against the Japanese and deserves credit for that. But now that he's in charge, he's proving to be as ruthless as the Japanese. If either man is suspicious of someone, they've already shown they won't hesitate to commit murder."

"War with the South?"

"I hope not but both men clearly want one Korea – a unified Korea. And I think they are both ambitious enough to kill – on a large scale – to get what they want."

"If there is war," Han said plaintively, "I hope we're not in it."

"Our age is against us."

"What do you mean?"

"We are too young to avoid military service."

CHAPTER 25

"Well, General, this will be our last ride together for a while. At least with me in the saddle." The horse was cantering spiritedly along the road from the Gudek's farm to Zyrardow. "Tomorrow we'll ride together again but you will be in harness and have more than one passenger. When we get back to the farm this evening, I'll put you in harness and give you a lesson in pulling a wagon. But," Thaddeus laughed, "let's be sure General Sosabowski never hears about this. He wouldn't look kindly on a lancer driving a farm wagon."

†††

"You don't have to leave," Tosia said, subdued, to Bernadeta. "You could stay as long as you want." She, Bernadeta, Jszef and Barbara were seated around the kitchen table.

"Your mother is right," said Jszef. "Our farm can support five people."

"Six?" Bernadeta murmured.

"Six?" Jszef said quizzically.

Tosia's sharpened eyes penetrated those of her elder daughter. "Are you sure?"

"No periods."

Jszef's eyes widened. "Am I understanding this correctly?"

Laughter erupted from Barbara. "Oh Father! You are going to be a grandfather."

Tosia pushed back from the table and stood. She hurried around the table, bent down and hugged Bernadeta. "That's wonderful, dear. Have you told Thaddeus?"

"He knows."

"And?" said Jszef.

"He is very excited to be a father. He says you are his role model."

"Me? Really?" Jszef's astonishment was evident. So was his pleasure. "I-I think I might weep."

Now all three women were laughing. Jszef dabbed at his eyes and began laughing with them. Then came sniffling, and the laughter subsided.

"You should have the baby here," Tosia said gravely. "On the farm. You'll need help."

"Experienced help," Jszef concurred.

Bernadeta's visage reflected clearly the immense affection she held for her parents. "That's our plan, Mama. To return to the farm when the baby is due."

Tosia's sigh of relief was deep. "That's good."

"What will you do in Warsaw?" Barbara asked.

"We can't be sure but Thaddeus has a plan. He is going to seek a teaching position at the University of Warsaw. Perhaps in history or political science. Or maybe French or English. If the Soviets still permit those fields of study. "

"He would be an excellent teacher," Jszef observed thoughtfully.

"And you?" Barbara asked. "I can't picture you sitting at home alone, just waiting months for the baby."

Bernadeta pushed back her chair, stood and curtsied with mock solemnity. "Thank you ever so much for that vote of confidence, little sister."

"You are most welcome, big sister." A pause. "If you miss milking the cows, pay us a visit." More laughter.

Bernadeta sat. "You know, Thaddeus has been teaching me English. He thinks I should try to find work at the American embassy. He thinks there is a shortage of English-speaking Poles."

"He has seen much more of the world than we have," said Jszef. "More than we probably ever will. He is a wise young man. And he makes friends so easily. Poles, Americans, British."

"You know what?" Barbara said brightly. "I think life with Thaddeus Metz will not be boring."

✝✝✝

Early the next morning outside the barn, Jszef and Thaddeus fitted General with the harness. Until now it had been used to fasten the ox to the tongues of Jszef's farm wagon, painted green with red wheel rims and in need of a post-war painting.

Tosia, Bernadeta and Barbara stood watching.

"There, boy, all set. I think you're up to pulling this load." Thaddeus was grinning. He reached for Bernadeta, grasped her waist and lifted. In the next instant she was perched high on the wagon's front seat. It was unpadded. "And now you, sir," Thaddeus said, gesturing to his father-in-law.

Jszef pecked Tosia and Barbara on their cheeks and climbed onto the seat. Thaddeus climbed aboard, easing himself onto the rear seat.

"I'll see you in a couple days," Jszef said to Tosia. His plan: stay with Thaddeus and Bernadeta until they found an apartment or room, see that General was properly fed and rested and then begin the return drive. Jszef removed the reins from the brake stick, lightly flicked them and clicked his tongue. General responded, stepping forward, northeast toward Warsaw.

With the sleeve of her white blouse Tosia dabbed at her eyes. Barbara wrapped her right arm around her mother's waist. "Try not to worry, Mama. Bernadeta and Thaddeus are both used to travels."

"I know…But there are dangers on the road and in Warsaw. And mothers never stop worrying. I sometimes think that's the real reason God made mothers, to worry."

Barbara squeezed Tosia. "I love you."

Tosia's concerns went beyond motherly worrying. In recent weeks she had been experiencing occasional stabbing pains in her abdomen. It could be an ordinary female malady, she speculated. Nothing major to worry about. *Maybe I should see a doctor to be sure. But that would only cause worry for Jszef and Barbara. Maybe the pains will go away.*

CHAPTER 26

When during life do we begin to learn about ourselves? Our strengths and weaknesses? Physical, intellectual, emotional and moral ones? Some individuals, we know, begin to acquire, store and use such knowledge early on. For others, however, such knowledge remains elusive until later – the very end – or never.

For many if not most, the teen years stand as the least likely for acquiring, absorbing and putting to productive use knowledge of self. Why should that be? Is there any stage of life during which a person – boy or girl – is more awkwardly self-conscious? More prone to embarrassment? More worried about fitting in with peers? More concerned about being accepted without reservations? More immune to healthy introspection?

Boys and girls seem equally affected. Raging hormones, blotchy skin, sprouting hair, enlarging breasts, monthly bleeding, swelling penises and more. For millennia they have undermined self-esteem, fueled self-loathing and proven effective preventatives to serious self-examination. Perhaps the clearest – and most tragic – evidence is the suicide rate among teens.

And yet for some teens, an epiphany – often resulting from trauma such as a crime against the family, the passing of a parent, the unexpected premature death of a friend – can accelerate the knowledge-of-self process and speed maturation. Such a happening can inspire leaps in self-worth, self-confidence and selflessness. When it happens, it rarely goes unnoticed.

For Edward Frantek, age 16 in early 1946, the trauma was seeing his sister Marzena's belly swollen daily by a half-Jewish fetus. At his trauma's roots were Catholicism and its unbending dictates as well as age-old, permeating anti-Semitism. His parents' outward and surprising acceptance of Marzena's condition did nothing to ease Edward's trauma. Instead it deepened and complicated it. Why not send her away? Or hide her in the family apartment above the restaurant? Or arrange to have her pregnancy ended? Well, not that; the church forbids it. But my dear mother and father must be mortified. Their shame must be bottomless. Yes, all right, the fetus's father was a hero. He saved Marzena from rape. Perhaps had spared the entire family from murder at the hands of the Soviet barbarians.

But Tomasz was a flawed hero. He had to be. Edward didn't know all the details of Tomasz's transgressions against humanity. But he was Jewish, he had survived Auschwitz, and Edward's imagination could fill in the blanks, if not altogether accurately.

It was all terribly complex and deeply troubling. That's one reason why today Edward was relishing so very much fishing in the Vistula with Karol, his friend and neighbor since elementary school. Fishing was enabling Edward to temporarily put aside such thoughts and concentrate on his gear and the finned catches he was angling for. So far each boy had landed one fish of decent size. Imagining his mother applying her culinary skills to freshly caught fish was activating Edward's salivary glands. First he would have to clean and gut the fish, but he regarded that as an acceptable component of the equation.

Both boys were wearing shirts – Edward's was green, Karol's blue – with sleeves rolled above the elbows. Both boys were hatless. They were thoroughly enjoying the sun's warmth on exposed skin. Both boys were lounging, half-sitting, half-lying supine. Edward stretched his lanky frame and groaned pleasurably.

For more than an hour Edward and Karol, using ordinary cane poles, had been tossing their lines into the water from the river's north bank. This stretch of the serpentine Vistula flowed west to east as it made its way erratically north to the Baltic Sea. The tranquil combination of sunshine and fishing's deliciously slow rhythm – preparing the line; affixing the sinker, hook and bobber; baiting the hook; casting; watching for nibbles – had Edward feeling more relaxed than he had in weeks.

"My parents were in your restaurant the other night," Karol remarked offhandedly. His father was a midlevel functionary in the agriculture section of Poland's puppet government.

"Uh huh. I saw them." Edward was more intent on watching his bobber for signs of a bite than for pointless small talk about the restaurant.

"They say your sister has put on weight – all of it around her middle."

"Edward's cheeks began burning, taking on the hue of his bobber – red. "So?"

"Is she eating more of your mother's cooking?"

"Not that I know of but I'm not her mother."

"So who is the mysterious man who knocked her up?"

The unexpected question smashed into Edward's brain with the force of a .45-caliber bullet. It sent heated blood rushing to his cheeks. The same blow was causing his stomach to knot as tightly as his face was blushing. His embarrassment was so overwhelming as to render him speechless.

Karol could see easily that his crudely put question had struck a raw nerve. Edward's reaction was visceral. He had flinched and grimaced. Karol was eager to satisfy his curiosity, but given his friendship with Edward decided not to press with more queries – unless, that is, he responded in a way that provided an opening.

Edward's initial shock was abating slowly and he was beginning to think more clearly. He remembered his father's counsel. Be discreet. But if asked don't deceive. Lies weave a complex web difficult if not impossible to escape without escalating damage. A guarded, partial truth is preferable to deception. "A hero," Edward murmured. "The baby's father is a hero." There, he thought, I've said baby, not fetus. Both were living beings, yes, but baby was somehow a more explicit, more personal descriptor.

Karol was momentarily incredulous but then remembered that Edward didn't make a practice of lying or exaggerating. He had, however, answered in a way that invited more questions. "Who is this hero?"

"The Nazis were after him. The Russians too."

"He was with the Home Army?"

"He killed enemy soldiers."

"Wow!" Karol was hugely impressed. "What's his name?"

"Tomasz."

"Last name?"

"Sorry. In due time, perhaps. It's not safe to tell yet." That, Edward knew, was true. The Nazis were gone, no longer a threat. But the Russians were a different story and, with Tomasz traveling with a former Home Army cell leader, still posed a danger. And disclosing too much about Tomasz – including his last name – could jeopardize Marzena's safety – emotional if not physical. Knowledge of his last name by sufficiently curious – nosy – people could facilitate tracking his origins – in particular his Jewishness.

"Was he staying with your family?" Karol asked.

Edward was feeling better. He was learning something about himself, and he found the new knowledge comforting. He could feel his embarrassment receding. Replacing it was a selfless determination to uphold his family's honor – his sister's – and to safeguard her. "Karol," he said firmly but not unpleasantly, "don't ask more questions that I won't answer. Not now."

CHAPTER 27

Kaz and Tomasz were on the road, driving a load of home-brewed beer west from the countryside toward Warsaw. They were nearing Praga, the community on the east, or right, bank of the Vistula. Soon they would be crossing the Slasko-Dabrowski Bridge into Warsaw's Old Town. The hulking brown ox pulling the weather-beaten wagon was plodding, one lumbering step after another. The pace of each roundtrip afforded the two men ample time for thinking and conversing.

Kaz's idea – finding farmers willing to produce beer and letting Kaz and Tomasz transport and sell it in Warsaw – had led quickly to brisk business. As Kaz had anticipated, Soviet soldiers were numerous and among their best customers. But the clientele spread rapidly among bureaucrats and other Poles with a few extra zlotys to spend on a bargain-priced luxury. Kaz and Tomasz occasionally were offered – but declined – barter goods. Demand among cash-paying customers was enough to assure a fast sale of the small barrels that made up a load.

On this day under a cloudless sky, as the wagon edged slowly along the rough rutted road, Kaz murmured, "I think it's getting to be time to move on again."

Tomasz turned to look at his friend and smiled knowingly. "To Zyrardow?"

Kaz nodded. "I've got money in my pocket now. Enough to last a while. I'm not sure what I'll find. I'm not sure if Bernadeta is alive. But I need to find out."

The front right wheel passed over a jagged egg-sized rock. The jolt was enough to lift Kaz and Tomasz a couple inches above their seat. Kaz reached up to adjust the black patch over his right eye.

"Won't you miss these rides?" Tomasz chuckled.

"The ruts and bumps, no. The companionship, yes."

"Our friendship, who would have guessed? Catholic and Jew."

"You and Michal and Jacob – especially Jacob – gave me a second life."

"If you can't find Bernadeta, if she was…" Tomasz swallowed to clear his rapidly thickening throat. "You can always come back to this. It's really your business."

"Our business."

"It was your idea and you made it work."

"I'm remembering something else – our escape – that was not my idea and you made it work."

"This is good, no?" Tomasz smiled. "Debating who should get credit. Maybe it is all God's doing." A pause. "Of course, in my case he has much to forgive before granting me any favors."

"In Catholicism we call it confession and doing penance."

"In Judaism we call it atonement."

"Do you think it makes a difference in God's eyes?"

"Not from what my eyes have seen."

"Nor mine."

✝✝✝

Dusk was giving way to darkness when the Gudek's wagon entered Warsaw from the southwest on Krolewska Street. Jszef pulled back on the reins and General stopped. The city's reconstruction had begun, albeit slowly, but even in the dim light the extent of the war's destruction was jarring. Skeletal structures. Bullet- and shell-pocked walls. Piles of dusty debris. Gaping potholes.

"Have you ever been to Warsaw before?" Bernadeta asked Thaddeus.

"This is my first time."

"It was once a beautiful city. It was founded in 1281. It has been our country's capital since 1596 when King Sigismund moved it here from Cracow."

"Perhaps it can be beautiful again. With time."

"I would like to see St. Ann's," said Bernadeta. "I've heard it survived the Nazis' razing of the city. Our Resistance cell lived there in the church basement. But that can wait."

"Where to first?" Jszef asked.

"It's getting late," Thaddeus replied. "In the morning we'll find the United States embassy. See about applying for a job for Bernadeta. Then visit the University of Warsaw. Check into teaching possibilities."

"The university is very close to St. Ann's," said Bernadeta. "They are on the same side of the same street, Cracowskie Przedmiescie. Actually, everything is fairly close together. Easy walking."

"Good," said Thaddeus. "At the embassy, at the university, perhaps we can get some suggestions on places to live."

"Do you think someone at the embassy will agree to see us?" Bernadeta asked. She wasn't so much worried – she felt perfectly secure with Thaddeus and Jszef – as she was curious.

"When they hear my English, I'm counting on that. If need be I will tell them about Dunkirk and Market Garden – and occupation duty in Germany."

"And tonight?" said Jszef.

"It's getting late. We'll ask about for an inn of some sort. But we might have to sleep in the wagon."

They did. Taking turns, two slept while a third kept watch. In the wagon, along with Thaddeus and Bernadeta's meager belongings, was the bread knife Thaddeus had used to slay the German guards in 1939. Jszef had thought to bring it only minutes before leaving the farm for Warsaw. Just in case. Thaddeus had brought the dagger and bayonet that Jszef had given him after Thaddeus and the cow pen soldiers had buried the two Germans. Just in case. The weapons had been Jszef's mementos from his days fighting the Russians during World War I.

†††

That night sleep came slowly to Tosia. Her brain seemed reluctant to shut down. She couldn't help imagining Bernadeta and Thaddeus as young newlyweds, parents in a few months, leaving the security of the farm for the big city and its unknowns. And Jszef, her faithful and caring husband for 28 years. He would make any sacrifice for his family. At last Tosia was drifting into sleep when pain went knifing through her abdomen. Her eyes snapped open. Involuntarily she groaned and curled into a fetal position, hands pressing hard against her stomach, fingers digging in. Long moments crawled by and then she felt blessed relief as the pain began dissipating. More moments passed and it disappeared. She breathed deeply and exhaled slowly. She was perspiring. And she was frightened.

Silently she began posing questions. What is it? An infection? Cramps from menopause? Worse maybe? Cancer? I'm forty-seven. My mother was dead by now. Heart attack at forty-six. My father was gone at fifty. Life is so short in Poland. Too much hard work. Too many diseases. Not enough good doctors or cures. Is my time coming to an end? I want to see my grandchild. My first grandchild. Please, God, grant me that. I don't want to tell anyone, but if I don't Jszef will be upset. I couldn't blame him. After all, if he was sick and didn't tell me, I would be upset and, yes, angry. What about Barbara? She is twenty-four. A woman. An intelligent, beautiful young woman. If I tell her, yes, it would help for her to be my confidant. Her and me. She is mature and strong. Bernadeta? She is twenty-seven. So very strong. But, no, I will not tell her. I won't write to her. Finding a job in Warsaw, dealing with pregnancy. That is quite enough, Tosia Gudek. I have been blessed. A good husband. Two wonderful daughters. We all survived the war. Whatever it is, I am grateful. Do you hear me, God? I am grateful.

†††

In the gray predawn two Soviet soldiers, Yuri Rykov and Ivan Godunov, both privates, could hear water falling on rubble. Both were feeling the effects of beer they had bought last night from Kaz Majos and Tomasz Dolata. The two young soldiers, against regulations, had begun consuming it before starting their watch duty. They had continued drinking from canteens they had filled from the barrel.

"A filthy Pole pissing in the alley," Rykov mumbled, smirking. They were on Moliera, a short street that bent like the inside curve of a quarter moon, just a couple blocks south of Old Town's central plaza.

"I could stand to piss too," said Godunov. "Let's surprise him. Get rid of some of the beer. Piss on his shoes."

Rykov swallowed a chuckle and with his elbow nudged his friend Godunov on the arm.

Unsteadily they edged into the alley. Rykov had to labor to suppress a giggle. About 25 feet into the alley, they stopped abruptly. Surprise showed clearly in their alcohol reddened eyes. A woman was squatting, her long dress hiked up, her back to them. Godunov placed his left forefinger against his lips to signal quiet. As the woman began to stand, pulling up her cotton underpants, Godunov stepped forward and reached out. Firmly he placed his left hand on her left shoulder, preventing her from rising. She was startled and began to pivot. Godunov's right hand held a PPsh submachine gun.

"A Polish bitch," Godunov said over his shoulder to Rykov who again was smirking with anticipation. "It's early but not too early."

Rykov lurched forward. "Let me get a good look at her. If we're going to fuck her, I want to see the merchandise."

Godunov released his grip on the woman's shoulder. "Stand up and turn around."

The woman was slow to respond. She also was feeling a not unfamiliar surge of anxiety.

"She doesn't understand Russian," Rykov said, alcohol slowing his words. "None of these ignorant Poles do. It's no wonder Hitler did away with so many of them. Worthless shits."

Godunov gestured forcefully with his left hand, and the woman slowly straightened and turned toward the soldiers. She could smell alcohol on Godunov's breath.

"Look at that scar," Rykov mumbled, squinting in the grayness. "Never fucked a scarface before."

They were right about one thing; Bernadeta didn't understand Russian. But her Home Army experience told her that they were posing a serious threat to her and the baby she was carrying. Her memory flashed back to the day in 1944 when Nazi Lieutenant Gerhard Blatz in Warsaw had recognized the scar he had seen at the Gudek's farm in 1939 when he visited the day after Bernadeta had helped Thaddeus and the other cow pen soldiers escape. Blatz was about to take her to interrogation when Kaz Majos intervened, wounding the lieutenant with a point-blank gunshot. Now, Bernadeta's mind was racing as it often had during her perilous years in the Home Army. Should I cry out? she asked herself. If I do, Thaddeus and Father will come running. But these soldiers have guns. Automatics. They would stand no chance.

"Get down, bitch," Godunov ordered her, gesturing with his gun.

Bernadeta backed against the remains of a brick wall. She squinted, peering farther into the alley, looking for a way out. In the dim light and with piles of rubble obscuring her vision she couldn't see whether the alley was a dead end. Still, she inched farther along the wall, not taking her eyes off her tormentors.

"Stop!" Godunov ordered. Then to Rykov. "Get her on the ground, on her back."

Rykov stepped around Godunov and moved closer to Bernadeta. His breath too reeked of alcohol. He slung his PPsh over his right shoulder, grasped Bernadeta's shoulders and began forcing her downward. She batted his arms away. He slapped her hard on the left cheek and was cocking his arm for a backhand slap.

"I wouldn't do that." The warning was coming from behind the soldiers, and though they didn't understand the words, they recognized the voice as Polish. The words had been spoken coldly and deliberately.

Godunov and Rykov could make out two men. The one who had spoken was the younger and larger of the two.

"Get out of here, you Polish pigs," Godunov snarled. "This slut is our business, not yours."

Jszef recognized the words as Russian and felt instant loathing. His jaws tightened, teeth pressing hard against teeth. The fingers of his right hand tightened around the grip of the bayonet he had brought from the wagon.

Thaddeus was experiencing a sudden, massive urge to protect.

Rykov stood and moved to Godunov's side. Rykov unslung his PPsh and pointed it toward Thaddeus and Jszef.

"One more step," Godunov warned, "and you are both stinking piles of Polish guts."

In the next instant Godunov saw tiny points of light exploding behind his closed eyelids before be blacked out and crumbled, his submachine gun clattering on the pavement. Bernadeta had slammed a hunk of jagged brick against the back of Godunov's skull, sending his uniform cap flying.

Startled, Rykov turned reflexively to see the source of Godunov's fall. In that moment Thaddeus lunged forward and slammed his right fist into Rykov's temple. Rykov staggered and swung his PPsh toward Thaddeus who grabbed and pinned Rykov's arms to his sides. "Stop," he commanded.

But Rykov, still gripping the gun, continued struggling to free his arms.

Thaddeus squeezed harder. He looked at Bernadeta, still holding the hunk of brick, and then at Jszef. "This isn't going to work. See if you can free the gun from his hand. Be careful."

"Too dangerous," Jszef said calmly, "for all of us." Jszef stepped in front of Rykov and said to Bernadeta, "Turn away." Then to Thaddeus he said, "Keep your arms locked in place." Jszef then firmed his grip on the bayonet and drove it, tip pointed upward, into Rykov's lower abdomen. The soldier's shriek was primal and long. Then he shrieked a second time. "You would rape my pregnant daughter," Jszef hissed. "Never again," and he applied hard twisting pressure. Rykov screamed a third time, then began whimpering. It was too late for pleading and he knew it. It took another full minute before Rykov felt the grip of death. He gasped for breath. Jszef reached down with his left hand and easily removed the gun from Rykov's grasp. Then his right hand pulled back sharply, freeing the bloodied bayonet. "Let him go," he grimly instructed Thaddeus. Rykov's knees buckled and he slumped to the pavement. Jszef sucked in a breath. "First Russian I've killed in nearly thirty years."

Bernadeta turned back toward the men, her face expressionless. In her days with the Home Army she too had executed enemy soldiers and knew that justice once again had been rendered.

"What about him?" Thaddeus asked, pointing toward Godunov. Blood was pooling around the soldier's head. He was dazed but still conscious.

"Let him be. If he lives, he won't remember much if anything," Bernadeta said analytically. "Too drunk, and the blow. And the darkness. If he does remember, he will be better off pretending to forget. He's smart enough to know that's better than trying to explain what happened to him and his friend." She let the hunk of brick fall to the pavement.

Thaddeus nodded and said gravely, "I am glad we all remembered how to be warriors."

CHAPTER 28

The newly arrived visitor didn't have to introduce himself. It mattered not that Barbara Gudek had never seen the man. One look at the black eye patch and blonde hair and she knew she was meeting Kaz Majos.

"You must be Barbara," he said tiredly. His six-foot, broad-shouldered frame was sagging noticeably. "Your sister told me about you and your parents." He bowed slightly, extended his right arm and they shook hands.

"You - Bernadeta wasn't sure what happened to you after the Uprising."

"Auschwitz."

His dry mention of the camp's name caused Barbara to shudder. Scant minutes before, she had been walking from the house to the barn where she was intending to lead the two milk cows to a small pasture to let them graze. She had seen the man walking slowly on the road from Warsaw. It wasn't an unfamiliar sight, with displaced persons constantly on the move.

"You - you survived." Inwardly Barbara scolded herself for the inane observation of the blindingly obvious.

Kaz wasn't even mildly tempted to reply curtly. The young woman appeared too sweet and shaken, and he was too weary. After weeks of sitting on the beer wagon, the 40-kilometer walk from Warsaw had exhausted him.

"Where is Bernadeta?"

Barbara felt a surge of awkwardness and she knew its source. "She's not here. You missed her. She's in Warsaw." Kaz sighed below his closed eyes. His head shook in dismay. "Is that where you've been?"

He nodded. "I've been working there. I - Do you know what she's doing there? Where she's living?"

Before Barbara could answer, she saw Jszef leading the ox from a field to the barn. When he saw Barbara talking with the stranger, he stopped and waved.

"He's my father. Come with me, please. I want you to meet him and my mother."

† † †

"Thaddeus Metz? The name, it's quite common. I'm not sure," Kaz said. He was sitting with Barbara, Jszef and Tosia at their kitchen table. He had gratefully accepted Jszef's invitation to eat with them and rest before beginning the long trek back to Warsaw.

"He was one of the soldiers Bernadeta helped escape from the cow pen," Barbara explained.

"Oh, yes, she spoke of them, of him, but I'm not sure it was by name."

"She didn't know his last name, only his first."

Kaz nodded. He tore a piece of bread from the fresh loaf Tosia had baked, put it in his mouth and chewed thoughtfully. He swallowed and then drank milk from a tall, roughly textured ceramic brown cup. He was savoring each bite and sip. "When did they marry?"

Barbara blushed. "Just…"

"Just recently," Kaz finished for her.

She nodded.

Tosia sliced more cheese and placed it on Kaz's plate. Her motherly instinct was rushing to the fore. "Kaz, we want you to stay the rest of today and tonight. You can sleep in our main room or in the barn. Wherever you think you would be more comfortable."

"Thank you."

"Actually," Jszef said, "you would honor us if you stayed a while longer. Bernadeta told us about how you led the Home Army cell. She told us about the risks you took. How you saved her from interrogation and probably worse. And Auschwitz, that…I'm sorry. I shouldn't have mentioned it."

"That's all right. It was everything you've heard and worse. I appreciate your hospitality, your kind offer. I don't want to impose but I will stay a while – a few days, if you like."

"Good," Tosia said, smiling warmly. "After you have finished your meal, Barbara can show you the barn. But take your time. And please, eat all you want."

Kaz smiled gratefully. "I can't remember the last time such simple food tasted so wonderful."

"Nature's best," Jszef winked. "Helped along by Mother Gudek."

Tosia blushed. "You were not a farm boy, were you?" she laughed.

"Always a city boy," Kaz chuckled lowly.

"Well," Jszef said cheerfully, "before you leave maybe we can put some of our farm on your bones and in your blood."

"I have a feeling I could do much worse."

CHAPTER 29

Democracy's whisperings were being heard in Berlin, Nazism's sacred seat. On October 20, 1946, Berliners were allowed to vote in free elections for the first time since 1933. Ernst Reuter, a member of the Social Democratic Party, was elected mayor. But those whisperings soon were muted. Reuter was barely sworn in when Berliners saw another harbinger of the long political winter they would be enduring. Officials in Moscow, at Joseph Stalin's behest, deemed Reuter "anti-Soviet" and vetoed his election.

Stalin was moving with dispatch to strengthen his hold on lands behind the iron curtain. He was expanding westward as Hitler had expanded eastward, but without having to butcher entire populations. Stalin knew he could continue imposing his will. He possessed three telling advantages – his army's rippling muscles, the zeal of satellite countries' secret police and acquiescent western heads of state.

In January 1947 in Poland, Stalin's bobbing puppets staged elections that were rigged so transparently that even sight-impaired citizens could see through the sham. Ambassador Lane knew then that Stalin's Yalta Conference promise of "free and unfettered elections" was a lie. Lane quit in disgust.

"Ambassador Lane is an honorable man," Bernadeta observed over supper with Thaddeus in their cramped second floor walkup apartment on Mostowa Street. Most of the street's buildings were three floors, with a few also having cramped lofts. Some of the buildings had gray granite fronts while others had blue, brownish orange and pinkish facades. Virtually all had red tile roofs. The street, stone-paved and running for three blocks down to the Vistula, is just a few blocks north of Old Town's brick-paved rynek or central plaza. Thaddeus and Bernadeta's apartment was in Number 22, one of the granite-faced buildings. The entrance was on the street's north or left side, about 70 yards from its high point at Freta Street from where it began its gently curving descent to the river. That put their home nearer the American embassy, just a few blocks to the north on Koscielna Street, than the University of Warsaw, about a 20-minute walk to the south.

Behind #22 and the other buildings on the street's north side was a garden about 30 feet wide. It was planted simply with trees and shrubs. Bernadeta and Thaddeus valued it for the touch-of-green view from their apartment's rear window and for the refreshing shade it provided on warm days.

"Have you heard who might replace him?" Thaddeus and Bernadeta were speaking English as they did each evening to strengthen her command of the complex, difficult-to-master language.

Thaddeus' plan had proven successful. He had won a position on the University of Warsaw's faculty, teaching French and English. Bernadeta was employed at the American embassy as a combination receptionist and clerk-typist.

"Stanton Griffis. At least that is the rumor."

"What do you know about him?"

"He is not a career diplomat," Bernadeta replied. "He is like so many American ambassadors. They are rich businessmen who have donated much money to their president. Being an ambassador is their just reward or," Bernadeta said wryly, "their just punishment."

Thaddeus chortled. "Joking in English – a sure sign you are feeling more comfortable with your second tongue. It is also clear that you are learning about American politics. Perhaps those lessons will prove useful sometime."

In fact, Griffis, who would be arriving in Warsaw in July, had been a shrewd and amiable investment banker who once controlled New York's Madison Square Garden and ran Paramount Pictures. He also contributed generously to Truman's Democratic Party.

"When President Truman nominated him, Mr. Griffis said, 'Poland will never become communist.' It makes one question his qualifications."

"Yes," Thaddeus agreed, "and someone should advise Mr. Griffis that never is a dangerous word."

"Like always?"

"Precisely."

They had finished eating and stood to clear their small table. Bernadeta shivered. "It will be nice when we can enjoy heat on cold nights. Coal remains in short supply and electricity is still a luxury. Of course," Bernadeta said dryly, "I am sure Stalin's communism will bring us all our wishes."

"Hmmm..."

"What are you hmmming about?" Bernadeta smiled, left eyebrow arched in suspicion.

"Our apartment isn't your barn loft and we don't have straw on the floor. But we are on the second floor and together we can supplement the rising heat."

"Should we wash and dry our dishes first?"

"That would only warm our hands."

"So true. We should warm our entire bodies."

"The baby won't mind?"

"Not yet. Soon but not yet. We just need to be " – Bernadeta paused, searching for the right English words – "to be not so athletic."

CHAPTER 30

Barbara covered her mouth, trying to suppress her giggling. To no avail.

"I told you I was a city boy," Kaz said jovially. "Look at my hands; you can see they were not made for this."

"You have to squeeze a little harder. Don't be afraid to hurt the cow. You need a rhythm." She giggled again.

The cow lowed its displeasure.

"She agrees with you," Kaz said. "Poor thing. This wasn't such a good idea."

"Ahem, it was your idea, sir."

"This poor cow would be better off if I was helping your father in the field."

"Move over," Barbara said. "Watch."

"Yes, Madam Milk Maid, whatever you say." Kaz eased off the milking stool and Barbara took his place. Kaz squatted beside her, watching intently and admiringly, mesmerized by Barbara's efforts. "I now understand why I've heard of milk maids but not milk men. You have the touch – and the cow appreciates it."

Without looking up Barbara smiled and said, "Father can handle these teats quite nicely. Who do you think taught me?"

"Bernadeta too?"

Instead of answering Kaz's question, Barbara spoke the words that came suddenly to mind. "She loved you. She said so." What Barbara didn't say was what Bernadeta had confided: while she had grown to love Kaz and given herself to him, she hadn't fallen in love with him, not as she had with Thaddeus.

"I waited too long," Kaz said with a hint of remorse tempered by time's passing. "Here, let me try again."

Barbara stood and Kaz reseated himself on the stool. He grasped the cow's teats and began working them.

"I want you to stay." Barbara hadn't been planning to speak those words either but wasn't sorry she had, her reddening cheeks notwithstanding.

Kaz looked up at the comely young woman in the brown ankle-length dress. He peered into her eyes and thought he could read her feelings. Kaz pulled his hands back and rested them on his knees. "Your sister and I-"

"I know. She told me. Don't leave."

CHAPTER 31

"So," the elder observed thoughtfully, "you married the woman you loved to another man."

Father Jack Brecker nodded. "Yes I did."

"That must have been a very difficult task. Why did you do it?"

"She asked me to."

"Because she wanted to cause you pain?"

Jack shook his head, pursing his lips. "No, because she is my friend. A friend who is easy to like and respect. And she loves me."

"White people can be very confusing – and confused. We Indians have seen this for hundreds of years. The explorers from Spain, they came looking for riches. They decided they must convert us – and then murdered us by the thousands. Then they built these beautiful white missions to make them feel better about their crimes. Their guilt must have been great because they built many missions – here in Arizona, and in New Mexico and California I am told." A pause. "Many of my people did become Christians. But not because they saw it as a religion better than our own. Often they saw it as a way to protect themselves from the Spanish conquistadors and their missionary priests. The priests...Some of them saw spilling our blood as a fair price for saving our souls." There was no trace of bitterness in the elder's recitation. He sounded much like a professor dryly lecturing a history class. "Perhaps," the elder added, smiling at Jack, "we Indians also can be confusing – and confused."

Jack reached out and twice patted the elder's left shoulder. The two men were walking a ridgeline on the sprawling Tohono reservation near Charco, a village at the reservation's western edge. They paused and surveyed the surrounding terrain.

"This is where I shot the mountain lion," Jack reminisced. He was recalling the incident in 1943 when he and friend Luke Haynes had used one of the elder's lambs to lure to its death a mountain lion that had been preying on the Indians' flock.

The elder nodded. "Your good shooting saved many of our sheep. We still depend on them for food and wool for our blankets. The ones we use ourselves and the ones we sell to the whites."

To Jack, the elder looked no older than when they first had met back in 1942. His six feet of height still were youthfully erect. He had neither gained nor lost weight. His straight, shoulder-length hair still was gray, not white. He had been born in 1887 when Geronimo still was on the loose. The legendary leader once had terrorized the area around Tucson where Jack's diocese, with Bishop Wilhelm Metzger still presiding, was based. In 1903 Geronimo had converted to Christianity, joining the Dutch Reformed Church.

"You know," Jack reflected, "for hundreds of years after Christ died priests were allowed to marry. They fathered children. Became family men."

"I did not know that."

"Most people don't. It's not something the church teaches."

"Married priests. That seems to me what nature intended," the elder observed quietly. The two men continued strolling along the rocky, sun-baked ridgeline. "Why did the church decide to go against nature?"

"Money," Jack shrugged. "Power."

"Oh hoh. The same reasons the Spanish were so cruel to my people – the same people they wanted to convert to the Catholic Church."

"For hundreds of years many priests acquired property and wealth. In some countries, like England, when a father died, by law his estate – his legacy – went to his eldest son. The Vatican wanted those estates to become its property."

"So, by forbidding priests to marry…As you say, money and power."

The two men continued walking in comfortable silence for a few minutes. Then the elder stopped. He slowly extended his right arm toward the distant horizon. "Tell me, my young friend, what do you foresee in that unnatural condition for priests?"

Jack's left thumb and forefinger rubbed his chin twice. "I think we will see fewer young men becoming priests. I think we will see more young priests leaving the priesthood to marry and become fathers – of their own children, not just God's. They will want flocks in their own homes, not only in their churches."

"Is this happening now?" the elder asked.

"Not yet. But soon, I think." Jack paused and laughed. "It will probably begin in California or New York. That's where so many things in our country seem to start. Skyscrapers. New fashions. Movies. Magazines."

"Have you voiced these thoughts with Bishop Metzger?"

Jack smiled. "Until today I haven't voiced them with anyone. He – and the church –would see them as radical. Even heretical." A pause. "Why do I share so much with you?"

The elder's coal black eyes twinkled youthfully and a sly smile creased his leathery face. "It is because I am so natural."

Jack's booming laughter echoed from the ridgeline. "And who among us mere mortals can resist communicating with nature?"

CHAPTER 32

Felix Glemp wanted to learn English. Danuta Ostrowski wanted a friend.

Felix was the kind of student who made Thaddeus glad he had sought to become a teacher. In fact, in some ways Felix reminded Thaddeus of his younger self – bright, eager to learn, willing to study hard.

Felix was born in 1927. He had grown to five feet nine inches. He had brown eyes and a shock of unruly brown hair that had a windblown look even on days when not the slightest breeze was stirring on the Vistula. Felix had an open friendly face and an engaging smile. His mother had died unexpectedly from a heart attack when Felix was 15. His father, a Warsaw constable before the war, had become a member of Poland's Moscow-directed and feared secret police.

In Thaddeus' class Felix's right hand shot upward often as he both answered questions and posed them. Felix sensed – correctly – that Thaddeus liked him and that further fueled his desire to learn and be noticed.

Danuta Ostrowski lived alone on the ground floor of the building in which Thaddeus and Bernadeta lived a floor above. She was born in 1886, and her growth had stopped at five feet two inches. In her youth she had been an effervescent, bright-eyed, pretty woman. Blonde hair, blue eyes, petite. Time as well as stress and deprivations during the Nazi occupation had exacted a toll, and now she was haggard, gray-haired and stumpy. Like virtually all Poles she had suffered much during the war. Her son Krzystof had been conscripted by the Nazis and sent east. He never returned and was recorded as missing in action. Her husband, like Thaddeus a lancer, had been shot out of his saddle on September 1, 1939, the day Germany invaded her homeland.

Danuta was grateful to the Soviets for driving out the vilified Nazis. She had not been accosted by liberating Russian troops. She couldn't be certain but speculated – to herself only – that her unattractive appearance had spared her the rape that had been visited upon so many Polish women and girls. In any event, in those first years following the war, Danuta couldn't abide anti-communist, anti-Stalin aspersions. To her, Stalin might not have been a saint but he was a savior.

She was lonely. On the day that Thaddeus and Bernadeta moved into their small apartment, Danuta saw an opportunity for forging friendship and knocked at their door. She had greeted them with a loaf of freshly baked bread and a cake decorated with pink and white frosting swirls.

"Please come in," Bernadeta had said. "We have little furniture but please sit and visit." She put the bread and cake on her small kitchen table.

"Thank you. Is it just me," she asked bluntly but not unkindly, "or is my new neighbor with child?"

"She is," Bernadeta beamed. "We are very excited. I'm so glad you asked. I've wanted to say something to someone about it."

"You can talk to me all you want. And if I can ever be of assistance – any at all – please let me know."

"I will."

"You can depend on me."

† † †

Despite Soviet meddling with the curriculum, Thaddeus was happy to be teaching at the University of Warsaw. During the Nazi occupation Poland's universities were closed. At the University of Warsaw much laboratory equipment and many collections – books, biological specimens, art and others – were seized and shipped to Germany. Many of the university's buildings were converted into barracks, and the Nazis used one as a stable, with tables and desks used to create stalls.

But the university didn't die. Many of its professors defied Nazi rules and risked death by teaching in homes, church basements and any other nook that could accommodate a few determined students. In this fashion, by 1944 some 300 faculty members were teaching about 3,500 students – most of whom also were serving in the Home Army. How dangerous was this underground instruction? During the occupation, 63 professors were executed.

After the 1944 Warsaw Uprising the Nazis destroyed about 60 percent of the 30 campus buildings and others were damaged. Windows were blown out, ceilings and walls collapsed, and a courtyard was used as a cemetery – with exhumation occurring in the months following the war.

Beginning in early 1945 campus reconstruction and rehabilitation commenced with faculty and students doing most of the labor. When they arrived on campus to begin their work, surprises awaited. In one building they found Russian soldiers bivouacked and cooking fish removed from formalin jars over an open fire. For fuel they were using the building's parquet floor. They also found a single horse – which they put to work removing debris and pulling materials needed for reconstruction. To keep the animal fed, university administrators scrounged hay.

A formal rededication of the university was held in March 1945 but was largely symbolic. Too much reconstruction work remained to be completed to resume operations. Briefly, university leaders considered moving the school to Lodz, about 100 kilometers southwest of Warsaw. Amazingly, by December 1945, a scant seven months after V-E Day, reconstruction had progressed enough to resume classes on campus for more than 4,000 students. There were no tuition fees, and 60 percent of students received grants for maintaining good grades. Taxes on Poles and generous contributions from Polish ex-patriates provided funding.

During the early postwar years professors enjoyed goodly amounts of academic freedom. Then beginning in earnest in 1949 came a gradual, grinding Stalinization with eroding freedom of instruction, use of ideological criteria in selecting faculty and isolation from western development and thinking. Faculty and students alike resisted.

By the time Thaddeus began teaching, the campus was largely resurrected, and administrators, faculty and students were again immersed in their academic pursuits. Two blocks of the university's buildings – massive, granite-faced, three-story structures with red and gray tile roofs – fronted busy Cracowskie Przedmiescie Street. Midway along this stretch was an imposing gateway bearing the address 26/28. On each side were thick, decorative granite walls that flanked double-wide black wrought iron gates topped with a single word – university – in gold-leaf letters. Beyond the gates lay a tranquil environment that had the look and feel of an institution dedicated to learning. Thaddeus found it immensely appealing. The campus grounds spread widely. Broad lawns planted liberally with trees separated many of the buildings, most of which were massive three-story structures with granite facades. Around the perimeter of one of the lawns were numerous park benches – wooden seats and wrought iron legs and arms – favored by students in warm weather. Broad, stone-paved walkways eased movement by students and faculty, and Thaddeus took pleasure in greeting other members of the academic community. Daily he was demonstrating his ability to win friends and admirers. He felt long-removed from his years as a soldier and blessedly so.

Behind the campus the ground sloped steeply down to the Vistula.

Each day, even on the coldest and windiest, when Thaddeus passed through the campus gateway, he felt a surge of warmth. To him the gateway represented much more than a physical entrance. It was the passage to opening fertile minds to new concepts, perspectives and facts. He saw his mission in much broader terms than helping students learn a different language. Yes, that was important. He could foresee the day when Poland and Poles would be profitably engaging the West, and knowledge of English and French would greatly facilitate such interaction. But as a teacher his real aim was to broaden and deepen students' thinking, to prod them to question tenets, regulations, proclamations and, most fundamentally and importantly, their own beliefs.

On many mornings when Thaddeus strode onto campus, a wish invaded his thoughts. It was a foolish one, he knew, and he chuckled at himself for even dreaming it – riding General from his apartment to the university so students and fellow faculty could admire and fawn over the gift from General Sosabowski that had carried him from occupation duty in Germany to the Gudek's farm where he found lasting love and a future.

Thaddeus considered himself fortunate to have won a faculty position. But unlike Danuta Ostrowski he harbored no affinity for the Soviets. In his English classes he occasionally permitted his pro-American, anti-Soviet views to emerge. It was risky. Gradually, in discussing the language his students were striving to learn, Thaddeus disclosed his friendship with Americans. In particular, he told them about Captain Jack Brecker, the army chaplain who had said Easter Mass for Polish airborne troops and later volunteered to join them on a hazardous crossing of the Rhine during disastrous Operation Market Garden. Father Brecker already had survived a crossing with the 82nd Airborne troops. Thaddeus had dissuaded Father Brecker from making a second crossing, explaining that because he didn't speak Polish his presence would be more hindrance than help. In telling his students about Jack, he said, "I'm not at all certain that Father Brecker believed me but he agreed to stay behind."

"Did you ever see him again?" Felix Glemp asked.

Thaddeus' head shook, his chagrin apparent. "I don't know if he survived the war. To me he was a symbol of what I believe to be good about Americans. They are a generous people. They volunteer to help other peoples and expect no reward for doing so. Not even thank yous. And from what I've learned, America has not received enough thank yous. Do you think Stalin ever thanked America for all the equipment and ammunition he received? For invading Italy and France and taking pressure off Stalin's armies? Do you see America trying to rule lands it freed? Yes, it is occupying Japan but is bringing its people democracy and economic growth. It is doing the same in western Germany and southern Korea."

"Stalin freed us," Felix said.

"From one tyranny but only to impose another," Thaddeus replied evenly.

"Maybe Stalin doesn't think we Poles are ready to govern ourselves," Felix countered mildly.

"Or," said Thaddeus, "Stalin's memory is keen. He remembers that free Poles defeated Russia in World War I and prefers to avoid another humiliation."

"My father has confidence in Stalin," Felix persisted, his voice taking on a sharpening edge. "He believes that Stalin will act in our nation's best interests."

Thaddeus briefly considered asking Felix more about his father – his history, his occupation – but concluded that his classroom was not the appropriate venue for such probing. Thaddeus picked up a book from his desk. "Let's talk about some words in English that are especially troublesome for students of the language. For example, w-i-n-d. Who can tell me the different pronunciations and meanings of this small word?"

✝✝✝

"I wish you would be more careful about what you say in your classes," Bernadeta said in English. "It worries me."

It was early evening and she and Thaddeus were dining in their apartment.

"Umm. Mrs. Ostrowski's cake is delicious. Eat your piece. Our baby surely will love it."

"Thaddeus!" she cried in exasperation. "I'm hearing rumors about the secret police. They are said to be asking people to snoop on others and report suspicious words and behavior. And I am hearing soon that the new government will be giving all of us Soviet hammer and sickle flags to display in our homes."

"Your source?" Before Bernadeta could reply, Thaddeus answered his question. "Mrs. Ostrowski."

"She seems to be very well informed," Bernadeta said defensively.

"Or willing to invent and share her inventions."

"She could be right about these things."

"She could."

She was. Within a short time hammer and sickle flags were distributed to Polish homes and snooping would become endemic.

"Well then, husband, humor your pregnant bride. Be careful what you say and where you say it."

Thaddeus sighed and smiled lovingly. Then he reached across the table and his forefinger brushed lightly against Bernadeta's chin. "You had a spot of icing on your scar."

✝✝✝

The Park brothers, still students themselves in secondary school, now were working part-time jobs. Min, nearing graduation, was working after school in Kaesong's cement block, bustling post office. He hoisted sacks of mail, swept the floor and gladly did whatever else was asked of him. Han, a year younger, was doing chores for area farmers. He helped fertilize rice paddies – an essential and smelly, dirty task with human excrement the fuel for growing food. He also sharpened tools and took produce to shops in Kaesong. Han used his work to give Sejong daily exercise, riding to and from jobs.

By now Min and Ahn Kyong Ae were a well-known item. They made an attractive, popular couple. Their fondness for each other was visible, even in a culture that strongly discouraged displays of affection. When together, their smiles and light touches spoke volumes.

On this day the two had met outside the post office after Min finished his work.

"If it is all right with you," Min said without preamble, "I would like to speak with your parents about marriage."

"With me?" Kyong asked with the soberest of expressions.

Min was taken aback. "Why, of course, with-" and then he caught himself as Kyong's teasing came crashing into his mind.

Her laughter erupted joyously. "You are so intelligent and yet in such matters so easily taken in. I wonder if all men are like that."

"Only," Min said, regaining his composure, "in the company of beautiful young women that they love."

"So you do love me," Kyong said impishly.

"I – I should throttle you – just like a traditional Korean husband." He reached for her arm and she turned, shrieking, and started running. Min pursued, laughing. They were in full view of numerous pedestrians on Kaesong's busy main street. Within seconds Min had captured his quarry. He grasped her shoulders and turned her to face him. Then he drew her to his chest. Passersby had stopped to gawk, taking in this decidedly rare and indecorous public behavior. Some were shocked while others were amused.

Before Min spoke, Kyong, beaming, said, "There is one elemental thing you have forgotten."

"Oh? What is that?"

"Asking me if I will marry you. Yes, you must seek my parents' permission, but a girl – this girl – would like to be asked first."

The fingers of Min's right hand scratched his head. "My inexperience in this matter is obvious."

"So is your male chauvinism. So Asian. So typically Asian." Kyong was speaking with good humor, but her points were not being lost on Min. "Put a woman in her place. Her subservient place. Take her and her feelings for granted. You have learned that lesson well, Park Min Shik."

For a long moment Min didn't know whether he should grovel or ignore. He chose the former. He cleared his throat with exaggerated solemnity. "Please permit me to represent new Asian male thinking. You are first in my thoughts and will always come first. You will walk with me, not behind me as custom dictates. You will eat with me, not after I have finished. Your thoughts will be spoken freely and respected."

Now it was Kyong's turn to be taken aback. Their teasing had quickly evolved into serious dialogue. "That thinking is radical. Welcomed – by me – but radical. I think it is possible you might just make a proper modern husband." A pause, then a twinkling of eyes that foretold more teasing. "Of course, that can happen only after you have asked me to marry you – and if I accept your proposal."

CHAPTER 33

As the calendar pages turned deeper into 1947, it was time for Bernadeta to fulfill her promise to return to the farm to give birth. Thaddeus, through the head of the university's Languages Department, had arranged the loan of a horse-drawn wagon. In the postwar years few Poles, other than top bureaucrats and military and police senior officers, had cars. Thaddeus' plan: drive the wagon with Bernadeta to the farm and then return the wagon to Warsaw with General walking behind and then providing Thaddeus with transportation back to his wife and her family.

"I'm a little nervous," Bernadeta said on the eve of their departure. Her protruding belly spoke of birth's imminence.

"I wish the road was smoother," Thaddeus replied.

"I don't mean the road, silly," Bernadeta said, rolling her eyes upward. "Men! I mean becoming a mother. Giving birth. It – I took many risks in the Home Army, but giving birth frightens me. Foolish, huh?"

"Not at all. We know it can be dangerous."

"I saw many births on the farm."

"Animals, not humans. Still, I think your mother will be a great help. After all, she gave birth to you and Barbara there."

"In her own bed. With no doctor present. Just father to help."

✝✝✝

Tosia and Jszef were readying themselves for bed. So were Barbara in her bedroom and Kaz in the main room which doubled as his sleeping quarters.

"You see what is happening?" Tosia said quietly, wanting to keep her voice confined to their room. "Between Barbara and Kaz."

Jszef smiled. "Who can miss it? Just like a young tree, you can see love taking root and growing."

"So," Tosia smiled wryly, "a trace of the young romantic still lives inside your aging self."

"Perhaps," he said, tilting his head upward and sniffing the air with mock imperiousness, "my youth is better preserved than you imagine."

Tosia laughed despite herself. "That no doubt explains why I still find you so attractively masculine."

Jszef huffed, threw back his shoulders and puffed out his chest. "For all the world to see."

✝✝✝

"Do you have everything ready for the trip?" Thaddeus asked, looking around their apartment. "Everything you need?"

"Yes. And I am so grateful that everyone at the embassy is being so understanding."

"True," agreed Thaddeus. "But I think the foundation of their understanding is your value to them. I think you have exceeded their expectations. Your speed in mastering English has impressed them. Plus your work skills and habits and your way with people. You would not be easy to replace."

✝✝✝

The sharp cry of pain penetrated the walls and caused Barbara to leap from bed and come running with Kaz just a step behind. Barbara hesitated briefly – "Father," – she called – "Mother" – and then pushed open the door to her parents' room. Her eyes widened in alarm. She saw Jszef standing in momentary shock over Tosia who was on the floor, curled into a fetal position and rocking slowly. Eyes clenched tightly and face contorted, she cried out again and then began moaning.

✝✝✝

"Oh, no!" Bernadeta cried fearfully. She was standing in their kitchen, hands resting on the back of a chair.

"What's wrong?" Thaddeus answered worriedly.

Bernadeta felt liquid running down her legs. "My water broke. Oh, my God, no!"

✝✝✝

"Let's get her onto the bed," Kaz said to Jszef, and the two men bent down on either side of Tosia, maneuvered their arms beneath her and lifted gently.

153

"Kaz," Barbara said with urgency, "go saddle General. I'll ride into town for the doctor."

† † †

Thaddeus helped Bernadeta to their bed and then went racing down the stairs. He pounded three times on the apartment door. A moment later it swung open.

"Mrs. Ostrowski. It's Bernadeta. There's a problem."

Mrs. Ostrowski said nothing. With surprising quickness and agility the stumpy woman followed Thaddeus up the stairs.

† † †

Doctor Kajma stood over Tosia, taking her pulse. Sweat glistened on her whitened face and neck, and her breathing was shallow.

Jszef, Barbara and Kaz stood mutely at the foot of the bed. Barbara's hands were clasped in prayer, her lips silently imploring God's grace. Kaz put his arm across Jszef's shoulders and squeezed lightly.

Only an hour had passed since Barbara had vaulted onto the saddle and General went racing toward Zyrardow. During the return Doctor Kajma had whipped his aging carriage horse to maximum speed.

† † †

Sweat was also glistening on Bernadeta's face. Her eyes were closed and her breathing seemed as shallow as her mother's 40 kilometers distant.

Mrs. Ostrowski was holding the mucus-covered, quiet infant. She looked at Thaddeus with crushing sadness. "Stillborn," she murmured. "A boy."

Thaddeus had killed men and seen countless others slain, but none of those deaths had prepared him for this trauma. His upper teeth bit into his lower lip and he forced a swallow. "Bernadeta?"

"I think she will live. Keep her face cool and her body warm. After I...take the baby away, I will try to find a doctor to come and look at her. I...Are you going to be all right?"

154

Thaddeus nodded. Then he reached down and gently laid his hand on his wife's forehead. It was hot.

†††

"It was a burst appendix," said Doctor Kajma. "There was nothing I could do. The poison – the infection – it had spread too far."

Jszef stood, sagging and benumbed. His left hand was at his neck, propping up his head. Barbara was weeping softly. Kaz's lips were pursed. Like Thaddeus he had caused and witnessed more deaths than he would ever want to tally. He knew he would never mourn even one of them more than that of this loving woman who had invited him to stay at the farm and given him precious time to find a love that he would hold dear for the remainder of his days. Standing between husband and daughter, one arm already across Jszef's shoulders, he wrapped the other around Barbara's waist and gently drew her to him. He foresaw never leaving the farm.

†††

A continent, an ocean and part of another continent away, Theresa Hassler Morton gave birth in Belvidere, Illinois to Marilyn Carter Morton. But not without difficulty. The baby's position in the womb – butt first – presaged a dangerous and painful breech birth. As a nurse Theresa knew the risks. With her approval and with Dean forewarned in the hospital waiting room, the obstetrician had performed a Caesarean section. The procedure drained Theresa. The first time she held the newborn, she found herself thinking *I'm not sure I can do this again. Or want to.*

During Theresa's pregnancy she and Dean had discussed possible names. With his unhesitating and full agreement she had proposed naming a daughter after Lieutenant Colonel Marilyn Carter, her commanding officer in the U.S. Army Nurse Corps. Colonel Carter had been fatally hit by shrapnel in a surgery tent outside Bastogne during the Battle of the Bulge. She had been an extraordinary leader, unflappable, an outstanding nurse, an understanding superior, a mentor and friend. Theresa still missed Colonel Carter and included her in her nightly prayers. As Theresa's new daughter sucked at her mother's left nipple, Theresa silently uttered a quick prayer: *may you be as strong, courageous and caring as your namesake. And live a longer life.*

CHAPTER 34

As with most new 18-year-old arrivals in late January 1947, Michael Cornelius and Kendall Thorne stood in awe at the main gate of the Royal Military Academy at Sandhurst, adjacent the town of Camberley. The gatehouse itself was no mean structure; it was white with five thick pillars fronting a portico that spanned two of its sides. Flanking the gate were two white stone rectangular pillars, each bearing the academy's red crest. The gate was wrought iron and wide.

And then there were the buildings. The first to come into view was massive Old College, built in 1812 and painted beige, two floors high and nearly the length of two football fields. It housed administrative offices, classrooms, meeting rooms and a dormitory – called an accommodation block. Positioned across Old College's front were Napoleonic era cannons, and supporting the main entrance were eight majestic pillars. Stretching across the front of and beyond the ends of the building was a sprawling, paved parade ground. From there across a wide expanse of rich green lawn, Michael and Kendall could see the library, also beige. Then there was the chapel, red brick with banks of stained glass windows and more the size of a large church. In addition there were dormitories – red brick and three floors high and containing the academy's other two cadet colleges, New and Victory. There also was a large gymnasium.

But it wasn't just the gatehouse and the buildings and the sweeping lawns, impressive though they were. After all, the boys had grown up in London in the shadows of such landmark structures at St. Paul's Cathedral, the Tower of London, the houses of Parliament, Westminster Abbey and Buckingham Palace. They had frolicked in Kensington Gardens, Hyde Park and Green Park. Instead it was the academy's history and overall aura – the aggregate impact of the handsome buildings, the spacious campus, the man-made lakes and perhaps most inspiring – and intimidating – the officer cadets and senior cadets in their khaki battledress uniforms and navy blue berets.

"Do you think we'll fit in?" Kendall asked nervously.

"From what Father told me," Michael replied, "we'll know soon enough. There's no jolly honeymoon period for new intakes" – as first termers were called.

In fact, the first five weeks for newcomers were especially and purposely hectic. Nonessential personal items – meaning virtually everything – were confiscated and returned only after those first weeks. Their days began with BRC – Breakfast Roll Call. Then from dawn to dusk new cadets were "chased." The intent: break down the newly arrived and then build them up in the mold of educated, skilled, disciplined British Army officers.

Michael and Kendall weren't in a military setting for the first time. In fact, before arriving at Sandhurst, they had spent the preceding three months – November through January – with other soldiers-to-be in basic training at Catterick Camp, a site in Yorkshire in the north of England. Their intent on completion of basic was to matriculate at Sandhurst.

Their classmates weren't exclusively British. Some came from Burma, Ceylon, Jordan and other Commonwealth countries.

"The literature made the course descriptions seem rather rigorous," K recalled.

"Demanding, actually, and meant to cull the unfit and underqualified."

Michael was right. The course work, divided into three six-month terms – with home leaves between – over two years, was meant to test intellectual acumen, physical ability and mental toughness. The military portion of the curriculum included training with weapons – principally with Lee-Enfield .303 bolt-action nonautomatic rifles – signals, transportation and tactics as well as military drilling and ceremonial parades. There also was a strenuous physical fitness program that required successfully completing the confidence area, or as it was known at United States Army training sites, the obstacle course. One section in particular of Sandhurst's course either inspired confidence or induced dread. It included a bridge-like superstructure made from wooden beams. Cadets had to climb the steeply sloping near end, maintain their balance while scampering across long narrow beams a dozen feet above hard ground, and then jump down from the high end. Falls were long, painful and bruising. Michael and Kendall both made it, with Michael's successful crossing captured for posterity in a black and white photograph that shows him smiling widely as he leaped joyously from the far end.

At Sandhurst sports also were strongly emphasized. Twice weekly, cadets were required to play soccer or rugby during winter and cricket in summer, and boxing sans protective headgear was compulsory for all cadets during their first term. Cadet teams competed in those sports against teams from Britain's Air Force and Navy colleges and from military academies in France and the Netherlands. Most Sandhurst cadets also played intramural sports.

Academic requirements included mathematics, science, at least one foreign language and military history.

In addition, away from the Sandhurst campus, cadets participated in field exercises in various training areas around England.

Cadets worked desperately to avoid failing any aspect of the coursework. Shortcomings were punished with extra drilling as early as 6 a.m. or suffering the embarrassment of wearing a white belt that shouted to everyone that a cadet was on restriction. Worse was being relegated which meant having to repeat a term. Worst of all was being RTU'd – returned to unit – the fate accorded those who failed any term a second time; they were unceremoniously drummed out of Sandhurst. During Michael and K's time at the academy one cadet – facing such a fate – committed suicide early one morning on the rifle range.

Once at Sandhurst, leaving campus required clearing a high hurdle. No cadet was permitted to leave campus during the first eight weeks and afterward not until he had "passed off the square." Translation: successfully being drilled and inspected as an individual on the main parade ground by the academy regimental sergeant major and the adjutant. For most cadets this was a fearsome experience. Many failed the first attempt and some twice. Michael and Kendall both would succeed on their first try.

Sandhurst is situated on 600 acres about 30 miles southwest of London. Much of its acreage is wooded parkland. Behind the campus and hidden from view are hundreds more acres used for firing ranges and field training.

The school's roots date to 1741when the Royal Military Academy was founded at Woolwich to "train gentlemen cadets" for artillery, engineers and signals units and later the tank corps. In 1800 the Royal Military

College was founded at Camberley as a continuing education school for staff officers. In 1802 the Royal Military College expanded its charter to train gentlemen cadets as line officers. By the time Michael and K arrived, the Woolwich and Camberley campuses had been consolidated into a single academy, a merger that occurred soon after World War II.

"This place reeks of history," said K. "They name cadet companies after famous campaigns and battles – Burma, Waterloo, Blenheim, Ypres, Somme, Marne."

"Not to mention," Michael added, "Normandy, Alamein, Burma and Rhine. I hope I'm assigned to Normandy since my dad fought there."

"Well, then, I hope I'm assigned there too."

K soon had to suffer disappointment. While Michael got his wish, K was assigned to Alamein.

In fact, Sandhurst's approximately 1,000 cadets were divided into the three colleges – New, Old and Victory – each with some 350 young men. They were identified by uniform lanyards or patches – red for Old College, blue for New and yellow for Victory. Each college included four companies. Michael's Normandy Company was part of Victory College – as was Kendall's Alamein.

"Are you still thinking of airborne as your military specialty?" Michael asked.

"I am. If I'm going to be in the Army, I think I'd prefer an extra dash of danger. A specialty with some panache. Jumping out of planes should impress the birds back in London. How about you?"

"I'm still leaning toward keeping my feet on the ground. Infantry. I guess I'll just have to win over the girls back home with my earthbound charm."

"You've no shortage of that, Cadet Cornelius."

"You are too kind, Cadet Thorne."

CHAPTER 35

Sitting at his desk in Pyongyang, Kim Il Sung was edgy. He was drumming his fingers on the leather desk pad. Moments later, fuming, he stood and began pacing. To be sure, Joseph Stalin had approved Kim's anointment as head of North Korea's provisional government. But now, in effect, the entire world was aligned against Kim. In New York City the United Nations had passed a resolution calling for general elections in both North and South Korea with the intended outcome a unified Korea. To Kim the result could be both a professional and personal disaster: he could lose to despised Syngman Rhee.

In that event, the capital of Korea assuredly would be south of the 38th Parallel in Seoul, not north in Pyongyang. Kim would be marginalized, if not an outright outcast. As much as Kim yearned for a unified Korea, what he wanted even more was power – lasting, unfettered power that was anathema to democracy.

Kim concluded that his next step – one that he deemed necessary – was one that he abhorred taking. He would phone Stalin. The notion of being a supplicant disgusted Kim. As a veteran guerilla leader he had shown his mettle repeatedly. For years he had acted independently. He had taken no orders and had sought no advice. Now he felt his future was dependent on a foreign despot, and the taste of that reality was unappetizing. He girded himself and placed the call.

"Our government is beginning to win control of our country," Kim said, tiptoeing into the conversation.

"I have been following developments in Korea," Stalin replied. "Molotov keeps me briefed." Stalin hadn't been expecting a call from Kim, but now that it had come he was guessing its purpose.

"But our progress is now in jeopardy," Kim continued, carefully modulating his voice, determined to avoid manifesting desperation. "The UN resolution calling for free general elections could defeat our mission."

"It could," Stalin said coolly, "if we were to comply with the resolution."

"You will not comply?"

"Of course we will not comply."

Kim was feeling the first glimmers of relief from his anxiety. "What will you say?"

"That there is corruption in the south. Which happens to be true. Rhee already is lining his pockets with government revenues."

"You will stall."

"Precisely."

Sergeant Kwon Oh Bum, Kim Il Sung's faithful guerilla aide, now was Captain Kwon in Kim's North Korean Army. The fledgling force was growing rapidly thanks to the munificence of Stalin who was supplying arms, armor, planes and training.

As much as the new army needed weapons and equipment, it also needed men. Captain Kwon's mission was clear: recruit young men – by whatever means deemed necessary.

Kwon looked to Kim as his role model. As the chief guerilla leader in the long struggle against Japan, Kim had not shied from action. Often he had led his men into combat. Kwon would do likewise in rounding up recruits. He would brook no evasions or excuses. He would not permit families to buy their sons exemptions. All young men would be expected to serve their Great Leader, Kim Il Sung. And simultaneously Kwon would see his own sun on the rise.

†††

Young men entering the Royal Military Academy at Sandhurst were, in fact, volunteers. But once cadets they sometimes found themselves targeted for a certain nonvoluntary experience. Inside Sandhurst it was regarded as a rite of passage from the freedom of civilian life to the rigidity of military discipline. Elsewhere it was called hazing. At Sandhurst, a school founded for the training "gentlemen," hazing – officially discouraged – could be decidedly ungentlemanly.

Elton Leighton was a Sandhurst first-termer who had been assigned to Normandy, Michael Cornelius's cadet company. Elton was a young man of average height and build who, like most newcomers, worked to make himself as invisible as possible to upperclassmen, the vaunted senior cadets.

Normandy Company cadets were housed in Victory College, at the far left when facing a row of adjoining red brick buildings that stood north of Old College and the chapel. In the center was the imposing Officers Mess, domed with a clock high on the face of its tower, and to the right, New College. Victory College was three floors high. Normandy Company occupied the building's left wing. Michael and Elton occupied rooms on the second floor.

The three stately buildings stood atop a rise, the highest point on the campus. Stretching across the front of all three buildings was another paved parade ground. Sloping down and away from the buildings was a broad lawn several hundred yards wide and interspersed with soaring shade trees.

Beyond that lawn and coursing through campus was the Wish Stream. The academy's magazine was named after it. Except for its location and a combination of intended and unintended uses, Wish Stream would have been an unlikely candidate for renown. It was only about 12 feet wide and at its center just waist deep. Its banks sloped steeply but were only about two feet high. Planned uses included cadets splashing through it as part of their confidence-building exercises and pulling on thick ropes in games of tug-of-war, losers getting a good soaking.

It was a cold, early March night and Michael and Elton were in their Normandy Company's latrine, brushing their teeth. They were wearing pajamas and slippers. Lights out would be in another 10 minutes.

†††

Half a world away Park Soon Im was examining her inventory. "Min, we need a few things for the shop. Knives mostly," said mother to her son. "Will you be working at the post office after school?"

"Not today, Mother."

"I didn't think so. Would you ride Sejong to Munsan and buy some knives from Mr. Choi? He has the best knives to be found in this area. It would save your father a bicycle ride."

Choi Chun Kuen and his wife owned a combination butcher and cutlery shop where they sold and sharpened knives of all sorts.

"Certainly."

"Good. I'll make a list and give you the money."

"I'll enjoy taking Sejong on a longer ride. Actually I'll just enjoy riding him since Han does most of it."

"Just one other thing. If you are stopped at the border – either by North or South Korean guards – be cooperative. Show them the list and explain your purpose. Don't give them any reason to detain you."

"Don't worry, Mother. I'll be my usually charming self." Park Soon Im smiled lovingly at her son who was grinning. "Anyway, I haven't heard of any problems with crossing. I know for a fact that letters and packages are still getting through. We see them every day at the post office."

† † †

Captain Kwon, a corporal and a private were squeezed together on the seat of a Russian-made military truck. The private was driving and the vehicle was headed south from Pyongyang to Kaesong. Rain had begun falling and the unpaved road was becoming increasingly squishy and unstable.

"Take it easy, private," said Kwon. "Just concentrate on keeping the truck on the road."

"Yes, sir."

† † †

Elton and Michael finished brushing their teeth. They tapped their brushes on the edge of the sinks and turned to exit the latrine. Elton was first to step into the hallway. Immediately two senior cadets, Robinson and Smythe, grasped his arms and pinned them behind his back. A third senior cadet, Kirkwood, slipped a black woolen hood over Elton's head. A fourth senior cadet, Driscoll, warned, "Don't resist, Leighton. You'll only make it harder on yourself."

Michael stepped forward. "What's this?"

"Don't interfere, Cornelius," said Driscoll. "Your turn will come – and sooner and harsher if you try to interfere."

The senior cadets shoved Elton and he went stumbling down the hallway toward the staircase.

† † †

Park Min, astride Sejong, had crossed the 38th Parallel without incident. Guards – North and South – had stopped him but only briefly. They

163

were bored, wearing slickers to keep dry, and showed no signs of genuine interest in Min or other travelers heading south and north.

Min was wet and glad to be nearing Munsan and the Chois' shop. He was hoping to dry out there before starting north with his cargo of knives.

"You don't mind the rain, do you, boy?" Min said. He reached out with his left hand and patted Sejong's neck. "But I'll see if I can find a stable to shelter you while I'm at the Chois' shop." The horse continued its easy walk, his hoofs kicking up sprays of grimy water.

✝✝✝

Outside Victory College the four cadets were guiding hooded Elton down the slope and through trees and on across the broad lawn toward Wish Stream. A dusting of snow covered the ground. At the water's edge Driscoll told Elton to remove his slippers, now partially covered with snow. Elton could hear the water gurgling.

"What are you going to do to me?" His mounting anxiety had elevated the pitch of his voice.

"We expect new cadets to immerse themselves in Sandhurst, and we are helping you expedite the process."

Elton stiffened and the senior cadets tried to muffle their laughter. They knew that policy proscribed hazing and detection could lead to severe discipline. Seldom, however, were violators reported; snitching was widely regarded as abhorrent. While Robinson and Smythe continued pinning Elton's arms behind him, Driscoll and Kirkwood removed their standard issue brown shoes and socks and rolled up their khaki pants above their knees. "Not good for our creases," Driscoll grumbled good naturedly. "We'll have to get someone to press them for us. Like Leighton here. Okay, Leighton, in you go."

Driscoll and Kirkwood took Elton's arms from Robinson and Smythe. They stepped into the cold water with Elton. "Kneel down," Driscoll commanded. "Now."

Elton began squatting and Driscoll and Kirkwood, impatient, pushed down on Elton's shoulders until he was kneeling, soaking his pajamas to his waist.

"Lower your head into the water," Driscoll ordered him. Elton hesitated and Driscoll placed his right hand on the top of Elton's head and pushed down roughly. Elton's face went under and Driscoll continued applying downward pressure.

✝ ✝ ✝

Captain Kwon, the corporal and the private stepped from the rain inside the Parks' general merchandise shop. He eyed Mr. and Mrs. Park. "Are you the owners?"

"Yes," said Park Bong Suk.

"I am Captain Kwon. Where are your sons? You have two."

"Why do you ask?" said Mr. Park. Mrs. Park remained mute, as Korean culture all but demanded in such a setting.

"We are conscripting young men for our army. They are badly needed for the defense of our country."

"Defense? But," Mr. Park said mildly, "there is to be a general election and a unified Korea. The Japanese are defeated. Who would be our enemy?"

"You are naïve," Kwon said icily. "And you ask questions that betray your ignorance. Now, where are your sons?"

Mr. Park considered briefly refusing to answer. But common sense told him that could bring a sharp rebuke, perhaps a physical one, from Kwon. Instead he asked, "Did you come from Pyongyang?" Kwon nodded. "Then you just missed Han. He is working after school on a farm north of town. He probably was in the farmer's house to stay out of the rain."

"Your other son?"

"Away in Munsan."

"What is he doing in the south?"

"We sent him there to buy supplies for our shop."

"When will he return?"

Mr. Park decided it was time to risk lying. "I don't know. He might stay with friends for a few days." His deception surprised Mrs. Park whose blank expression remained unchanged.

"We will be back for him. In the meantime we will get your other son."

"Will you bring him here?" Mrs. Park asked meekly. "So that I can say goodbye."

Kwon looked sharply at the woman, her hands clasped in front of her white apron. He clearly wasn't accustomed to being questioned by women. "Briefly, yes," Kwon replied coldly. "Then we will take him to begin training."

"How long will he be away?" Mrs. Park asked, chancing a second question, aware that Kwon was regarding her queries as an affront.

"His term of duty will be three years – unless he is needed longer. As I said, we will return in a few days for your other son."

✝✝✝

Michael had stayed behind in Victory College, watching the departure – an abduction in his mind – from a second floor window. What he was witnessing, he knew, wasn't condoned by academy officials. With each passing moment his unease with himself was increasing. Within a couple minutes his acquiescence to Driscoll's warning was leading to self-reproach. Then to anger. His lips pursed and his jaws clenched, Michael felt a force pulling – or pushing – him toward the stairs. He decided to descend and leave the dormitory.

✝✝✝

"I do not want my sons in the army." Mrs. Park enunciated crisply and with authority. Her words and tone took her husband aback. Totally unaccustomed to being addressed so abruptly by his wife, he merely stared. In Korea, male dominance flourished. Wives treated husbands with the utmost deference. A culture 5,000 years in-the-making dictated that wives insisted on nothing at any time. Even their suggestions and requests generally were circuitous. Yet with Mrs. Park's concern centered squarely on the welfare of their sons, Mr. Park's gestating rebuke for wifely disrespect quickly evaporated.

"I don't know that we have much choice," he replied evenly. "Kwon and his men are on their way to get Han, and Min will be back late tonight or early tomorrow."

"Bong!" Mrs. Park exclaimed, barely restraining herself from shrieking exasperation. "Min need not return tonight or tomorrow."

166

"What-"

"Get word to him. Somehow. A message with someone headed that way. Someone we can trust. Let Min know that he is to stay with the Chois. For as long as necessary. It doesn't matter how long. He must stay in Munsan as long as there is the threat of conscription. There is going to be fighting. Can't you sense that?"

"I don't know. I - Perhaps I should go myself."

"Perhaps that would be best." She was trying to calm herself.

"What do you think I should tell Min? If I tell him Han is to be conscripted, he might insist on returning."

"You are right. You needn't tell him everything. Just that there are rumors about conscription and possibly another war."

Mr. Park was experiencing rising admiration for his wife, for her decisive thinking. "I will take our bicycle. Faster than walking and the rain is easing. Perhaps the road won't be too sloppy."

"You might need a reason for crossing the frontier."

"Write me a note like the one you wrote for Min."

"I will do so now."

"Hmmm..."

"What?"

"When I get close to the border checkpoint, I am thinking it might be better if I leave the road. Lay my bicycle against a tree or on the ground and walk through the forest across the 38th Parallel."

"Why?"

"I'm not sure. Maybe because Captain Kwon would kill me if he learned what I had done."

"Yes, I can see he is a hard man. But what you are considering could be dangerous. If you are caught in the forest, they might think you are a spy. An enemy agent."

"They might. That's a decision I'll make while I'm riding."

✝✝✝

Michael removed his slippers and stepped onto the snow-covered parade ground in front of Victory College. Telling himself to ignore the snow working its way between his toes, he crossed the parade ground, stepped gingerly down the snowy slope and began walking across the expanse of lawn toward Wish Stream. For a moment he thought, This could get me dismissed. Then he thought of his father and the hand he lost while serving and continued walking, picking up his pace.

✝✝✝

His hooded face under the water and no longer able to hold his breath, Elton felt the onset of panic. He thrashed his arms and tried to raise his head. Driscoll held it down for another terrifying moment. Then, grasping Elton's pajamas at the neck, he raised his head. Elton gasped for air. Then Driscoll again shoved his face below the surface.

✝✝✝

It was dark now as Mr. Park peddled his bicycle south on the road toward Munsan. He tried to keep the bike in the center of the road at its crown where it was firmest. Only the moon and stars were lighting the way. I can hardly believe this is happening, he mused. We are freed from thirty-five years of Japan's tyranny, and now we have fellow Koreans acting as imperialist as the Japanese. It is sad and it is maddening. Where will it end?

✝✝✝

As Michael neared the water, he could hear Robinson and Smythe struggling to muffle their laughter. He also could hear Elton's arms and hands slapping the water. Michael inhaled, reached out and shoved hard against Robinson and Smythe's backs.

"What?" he heard Robinson exclaim as he and Smythe went stumbling down the steep bank into the stream. Michael followed them into the water. Their large splashes surprised Driscoll who looked to his right. At that moment Michael reached down, cupped his right hand under Driscoll's chin and jerked it up. Driscoll released his grip on Elton's pajamas. Elton raised his head, coughing and sputtering.

"Get out of the water," Michael ordered Elton. "Now. Pull the hood off."

Still coughing and expelling water, Elton pulled off the black hood and crawled from the stream and up the bank. As he did so, Michael released his grip on Driscoll's chin, positioned his right foot against Driscoll's chest and shoved him under the surface.

168

"You meddling shithead," Kirkwood sneered. "We'll have you up on charges for this. Or worse."

Michael lifted his foot from Driscoll's chest, and he rose coughing and sputtering as Elton had. Michael turned toward Kirkwood and put his nose less than an inch from Kirkwood's. Michael was feeling the confidence and calm that accompanies being in the right. He half-hissed half-growled, "You say one word of this to anyone – anyone – and your ass will be in a sling. My sling. And if you try this with any other cadet in Normandy Company, I shall personally see that your nose never breathes freely again – under water or not."

Smythe and Robinson, standing in the water, were watching mutely. As Driscoll was rising to his feet, Michael gave him a hard shove, sending him backward and falling into the center of the stream. "Cowardly bastard," Michael snarled.

Then he was out of the stream and helping Elton to his feet. Elton found his slippers and picked them up. Without looking back, the two went walking slowly back across the lawn toward Victory College.

Moments later the four senior cadets were out of the water, standing and watching Michael and Elton, their forms outlined against the snow.

"Cheeky blighter," Driscoll hissed, spitting the last of the water from his mouth.

"He's that," Kirkwood said. "He's also a leader, and I wouldn't mind having him with me in a scrap."

CHAPTER 36

Reunions. With family members, schoolmates, old friends and long ago loves. They can generate anticipation – and trepidation – that is palpable. Who will be there? Will they recognize me? Will I recognize them? What will people think and say? What will I think and say?

Greetings at reunions are often visceral; bear hugs and kisses abound. And reunions are vocal; shrieks of joy, soft weeping and shouted laughter punctuate the proceedings.

Attending a reunion can be like uncorking a bottle of champagne; a lot of deeply buried memories come bubbling to the surface. Reunions generate new memories that, when banked and later recalled, can keep people smiling for decades.

Unexpected reunions? They can be even more charged, stunning the principals and sending currents of emotion that seemingly can light up rooms.

On a glorious autumn morning in 1947 at the University of Warsaw, Thaddeus Metz came striding vigorously onto campus. He looked up at the canopy of gold and red leaves and smiled contentedly. He was in his element. Minutes later after organizing papers on his desk, he had just begun addressing his English students. It was 9:05 a.m., as Thaddeus would long remember. The door to his classroom began edging open, creaking on hinges that needed oiling. Thaddeus turned to see who was entering his cherished academic domain. One look had Thaddeus rocking back on his heels, his hands reaching out behind him for support against the chalk-smeared blackboard.

"Ho, ho, ho," a bass voice boomed, "our captain is losing his balance and his wits." The visitor, wearing gray pants frayed at the cuffs, a brown long-sleeve shirt and a brown corduroy jacket, began striding across the front of the room. Two more men similarly attired and smiling broadly were following.

Thaddeus regained his balance and pivoted to face the arrivals.

"He has no voice," the visitor said, lowering the volume of his own. "How can he possibly teach these young people if he cannot speak? Students," the visitor said gravely, pausing and turning to face them, "does this man actually teach you? Does he have a magic technique for teaching without talking?"

The mouths of several students were agape, and all were as silent as Thaddeus. This sort of interruption was not only unexpected but unprecedented.

"This man, your teacher," the visitor continued, "once had no difficulty talking. In fact we often followed his words – jumping out of airplanes and crossing rivers under fire."

"Marek!" It was Thaddeus finding his voice and rushing into the outstretched arms of Marek Krawczyk, a former fellow cow pen soldier.

Tears began leaking from eyes and there followed quickly two more massive hugs with two more former cow pen soldiers, Henryk Wyzynski and Jerzy Pinkowski.

Thaddeus, despite the arms encircling him, felt on the verge of collapse. Marek could feel Thaddeus' knees buckling and braced him up. "Here, here, it's one thing for students to see their teacher weeping but entirely unseemly to see him flat on the floor. We cannot permit that."

Thaddeus brushed tears from his cheeks and inhaled. "I'm all right now. Really."

Marek, Henryk and Jerzy all pushed away from Thaddeus, and Marek said, "Let me look at you. A proper specimen of manhood you are. Yes, I can see why you made a fine lancer and an equally fine paratrooper."

"How-" Thaddeus paused and turned to face his students, most now looking on with smiles of amusement and affection. Felix Glemp was watching with narrowed eyes. This was a new side, entirely unexpected, of their English teacher. What are we learning about him, Felix wondered, and his history? "Excuse me," Thaddeus sniffled, "these men. They are friends, very dear friends."

"Did you know, students, that your teacher also was a soldier?" Marek asked. "That he fought the Bosche? That he was captured – with us? That he led our escape from a cow pen where the Nazis had put us with two smelly beasts? Did you know any of that?" A few students shyly shook their heads. "I thought not. He is far too modest a fellow. Well, we all escaped to France and fought with the French and English. The French, they had some good fighters but were poorly led. But we Poles, we had great leaders. Captain Metz. General Sosabowski. Lieutenant Colonel Jachnik. Did you know that your teacher was the very first man to volunteer for General Sosabowski's airborne brigade in England?" Several students shook their heads. Felix Glemp continued watching with rapt attention. "You've heard of General Sosabowski?" Most nodded in the affirmative. "Good! You should have. He was a great leader. A Polish hero."

One of the students in the front rank chanced a question in a barely audible voice. "Is General Sosabowski still alive?"

"Very much so," said Marek. "He is living in England, satisfactorily I might add. He has made a good life for himself."

"Why didn't he return to Poland?" the student asked, still speaking barely above a whisper.

"Too risky," said Marek. "The Soviets were…were doing unkind things to many Polish officers. Surely you've heard the stories. The Katyn Forest massacre. Stalin ordered the murder of thousands of Polish officers. And who knows how many more he sent to the Gulag? There to perish. Certainly you know these things."

The student shrugged his shoulders and murmured, "I guess so."

"The danger is less so now, although snoops are everywhere and only too willing to tattle on good Poles to our Soviet overlords. Despicable."

At this, Felix unconsciously slumped down in his chair.

"Marek," Thaddeus said sincerely, "I know my students are enjoying this interlude, but-"

"Yes, I know," Marek interrupted. "We are disrupting your class. Depriving these wonderful students – the future of our country – of valuable learning time. We will leave."

"Wait," said Thaddeus. "Meet me outside after class."

Marek laughed. "You didn't think we were going to invade your classroom – conquer it – and then retreat never to be seen again?"

"Well, no, I guess not."

"We will wait outside for you – and for any of your students who would like to continue their history lessons from the men who lived it."

✝✝✝

"Bernadeta will be thrilled to see you," Thaddeus said to Marek, Henryk and Jerzy.

The four men had been walking leisurely for about 30 minutes, moving north from the university. Along the way they passed considerable reconstruction. Perhaps the most remarkable such project was the erection of a new King Sigismund's Column adjacent the Royal Castle, also being reconstructed. Thaddeus and his companions paused to observe the work, which would be completed two years later in 1949. The original column, 70 feet high and topped by a statue of the ruler who moved the nation's capital from Cracow to Warsaw in 1596, had collapsed under the weight of Luftwaffe bombardments. After the war the decision was made to construct a new column and crown it with the statue that had survived intact. A second decision was made to leave the collapsed column on the ground where it fell. By the time Thaddeus, Marek, Henryk and Jerzy were walking by the site, Poles had taken to touching the fallen column, believing – or hoping – it would help them fulfill wishes. In effect they were turning the old column into what was perhaps the world's largest and longest good luck charm.

"Should we touch it too?" Henryk asked with evident good humor.

"Don't you think we already used up our supply of good luck?" Marek replied jovially.

"Perhaps," Henryk said, scarcely able to suppress a grin, "but it couldn't hurt to re-stock."

Laughter all around. And then, one by one, the former cow pen soldiers, survivors all, stepped beside the fallen column, reached down and patted it.

"We Poles are a superstitious lot," Marek grumbled good-naturedly. "We mix our belief in God with belief in pagan spirits."

"Ahem…I prefer to think that only makes us exceptionally faithful," Thaddeus said with mock gravity.

"Spoken like a genuine academic princeling," Marek teased.

With each passing minute the reunited cow pen soldiers were increasingly reveling in their camaraderie.

Now the four men were turning onto Mostowa Street and proceeding slowly toward the apartment building that was home to Bernadeta and Thaddeus and was just 50 paces ahead on the left.

"She will probably be as shocked as you were," Henryk laughed and slapped Thaddeus on the shoulder. "She obviously made a strong impression on you back in 1939."

"Fortunately for me, I assure you." The men laughed. "We have no phone so I couldn't warn her."

"All the better," Jerzy said.

"How did you find me?" Thaddeus asked.

Marek smiled slyly. "It wasn't difficult. We asked your sister-in-law."

Thaddeus' eyes widened. "You've been to the farm?"

"It was the first place we went after returning from England."

"England?"

"After occupation duty in Germany we decided to visit General Sosabowski. And to be honest we were considering staying in England. That's what so many of our fellow paratroopers have done. Colonizing the British Isles, you might say. Did you know that?"

"No."

"As you do know, many of our men formed attachments to local women while we were training in Scotland and England. In recent months," said Marek, "there have been many Polish-English and Polish-Scottish weddings – exchanges of vows bringing together hundreds of Polish Catholics and British Protestants. A few years ago, who would have guessed that?"

Thaddeus smiled. "A perfect or imperfect irony, depending on your point of view. How is General Sosabowski?"

"He is doing well. He's working in a factory. Close to where many of our men found jobs in brickyards near Peterborough." Peterborough had been the Polish Parachute Brigade's second training site, after Upper Largo in Scotland. "He asked us to bring greetings to you."

Thaddeus nodded. "A wonderful man. A great leader."

A pause. Then Marek said softly. "At the farm we rode your horse. General. A fine name. We hope you don't mind."

"Of course not."

"Barbara rides him daily and is a fine horsewoman," said Henryk. "But we lancers couldn't resist climbing into the saddle once again."

"Did you run him hard?"

Marek, Henryk and Jerzy all laughed.

"Do you think lancers – even former lancers – would ride him as would a child just learning the basics?" Marek asked rhetorically.

Now it was Thaddeus who laughed loudly.

As they neared Number 22 Mostowa, a woman was approaching from the opposite direction.

"Mrs. Ostrowski!" Thaddeus called to his downstairs neighbor. Thaddeus waved vigorously, and Danuta Ostrowski replied with a tentative wave. "Mrs. Ostrowski, I want you to meet three friends."

The short woman stood facing the four much taller men.

"Pleased to meet you, Ma'am," Marek said and bowed slightly.

She smiled and nodded.

Thaddeus completed introductions and then added, "Marek was wounded at Dunkirk."

"So," said Marek, "was Captain Metz."

✝✝✝

Moments later Mrs. Ostrowski heard two piercing squeals in the apartment above her head. Her curiosity was fully aroused. Just who are those three men, she wondered, and why did they cause such an outburst from Bernadeta? Would she greet strangers that way? Even if they are friends of Thaddeus? Somehow, somewhere they must have met in the past.

CHAPTER 37

A pair of tugboats was laboring to ease the huge liner to its berth at Southampton. The vessel wasn't particularly posh, but Lucy Crispin had been comfortable on the long voyage from Wellington, New Zealand westward around the Cape of Good Hope and north past the Horn of Africa. The seas had been calm throughout the journey and Lucy was thankful.

Standing at the rail Lucy was tingling with excitement. Fascinated, she watched crewmen scrambling to tie up the liner and lower the gangway. My grand adventure continues, she reflected. Half way round the globe from comfy New Zealand to this land of my family's forbearers. Next stop, the local rail station and a train north to London. I don't know a soul here, but I don't feel frightened or alone. Well, not yet anyway. Too much to take in now. In just a bit I shall be collecting my luggage and moving on. She smiled. If I'd brought everything Mother and Father wanted me to carry, I'd need my very own freight car. Less will be better. Fewer encumbrances. After all, I'm here to learn nursing, not furnish a large flat. Lucy reached up with her slightly withered left hand and patted her curly light brown hair. This humidity should keep my curls firmly furled.

At St. Thomas Hospital, located near the houses of Parliament and Waterloo Station, Sister Esmerelda greeted Lucy warmly. "Welcome, my dear. We have been expecting you."

"I am thoroughly delighted to be here."

"You are the second young woman we have welcomed from afar."

"There is another New Zealander here?"

"Oh, no," Sister Esmerelda explained, "I'm afraid I am talking history. Sorry. I'm referring to an American. Theresa Hassler. She arrived here – already a qualified nurse – back in 1940. Just in time to be helpful during The Blitz. She was the epitome of aplomb."

"She sounds like a remarkable woman," said Lucy.

"Theresa became a legend," Sister said with a hint of wistfulness. "During the Battle of Britain she lost her beau. An American flyer who volunteered for the RAF. Walker was his name as I recall. First name Hal. Shot down or so we think."

"You think?"

"He was never found. Nor his plane. So very sad."

"What did Miss Hassler do?"

"She soldiered on. Then after the war she returned to America."

"Did you ever hear from her again?"

"Oh yes," Sister smiled. "That's how she really made her legend. You see, she returned to London. Here to St. Thomas. Said she had come to regard London as her adopted hometown."

"She's here now?"

Sister shook her head. "The legend continues," she smiled. "An American officer, one she had patched up during the Sicily landings, came looking for her. Took her back to America."

"Married?"

"Yes," Sister beamed. "Theresa sent us an invitation to their wedding. Of course we couldn't afford to attend, but she was so thoughtful, don't you think?"

"Yes, very."

"Come with me to my desk. I'll show you a picture. Theresa recently became a mother, and she sent us a picture of her with the baby and her husband." Sister Esmerelda turned the picture over and read the caption. "Dean Morton's his name. Fine man. They named their daughter after Theresa's Nurse Corps commander who was killed at Bastogne. As I said, Theresa is a legend here. And deservedly so." A pause. "One other thing, Miss Crispin. Your left arm and hand."

"As you will see, Sister," Lucy said confidently, "it's a disability I've learned to cope with."

"Min can stay as long as you feel it advisable," Choi Chun Kuen assured Park Bong Suk.

Min was standing by silently, observing closely and listening respectfully to his father and his business acquaintance.

"It could be a long time," Mr. Park said.

"The times are uncertain," Mr. Choi replied. "If we can provide a little certainty, it will be our pleasure."

"Here," Mr. Park said, "take this." He handed Mr. Choi a thick packet of won, Korea's currency. "It's for the knives Min was to buy."

"This is too much," Mr. Choi said.

"Use the rest to feed Min."

"Min can pay for his keep by helping us in the shop and running errands," Mr. Choi replied. "We are confident he is a good worker."

"Then use the extra won to feed and stable Sejong."

"That is agreeable." Mr. Choi bowed. A pause. "Stay the night with us. Please. You would honor us with your presence."

"Thank you," Mr. Park said, relieved at not having to begin the return trip in darkness. "But in the morning I will depart early. Or my wife will worry."

"So true," Mr. Choi agreed. He nodded, smiling at his own wife. "That's what you would do too."

"Let me prepare supper for four," Mrs. Choi said.

"You are too kind," Mr. Park said and meant it. He was deeply grateful for the Chois' enthusiastic willingness to shelter his son and to provide overnight accommodations for himself.

"One more thing," said Mr. Park.

"Yes?"

"Please bear in mind that as long as Min is here, our home is now his home."

Lucy Crispin was in need of a home and, on the advice of Sister Esmerelda, had gone walking to nearby Carlisle Lane. She pushed open the door to a bicycle shop and entered. Several new bikes in an array of colors were on display, and there were racks of spare parts. A man, balding and appearing to be in his early 50s, was standing behind the sales and service counter.

"Are you Mr. Turner?"

"Ronald Turner, miss, one and the same."

"My name is Lucy Crispin. I've come to St. Thomas from New Zealand to study nursing. I need lodgings and Sister Esmerelda recommended that I seek you out."

"Ah, the good sister," said Ronald Turner, stepping from behind the counter and moving toward Lucy. "She has made a wise recommendation. As she usually does. By the way, did you know she rides bikes?" Lucy's reply was a look of surprise. "That's right, sisterly habit and all. Sister Esmerelda is more than she seems." Mr. Turner extended his right hand and Lucy shook it.

"You have space available then?"

"I do. A room twice occupied by another young woman from abroad."

"Theresa Hassler?"

"So," he smiled, "you've already heard of our legendary American nurse. You would do well to follow in her footsteps. An exceptional young woman. Say," said Mr. Turner, "do you ride bicycles?"

✝✝✝

Early the next morning Park Bong Suk began making his way north from Munsan. As he neared the frontier dividing south from north, he veered from the road and once again began edging through the forest. Moments later he stepped on a dry branch and to him the cracking seemed as thunderous as an exploding artillery shell. He froze as adrenalin sent fear surging through him. He waited, heard nothing more, breathed in relief and resumed his stealthy border crossing.

Once across the 38th Parallel and past the south and north checkpoints, Mr. Park located his bicycle. It was wet from the previous night's rain and the morning dew. He stood the bike upright, removed his vest and used it to wipe the seat. Might as well ride in comfort, he mused. Then he positioned the bike on the road and began peddling north to Kaesong.

I wonder when I'll see Min again. At least he's safe from the clutches of Captain Kwon and Kim Il Sung.

CHAPTER 38

Tentatively Park Han stepped into his parents' small shop. From floor to ceiling shelves were jammed with foodstuffs and household goods. His father was standing on a small stool, stocking high shelves. His mother was filling large glass bowls with hard candies that were grouped on the sales counter.

"You should be at school," Mrs. Park said.

In the next instant, before Han could reply, Captain Kwon followed him inside. "His schooling is finished," he said brusquely. "At least his civilian schooling." Seconds later the other two soldiers entered the shop.

Mrs. Park blinked, her eyes shifting from her son to Kwon and back.

Han looked over his shoulder at Kwon and then back toward his mother. They moved closer to each other and embraced, awkwardly, not accustomed to showing affection in front of others.

Mr. Park stepped down from the stool and moved around the end of the sales counter toward his son. They bowed to each other, and then Mr. Park grasped and squeezed his son's right forearm.

With Kwon's impatience visible, mother, father and son were finding speaking difficult. Finally Mrs. Park said simply, "Be careful."

"I will."

"Come on," said Kwon. "It is time you begin training to become a defender of our Great Leader." Then he spoke to Mrs. Park. "We will be back soon for your other son."

CHAPTER 39

Dean Morton was sitting in their living room in the yellow upholstered recliner rocker. He was reading the *Belvidere Daily Republican's* Saturday edition sports section and sipping freshly perked coffee. He was wearing blue jeans and a gray sweatshirt. His feet were bare. It was a little after 8 a.m.

Theresa, limping as always from her war injury, came walking into the room. She was holding little Marilyn and looking sunrise fresh in a yellow skirt and white blouse. For a few moments she stood silently, five feet in front of Dean, engrossed in his reading. Then she cleared her throat.

He looked up. "What? Did I forget something? Is it my turn to change the baby?" He started to rise.

"Don't get up. You are too funny," Theresa smiled.

Marilyn gurgled and Theresa shifted the baby from her left shoulder to her right. "No. I just want to ask you something."

"You've got my attention," Dean smiled.

"Have you ever thought of adopting?"

"No."

"Would you?"

"Umm. I guess so."

"Good."

"Uh huh. Now, what brought this on? What am I getting myself into? I mean, Marilyn is still a baby. Not even walking yet. And unless there's something you haven't told me, Nurse Morton, we are capable of producing more little Mortons."

"I'm keeping no secrets," she smiled. "I was reading a *Newsweek* article about adopting. It got me to remembering the children orphaned in London during The Blitz. It was so sad. And that got me to thinking about children in this country, ones given up for adoption by unwed mothers. There must thousands of them every year. Without a loving home..."

"I see," Dean said. "Your motherly instincts and nursing sensibilities have been aroused. A powerful combination."

Theresa smiled. "I can't deny it."

"Sit down."

Theresa sat on a brownish upholstered easy chair and perched Marilyn on her lap facing Dean. "I want more children. You know that. At least two."

Dean nodded. "I know and I'm still okay with that. But why bring it up now?"

"I'm not sure I want to go through another delivery like the first one. It was scary and it was hard. The Caesarean was no picnic. And I think it would be nice to give a home to a child who needs one. And from what I've read and heard, the adoption process takes a long time. The home study includes several interviews with both of us – together and separately. And there's paperwork."

"So let me see if I'm reading this right. If we're going to adopt we should get the process started. Is that what you are saying?"

"Right."

"I don't know," Dean said, working to maintain a sober expression. "Do you think I could hold a kid in each arm?" He was alluding to the lingering effect of his chest wound.

After the war, Dean, with assistance from his congressman father Raymond's government connections, went looking for Theresa and found her at St. Thomas Hospital in London where she had returned after a brief homecoming. Dean had proved persuasive, and their wedding followed soon after. Dean then went to work as the head of his Republican father's district office in nearby Rockford. Dean's health was fine, but the wound restricted motion in his right shoulder where residual stiffness and pain kept vivid his memories of war's horrors.

"Oh, I think you'd make the effort," Theresa replied casually. "At least for family photos."

"Once a year in front of a camera. Holding a brood. For posterity's sake. Yep, you're right."

"You know, I love you."

"Hmmm…From time to time you have reminded me of that."

"And?"

"I like the reminders – the ones I hear and the ones I get in bed." He was grinning with mock lasciviousness.

"And I think I know which kind you like best," Theresa replied with exaggerated coquettishness. "I don't know if you should be hearing this, Marilyn."

"Action is a language I understand and appreciate better than words."

"And you're ready for some weekend action?"

"It's not too early. After all, I've had my coffee and read the sports."

"Well, sport, let me put Marilyn in the playpen."

Dean put the newspaper aside and he and Theresa both stood. She then lowered Marilyn into the playpen. The baby whined and Theresa patted her reassuringly. She looked up at Dean and grinned. Mindful of the discomfort Dean still felt in his right shoulder, she punched him lightly on his left. She loved her husband dearly and seldom spent more than fleeting seconds thinking of her earlier loves, Jack Brecker and Hal Walker.

"That was a reminder of how much I love you," she smiled, eyes glistening. "Taking care to punch you on your good shoulder. How many wives would be so considerate?"

"The only one I care about," Dean said, wrapping his arms around her waist and drawing her close.

"That's very reassuring, Mr. Morton. Now, before it slips our minds, let's see that you get your favorite reminder."

CHAPTER 40

In November 1947 the first Siberian gusts sent cold probing fingers across the Korean peninsula. Winter was in the winds, but to the Parks – Bong Suk and Soon Im – the coming arctic temperatures foretold more than daily shivering and layering on clothing.

Captain Kwon Oh Bum and two privates came barging into the Parks' general merchandise shop.

"Where is your other son? Min?" he asked without preamble, his piercing black eyes clearly reflecting mounting exasperation. Kwon was carrying a worn leather briefcase and a Russian-made sidearm. The two privates were holding Soviet-supplied PPsh submachine guns.

"Still in Munsan," Mr. Park replied soberly.

"Have you talked with him?" Kwon placed his briefcase on the floor and removed his leather gloves.

"No. We received a letter," said Mr. Park. That was a lie.

"And?"

"He has taken a job there. In a butcher shop." That was bordering on truth.

"He is not finishing his last year of secondary school?" Kwon asked pointedly.

"He believes the job is a good opportunity to learn a trade." Another lie.

"Does he know we want him?"

"I wrote to him about his brother." A third lie.

"And still he does not return." Kwon blew out a short breath of disgust. "Not much of a brother – or a son." Kwon's sarcasm was as biting as the northwest winds cutting in unencumbered from the Yellow Sea.

"He is a fine son and a fine brother," Mr. Park said grimly, his bile rising.

"I think you are lying," Kwon said accusingly, not minding at all that he was provoking the humble shopkeeper.

"I-"

Kwon stepped toward Mr. Park and slapped his left cheek with the gloves. Mrs. Park flinched. Mr. Park's jaws clenched and he refrained from rubbing his stinging cheek. Kwon was hoping Mr. Park would lash out. He decided to keep pressing the issue. "I could kill you – or both of you – and suffer no consequence." Mrs. Park was hoping fervently that her husband would say no more. "Our Great Leader demands loyalty from his people. He does not tolerate subversion or evasion. Nor do I."

But Captain Kwon was not blind to certain realities. He knew that killing the Parks or even inflicting severe physical harm would become instant news that would spread faster than wind-blown seeds and have more parents sending their sons into hiding.

"We mean no disloyalty," Mr. Park said with forced contrition. Mrs. Park allowed herself to inhale and exhale carefully, as though her resumption of breathing could trigger another outburst.

"Here is what you will do," Kwon said, enunciating each word with menacing precision. "You will get word to Min. You will tell him that he owes a duty to our Great Leader to join our army in defense of our country and its provisional government. Further, you will tell him that if he does not return promptly, training for his brother Han will include some very special exercises. This is not negotiable." A pause. "Need I say more?"

Mr. Park shook his head.

Kwon gestured toward the shop's door, and his two men exited. Then, glowering, Kwon picked up his briefcase and backed from the shop, his black eyes radiating contempt.

✝✝✝

"What are you going to do?" Mrs. Park asked worriedly.

"I will tell you what I am not going to do," Mr. Park replied, his anger still evident. "I am not going to tell Min anything about threats to his brother." Mrs. Park nodded, absorbing her husband's thinking. "If I do," Mr. Park continued, "Min will return at once and you – we – will get precisely what we do not want – two sons in Kim Il Sung's army.

CHAPTER 41

"A letter from my sister," Bernadeta said excitedly, looking at an envelope postmarked Zyrardow. She and Thaddeus had arrived at their Mostowa Street apartment together, Thaddeus having stopped at the American embassy to meet her on his walk north from the university. Bernadeta sliced open the envelope with a paring knife, tossed it on the small kitchen table and began reading the letter written in Barbara's neat hand. Minutes went by and then she uttered simply, "Oh my."

"Bad news or good?" Thaddeus asked in English.

"Here, my husband. Read it yourself." Bernadeta's eyes were glittering.

December 2, 1947

Dear Bernadeta,
Father and Kaz and I would like you and Thaddeus to join us for
a special Christmas celebration. This is Father's idea. He wants our
family together for the holiday and to commemorate the gravesite he and
Kaz have built for Mother. You will like what they have done.

Father had another idea. A good one we think. He would like you and Thaddeus to invite the three cow pen soldiers. He respects them immensely and believes they might enjoy this special time at our farm. He says if they have wives and children to invite them too. We might have to evict the cows and the ox and General for everyone to have a place to sleep. Ha ha.

There is more! Father has said that Christmas – Christmas afternoon – would be the perfect time for me and Kaz to marry. Naturally we agree. Ha! Ha! This will mean more sleeping space for everyone else. Ha!

This is so exciting!! I was worried that Mother's passing would bring a black cloud over this Christmas season. But then Father always has been full of surprises. I am so glad I was wrong.

Here is our plan. I hope you and Thaddeus approve. Two days before Christmas, Kaz will drive our wagon into Warsaw to collect you and the others. Our ox will complain about the heavy load, no? He will also bring General, so Thaddeus can ride him back to the farm. Bring blankets!

Please give my love to Thaddeus.
Your loving sister,
Barbara

"This is wonderful," Thaddeus said, eyes sparkling. "I will contact Marek, Jerzy and Henryk right away. I am certain they will want to join us. And they will want to take turns with me riding General."

"They are all still single?"

"Unless one of them has his own holiday season surprise for us."

"There is someone else I would like to invite," Bernadeta said excitedly. "Mrs. Ostrowski. She must be so lonely at holidays."

"Agreed. She will be thrilled, I'm sure. Such a wonderful friend."

✝ ✝ ✝

The train was slowing as it entered cavernous Waterloo Station just across the Thames from the houses of Parliament. The station was the terminus for trains arriving in London from the south. Michael Cornelius and Kendall Thorne were excited to be coming home for Christmas. The regimen at Sandhurst had lived up to its billing; it had been grueling – physically and mentally – and Michael and Kendall were ready – more than ready – for a respite.

The train came screeching to a stop, steel wheels straining against steel rails, and Michael and Kendall stood and retrieved their bags from the overhead rack. The doors opened and the pair of cadets stepped onto the concrete platform. Most alighting passengers began scurrying down the platform toward the sprawling arrivals area. Michael paused. He looked up at the station's high ceiling, pulled in a deep breath through his mouth and smiled. He wanted to absorb slowly the sense of being back in his hometown.

"London air," Kendall observed dryly, "a bit less pure than at Sandhurst."

"So true, but soupy though it often is, it is still *our* London air, and it feels good to be breathing it."

Michael and K walked unhurriedly to the arrivals area and then exited the station on Mepham Street and paused. Which way to go home? Michael asked himself. A taxi? Hmm…costly. "I think I will circle around the station and catch the tube at Lambeth North to Bayswater," said Michael. "Then it's only a short hike to our home on Ilchester."

"Here's where we part then. I'll just catch a bus to my neighborhood."

"Right. Let's stay connected during the holidays."

"Perhaps tipple together on New Year's Eve at Trafalgar Square."

"Once again aboard the lions."

"The young lions aboard the old lions. To us!"

Michael and K tossed each other salutes, British style, palms outward. Then   Michael hefted his bag and began walking southeast to Waterloo Road where he turned southwest onto Lower Marsh. The street was busy with holiday shoppers ambitiously searching for gifts even as Londoners still were coping with one of the lingering vestiges of the war – rationing certain foods and merchandise. The last ration cards wouldn't be retired until 1954.

At the end of Lower Marsh where it met Westminster Bridge Road, Michael saw a sign for Turner's Bicycle Shop and, on a whim, crossed the road into Carlisle Lane. Standing now in front of the shop, he was thinking, If I had one of those bikes, I just might try balancing my bag on the handlebar and peddling my way home. He smiled at the thought, shrugged, pivoted and began retracing his steps to Westminster Bridge Road. Once there he would turn right and be but a block from Lambeth North tube station.

Approaching from the opposite direction was a curly haired young woman. In her right hand she was carrying a cloth bag containing groceries. In her slightly clawed left hand she was holding a bottle of chianti, a Christmas splurge for herself. Tucked between her left arm and chest was a folded newspaper. With little warning on the congested sidewalk, she found herself bracing for a collision. Two boys, both laughing heartily, came charging toward her. One was chasing the other. As the woman moved to the left to dodge them, the newspaper slipped free and fell to the sidewalk. The boys took no note as they went racing by, one so closely that the woman felt his sleeve brush hers. She shook her head slightly and smiled.

As she began bending her knees, a voice said, "Let me."

The woman looked up. "Thank you."

Michael lowered his bag to the pavement and squatted to pick up the paper. "*The Daily Telegraph*. A favorite of conservatives and the military." He stood. "You don't look the military sort so perhaps you're for the Conservatives."

"Actually," Lucy smiled, "I'm for common sense, and that seems to be *The Telegraph's* forte."

"Well put," said Michael. "I confess to being in the military" – as Lucy could see plainly by his Sandhurst uniform – "and most would judge me conservative. Like my father, I'm afraid. This apple didn't fall far from the political tree. Now, what remains open to question is how many people would accuse me of harboring a surfeit of common sense."

Lucy laughed delightedly. "What doesn't seem open to question is your willingness to help a young woman and engage her in chatter in a public setting."

"Guilty as charged," Michael grinned. "Although I must also confess to having no precedent for my chivalrous behavior."

"Thank goodness," she said cheerfully, "for your willingness to establish a precedent."

"You live near here?"

"You just passed by my lodgings." With a forward nod of her head she gestured in the direction from which Michael had materialized. "I've a room above the bicycle shop."

"Do you ride?"

"Not as yet here in London. Actually I'm more accustomed to riding a horse, but there seems little opportunity for that here."

Michael chuckled, his memory flashing back to the day a mounted bobby had given him a ride around Trafalgar Square, less than a mile from where they now were standing. "Bikes or horses, perhaps we could ride together during these holidays. If I'm not being too presumptuous." Michael extended his hand holding the newspaper and helped Lucy tuck it back beneath her arm. She saw Michael still holding out his right hand and, awkwardly, the grocery bag suspended from her arm, took it and shook politely.

"My name is Cornelius. Michael Cornelius."

"Mine is Crispin. Lucy."

"Merry Christmas, Lucy."

"Merry Christmas to you, Michael."

†††

In Arizona dawn on Christmas morning had not yet arrived at Charco on the Tohono Reservation. In the darkness Jack Brecker and the elder were standing on the earthen road and leaning against Jack's dusty gray Studebaker in front of the village chapel.

"Should we begin Christmas in our traditional way?" Jack asked.

"Tradition is important to our people."

Jack smiled and then twisted and removed the metal cap from his thermos bottle. The elder had a gray metal mug and Jack poured black coffee, steam swirling upward. Then he poured some for himself into the cap-as-cup. The elder sat his cup on the hood of Jack's car and removed a pack of Camels from his woolen vest pocket. Jack produced a silver Ronson lighter – army issue – and held the flame to the end of the elder's cigarette, then to his own. As the cigarette tips glowed orange, stars shown brightly in the dry desert sky. Both men contented themselves with long drags on the cigarettes and then sipped coffee. Jack, savoring the taste, ran his tongue across his lower lip.

"Five years," Jack reminisced. "Five years since our first Christmas morning coffee and cigarettes."

"They were our first gifts to each other," remembered the elder. "They were perfect gifts."

The two men were recalling Jack's first Christmas as pastor in nearby Ajo from where he also served the Tohono Reservation Indians. On December 25, 1942, Jack had said midnight Mass in Ajo's Immaculate Conception church, slept for a few hours and then driven to Charco to say a 5:30 Mass. The elder had been waiting and their time together, spent sipping and smoking while awaiting congregants, had laid the foundation for their friendship. From that first meeting conversation between the two men came easily.

"This Christmas will be a little different," said Jack.

"Oh?"

"After saying Mass for your people, I'm flying."

"I think I can guess your destination."

Jack sipped and smiled. "Your hunches are famously accurate."

The elder smiled knowingly. "I only take the time to study people. Especially my friends."

"You are an excellent student."

"Who will say your morning Mass in Ajo?"

"No one. Two weeks ago I asked my parishioners how they felt about attending a Christmas Eve Mass or midnight Mass so that I could leave right after saying Mass for your people."

"They would not deny you a special Christmas with your family. You are flying to Ohio, aren't you?"

"Yes. My family in Shelby is having a big Christmas reunion. They asked me if it was at all possible to join them. They really didn't think I could make it, but they wanted me to know about it. So I phoned Bishop Metzger and explained."

"The bishop is a good man. We will be sorry when he leaves. My people still speak well of him for saying the dedication Mass for our chapel."

"He is very understanding. And as a native Ohioan himself he was glad to let me."

"You should have asked my people the same thing. They would have said yes."

"I know."

"You could have said Mass here at Charco yesterday afternoon. Then you could fly even earlier. You would be in the air even as we are speaking. You know my people think well of their desert priest." The elder reached out with his left hand and placed it on Jack's right shoulder.

"I thought about asking but only briefly."

"Why?"

"Tradition." Jack smiled. "Christmas morning coffee and cigarettes here at Charco with you. What would Christmas be without it?"

The elder removed his hand from Jack's shoulder and picked up his mug. Then he elevated it toward Jack's, and the two men clinked cups and nodded.

"Does your family know you are coming?"

"I thought about surprising them but was worried that the shock might be too much for my parents. And I know my mother would be hurt if she didn't have time to fix my favorite foods and desserts."

"Can you fly fast enough?"

"I estimate twelve to fifteen hours in the air, with good tail winds. Plus refueling stops. It will be late when I arrive. So they are having the reunion the day after Christmas."

The elder inhaled his Camel. "I am getting old," he said, eyelids blinking away rising smoke. "I think we will not have many more of our traditional Christmas mornings."

"Pshaw. You are not so old."

"Sixty. That is old for an Indian. I have seen many, many full moons. Our young people see me as an ancient." He smiled wryly.

"But you still stand tall and strong. And you love life. That is important. Plus your people need you – your leadership."

"Some nights I can hear my ancestors. They are saying it is getting close to my time to join them."

"Is something wrong?" Jack's voice betrayed deep concern.

"Some days – some nights – I feel empty. This is hard for me to explain. I feel like my body is here but my spirit – my soul – is somewhere else. With my ancestors, perhaps." The elder sighed shallowly and sipped his coffee. Then he faced Jack and smiled. "I am sorry. Christmas morning is about birth."

✝✝✝

"Do you think we should celebrate the new year?" Park Soon Im asked her husband, Park Bong Suk.

"It would be difficult to enjoy a celebration without Min and Han."

"That is what I was thinking too. The new year should be about hope. The birth of new hope. Or renewal. Min is still safe in Munsan but I worry about Han."

"Captain Kwon?"

Mrs. Park nodded. "He will return again to ask about Min. You made him angry, and I think he is a man who feeds on anger. And who doesn't forget."

✝✝✝

Bernadeta and Barbara, with Mrs. Ostrowski gladly helping, were up early and busy in the kitchen. They were preparing a magnificent Christmas breakfast. They made light, fluffy biscuits, and they fried thinly sliced potatoes with onions. They cracked two dozen eggs and scrambled them with pepper and farm fresh cheese.

They didn't have to awaken anyone. The aromas emanating from the kitchen opened eyelids and aroused appetites, including ones whose owners had slept in the barn.

Barbara and Jszef had decided on sleeping arrangements. Jszef in his own bed. Barbara and Bernadeta again sharing a bed. Mrs. Ostrowski in the main room on a worn, rose-colored settee. Kaz and Thaddeus in the barn's loft and Marek, Henryk and Jerzy on pallets of straw in the stalls vacated by the milk cows, the ox and General who had spent the night tethered outside the barn. Thaddeus and Kaz had offered to sleep in the cow pen, but Marek, Henryk and Jerzy had insisted they take the loft.

Christmas Eve in the loft. Thaddeus, the former lancer and paratrooper, and Kaz, the Resistance cell leader and Auschwitz escapee, had first met just hours earlier. Both had loved Bernadetta.

Inside the house in their room Bernadetta and Barbara wondered what their husband and husband-to-be might be discussing. The men had shaken

191

hands cordially. There had been no sign of tension. But their introduction had been in the presence of the others. Now they were alone together and away from curious ears.

Inside the barn, Thaddeus and Kaz had climbed the wooden ladder to the loft. There they built mats of hay, lay down and arranged blankets over them.

"You don't remember me, do you?" said Kaz.

"From where?"

"We rode in the same lancer regiment. Here at the farm, when I first heard your name, my memory was foggy. But when I saw you this afternoon, it all came back."

"I'm sorry for not remembering you. I apologize."

"Not to worry. We were a thousand men."

"On the first day of the war."

"I saw you spear the German."

"Oh."

"After the battle, I saw you riding south. I rode north."

"It would seem we both rode well."

In the darkness both men smiled.

"So," Kaz whispered, "what do you think they are talking about?"

"Us, no doubt."

"Just as we are talking about them."

"It's the nature of things."

"Agreed," Thaddeus whispered, not wanting to disturb the three former cow pen soldiers sleeping below. "They are probably anxious about how we'll get along."

"The past is past," said Kaz. "Theirs and ours. There is no need to talk more about it."

"Agreed." A pause. "I am glad that you and Barbara found each other. She seems very happy."

✝✝✝

Early on Christmas afternoon Father Kowalski arrived from Zyrardow. There would be a second wedding in the barn. This time, though, there would be no assemblage of area friends; they were celebrating Christmas with their own families. The only other wedding guests in addition to those who had breakfasted together were General, the two milk cows and the ox, all having been led back inside the barn.

"We can't have you miss this," Thaddeus had said while leading General to his stall. "You are family."

Once again Father Kowalski had responded to incentive to perform another barn wedding. The promise of another post-ceremony feast and his own cake to take back to his rectory had proven persuasive. This time there would be no six monthly deliveries of milk. Instead, Jszef presented Father Kowalski with one of the farm's new laying hens, purchased with zlotys Kaz had brought from Warsaw.

✝ ✝ ✝

What is it with the men in my life and flying? Theresa Morton was wondering. Dean's not a pilot like Hal and Jack, but he enjoys being in the air. He loves flying back and forth to Washington with his dad. I know they value their time alone together. Sometimes I worry but I know Mr. Morton – Dad – is an experienced pilot.

Those reflections were occupying Theresa's thoughts amid a joyous gathering of family and friends in her parents' – Joe and Eleanor's – large living room on Grand Boulevard in Shelby. It was the house Theresa had grown up in and had changed little. The major difference: wall-to-wall carpeting – gray with red roses – had replaced area rugs in the living and dining rooms. The occasion was the night-after-Christmas family reunion. Present were both the Hasslers and the Breckers, the latter because of the Bridgett Hassler-Tom Brecker union and the resulting twins, now more than three years old.

Champagne corks were popping and laughter was ricocheting off the walls. Laughing loudest, his booming roars infectious, was Jack. As was his preference, he had eschewed landing at Shelby's small airstrip and instead had touched down in a wheat field behind the Sacred Heart Seminary just five miles southeast of Shelby. His reasoning: at 6:00 in the morning on the day after Christmas the airstrip would be devoid of people. But at the seminary young priests-in-the-making would be milking cows and doing other chores, and they would gladly announce his arrival to any faculty who had not heard the plane's approach. One of them then would enthusiastically drive Jack to his parents' house on Raymond Avenue.

From takeoff in Ajo the journey, including stops for refueling and rest, had taken 22 hours. After breakfasting with his mom, Virginia, and dad, Anthony, Jack had slept until noon. Then he arose to give each a special Christmas present – for Virginia a turquoise pendant fashioned by the elder and for Anthony a blue woolen shirt-jacket, a product of the Charco villagers.

"It's gorgeous," Virginia had marveled. "The turquoise is so highly polished. And the silver setting is absolutely lovely. I'll treasure it all the more, knowing your friend made it."

Anthony stood and slipped on the shirt-jacket. "Perfect fit."

"I showed the Indians a picture of you and me standing together to give them an idea of your size."

"I always knew your higher education would be good for more than priestly duties." Anthony chuckled at his own small joke. "I'll be wearing this a lot this winter. Please tell your Indian friends thank you."

"Oh, yes," Virginia bubbled. "Please tell the elder how grateful we are – and how skilled he and his people are. Not to mention generous."

That night during the party at the Hasslers, as Jack looked around the room at the happy faces, his eyes fell on Theresa. She appeared beatific. She was holding little Marilyn who, amazingly to Jack, was sleeping soundly amidst the tumult. On the floor in the center of the room, Bridgett and Tom's twins, Theresa and Jack, were providing entertainment by their very presence. A new dollhouse with its miniature furniture was occupying Theresa. Enthralling Jack was a tin windup motorcycle with permanently affixed rider, a gift from his maternal grandparents. Repeatedly, Jack turned the key and then watched the tiny motorcycle scoot in endless circles on the carpet.

Jack was relieved that no one in the room knew of his Bastogne liaison with Theresa. Knowledge of it would have created unwanted tension, perhaps even scuttled the party. His middle brother Paul might have half-suspected that intimacy had occurred, but he was too much the good brother to have queried Jack. A year after the Battle of the Bulge, Paul had been thrilled that Jack had been able to journey to the Alsacian village of Ribeauville, just days after having stayed with General Patton beside his death bed, to perform his wedding to Lea Peiffer. She was the Resistance fighter Paul had met outside the gate to Natzwiller-Struthof, the Nazis' only death camp in France. Paul's airborne company had been ordered to liberate the camp, but the Germans already had vacated it. Lea's group of partisans, knowing the camp had been abandoned after the liberation of Paris, had journeyed to the camp to protect it from looting as a first step to creating a memorial. Love had taken root with not uncommon wartime urgency. Paul and Lea now were living in Shelby, and Paul occasionally still marveled at how chance had brought them together. Their plan was to spend the next Christmas – 1948 – with Lea's parents in Ribeauville in their 440-year-old house, built to last with stone walls and thick floor and ceiling beams.

As Jack sat reflecting on his Army service in Europe, his thoughts turned to Thaddeus Metz. Jack smiled when he thought of the care package his mom and dad had sent to Thaddeus and his fellow cow pen soldiers in December of 1944. He knew the package had arrived because subsequently his parents had received a thank you letter written by Thaddeus and signed by all the cow pen soldiers. Earlier in a letter to Anthony and Virginia, Jack had suggested filling the package with canned meats and tuna fish, crackers, cookies and cigars. He also had asked Anthony and Virginia to include some cash that the cow pen soldiers could use to buy liquor to sip while eating and smoking.

Is Thaddeus still alive? Jack wondered. If you are, where are you? Poland? That could be a very dangerous place for a former Polish officer. Jack had read of the Katyn Forest massacre, and Stalin's purges were a matter of record. If you are alive, Thaddeus, I wonder how you are spending Christmas. And if you are alive, it would be nice to cross paths with you again, my friend. The Polish lancer and the desert priest. An unlikely pairing but we made a good team, didn't we?

"I think it's time for a toast or two," Dean announced. "Everyone have some bubbly? Good." Everyone stood. "I would like to go first." The room quieted, except for the twins and the windup motorcycle. Dean elevated his fluted champagne glass and the others did likewise. "Here's to a wonderful family. I am so happy to be part of it."

"Here, here" came the chorus.

"Jack," Dean asked after sipping his champagne, "would you please do the next one?"

"Sure." Jack's left thumb and forefinger rubbed his chin. Then he raised his glass and spoke slowly. "To all of us here tonight, may we be grateful for God's blessings. And may we not forget our friends made during the war, those who survived, those who perished and those whose fates are unknown. May we always remember the sacrifices made by numerous individuals to preserve precious freedoms for millions of others. They deserve our lasting gratitude."

This time, thickened throats and misting eyes reduced the chorus of "here here's" to gentle murmuring.

CHAPTER 42

"Goosebumps are forming on my goosebumps." Cadet Kendall Thorne wasn't seeing any humor in his shivering dilemma. Instead, his teeth were chattering behind a contorted face and bluish lips.

Early January 1948 had brought colder than normal temperatures to southern England where the Gulf Stream tends to keep winters milder than in northern Europe. On this night heavy layers of clouds were blocking any illumination from stars or the moon, and a thin dusting of snow covered the Royal Military Academy campus.

Michael Cornelius removed his bathrobe, rolled it up and laid it on the ground next to Kendall's. Both men, still not 20, were naked and standing beside Wish Stream.

"The snow feels good under our feet, don't you think?" Michael managed to smile through quivering lips.

"You can still feel your toes? Tell me again, Cadet Cornelius, why are we doing this?"

"It's invigorating."

"You could call it that. Or you could call it bloody bonkers. What if we're caught? We could be drummed out of here."

"We won't be. Do you seriously expect anyone else to be out here at this time of night? On a night like this?"

"Precisely. Why did I let you talk me into this insane stunt?"

"Because I am your closest friend, and you know you can trust me in all matters large or small."

K had folded his arms across his chest and pressed his legs together tightly. "Tonight, my friend, you are testing that trust to the limit." Michael managed a half-frozen chuckle. "Pray tell, what exactly is behind this madness?"

"I've been in Wish Stream only twice before," Michael replied.

"Right. As part of the confidence course and the affair with Elton Leighton and the senior cadets."

"Right. During the holidays in London I did some thinking."

"When you weren't courting that Crispin girl."

"We weren't together every minute."

"You certainly didn't have much time for me, your so-called closest friend."

Michael ignored K's jibe. "Anyway, it occurred to me that I should revisit Wish Stream. Make a genuine wish. Doing it at the beginning of a new year seemed appropriate timing." He rubbed his palms vigorously against his shoulders and chest. "I confess I didn't expect this cold snap."

"Why naked?"

"Fresh beginning, as it were. Purge the bad, make way for the good. And I thought, why keep this re-birthing ceremony to myself?"

"Well, of course, you never were the selfish sort." K's sarcasm was as cold as his now pinkish skin.

"You've noticed," Michael replied impishly. "Why, if word gets around campus, we might begin a new Sandhurst tradition."

"The Cornelius re-birthing. So you decided to share this eponymous moment, as it were, with your dearest friend. And perhaps your most pliant."

"Spot on, old chap."

"How much time will be required to start this dubious new tradition?"

"Just long enough to cleanse your mind of past transgressions and impure thoughts."

"Gawd, an all-night immersion."

Michael mumbled another half-frozen chuckle. "Then we'd better not delay." He unfolded his arms, sucked in a breath of frigid air, stepped to the stream's steep bank and leaped, drawing up his legs and clutching his knees. A second splash quickly followed his.

"Oh my freezing lord" were K's first words as he stood dripping.

Michael, standing a few feet to his left, reached down, cupped his hands, scooped up water and splashed it against his face. "Bracing."

"My balls," Kendall said in wonderment, "I think they've shrunk to the size of peas. Can't feel a thing." He then reached down with both hands and sent a spray of water in Michael's direction.

Michael retaliated and both cadets began laughing through gritted teeth. Then Michael lunged toward K, grasped him at the shoulders, pulled hard and both men went down. Moments later they struggled to their feet, K spitting water.

"I think we've met all requirements," Michael said.

"Agreed. My memory has been erased. I can't remember a single sin."

"Onward to a guilt-free future," Michael laughed as he went high-stepping toward the bank. Out of the water both men quickly unrolled their robes, pulled them on and went running across the snow-covered expanse of lawn toward Victory College and their rooms in Normandy and Alamein companies. "And," Michael said to his friend, "may it never again be as cold or as dark as this night."

✝✝✝

The next morning in Moscow was typically arctic. The temperature was 16 degrees below zero Fahrenheit, and more than a dozen inches of new snow gave the city a certain shapelessness. Winters arrive early in Russia, quickly tighten their grip and often resist letting loose until well after spring's calendar arrival.

Inside the Kremlin the temperature was warmer but the political climate was decidedly chilly. "There are more machinations in New York. The United Nations is urging us again to permit a free election in North Korea," Molotov said to Joseph Stalin in his birch-paneled office. "I am concerned. If we keep delaying, South Korea will hold its own elections, and Rhee will use that as a pretext for claiming sovereignty over all of Korea."

Stalin struck a match and lit his briar pipe. He puffed thoughtfully. "How strong do you see the United Nations?"

"No stronger than the United States," Molotov replied derisively. "The UN is an organizational puppy. It will follow the lead of its master – the U.S."

"I agree," said Stalin. "And I don't think the U.S. is ready to pick a fight with us."

"I concur."

"We will move now," said Stalin. "Forget elections. We will announce that Kim Il Sung is now premier of North Korea. The provisional government will become his. Do you think he is strong enough to rule permanently?"

"Yes. With adequate backing."

Stalin puffed again, gray smoke swirling toward the high ceiling. "I agree. He has combat experience. He knows what it is like to sacrifice, to win, to keep control. He already has begun forming an army – with our assistance. He is tough-minded and I think will be as cruel as situations demand."

"And," Molotov added with rising enthusiasm, "he is still willing to toe our line. Did you know he is now wearing the uniform of a Russian major?"

"He's smart," Stalin observed. "He knows he'll have no other choice. The world will see him as a dictator, but in reality he will be our dictator."

† † †

In Warsaw winter had struck with a fury equal to the blow it had delivered in Moscow. And the political climate was just as chilly.

Dominik Szota was sitting comfortably in his office in the gray building on narrow Podwale Street, which curved like a leather belt around the waist of Old Town from northeast to southwest and was just three short blocks from the rynek or central plaza. Szota saw himself as ideally suited to his new job. It required a wintry personality. Before the war he had served as a detective in the city's police department. Tall and bald he had eaten too much rich food and drunk too much Polish beer. His jowls hung heavy and his belly forced his wide black belt downward. He wore glasses with steel rims that matched the color of his neatly trimmed mustache.

During the Nazi occupation his job remained essentially unchanged. Except instead of investigating crimes against people and property, he was searching out members of Poland's Home Army and reporting suspects to the Gestapo. He knew if caught by the Home Army, his death would follow swiftly. Still, Szota hadn't much troubled himself with thoughts of betrayal. His objective was to preserve his quality of life and that of his family. Among other things, that meant continuing to eat and drink well when many other Poles were starving.

Now in January 1948 he was working under the aegis of the Polish puppet government. Szota's mission was to recruit snoops – people willing, for political pats on the head preferably, for a price if necessary, to tattle on fellow Poles. That their reports could lead to arrest, incarceration, torture and possibly execution deprived him of no sleep.

When initiating contact with potential snoops, Szota often was rebuffed. He wasn't surprised or distressed. Most Poles were chafing, resenting their Soviet overlords and their weak-kneed, greedy Polish minions. But many of them will eventually agree to cooperate, Szota told himself confidently. I'll make sure to feed the rumor mill with names of snoops. It won't matter if they've actually agreed to spy on their neighbors and friends and co-workers. As word spreads, more and more of my countrymen will agree to snoop and tattle. Not all but enough. Enough to safeguard control. They will come to regard it as a matter of self-preservation if not duty. Tell on my neighbors before they tell on me – even if there is nothing of substance to tell. Paranoia, Szota's police experience told him, was a powerful motivator. Blame someone else before they can point at me. I'm aiming to recruit a good mix. Everyday people. Shopkeepers, housewives, students, government workers. People with grudges, with scores to settle. Or just a primitive streak of meanness.

✝✝✝

"It's a shame," Thaddeus was saying to a group of seven of his English students after class. They were standing in front of the off-white classroom building, fronted by denuded trees standing firm against icy blasts from the north and west. Snow blanketed the university grounds and each word spoken was accompanied by crystallized breath. "Everywhere the communists are in control. Freedoms are becoming as extinct as dinosaurs. Korea, China, Hungary, Czechoslovakia, Poland. What is more precious than freedoms?"

"Our lives," said Felix Glemp. "We saw that under the Nazis."

"How much are lives worth without freedoms?" Thaddeus asked evenly. "How many of our fellow Poles have willingly sacrificed their lives to fight for freedoms?" A pause. "How many of us would risk our lives for a free Poland?"

"I still say we are free," Felix responded with a hint of agitation. "We are free of Nazi oppression. We are free to come here to university. We are free from hunger."

"All of us?" Thaddeus asked.

"Well, most of us," Felix conceded grudgingly.

"Those are important freedoms," Thaddeus replied calmly, not wanting to sound patronizing. "But do we have freedom to elect our government? A democratic government? Are we free to criticize our government without fear of reprisal? Are we free to travel outside Poland – wherever and whenever we choose? I think we are all Catholics. Correct?" Heads nodded. "Are we free to worship? The Nazis killed many of our priests. The Soviets are persecuting them. Why? They fear them. They see them as threats to controlling the rest of us. They see the clergy as engines of freedom."

"You are looking only at the dark side," said Felix, shivering, crossed arms holding books against his chest and hands tucked in his armpits.

Thaddeus pursed his lips before replying. "The Nazis were darkness personified. Their willingness to inflict and perpetuate evil knew no bounds. Their defeat meant the return of light. But I see that light dimming under Soviet control and darkness again descending on Poland. And when it falls, I fear that new light will be a long time returning."

CHAPTER 43

"Our troops fought to free Europe from Hitler and they succeeded. But as you know, not without considerable sacrifice."

Bishop Wilhelm Metzger was sitting at his modest desk in his spartan office next to the cathedral. He nodded, wondering where this conversational thread was heading. Bishop Metzger, a native of Toledo, Ohio, had been presiding over the sprawling Tucson Diocese when newly ordained Father Jack Brecker arrived in the summer of 1942 from the Vatican-administered Josephinum Seminary in Worthington, Ohio. When the Holy See dispatched Jack to Arizona, it still was officially designated as mission territory. Jack's job had been dual: build parishes and minister to the Indians.

The two men had grown close to each other, and Bishop Metzger had willingly released Jack from his parish and mission responsibilities to volunteer for the Army's Chaplains Corps.

"Go on," said the Bishop.

"When Hitler invaded Poland," Jack continued, "you'll recall that Britain and France honored a pact they had with Poland and declared war on Germany right away."

"Yes, go on," said the Bishop, curious and growing amused. "There's more. I know you well enough to know that, Father Brecker."

"Yes, well, did you hear about Winston Churchill's speech in Fulton, Missouri? The one where he talked about Russia lowering an iron curtain between eastern and western Europe?"

"I did. Unsettling."

"Exactly. We – our troops – and our allies didn't sacrifice to free Europe from Hitler only to see it enslaved by Stalin."

"Agreed. But did you expect America and its allies to go to war against Russia?"

"No." Jack sighed audibly. "We were warred out. Stalin isn't sending millions of Jews to gas chambers and murdering Polish priests. There aren't that many left – Jews or priests. But we've heard about his purges. And the good Lord knows he's repressing religion. It's not safe for a priest to say Mass anywhere behind the Iron Curtain. They can be arrested with impunity. Tortured. The church is being forced to go underground."

"A tragedy. Made more so by all the aid the West – the U.S. – gave Stalin to save Russia from Hitler."

"My Polish friend – Thaddeus Metz – was right. You can't trust Stalin. No more than anyone could trust Hitler."

"Where is this going, Jack?"

"I've been studying Polish."

Bishop Metzger's eyes widened in surprise. "Where? Who with? Why?"

Jack relaxed and grinned. "I asked Walt Hunter – my friend the airborne captain – if his dad might be able to find someone who could help me learn Polish. I thought, with his business connections, he might be able to help."

"And he did."

"Mr. Hunter is one determined and resourceful man," Jack said admiringly.

"He didn't get to be a mine owner without certain abilities," the bishop observed. "And you know firsthand his generosity." Bishop Metzger was alluding to Elgin Hunter's having given Jack his plane after he returned from Europe to help him more easily serve his congregants and having helped fund the Indians' new chapel at Charco.

"Right. Well, he went and hired a new manager who is fluent in Polish."

"Where on earth did he find him?" The bishop made no effort to mask his astonishment. "How did he find him?"

"Just as I suspected he might. Through his network of contacts. Actually he located a poorly paid engineering professor at Roosevelt University in Chicago and made him an offer he couldn't refuse."

"I can imagine," Bishop Metzger said wryly. "Enough money to lure him from the shimmering shore of Lake Michigan to the barren vista of a strip copper mine. What is your intent, Jack? If I know you at all, this is more than a purely academic pursuit."

"I'd like to see if Thaddeus Metz and the other cow pen soldiers survived the war. If they did, I'd like to see how they are doing under the communist regime."

"You obviously feel very strongly about this."

"Very."

"Father Brecker, you are one of the most level-headed priests – men – I know. You said yourself how unsafe it is for priests in Eastern Europe. How do you propose to find them? If I should grant you permission to try."

"I would need another leave."

"Yes, well." Bishop Metzger cleared his throat. "The Vatican didn't overly question my judgment when I granted you leave to become an army chaplain. But it doesn't seem likely that the communist government would grant an entry visa to an American Catholic priest. They would see that as an invitation to upsetting their precious order."

"No doubt," Jack agreed. "But they probably would grant one to an embassy official's new aide." Jack's smile hinted at conspiracy.

"Father Brecker, whatever you say next is not going to surprise me. Now, go ahead and satisfy my curiosity."

"A woman from Shelby is married to a man whose dad is a congressman." Jack was alluding to Theresa Hassler and her father-in-law, Raymond Morton. "I talked with Theresa and her husband Dean at Christmas. They said – assured me actually – that Congressman Morton would be happy to pull strings at the State Department. He did. My diplomatic passport needn't include the word 'Reverend.'"

"A diplomatic passport." The bishop slowly sighed. "And your diplomatic role?"

"The embassy in Warsaw could use an administrative aide fluent in Polish."

"I see," the bishop said, eyes closed in thought. Methodically he began tapping a pencil on his desk. "I must tell you I have some other plans in mind for you."

"Oh?"

"A conference in Rome is coming up soon for mission priests. From all over the world. Africa, Latin America, Asia, here. It will last two weeks. The first week would be the actual conference. The second would concentrate on advanced theological studies. I thought you would find this an appealing opportunity. Theologically and socially, getting to know priests working elsewhere."

"It is," Jack said sincerely. "I've wanted to see Rome ever since I arrived at the Josephinum from St. Joseph's Seminary. I am flattered that you would recommend me."

"You are welcome. You also are qualified and deserving, and being a graduate of a pontifical seminary, I had a feeling that the Vatican would look favorably on my recommendation."

Jack's left thumb and forefinger tugged at his ear. "Going to the conference would crimp my plans," Jack said contemplatively. "But the delay doesn't ruin them. If you approve them. When is the conference?"

"A few months from now. In June. But you know, going to that conference could actually make getting to Poland a little easier on you and your wallet."

"How's that?"

"Well, if you go to Rome wearing your collar, your expenses will be covered, and you'll be a lot closer to Poland than here in Arizona."

"You're granting my leave?"

The bishop smiled. "By agreeing to go to the conference and going to Poland from there, you will have four more months to polish your Polish – excuse the play on words."

CHAPTER 44

Standing in the butcher and cutlery shop on the busy main street in Munsan, Park Min was reading a letter from his mother and frowning.

Choi Chun Kuen was watching with concern while pausing from sharpening a carving knife.

When Min finished reading, his hands fell to his sides. His head shook forlornly.

"What is it?" Mr. Choi asked with deep concern. In the months that Min had been living with the Chois and working with them in the shop, Mr. and Mrs. Choi had developed warm, parental feelings for their young friend.

"My brother. He has been conscripted by the North Korean Army. Mother fears there could be another war. She admits there is no evidence, just her intuition. She delayed telling me but is telling me now so I don't return on my own and be conscripted. She is urging me to stay here until the situation becomes clearer. If it is all right with you and your wife." A pause. "Here," said Min, handing the letter to Mr. Choi, "you can read it yourself."

Mr. Choi did so and then said, "Your mother is wise. It is safer here. We want you to remain with us."

"I'm worried about my brother. He can handle military training. I have no doubt about that. He is strong. But if there is a war…But with whom? Japan is defeated. Russia and America each control half of Korea." Then the epiphany. "A civil war. North against South. That's the war Mother is worried about."

"A civil war?" Mr. Choi said.

"Yes. If Kim Il Sung or Syngman Rhee wants a united Korea badly enough, one might begin shooting at the other. My brother could be caught up in that."

"We always have been one nation," said Mr. Choi. "It would be too tragic if we are forced to fight each other. I don't think I could be part of that."

Min took the letter back from Mr. Choi and read it again. He shook his head. "Mother is wise. But I am feeling a need to return to Kaesong. To be with my parents. Perhaps to see Han. And there is my girl friend. It's been so long since I've seen Kyong. I really miss her. If there is war, she…" Min's words trailed off in a welter of worry.

"But if you go back you will be conscripted," Mr. Choi said. "That cannot help. It will cause greater worry for your parents." A pause. "You have too much to worry about. You need to clear your mind," Mr. Choi said kindly. "Leave the shop. Take a long walk. Or better yet, take Sejong for a ride. A long one."

✝✝✝

Half an hour later Min was saddling Sejong in a nearby stable. Sunbeams were slanting in through the open doorway and gaps and cracks in the unpainted siding. The meadows and hills around Munsan were greening with the onset of spring, with the earliest wildflowers straining to open.

With athletic grace Min inserted his left foot in a stirrup, swung onto the saddle and patted Sejong's neck. He liked the feel of the aged leather beneath him. "Life has become very complicated." The horse tossed its head up and stepped spiritedly from the stable onto the dirt road. "I can't find any easy answers. None at all. Maybe there aren't any. What do you think, Sejong? Should I stop looking for them?"

Min turned Sejong south and the horse, eager for exercise, began cantering from town into the countryside. "No matter what choice I make, there will be consequences. Unavoidable ones. Bad ones." He sighed. "Well, Sejong, if I am going to clear my mind, we need to move a little faster. To feel the wind in my face. Ready?"

Simultaneously Min tapped Sejong's brown flanks with his heels, flicked the reins and said, "Let's go."

Within moments horse and rider were flying down the road, the wind whipping Sejong's brown mane and Min's black hair.

✝✝✝

The plane was flying at 5,000 feet, and the rush of the wind and the drone of the engine were pleasantly hypnotic. Raymond Morton was at the controls, his son Dean in the adjoining seat. They had departed National Airport, just across the Potomac River from Washington, D.C., at 9 a.m. eastern time, 8 a.m. central. They were bound for their hometown of Belvidere.

"Jane won't have much to worry about today," Raymond smiled. "Nor Theresa. Smooth sailing ahead. That was the forecast."

Raymond and Dean already had soared over Maryland and Pennsylvania's Allegheny Mountains and were nearing the eastern end of Lake Erie. "Not a cloud to be seen."

"Perfect flying weather, Dad."

✝✝✝

Flawless flying weather notwithstanding, Jane and Theresa Hassler Morton felt nagging twinges of anxiety whenever either of their husbands went wheels up. Jane's worries resulted from a decades-long fear of flying. She realized it was a phobia with no rational explanation, but it was plenty real. She went aloft only when necessary, and she knew the coming color of her knuckles as her hands would grasp seat arms like a pair of vise grips.

Theresa's worries were born of experience and were more sharply and deeply etched. She would never forget two of Hal Walker's flights – the

207

one in which he had to use his sidearm to shoot off the latch that released his canopy and enabled him to parachute before crashing – and the final one in which he was last seen dueling German fighters over the English countryside and speeding and swerving out over the English Channel on September 7, 1940. Hal and Theresa had been intending to marry.

And then there was her first love, Jack Brecker. His passion for flying had taken root during his first practice jump with the 82nd Airborne. Theresa no longer thought of Jack daily. But when Dean took to the skies, images of Jack at the controls of his yellow and blue-trimmed Luscombe two-seater sometimes popped into her mind. She would visualize him flying over Arizona's unforgiving mountains and deserts or piloting his way cross-country to visit family in Shelby. Occasionally while Theresa slept, those images invaded her dreams. More than once the dreams transformed into nightmarish visions of Jack's plane plummeting to earth.

Theresa had flown with Hal and Jack, once each, and she had gloried in both experiences. But they counted for little in the way of reassurances whenever Dean was in the air.

† † †

Jack was in the air. It was 7 a.m. in Arizona, and he had as his passenger the elder.

"This is very special," the elder said to Jack. "I never again thought I would see God's scar." The Indian was referring to Grand Canyon and his first aerial view of the wondrous slash in the earth since April 1946. That was soon after Jack had earned his pilot's license following his return from Europe. During that 1946 flight the elder had dubbed the magnificent canyon God's scar.

"You know I'm going to Rome and then to Poland to look for my friend."

"The Polish horseman."

"Right."

"It would be nice to ride with him sometime."

"Wouldn't that be something? An Indian riding across the Polish steppes with a former lancer. Your people would still be talking about it in the next century."

"I could tell his people that great spirits lifted me and carried me across the wide sea to their land."

"Some might be tempted to believe you."

Jack and the elder chuckled.

"Ah," sighed the elder, "look at those colors down there. More than in any rainbow."

"I wanted to see the canyon again from up here and not alone. I wanted to share the view with someone, and I couldn't think of anyone who would appreciate it more than you. Someone with a special place in his heart for this beautiful land."

The elder smiled. "I think you now have that same kind of feeling." As always, his words were spoken unhurriedly with unforced precision. "You, the desert priest. This desert, these mountains, that canyon. I believe they now mean as much to you as my people. The people you serve so well." The elder felt sudden tightening in his chest and squeezed shut his eyes in concentration. He was determined not to grimace or gasp. Not now. Not while flying with his friend above God's scar.

"Dean, look at that."

A well-spring of alarm was beginning to raise the pitch of Raymond's voice. "To the northwest. It's coming fast."

Dean looked up from congressional hearing notes he was studying and saw the fast-approaching storm's leading edge. "Mother Nature looks peeved."

The storm was black and roiling, and it was being pierced by bolts of lightning that were stabbing the lake's churning waters.

"I take it that wasn't in the forecast," Dean said.

"Too often bad stuff isn't," Raymond complained gruffly. "I've been saying for as long as I've been flying that we need more sophisticated weather forecasting technology."

"It's so peaceful up here," said the elder, the tightening in his chest having abated. "Even with the engine. A man can forget his earthly problems."

"Does tend to free up the mind," Jack replied. "I do some of my best thinking up here." He turned to the elder and grinned. "This is where some of my best sermons take shape. If I told my congregation that, they might regard my homilies as a trifle on the airy side."

The elder chuckled lowly. "Your voice and your mind. They are solid as the earth beneath our feet."

Jack dipped the plane and began descending lower over the canyon. He could feel a strong updraft trying to slow the descent.

††††

"It's almost on top of us. Do you think we can swing south and outrun it?" Dean asked. The storm was blowing southeast like a steam-billowing runaway locomotive.

"We're gonna try."

Raymond turned the wheel to the left and the little plane began responding. Dean felt a twinge in his chest and cringed. His dad didn't notice his pained expression, the occasional result of the wound Dean had suffered on Sicily's beach.

††††

Theresa was walking through the hallway leading to their home's bedrooms and bathroom when her eyes caught the small cross Jack Brecker had given her in 1946 in Cleveland on the day he confirmed he was remaining in the priesthood. His choice hadn't surprised Theresa, but it pained her as acutely as the shrapnel that had sliced open her hip near Bastogne. Jack, standing alongside the lagoon in front of Cleveland's Museum of Art, had removed the cross from a small bag and handed it to Theresa. The cross was made from a brass shell casing. Polish airborne troops had given the cross to Jack as a token of gratitude after he had said Easter Mass for them in 1944. Both the horizontal and vertical beams measured about six inches. On the horizontal the Poles had etched Fr. Brecker and on the vertical Polska. Knowing the cross' origin, Theresa had been touched deeply when Jack presented it to her.

This morning she reached up and removed the cross from the small nail holding it in place. In Marilyn's bedroom Theresa heard her daughter waking and whining and said a quick silent prayer for Dean's deliverance.

Blackness was shrouding the small aircraft. It began bouncing and shaking erratically in air so turbulent that Dean and Raymond could have been excused for thinking they somehow had been transferred to the inside of an electric clothes dryer. Then the plane shuddered violently as a blinding white flash flooded its interior.

"Lightning," Raymond muttered, hands struggling to control the bucking, complaining craft. "This isn't good." His armpits were leaking sweat.

"You're doing fine." Dean, also beginning to sweat, knew it was imperative to keep calm.

Another white flash exploded just outside the plane, close enough for it to begin faltering.

"Damn," muttered Raymond.

Dean looked at the altimeter. The plane was starting to lose altitude. "Controls shot?"

"I think so." A pause. "Hold on. We're going down. Jesus." Raymond continued struggling, refusing to give up. He pulled back hard, trying to elevate the plane's nose. "Maybe I can get her on a glide path." He grunted from the exertion. It was futile. Lake Erie's mean waters were where they shouldn't be – straight ahead.

Dean grabbed the leather-bound flight log and a pen. He opened the log and quickly scribbled: *Theresa, I love you with all my heart. The kiss of life meant everything. Dean.* His racing mind was again recalling the kiss his wife had given him in Sicily. He slammed shut the logbook and reached over to pat his dad on the shoulder. "It's okay."

That evening in Ajo, Jack was in his rectory office, studying a globe and mulling his June trip to Italy and Poland. His right forefinger was poised over Warsaw. He was half-listening to a radio newscaster: "A congressman and his son were killed today when their light plane crashed into Lake Erie during a storm." Jack paused to listen. He offered a simple, silent prayer: Lord, in your mercy, please grant those two men salvation. "Raymond Morton," the newscaster continued, "Republican from Illinois, was piloting the plane. His son Dean, a World War II veteran, worked in his father's district office in Rockford, Illinois. The two men were returning home from Washington, D.C."

"Oh, my Lord," Jack murmured. He turned away from the globe and began walking, wobbly-kneed, to his wood desk chair and plopped into it. "Those poor men, Lord, have mercy on them. Please. They were good men. Let them rest peacefully in your embrace for all eternity. And their wives and family, in your mercy-"

Jack's phone rang. He let it ring a second time. Then he picked up the heavy black receiver, sighed and shook his head to clear it. What now? he was thinking. "Father Jack Brecker speaking."

"Can you do the funerals, Jack?" The caller didn't have to identify herself. "It would mean so much...so much to me. You married us. And..."

† † †

After the burial family and friends gathered at the Mortons' home in Belvidere to share food and memories. As the afternoon wore on and guests began saying their goodbyes, Theresa asked Jack to step outside. They exited the house through the rear door and walked down three steps to the backyard. Theresa eyed a children's swing set that her in-laws had bought to entertain grandchildren. "Let's sit on those," Theresa said, pointing to the swings.

"I haven't sat on one of these since our playground days at St. Mary's," Jack smiled.

"Over twenty years ago," Theresa said wistfully. "We were just kids."

"Remember how high we used to swing? I liked going so high that the chains would go slack."

"You were the class daredevil."

"Maybe that's why I took to jumping out of planes." Jack winked. "Always the fool."

"Hardly. Do you remember that Saint Christopher medal I gave you back in 1932 when you were going off to seminary?"

"Remember?" Jack reached beneath his priestly collar and extracted the medal. "I still wear it."

"The same one?"

"I've never had it off."

"Maybe I should have bought them for Hal and Dean," she said somberly.

"Don't do that, Theresa," Jack cautioned, shaking his head. "Don't blame yourself. It's poisonous. I don't know if this medal has saved my life. But it has given me a sense of inner peace in dangerous situations. That's been it's real value."

"Thanks, Jack." She blinked back welling tears. "That helps. You're a true friend. Probably the best I've ever had."

"You can always count on me."

"I know."

"Hey!"

Theresa smiled questioningly. "Hey what?"

"Let's see how high we can go on these swings."

"Oh Jack."

"Come on. I'll bet Dean would think it's a good idea. It'll be good for a laugh or two, and I think we can use those."

"Maybe you're right." Theresa began walking the swing seat backward. Jack did likewise. She was already laughing. "Ready?"

CHAPTER 45

May 10, 1948

The United Nations had lost patience with Joseph Stalin. Member nations were exasperated by his repeatedly reneging on his promise to permit free elections in North Korea. Under UN auspices voting proceeded in South Korea, and its people elected a national assembly.

"It's good that our fellow countrymen in the south were allowed to vote and form their own government," Mrs. Park said pensively. "But I fear what it might mean for our sons."

"You still see war coming?" said Mr. Park.

213

"It seems unavoidable. I have no doubt that South Korea's parliament will elect Syngman Rhee president. He is ambitious and strong willed. His ego would probably fill our shop and those of our neighbors." Mr. Park chuckled lowly. "Kim Il Sung is much the same. Even if they haven't met and never do, they probably loathe each other. Certainly they don't trust each other. It's all so sad."

✝✝✝

Kyong was standing near the stable where Min and Han had kept Sejong before Min rode him to Munsan. Everyone knows how much I miss Min, she was reflecting. My parents. His. Sometimes the pain is so great it hits me like a brick. I know it's safer for him in Munsan, but that doesn't make the pain any less. And Munsan, it's not far. Only about 18 miles. Maybe I could walk there. See him. Stay with him. Mother and Father would never approve. They would say it's too dangerous. And staying with Min when we are not married...They would be mortified. Should I sneak away? No, that would humiliate them. They would lose much face. Oh, Min, I love you. I love you so much it hurts. Come back to me. Please. Soon.

✝✝✝

May 11, 1948

Tomasz Dolata turned to look back over his shoulder. He shook his head in amazement. He was driving the horse-drawn beer wagon into Warsaw. He now owned the horse and wagon, having purchased it from one of the farmers whose brew he bought and then sold in Warsaw. Tomasz also owned the following wagon, and its driver was Tomasz's first employee. A gentile, in need of work and food. The horse and wagon were proceeding slowly over a road so rough that Tomasz sometimes told people it was like driving over a washboard.

I can hardly believe I'm a successful businessman, Tomasz mused. It's no wonder I sometimes still pinch myself. Just to be sure I'm alive. A sonderkommando. Auschwitz. I thought I would draw my last breath there. Then in the cellar at the Franteks. Catholics. Marzena, how are you doing? Do you still think of me? Miss me? I miss you terribly. Your family too. They were so kind to me. A Jew.

214

The bumping of the beer-filled barrels against each other and the wagon's sides was a comforting sound. It signaled growing prosperity, increasing self-esteem and confidence. Me, a success in commerce. Tomasz shook his head dubiously. The son of a shop owner. Helping my father for a few zlotys a week. I hope he and mother are resting in peace. I think they would be proud of me. Their Jewish son successful because of the generosity of a gentile in a land of gentiles. There are so few of us Jews left in Poland. A few thousand, maybe. I think Mr. Frantek might have been right. Maybe I don't look so Jewish. Maybe if I looked more Jewish my customers wouldn't be so eager to buy. Maybe. But I do have a tasty product, and I sell it at a fair price. That is the key. Maybe my customers do see me as a Jew but overlook it because of my product and my price. I am making very good money. More than I ever imagined. And yes, Kaz, I am saving a fair portion for you. Just in case.

May 11, 1948

Slowly Marzena descended the stairway to the basement of the family's restaurant, Polska Kopernika. Her father Jacek had asked her to fetch two bottles of riesling. She sighed deeply. In the basement her eyes fell on the handsome chess set, its meticulously carved black and white pieces arrayed and waiting to be moved. She stepped to the small table and paused, hands at her sides. Then she reached out with her right hand and picked up the black king. Gently, she rotated the polished piece twice and studied it as never before. Tomasz, she spoke to the king, where are you? Warsaw? Or have you moved on? Left Poland? Are you all right? Did you find work? Do you know how often I think about you? Jew? Catholic? Why should it make such a difference? Is this what you want, God? Two people in love, pulled apart because they are accidents of birth. Because they both believe in you but worship you differently? Can this be your will?

These same questions had become part of a daily, silent recitation. Each day brought no answers, but each day the questions took on more weight. Marzena was feeling the burden of that weight, seemingly as heavy as a crushing millstone. Her chin drooped and her head shook forlornly. She firmed her grip on the king and caressed it with her thumb. You have been my king, Tomasz. I haven't met anyone like you. No one. Will I ever? Mama has been so patient with me. So loving. She must have talked to Father and Edward because they don't say anything. Not about Tomasz, not about men, not about my baby.

I just feel so sad. So tired. Every day. The days are so long, so dark – like night – and heavy. Everything seems so awfully heavy. Sometimes I just feel like I can't go on. Or want to. Her throat began constricting. I – There's no purpose.

Marzena sighed audibly. She put the king on the board, precisely into its square. She looked up at the ceiling and focused on a water pipe. She stared at it, thinking. Then she looked down at one of the chairs. It would be a sin. A mortal sin. The church says so. I would go to hell. For eternity. But can that be any worse than this?

✝✝✝

Minutes later Jacek was wondering why Marzena was taking so long. His customers were becoming impatient. His lips pursed and frowning, he walked to the top of the basement stairs and cupped his hands around his mouth. "Marzena," he called, loudly enough for her to hear but not so loudly as to antagonize customers. No reply. He called her name again. Still no reply.

Strange, Jacek thought. He began descending, his mind formulating a fatherly rebuke. Seconds later he reached the bottom of the stairs. "Oh, my God!" he gasped and went racing toward the dangling figure. With his left arm he reached for the overturned chair and righted it. With his right arm he gripped Marzena's legs around her thighs and lifted, just enough to put slack in the apron she had used as a rope and noose. Then he positioned the chair and, straining, managed to stand on it. He unknotted the apron-as-noose. Then holding her with both arms, he stepped down from the chair and lowered Marzena to the floor. "Please, God." With the thumb and fingers of his right hand on her left wrist, he was searching for the faintest of pulses and holding his breath.

✝✝✝

Illinois' governor wasted no time persuading the state legislature that there could be only one choice to complete Raymond's term: Jane Morton.

216

The day after the funeral, held jointly for Raymond and Dean with Jack Brecker officiating, the governor phoned Jane with his proposal to name her to succeed her late husband. "I just want you to know what we're thinking. I've checked with state legislative leaders and they wouldn't oppose your appointment. But take your time. Just let me know one way or another when you feel up to it."

"First of all, Governor, thank you," Jane replied. "This is very thoughtful of you." She also was thinking that with this gesture the governor was accumulating additional political capital. That probability didn't offend her. "I really don't need to think about it though. I know Raymond would want me to say yes. And so I will."

✝✝✝

Han was lying prone on the hard-packed ground. He squeezed off a shot. Then another. Both hit their mark – a piece of wood about 18 inches square and affixed to a wooden stake about 100 yards distant on higher ground.

"Good shooting, soldier." Captain Kwon was overseeing the firing range. "I wonder if your brother could shoot as well." Han had been in the army long enough to know that a reply was neither expected nor wise. "He's a coward. A shame for his parents. Afraid to return to the north and serve his country."

By now Han also had learned enough about military tactics to understand that virtually none of his training was geared to defense. Everything was structured toward learning to advance, to outflank and overrun enemy positions. War is coming, Han knew. I don't know how soon, but our training is too intense for mere garrison duty.

✝✝✝

Jacek, nearly consumed with fear, began carrying Marzena up from the basement, simultaneously calling, "Maria! Come here! Marzena is hurt badly. She is barely breathing."

As he reached the top of the stairs, two customers stood and one, gesturing toward their table, said, "Put her here." He and his companion quickly cleared the table, shifting wine glasses and salt and pepper shakers to an adjoining table.

One look at her husband and daughter and Maria, exiting the kitchen, almost fainted. In another moment, feeling nauseous, she was hovering over her supine daughter. "What's wrong?"

Jacek, eyes focused on Marzena but aware of staring customers, replied, "An accident."

Marzena coughed twice – small coughs – and worked to clear her throat. Color was returning to her face.

"Are you all right, dear?" Maria murmured. She could see the strangulation mark on her daughter's neck.

Again Marzena cleared her throat. "I think so." She tried to sit up on the table and Jacek assisted.

"Let's get her upstairs," he said and helped Marzena off the tabletop.

✝✝✝

"I'm so sorry. I didn't mean to frighten you." Marzena now was resting on a settee between her parents. "Daniel-"

"Your baby is fine. Asleep."

"I can't believe…"

"There, there," Maria said, comforting her daughter with gentle pats on her left shoulder. "You are alive. That is all that matters."

"I – I just miss him so much. He has been gone so long. He doesn't even know about Daniel. I couldn't-"

"You don't have to explain," Maria murmured.

"I think I need to."

CHAPTER 46

June 24, 1948

"Is everything ready?" Joseph Stalin asked Vyacheslav Molotov, his long-time foreign minister. Stalin, feeling edgy, ran his right forefinger around inside the tight-fitting collar of his military tunic.

"Yes, Comrade Leader," Molotov replied confidently. "All preparations are in order. Everyone is waiting for your final command."

"They have it." Stalin tapped ashes from his pipe into a large brown ceramic tray. Then he stepped to a tall window and looked down at the sun-splashed pavement. Without looking back at Molotov, he said, "Tell everyone to move now."

"Yes, Comrade Leader."

Within minutes the Soviet Union's surprise blockade of Berlin would be underway. Soviet soldiers would begin closing off rail, highway and water routes that linked West Germany to East Germany where Berlin was situated deep within Soviet-controlled territory.

Stalin's purpose was clear: force United States, British and French troops to abandon their respective occupation sectors in Berlin. Force all Berliners to accept communism and communist control.

Stalin turned away from the window and peered unblinkingly into Molotov's eyes. "Do you still stand by your estimate on how long West Berlin food supplies will last?"

"Yes, Comrade Leader. Within a few weeks the people will be out of food. They will pressure the U.S., Britain and France to pull out."

Stalin nodded. "Good." A pause. "For the last one hundred and fifty years, the West has been attacking Mother Russia," Stalin reflected while returning to his desk. "First it was Napoleon. Then Germany in the Great War. Then Hitler. Enough!" His right fist slammed his leather desk pad. "The only way to prevent another invasion is to control Poland – we are well on our way – and Germany. And the only way to stop those barbarian Huns is to keep them from rebuilding their economy and depriving them of their traditional capital."

Following World War II – or the Great Patriotic War as Moscow termed it – the Soviets had seized 85 percent of Germany's industrial equipment that had survived the war's destruction and transported it to Russia. Stalin called the seizure reparations for damage Germany had inflicted on Russia's industrial capacity. But western leaders, including President Truman, saw it for what it fundamentally was: a prophylactic for warding off a German rearmament.

"The blockade is a bold move, Comrade. It is worthy of your unsurpassed leadership."

Stalin recognized sycophancy but didn't forbid or discourage it. Reason: he didn't want anyone in his inner circle, including those who worked most closely with him, to feel comfortable. What was unsurpassed was his paranoia. "Too bold for Truman to retaliate?"

Molotov already had counseled Stalin that he fully expected a strong verbal rebuke from the United States, Britain and France but no military retaliation. But he sensed that the boss, even as he was issuing his final command to launch the blockade, wanted a final reassurance. Molotov felt confident providing it. "Yes, Comrade Leader, Truman will bluster but he will dither. So will Atlee and DeGaulle, although we might expect a display of some of his Gallic thunder." Stalin chuckled lowly. "Neither has the stomach to go to war again. West Berlin will soon be ours, and its people will come to heel."

"The United Nations?"

"As I've said before, the UN is no stronger, no bolder, than the United States."

✝✝✝

General Lucius Clay, commander of the U.S. occupation zone in Germany, responded speedily. As soon as he was advised of the blockade, he drafted a proposal and convened a meeting. "President Truman will probably find my proposal too bold for his liking," Clay told his staff. "But it just might force him to consider a strong response of some kind. And fast."

"What do you have in mind, General?" asked an aide.

"We'll form up a large armored column. Start putting it together right after this meeting. Load it with food and medical supplies. We'll drive it right down the autobahn from West Germany across East Germany to Berlin. I'll characterize the column as a peaceful one. One that we have a moral right to use to preserve the freedom of West Berliners and feed their families."

"And," asked the aide, "if the Soviets attack the column?"

"My proposal includes a request for authorization to fight back."

"How soon do you plan to advance this proposal?"

"How fast is our fastest typist?"

✝✝✝

Incredibly, within 30 minutes President Truman was handed a cable with Clay's proposal. He appeared to waffle. His initial reply: "It is too risky to engage in this due to the consequence of war."

220

The timidity of Truman's reply to Clay's proposal came as no surprise to Molotov or Stalin. They were exultant with this confirmation of their assessment. What would genuinely surprise them happened within the next few hours. Truman began entertaining second thoughts. He reconsidered the situation and resolved to defeat the blockade. Moreover, he intended to be creative in doing so. Said Truman to an aide: "Tell Clay to confer with LeMay about the feasibility of an airlift. Cable him now," Truman said, jaws firmly set. "We'll show Uncle Joe a thing or two about American ingenuity. Not to mention Missouri backbone."

Curtis LeMay was commanding general of United States air forces in Europe. Before June 24 ended LeMay appointed Brigadier General Joseph Smith as task force commander of an airlift.

✝✝✝

"An airlift!" Stalin sputtered. "What foolishness is that?"

Molotov gulped before replying. "They must be recalling how an airlift was used to supply Chinese troops during the Great Patriotic War. They called it 'flying the hump.' Their planes ferried supplies over the Himalayas."

"That worked, didn't it?" Stalin asked accusingly.

"Yes and no. They kept Chinese troops supplied, but the Allies lost many planes and men."

"Well," Stalin said acidly, "there are no Himalayas between West Germany and West Berlin. And we can't start shooting down American planes or even that puny Truman would respond with force. Perhaps order more atomic bombs. We cannot risk that."

"No, Comrade Leader."

"So," Stalin challenged Molotov, "I think you have miscalculated."

Molotov felt sweat breaking out and running down from his armpits. Though he had long served the boss well, he knew that longevity was no protection against Stalin's killer impulses. He could easily imagine Stalin forcing him to sign his own death warrant. His entire family and circle of friends could be at risk.

"Yes. Clearly. And I am abjectly sorry."

"Do you care to hazard an estimate on how successful this airlift might be?"

Molotov, forcing another swallow, was struggling to maintain his composure. "There are more than two million people in West Berlin. How can the Americans possibly fly in enough food and supplies? Where would they get the planes? They will try but their effort will prove too feeble."

† † †

June 26

In the morning 32 C-47 cargo planes lifted off from West Germany. They were hauling 80 tons of cargo – flour, milk and medicine. Truman, Clay, LeMay and Smith expected the airlift would cause Stalin to end the blockade within three weeks. They were wrong. Smith dubbed the airlift "Operation Vittles" because, he said, "We're hauling grub."

† † †

June 28

Britain joined the airlift. Within 90 days so did the French – after hurriedly building a new airbase in their sector which eventually would become Berlin's main international airport.

† † †

June 29

"Can anybody on earth now doubt Stalin's intention? He clearly has designs on empire," Thaddeus observed with pained frustration, "and one that will long outlast Hitler's. Stalin's blockade of West Berlin confirms my worst fears. Free elections and freedom for Poland is but a sad wish. An evaporated dream."

"Still," said Danuta Ostrowski, trying to placate her upstairs neighbor, "we remain free of the murderous Nazis. We have Stalin to thank for that. We must remember that."

Mrs. Ostrowski was seated with Thaddeus and Bernadeta around their small table, dining together. Since Mrs. Ostrowski had assisted Bernadeta with the stillbirth, she had taken to hosting Mrs. Ostrowski at supper once weekly. She enjoyed the older woman's company.

Thaddeus understood Mrs. Ostrowski's thoughts and feelings and sympathized. Many Poles shared her sentiments. But many others, like

Thaddeus, wanted freedom from all oppression. He replied gently. "We Poles will never forget Hitler's villainy. It is an indelible blot on humanity. But I yearn for a different Poland. One where on Sunday mornings I can get up and go to Mass in our neighborhood church. One where I can shake hands with the priest on the church steps. Without fear. I yearn for a Poland where I can fill out a ballot and drop it in a ballot box and know that it will be counted – and count for something in Poland's best interest. Is that too much to wish for?"

"For now," Mrs. Ostrowski said softly, "I am afraid so. I think it wise to accept our current situation and make the best of it."

Despite the gentleness with which their words were being spoken, Bernadeta sensed underlying tension. She valued dearly Mrs. Ostrowski's friendship, but she also shared Thaddeus' thinking. Like her husband she had risked and lost much in fighting to win her nation's liberation from Nazism. Now it was communism that was strangling precious freedoms. She refrained from speaking any words that might add to the tension. "Let me get the cake and pour more tea."

✝✝✝

June 30

"You are under arrest. Do not resist. Come with us."

Dominik Szota and two uniformed officers were confronting Thaddeus Metz on the tree-shaded walkway in front of his classroom building. Classes had recessed for the summer, and Thaddeus had strolled for 30 minutes from his apartment on Mostowa Street to the university to clean his classroom and clear out his desk. He was carrying a large cloth bag with his personal items.

"Why?" he asked. "I don't understand. What are the charges?"

"You have been subverting our government," Szota replied with little trace of malice. In fact, he sounded almost avuncular. "You have spoken treasonous words and spoken them often." Szota sounded bored, as though reading from an oft-used script. "Here with your students and friends and in your neighborhood."

"I have spoken the truth. That is all."

The detective shook his head wearily. "I am not going to debate you here. You will receive a trial."

Thaddeus had to refrain from snorting his derision. But thoughts of Bernadeta and worries for her safety stopped him. "May I please inform my wife?"

"She will be apprised – in due time. Now, Professor, please come with us. We would prefer not to use force," Szota said unctuously. "After all, we both are Poles."

Thaddeus inhaled deeply and then let his breath escape slowly. He realized instantly the seriousness of his predicament. Which, he knew, could ensnare Bernadeta. He began walking across a broad lawn between the uniformed officers. Szota was leading the way to an unmarked black sedan parked outside the university's main wrought iron gate on Cracowskie Przedmiescie Street. As they passed through the gate, Thaddeus looked back at the campus he had grown to love. Will this be the last time I see it? Will I ever teach again? Will I live to see another sunrise? Then at the car, as he bent to enter through the rear passenger side door, he saw a familiar figure standing on the sidewalk about 30 feet away in front of one of the university buildings. It was Felix Glemp, arms crossed, watching expressionlessly.

CHAPTER 47

It was late June and the Saturday after the first of Jack Brecker's two weeks in Rome. The morning was sun-dappled and the air pleasant, not yet far along on its march to a high temperature of 91 degrees. To Jack it seemed an ideal time to set out on a long leisurely hike from his cramped room – more the size of a prison cell – in tiny Vatican City, covering only 109 acres and an independent state since 1929. I've been wanting to see some of Rome's most historic sites, Jack was thinking, and get a little exercise at the same time.

Had this been a Saturday in Arizona, Jack would have been wearing blue jeans, an open-necked shirt and a large kerchief around his neck. But as he was at the Vatican he observed protocol and settled for wearing lightweight woolen black trousers, black shoes and an ankle length black cassock with white collar covering a white t-shirt.

As he exited Vatican City, walking east toward the snaking Tiber River, on Jack's left was magnificent Castle San Angelo, dating to 134 A.D. and built by Emperor Hadrian as a mausoleum. In 403 Emperor Honorius fortified the circular structure, building a high crenelated wall, to defend against threatening barbarians.

Across the river Jack cut southeast, strolling toward the Piazza Venezia. From there his eyes took in semicircular, two-story Trajan's Market – perhaps the world's first shopping mall, once having housed some 200 retail shops as well as warehouse space. The market flanked 2,000-year-old Trajan's Column. On his right were the column-studded remains of the Roman Forum with its imposing Arch of Septimius Severus, built in 203 A.D. And just ahead was the Colisseum, completed in 80 A.D. – 161 feet high, 600 feet long, 500 feet wide and seating 45,000 spectators. And adjacent to the great arena was Constantine's Arch – dedicated in 315 A.D. and 65 feet high with three arches.

Jack couldn't help marveling at the design and construction of those ancient wonders. The Romans were truly blessed with some remarkable architects and building contractors, he mused. They didn't have modern blueprints and slide rules. They didn't have high-rise cranes and motorized vehicles and equipment. They were clearly very brainy and capable men. Of course they did have plenty of cheap labor – slaves. And they were actually lucky in two respects. They had to build with stone – no steel, glass or concrete slabs at their disposal – which was bulky and hard-to-handle, but that enabled them to build to last. And they had this marvelous Mediterranean climate that allowed them to work the year round and that has helped preserve their creations. On the other hand I can't help wondering how increasing car and bus traffic with its pollution might be damaging them. Sad. It's fascinating; they didn't believe in God and hadn't been introduced to Jesus Christ. But it seems as though they had the Lord's endorsement.

Jack stopped to admire Trajan's Column, 100 feet high and built in 113 A.D. with an interior staircase winding to the pinnacle. The granite column was covered with intricately detailed carvings that, beginning at the base, spiraled upward and depicted Trajan's numerous military conquests in what are now Romania, Hungary, Algeria, Iran, Germany and Spain. No doubt, Jack mused, Trajan must have concluded that his gods were squarely on his side, admiring his military genius. As he gazed at the column's top, he couldn't help smiling. From his readings he knew that a statue of Trajan initially crowned the column and that in 1588 it was replaced by one of St. Paul. So, St. Paul, Jack reflected with amusement, how do you feel about standing for centuries atop a shrine a pagan built to glorify himself? Well, at least it puts you a hundred feet closer to heaven.

As Jack turned to move on, he heard shouts coming from behind Trajan's Market. They were boyish and echoing. Jack smiled again and paused. Curiosity was tugging at him and winning out over his planned straight-line stroll. He walked to the east end of the market and turned left onto an ancient narrow street. The shouts were louder. He continued north for perhaps 50 yards to an even narrower street, Via Tor dei Conti read the sign. He turned left onto the street, paved with millennia-old stones, and almost immediately a dirty white soccer ball came bouncing toward him. Sprinting after it was a laughing, black-haired boy whom Jack guessed to be about 12.

Jack had never played soccer but he was a superb athlete, with baseball long his first athletic love, followed closely by football. During his days at the Josephinum Seminary in Worthington, Ohio and later in Arizona during baseball spring training, Jack had played catch with famed Cleveland Indians shortstop Lou Boudreau. During Jack's time with the 82nd Airborne in England he had played baseball games with young paratroopers and impressed the soldiers with his batting, throwing and catching. Despite his absence of soccer experience and skills Jack instinctively turned his right foot sideways and stopped the oncoming ball.

The chasing boy pulled up. Smiling widely, black eyes peering upward, something caused him to ask, "Vuoi giocare con noi?" Translation: "Do you want to play with us?" The boy clearly was not put off by Jack's cassock and collar.

Jack didn't speak more than a few words of Italian, but his fluency in Latin and Spanish enabled him to understand the boy's invitation. "Si." He smiled kindly. This could be a fun diversion, Jack was thinking.

The boy picked up the ball, took hold of Jack's left forearm and led him farther up the street. Nine other boys were watching. Smiling – Jack long ago had learned the value of smiling warmly to overcome language hurdles – he pointed to himself and said, "Padre Brecker. Da America." Then he extended his right arm to the first boy and they shook hands. Then one-by-one, Jack shook nine other right hands of smiling soccer players. The game was on.

Jack's early missteps had the boys laughing, and he was laughing with them, his bass voice echoing up and down the narrow street. Soon, though, their amusement turned to admiration as they saw Jack's determination to play with gusto. When after a few minutes he removed his collar, hoisted his cassock and stuffed the priestly symbol into his trouser pocket, the boys cheered.

Minutes later, after studying the boys' highly skilled moves, Jack attempted to head and chest-trap the ball – with techniques he knew were as comical as they were ineffective.

There were no goal nets, but there were two goalies whose chief mission was to prevent the ball from escaping the street. Quick-footed with sure hands, they were successful far more often than not.

Jack towered over the boys who were reveling in his unexpected company. "Padre Gigante" one of the boys called to him, and immediately Jack had a nickname. A rousing chorus of "Padre Gigantes" began rising to the tops of the buildings lining the street. Soon, curious neighbors and parents were peering down from windows and balconies, virtually all bedecked with colorful flower boxes, at the American priest dashing about, exuberantly and noisily playing with their sons.

After about 20 minutes sweat was streaming down Jack's ruddy face, and he could feel his white t-shirt clinging clammily to his chest and back. He held up his hands and play stopped. "No mas," and the boys understood his Spanish. "Padre Gigante esta cansado," he continued in Spanish. He blew out a breath and turned his palms outward in a sign of surrender, and again the boys understood.

He began shaking hands and said, "I am going to see the Colisseum."

"Il Colossseo?" the first boy asked.

"Si."

The boy turned to his friends and for a few moments they engaged in discussion that Jack could see was serious. Then the first boy took Jack by his right arm and said, "Veniamo con te, Padre Gigante. Ti guidiamo fino al Colosseo e ogni altro posto che vorresti visitare. Roma e la nostra citta."

Translation: "We are going with you. Come, Padre Gigante. We will lead you to Il Colosseo and anyplace else you want to see. This is our Rome."

Jack didn't catch all the words but understood their gist. In the next moment one large American priest, 10 laughing Roman boys and one bouncing soccer ball were leaving Via Tor dei Conti.

✝ ✝ ✝

Thaddeus Metz wasn't sure where he was. He knew only that he was sitting on a wood chair, hands bound behind his back, in a dimly lighted room, and that he was bruised and in pain.

"A confession would spare you this nastiness," intoned Dominik Szota. "Just a brief confession."

"To treason?"

"You have spoken against our government. The state. You have incited opposition."

"If I have incited anything, it is independent thinking and patriotism."

Szota shook his head and then nodded.

One of the uniformed officers stepped forward and with his leather-gloved right hand viciously slapped Thaddeus' face twice. Blood began seeping from a reopened cut over Thaddeus' left cheekbone. The other officer stepped in front of Thaddeus, bent low and punched him in the abdomen. The air in Thaddeus' lungs came rushing from his mouth, and he coughed and then gasped, trying to draw in air.

"If I confess?"

"You will serve a prison term. A long one. Or..."

"Or face a firing squad or the hangman's noose."

"I cannot say. That will be a judge's choice."

"A Polish judge answerable to Soviet orders. Unjust choices at best."

"You committed the crime. A crime codified in our Polish laws."

"Polish laws the work of Soviet masters."

"Laws nevertheless and my job is to enforce them."

"Who is my accuser?"

"Does it matter?"

"If I choose a trial, I will see him."

"Trial?"

"If I don't confess…You said there would be a trial. When you arrested me."

"Yes, well, a trial of sorts."

"A mockery of justice. So, who is my accuser?"

"Someone you know."

"I think I know. One of my students. And I think I know which one."

Szota shook his head. "No. After you were accused, we talked with your students."

"All of them?"

"I think so. None would speak against you. Amazing, really."

"Because you threatened them."

"A little."

"Their families."

"Them too."

"Then who?"

"As I said," Szota smirked, "someone who knows you well. Someone you are close to."

"Knows me well…" Thaddeus' mind began reviewing the names of fellow faculty members, soldier friends, neighbors. *I can't believe any of them would turn on me. For what reason? What is there to gain? Favor with Szota's secret police? What have I done that someone would betray me? Whose feelings did I hurt? It makes no sense.*

"Enough of this," Szota said wearily. Turning to the uniformed officers, he said, "Take him back to his cell. We'll resume his interrogation tomorrow."

The knock on the apartment door was tentative, certainly not Thaddeus' and too timid for Mrs. Ostrowski's. Bernadeta stepped toward the door. That Thaddeus was late was causing her no concern. She knew well his penchant for stopping to chat with students and friends. His approachability was one of the factors in his widespread popularity. And with no phone, alerting her likely wouldn't have entered his thinking. Bernadeta opened the door. "Yes?"

"Are you Mrs. Metz?"

"Yes. And you?"

"My name is Felix Glemp. I am one of your husband's English students."

"Oh. Come in, please."

Felix bowed slightly. "Thank you."

His politeness impressed Bernadeta. "Please, sit down. Would you like tea?"

"No, thank you." Though seated, Glemp appeared ill at ease, sitting straight on the chair's edge, slowly twisting his hands.

Bernadeta noticed and ascribed it to his youth and his natural discomfort at being in the home of one of his professors. "What brings you to our home? Did Thaddeus ask you to meet him here?"

"No, Ma'am. He, uh, Professor Metz has been arrested. By the secret police."

In the next instant before Bernadeta could reply, icy dread went spreading through her torso and she shivered. Her head shook in momentary denial, and her left hand rose to her face, covering the scar that ran downward from the left corner of her mouth. "When?"

"A few hours ago. At the university."

"Did they hurt him?"

"The police were polite."

"Do you know where they took him?"

"Yes. Their station on Podwale Street, on the edge of Old Town."

"How do you know?"

"My father." Felix grimaced, shame shadowing his face. "He – he was able to find out."

"How?"

Felix averted his eyes. "He is with the secret police."

Bernadeta gaped. "Did he...Is he the one who arrested Thaddeus?"

"No."

"What will happen? Does your father know?"

Felix hesitated. "A trial, probably. Perhaps."

"A show trial. Does your father know the charge?"

"Slandering the state."

"Oh, my God. I warned...How did you find me? Oh, your father."

"Yes."

"Why did you come to tell me?"

"I respect your husband."

"Is that why your father told you?"

"Yes."

"Does Thaddeus know that?"

"Hah. I am probably his biggest headache." This flash of self-reproach relaxed Felix. He leaned back on the chair. "Sometimes I almost make him scowl."

"Why?"

"We disagree on things."

"Politics?"

"Yes."

"I thought so." A pause. "What should I do? What *can* I do?"

"You work at the American embassy."

"That's right. How-" She cut herself off, knowing the answer to the question she was about to ask.

"Go there. Tell them. That is what my father advises."

CHAPTER 48

"Is there nothing we can do?" Bernadeta asked plaintively. She prided herself on being a woman of action, and it was tearing at her to be doing nothing and feeling helpless to do anything.

"I'm afraid not, at least not now," said newly arrived Ambassador Stanton Griffis. Bernadeta was seated in one of the ambassador's leather guest chairs across from his ornate desk. "You say he is accused of slandering the Polish government. That is a purely domestic matter. Neither you nor your husband is an American citizen. We have no grounds for intervening. I am sorry." Griffis was tall and amiable and, Bernadeta was concluding, sympathetic but not willing to ruffle official feathers. Neither did she regard him as overly politically astute. She was recalling his proclamation earlier in 1947 that "Poland will never become communist."

"Mr. Griffis, I realize that I am only a lowly receptionist and a clerk. And my husband, he is only a young university instructor. But for humanitarian considerations, cannot you make a formal inquiry to the Polish government? Cannot you remind it of the freedoms we fought for? Freedom of speech."

"I'm sorry, Mrs. Metz. But as I understand the parameters of my position, this situation lies beyond my purview. Any action I take could embarrass our government at a sensitive time in American-Polish relations."

"I am sorry too. I wish my English was more skillful. So I could express myself more...better."

"Your English is fine and I understand your concern."

"Do you, Mr. Griffis? Do you really? My husband is a prisoner of our own Polish government. For speaking his mind. Nothing more. They – the secret police – have not permitted me to see him. I can guess what the secret police are doing to him. Can you?"

✝✝✝

Thaddeus' bruises from the first beating had not yet faded, much less disappeared. His left eye still was swollen.

"I really have no desire to see you suffer more," Dominik Szota told Thaddeus. "Confess to your crimes and we can end this unpleasantness."

Thaddeus felt an urge to lash out angrily. But he retained a measure of calm, foremost because of his worries about putting Bernadeta in jeopardy, if she wasn't already in danger. "I consider myself an honest man. If I had committed a crime, I would have confessed."

Szota sighed and removed his steel-rimmed glasses. With a fresh kerchief he polished them. Then he nodded to the uniformed guards. One stepped behind the chair Thaddeus was sitting on and grasped the chair's back. The other stepped in front of Thaddeus who knew what was coming. He tensed his abdominal muscles. The guard closed his right hand into a fist and drove it into Thaddeus' midsection. Thaddeus' mouth opened wide, and he could feel air rushing from his lungs. His eyes began watering.

"This can get worse," said Szota, hands folded and resting on his ample belly. "And in time it could become worse for your wife."

Szota's reference to Bernadeta sent fear rippling through Thaddeus. He struggled to regain his breath. "My wife" – he coughed – "works at the American embassy. You wouldn't-"

"Yes, we would," Szota cut him off. "We think we know the measure of the man that is Ambassador Griffis. He is tall but we nevertheless see him as a small man."

✝✝✝

Two young men, hands and legs bound, were lowered roughly from the rear of the army truck by a squad of North Korean soldiers. The men, their balance precarious, toppled to the ground. It was nearly 1 p.m. and Park Han was sitting on the dusty training camp ground, eating his midday meal of rice and kimchi. His rifle lay beside him.

Captain Kwon approached the two helpless men and kicked their feet. "Our newest volunteers," he grinned contemptuously. "Remove their bindings," he instructed a soldier who obeyed instantly. "Get up on your feet," Kwon ordered the two conscripts whose clothing, though grimy, was of good quality.

They had tried to evade conscription, Han knew. He had seen other "volunteers" arrive at the training camp similarly attired and bound. These arrivals looked urban and soft. Their lot would not be easy. Kwon would see to that.

The captain studied the arrivals. "Straighten your backs," he barked. "You need to look like soldiers even if you are sorry prospects for our People's Army."

Both men did so but one complied with a look of unmistakable contempt. Kwon's eyebrows arched. He removed his sidearm from its holster and placed its muzzle against the young man's left temple. For a pregnant moment Kwon did nothing. Unwaveringly, he stared into the conscript's eyes which were blinking rapidly. Then Kwon rotated the gun so that the muzzle pointed upward while remaining pressed against the youth's head.

"You will learn to be a soldier. That is something I know you despise. No matter. You failed your first lesson in obedience when you resisted our invitation to come here. Your next lesson will begin now."

Kwon squeezed the trigger. The flame from the muzzle singed the young man's hair while the gun's report thundered inside his skull and sent him staggering. Kwon followed and confronted the conscript and positioned his nose a scant inch from the youth's.

"Do you think you will need a third lesson?" Kwon's boiling anger was quivering his own chin.

The man shook his head. "No."

"No, sir!" Kwon barked, correcting the conscript.

"No, sir," he replied with a meekness that pleased Kwon.

As Han watched Kwon impose his terror, he was feeling both disgust and despair. This is our nation's future? he asked himself silently. This is what we waited so long for? To be rid of Colonel Fukunaga and the cruel Japanese and to be under the thumb of Kim Il Sung and Captain Kwon? Han eyed the rifle at his side. He had just come into camp from the rifle range, and his ammunition pouch contained a live clip. He placed his right hand on the trigger guard. Kwon and his sergeants have taught me well. Insert a clip. One shot, maybe two, and I could end his miserable life – and the misery he brings to so many boys and their families. Volunteers. That's what Kim Il Sung calls us. What hypocrisy.

Han fingered the trigger. He visualized Kwon shot, blood squirting from the wound, and crumpling. It would be easy. I can do it. Yes, I know. If I kill Kwon, I'm a dead man. The clip remained in the pouch.

✝ ✝ ✝

At Bernadeta's reception desk in the ornate, lavishly marbled embassy lobby, she was staring emptily at her weekly report that detailed visitors, their stated purposes and embassy staffers they met with. Her mind was elsewhere – on nearby Podwale Street. She was imagining a grimy jail cell where the man she loved was enduring daily torture and death threats. She also knew that Thaddeus had been warned that her safety was in peril. These things she knew because of reports delivered by Felix Glemp, courtesy of his detective father. Bernadeta was grateful. She knew the father was risking his own safety, never mind his job with the secret police, by funneling information to her.

A tall black-haired man approached and stood in front of her desk. He was holding a large brown leather suitcase with his right hand and a smaller satchel – also brown leather – with his left. He could see Bernadeta was preoccupied. She was taking no notice of his looming presence. He stood patiently for nearly a minute and then cleared his throat.

Bernadeta looked up. "Oh, I am sorry, sir. I was – never mind. How can I help you?"

The man lowered his load to the marble floor. Then he slipped his hand into the left inside pocket of his suit jacket and removed his blue-covered passport. He handed it to Bernadeta. She could see immediately that it was a United States diplomatic passport. The handsome man was wearing a black suit, white shirt and blue, black and gray regimental striped tie. She couldn't see his shoes but assumed they also were black. Appropriate diplomatic attire from top to bottom.

"As you can see, I'm an American. I've been posted here as an aide."

"Welcome to Warsaw, sir."

"Thank you kindly."

"Who is it you wish to see? I will phone him for you."

"I'm hoping you can direct me to the right person."

"I do not understand. You are posted here to work with someone. You have diplomatic orders?"

"Yes." The man didn't want to lie or even be sinfully evasive. "There is something else. I'm looking for a Pole. A man. A friend. I suppose I should go to a Polish government office, but I have no idea which one. I thought I'd better report in here and ask for guidance."

"Who is it you are searching?" Bernadeta blushed. "I am sorry. Sometimes my tongue gets tangled in English."

The man smiled and she could see his eyes radiating kindness. "Not to worry. The man I'm looking for was a Polish soldier. I met him in England and Scotland and again in the Netherlands. That was 1944."

Bernadeta nodded pensively. "Many of our Polish soldiers escaped to the West so they could fight the Germans again."

"Yes, I know. About one hundred sixty-five thousand Poles made it to France and England. They fought bravely in the Netherlands, France and Italy. They took Monte Casino in Italy."

"You know much about our Polish soldiers."

"The ones I met were dedicated, courageous men. I was very impressed, as were my fellow Americans."

"You were a soldier too?"

"A chaplain."

"A priest?" Her eyes narrowed as she studied his necktie. Could this be so?

"Yes. With our 82nd Airborne Division."

"But no longer a priest?" She blushed again, embarrassed by her own intrusiveness.

"This," he fingered the necktie, "notwithstanding, I'm still a priest."

A sense of improbable recognition was beginning to take shape in Bernadeta's mind. What she was starting to consider seemed incredible. Haltingly, she asked, "What is the name of your friend?"

"Thaddeus Metz."

Bernadeta blinked. Twice. She felt a chill go racing up and down her spine. She looked again at the name on the passport. Her head shook.

"Is something wrong?" Jack asked.

Her head shook again. "No. It is only that – that this is so like a miracle."

Jack smiled. "Miracle?"

"You are a friend of Thaddeus Metz. Once a Polish lancer. Then a paratrooper with General Sosabowski."

"Yes!" Jack was beaming. "You know him."

"He is my husband."

† † †

In a small room off the embassy lobby Jack Brecker and Bernadeta Gudek Metz began to get acquainted. After telling Jack that Thaddeus had spoken often of him, she phoned Ambassador Griffis and was told by his secretary to escort Jack to his office.

† † †

"Frankly, Father Brecker, I'm not sure I approve of this deception. Your motive is honorable, but your method questionable," Griffis lectured mildly. He wasn't at all intimidated by Jack's priestly credential, but he recognized that Congresswoman Morton had won State Department support for Jack's ruse and, though Griffis had been appointed by President

236

Truman, he knew that bucking State could prematurely end his Warsaw posting.

"Frankly, Ambassador Griffis, I'm not happy with it either. Deception wasn't central to my seminary studies." Jack's disarming candor was softening Griffis' steely reception. "I'm sorry for upsetting you. But my bishop and I both recognized that an American priest – any priest actually – wouldn't be entirely welcome in Poland."

"Nicely put, Father Brecker. Or while you are here, shall I address you as Mr. Brecker?" Griffis smiled wryly as did Jack. Bernadeta was enjoying being a spectator to this strange introduction.

"That might be better," Jack allowed.

"I take it you would like some time with Mrs. Metz."

"Yes, sir."

"Very good. Mrs. Metz, my secretary will send someone to fill in for you at the reception desk while you are meeting with Mr. Brecker. Oh, and Mr. Brecker, you'll need quarters while working as an aide here. We have rooms – small ones – for staff here inside the embassy."

✝✝✝

"How long has Thaddeus been jailed?" Jack asked.

"Eight days."

"What's next?"

"Next?"

"In the legal process."

"Whatever the secret police decide," Bernadeta said cuttingly. "Our legal system is no system at all. Our secret police are very much like the Nazis. They are the law and it can change – does change – at the whim of the secret police. Our government is a sham. Our leaders do what they are told – by Stalin or the secret police. We fought to free Poland but now we are prisoners in our homeland. Excuse me, Father. Er, Mr. Brecker. I did not mean to lecture you."

"I'm not offended." Jack bit his lip. "What do you think might happen to Thaddeus?"

"He will be in jail for a long time." Her voice caught and she took a moment to compose herself. "If he confesses or not. Perhaps worse. He was a Polish Army officer."

"I see." And Jack did. He knew about the fate of thousands of Polish officers at the hands of the Nazis and Soviets. The fingers of Jack's left hand covered his mouth and then rubbed his chin in contemplation. "We have to help him."

"Pray?"

"That too. But more than that."

"But how? Our embassy can do nothing. That is what Ambassador Griffis has told me."

"I don't know. Let me think about it."

✝✝✝

That night in an embassy room no larger than a monastic cell, Jack lay staring up through the blackness at the ceiling. The small window was open, admitting cool night air. Jack was wearing boxer shorts and a white t-shirt and was covered only by a thin sheet. His fingers were laced together behind his head on a thin pillow. A solution, he was thinking, for almost any problem there is a solution. The secret police. They are the problem. Who do they answer to? The Kremlin, ultimately. But locally, who might hold some sway over them? Not the puppet government? Surprise and intimidation were concepts creeping into Jack's thinking. Not my style but they could be the key. Who – or what – might intimidate them, even if only briefly? Jack closed his eyes. How much risk would I be willing to take? Could I do something alone? No. I would need help. Jack pushed back the sheet, swung his legs off the narrow bed and knelt in prayer. Dear Lord, I trust you can forgive me for the deception that got me into Poland. Now in advance, I ask you to forgive me for deception that I hope will get someone out of Poland.

✝✝✝

In the cutlery and butcher shop in Munsan, Park Min was sharpening a knife. It was a trade he was learning from shop owner Choi Chun Kuen. Min liked the work. He found it satisfying. He could see and feel the results in shiny, sharpened blades. Customers were appreciative. He also found the work relaxing and conducive to thinking.

At this moment he found himself wondering whether there was any way to extricate his younger brother Han from the North Korean Army. Is it possible? If it is, what would happen to Mother and Father? Could we manage to get the whole family south of the 38th Parallel? Safely? Would Mother and Father give up their shop in Kaesong to escape to the south? It's their livelihood. It's where their friends are. They don't have much money now. If they left Kaesong, they would have little or none. And Kyong. I wonder if she misses me as much as I miss her. I wonder if she would leave her parents if there was a way to get her here. Probably not. Her parents would lose face, and she wouldn't let that happen. Even if she still loves me and I hope she does. I still love her, more than anything. Sometimes I ache, thinking about her. So many questions. So few answers. I feel trapped. We're all trapped. There's no way out.

✝✝✝

"There might be a way out," Jack said to Bernadeta the next morning in the small embassy meeting room. "We would need help. Help we can rely on."

Bernadeta peered into the priest's brown eyes. They reflected seriousness of intent and penetrating intelligence. She was coming to understand quickly why Thaddeus so liked and respected him. She could see that Jack was determined to help a friend in need. What she found remarkable was that their friendship had taken hold and endured after spending so little time together. A few minutes in a tent where Thaddeus was introduced to Jack in 1944. Then a plane ride from England to Scotland to say an Easter Mass. Then a half hour together before the Polish paratroopers began crossing the Rhine during Operation Market Garden. No more than four or five hours total. Amazing, Bernadeta was thinking. Then she thought about how little time had been needed for her and Thaddeus to form a bond – a bond that somehow had withstood seven years of separation. Just a few hours that afternoon and evening on the farm in 1939 when she had helped Thaddeus and the cow pen soldiers escape. She smiled. "What kind of help?"

"Forgery."

Bernadeta's eyes narrowed. "Of what?"

"Military orders. Polish Army orders."

"And?"

"Polish Army uniforms. And men to wear them, men we can trust."

Now Bernadeta's deep blue eyes widened. "Father Brecker. I am sorry. Mr. Brecker."

"Call me Jack, please."

"I do not know if I can. We Poles revere priests."

Jack chuckled. "I'm not looking for reverence. Whatever makes you comfortable."

"Thank you, Father. I do not know yet what you are thinking, but my experience in the Home Army says it includes much danger."

Jack nodded. "Probably. I am willing to take such risk. Do you know anyone else who might be?"

† † †

A day later, hands on her hips, Bernadeta looked at the small table in her apartment's kitchen. She had set five places for tea and cake. She looked at the small wind-up clock on the kitchen counter. Nearly 7 p.m.

A knock at the door. Bernadeta stepped quickly to open it. "Father, come in, please."

"Thank you." Jack, wearing his black suit and striped necktie, bowed slightly and stepped inside.

"Did you have any difficulty finding our apartment?"

"Not at all. Just three blocks from the embassy. Your directions were perfect." He was holding the small piece of paper on which Bernadeta had sketched a map. "I should tell Ambassador Griffis that you would make an excellent cartographer."

"Please?"

"Cartographer. A drawer of maps."

"Oh." Bernadeta blushed. "Please, sit down. It seems so strange – good but strange – to have a priest in our home – an American priest. My friends would not believe it. Of course, I cannot tell them."

"Snoops?"

"One can never be certain. Besides," she smiled wryly, "you are now Mr. Brecker."

Another knock at the door.

"Excuse me," Bernadeta said, standing and moving to open the door. Three strapping men each bowed slightly and stepped inside. In the next sliver of time involuntary double takes had four heads bobbing and shaking.

Then the first man's mouth opened to speak but no sound emerged. He forced his mouth shut, his tongue flicking his lips. He cleared his throat. "Father Brecker. Is it you?"

"Yes," Jack smiled kindly, "it's me." Jack closed the distance to the man and extended his right hand. "It's very good to see you again, Marek." That Jack was addressing Marek in Polish was adding to the men's astonishment. He shook hands with Marek, then with Henryk and Jerzy.

"We are shocked to see you here, Father," said Henryk.

"Likewise," said Jack. "Bernadeta told me she invited friends but not cow pen soldiers. And I must apologize. I don't know your surnames."

"Krawczyk," Marek laughed, his fingers pointing toward himself. "And Henryk is Henryk Wyzynski and Jerzy is Jerzy Pinkowski." A pause. "Your Polish is excellent, Father. Our English is poor. We have not spoken it since leaving England. Please forgive us."

Jack's head shook. "No need. Do you remember Captain Walt Hunter, my friend?"

"Yes, of course," Marek said. "How is Captain Hunter?"

"He is fine. His father arranged for me to take Polish lessons from a Polish engineer he hired to work for his mining company."

"How wonderful. You have been a good student," Marek said, eyes twinkling.

Jack laughed. "Tell me," he said, "what about the other cow pen soldiers?"

"Ah. Some of us didn't survive the war," said Marek.

"Stephan?" Stephan had assisted Jack when he had said Easter Mass for the Polish paratroopers at Upper Largo.

Now it was Marek's head that shook, and sadly. "I am sorry, Father. Stephan was killed the first night we tried to cross the Rhine. Black Friday." Marek was referring to Day 6 in the September 1944 disastrous Operation Market Garden, British Field Marshall Bernard Law Montgomery's hurriedly and ill-conceived plan to end the war by Christmas. Stephan was killed by German machine gun fire while in a rubber raft in the middle of the river.

"I am so sorry," Jack murmured. "I am certain he is resting in peace in the company of our Lord."

"I think he must be," Marek said somberly. "He was a good man, and you gave us a blessing before the crossing. Do you remember?"

"Yes." And Jack did. And fleetingly he found himself wondering just how effective that blessing had been. Only 52 Poles in those rubber rafts made it across the Rhine that night. The next night 150 more made it across in their futile attempt to relieve British General Roy Urquhart's besieged men near Arnhem. In all during that operation, the First Independent Polish Parachute Brigade lost 378 men killed in action, with many more wounded, captured or missing and presumed dead.

"Bernadeta said we might be able to help Thaddeus so naturally we have come," Jerzy said. "But you – there was no time."

Jack smiled. "You are quite right." He then explained his desire to locate Thaddeus, to learn whether he had survived the war and how he was faring. He told them he had come not from the United States but Rome. Only chance had him arriving in Warsaw so soon after Thaddeus' arrest.

The cow pen soldiers were touched deeply.

"You are a loyal man," Henryk observed. "To us Poles loyalty is very important."

Jack nodded his appreciation of the compliment.

"You have a plan?" Marek asked.

"Yes. Yes, I do. But I must tell you straight away that it is dangerous."

Marek chuckled. "We would expect nothing else. Tell us how we can help."

Jack looked at Bernadeta. "We need documents. Polish Army orders. Polish and U.S. passports for Thaddeus."

"I can arrange for the embassy to provide those," Bernadeta said quietly.

"And," said Jack, "we'll need Polish Army identification papers for you three and me."

"The embassy can provide those as well," Bernadeta replied. "Our staff includes certain specialists, and they are my friends. We just need to make sure that none of this reflects on the ambassador."

"And us?" Marek asked.

"We need a Polish Army officer's uniform. A major's uniform or a colonel's would do nicely."

"Not a problem," said Marek. "We can even get you one without bullet holes or bloodstains."

"Can you get it without stealing or killing?" Jack inquired pointedly – and then quickly added, "I'm sorry I asked."

"Don't worry," Marek said soothingly. "Just a little bribery. Nothing that would compromise God's commandments or your priestly sensibilities."

Laughter erupted around the kitchen table. Bernadeta took the merriment as a cue to pour tea and cut the carrot cake. For the first time since learning about Thaddeus' arrest, she was experiencing a lightness of being.

"We will also need Polish Army uniforms for all of you. Perhaps a sergeant and two privates."

"We still have our own uniforms," said Marek, "and they still fit. But not if we keep eating Bernadeta's cake. It is delicious."

"About the bribery," Jack said.

"Is it a sin to pay bribes to save an innocent man's life?" Jerzy asked.

"I credit the Lord for being understanding and forgiving," Jack said, smiling wryly. "I think he would see it as a bribe of merit if not holiness. I was only going to ask if the bribe could be paid in a way that it would not be traced back to Thaddeus or Bernadeta."

"In that case," Marek said, "I will tell you that I think another small bribe could secure Polish Army pistols – the VIS. An automatic. To complete the uniforms."

"Good thinking," said Jack.

"The cake is scrumptious," said Henryk. "Unlike Marek," he teased, reaching to pat Marek's stomach, "I could eat much of it and still fit in my uniform." More laughter around the table.

"Thank you," Bernadeta said. "For you men I wanted it to be perfect." She blushed and so did the cow pen soldiers.

"We could fail," Jack murmured.

"We were soldiers, Father," said Marek. "We know what can happen after a battle begins."

"Chaos?"

"Chaos. We have seen plans become chaos and we have experienced defeat."

"You already have sacrificed much for your country."

"But never enough for a friend."

From the living room window in her ground floor apartment Mrs. Ostrowski had seen Bernadeta's guests arriving. One man had arrived first and then soon after the other three together. Her curiosity had risen faster than the mercury on that hot July day. Why had they come? Was this a simple party or reunion? Why didn't I know about it?

Now they were leaving together. Why had they stayed so long? And those outbursts of laughter. What brought them on? Simple jokes? Or more criticism of our government?

Should I or shouldn't I? Mrs. Ostrowski quizzed herself. Thaddeus is so nice and Bernadeta is so sweet. But those men. One a complete stranger in a black suit. That was odd. The other three Thaddeus once introduced to me, but I know nothing about them. Not really. And the first time Detective Szota was so grateful. He even sent me fresh blood sausages. I wonder what happened afterward. I haven't heard from him since. And I haven't seen Thaddeus for several days. Bernadeta has said nothing about him being away.

CHAPTER 49

Bernadeta wasn't worried for herself. If she hadn't miscarried and instead had a baby to mother, she knew she would be concerned for her personal safety. But not now. She had taken bigger risks – many of them – during the Nazi occupation. I was prepared to die more than once, she reminded herself. I could die for my country. I could die for my friends. I can die for my husband. But Father Brecker and the cow pen soldiers. This is a different situation. Much different. Even if they succeed, it won't change the big picture. Poland will not be free. We will still be squashed under Stalin's boot. If they are caught and judged to be spies or traitors, they will simply disappear. Without a trace. Being a priest will not spare Father Brecker. Not at all. Not for a second.

✝✝✝

"I'm really sorry we have to be less gentle today," Szota said unctuously. "But you see, we really must know who was visiting your wife. Who are they?"

The first time the woman's information was explicit, Dominik Szota recalled. Metz had slandered our government. She heard him – in his own kitchen. But this time her report was so vague. Metz's wife had visitors. Four men. On the same evening. One a stranger. The other three friends of Metz. What to make of it? Maybe nothing. But maybe something. I'll send her another little gift. No card. Nothing in writing. Just a small gift delivered by one of my men with a word of gratitude. So little can go so far.

Blood was oozing from a gash under Thaddeus' left eye. He wanted to dab it, but his hands were again bound behind the chair's back. "Think about it, Szota. How could I possibly know who visited her? I have had no contact with my wife or anyone else since you arrested me."

"You are a resourceful man," Szota said sincerely. "Nothing you accomplish would surprise me."

Szota removed his eyeglasses, nodded and a uniformed policeman wearing brass knuckles stepped in front of Thaddeus and drew back his right arm. Thaddeus saw the fist coming and ducked. The blow struck high on his forehead, splitting his skin in a second place. A knot began forming and the pain was so great he thought his teeth might fall out. He gritted them until the initial wave of pain subsided.

Who could those four men be? Thaddeus wondered. And one in a black suit. Undertakers wear black suits. Perhaps Szota has told Bernadeta I am dead. That wouldn't surprise me. Through the pain, Thaddeus felt anger surging.

"You enjoy this, don't you, Szota," he said accusingly.

"Quite the contrary. I would much prefer to be at my desk. Drinking tea. Reading a newspaper. This basement is too dark and damp for my taste. But my job demands sacrifice and I accept it. You seem like a decent fellow, and I think I might even believe you. I would like to but I can't afford that luxury. It would cost me my job."

"Other jobs don't require torturing fellow Poles."

"They don't pay as well."

✝✝✝

Four days later the double wooden front doors of the secret police station on Podwale Street swung open. A Polish Army major followed by a sergeant and two privates stepped through the doorway and stopped. The major was carrying a thin brown leather attaché case. He surveyed the large room.

At the nearest desk a police sergeant was staring wide-eyed. The major, back ramrod straight and projecting an arrogance that was nearly palpable, went striding to the sergeant's desk. His men, grim-faced, followed. The major snapped open his attaché case with a pronounced flourish and removed a single sheet of paper. "My orders," he said crisply, handing them to the desk sergeant whose eyes remained riveted on the handsome major. "You are to carry them out immediately."

The sergeant finally looked down at the orders but, stunned by the sudden appearance of the four soldiers, had difficulty concentrating on the words. "I...This is...There is no precedent."

"Those are military orders. This is now a military matter. It should have been from the start. You have overstepped your authority. You are to obey these orders at once. Is it possible for me to be more clear?" Beneath Jack's commanding façade his intestinal juices were churning as violently as a storm-tossed sea.

Marek, Henryk and Jerzy were struggling to mask their amazement. Even after their rehearsal they were astonished not only by Jack's command of Polish but also by his acting ability. Father Brecker, you make a convincing liar, Marek was silently lauding him. I would believe you and I am a practicing cynic. For his part Jack was hoping that the sergeant wouldn't take to debating the limits of authority – or possibly worse, run off to confer with a superior.

"No," the desk sergeant sputtered, "your orders are clear."

"As they should be," Jack said with studied arrogance. "Bring me Metz. Two of my men will accompany you. Unholster your guns," Jack directed Henryk and Jerzy. "Metz could be dangerous." What Jack was thinking – and this thought hadn't been part of his plan – was that drawn VISs would fatten the intimidation factor. He also was hoping that he wasn't overplaying his role.

"My superior," the sergeant muttered defensively, "I think I should-"

"You are wasting valuable military time and resources," Jack cut him off. "You can show him these orders and explain later. If he still has questions, he can ask me himself. Now go."

Not five minutes later Thaddeus came shuffling into the large room. His head was bowed and eyes were closed against the unaccustomed light. The desk sergeant was leading him, and Henryk and Jerzy were supporting Thaddeus who, when seeing the army uniforms, had concluded he was being taken to another torture site or to his execution. Should that be his fate, he was determined not to plead or to say anything that might pose more risk for Bernadeta.

Henryk and Jerzy had holstered their guns. Jack and Marek both wanted to reach out to Thaddeus but retained their military bearing. Jack was hoping fervently that Thaddeus would not recognize him. Don't look up, he pleaded silently, not till we get outside. But if you do, I'm praying that the years and this uniform will disguise me as well as a Halloween mask.

Outside the police station Henryk and Jerzy eased Thaddeus onto the rear seat of a brilliantly polished black sedan they had borrowed from the embassy – and outfitted with confiscated Polish military license plates. Marek slid behind the steering wheel. Jack sat on the front passenger side and refrained from looking back.

At the station doorway the desk sergeant watched the car pull away from the curb. He looked again at the orders and shook his head. I feel sorry for you, Metz. If you think you had it rough here, I can only begin to imagine what will happen to you now.

Moments later Marek braked the sedan in front of the American embassy on nearby Koscielna Street. Henryk and Jerzy helped Thaddeus from the car. Jack removed his Polish Army officer's hat and nodded to the two U.S. Marine Corps guards who smiled knowingly and stood aside to let the five men pass. An embassy staffer then quickly scurried to the car to begin changing back the license plates.

Inside the embassy's front door Bernadeta looked up from her reception desk, saw Thaddeus' battered features and immediately verged on dissolving into tears. Instead, she swallowed hard, clenched her jaws, firmly grasped the edge of her desk and stood. Then, shakier than during any of her Resistance missions, she stepped around the desk, advanced slowly and gently embraced her husband. Thaddeus could feel his warm tears leaking onto Bernadeta's cool white blouse.

✝✝✝

Later that day Dominik Szota was sitting at his scarred wooden desk. He was studying the orders directing the handover of Thaddeus Metz from the secret police to the army. His head shook slowly and he quizzed himself. I don't understand. What does the army want with him? He is merely an instructor of English. Could that be it? His English speaking ability? Even so, I can't recall the army ever seizing a secret police prisoner – except to carry out an execution and we usually handle those ourselves. I'm going to do some checking into this.

✝✝✝

In Jack's cramped bedroom at the embassy a subdued but nonetheless joyous reunion was underway. Thaddeus was semireclining, head and upper back resting against pillows on the bed. He stretched his bruised, blood-crusted face but refrained from touching it. Jack was perched at the foot of the bed, Bernadeta was sitting in the room's only chair, and Marek, Jerzy and Henryk were lounging on the floor, their backs against the wall.

"Ambassador Griffis is bringing us some champagne," said Bernadeta.

"I would prefer scotch or vodka," Thaddeus murmured.

"I'll tell the ambassador," Bernadeta said, rising.

"And cigars," Jack said. "We could use some good cigars."

"I'll go with you," Marek said, quickly getting to his feet. "You could use an extra pair of hands, and if I stay here I might cry tears of happiness in front of my fellow cow pen soldiers and the desert priest. Unseemly, don't you think?"

Hearty laughter filled the room.

"I can never begin to thank you," Thaddeus said softly, struggling to keep his voice from faltering.

"Don't start that, or I *will* cry," said Marek.

More laughter but less hearty.

"My cow pen friends, you saved my life at Dunkirk and now here in Warsaw." Tears did begin filming eyes and not only Marek's. "Father Brecker, I can hardly believe you are sitting here. You are like a warrior angel who appears from nowhere to slay enemies and rescue innocents. We have shaken hands but let me salute you, captain to captain." Thaddeus brought his right hand to his forehead and snapped off a crisp salute. Jack, still in the Polish major's uniform, returned it.

The answer just might be with Metz's wife, Szota was thinking. She could be the missing piece of the puzzle. She works at the American embassy. She no doubt has many contacts. Perhaps some in the Polish Army. She hears much. I think I should bring her in for interrogation. Yes. That is what I will do. No arrest. Nothing official. I'll see if my inquiries turn up anything during the next few days, and then I'll go to her apartment. Myself. If she knows the army has taken her husband, she is probably even more frightened than before. She won't resist. She won't dare to.

Thaddeus held his glass while Marek filled it with Chivas Regal.

"Ambassador Griffis sends his best," Jack observed.

"As well he should," Marek declared. He then handed one of the Macanudos the ambassador had furnished to Thaddeus and reached inside his right trouser pocket for matches. He lit the cigar and the rich aroma of exquisite tobacco quickly filled the small room.

Once all glasses were filled with scotch, vodka or champagne, Jack said, "A toast." Glasses were raised. "To precious freedom and all the sacrifices we and others have made to fight for it. May it be the destiny for Poland and all her people."

Glasses clinked and first sips were gratefully taken.

Marek then lit cigars for Jack and the cow pen soldiers.

"Where now, Father?" Thaddeus asked.

Jack sighed. "My friend, I don't think you'll be able to stay in Poland. It will be too dangerous for you and Bernadeta."

A pregnant silence ensued. Thaddeus broke it. "I agree. Szota will track me down. He'll start with my parents, my colleagues at the university and my students. He'll learn soon enough that the army doesn't have me. He can't see Bernadeta here at the embassy, but I'm sure he will go to our home. Then maybe to her family's farm. They all will be in danger. How much time do you think we have?"

"A little," Jack answered. "I think he'll start by checking – discreetly – with the army. It's a bureaucracy – like the Vatican," he grinned. "It should take him a few days to figure out that the orders are fake."

"In the meantime?"

"You need to stay here at the embassy. Regain your strength. Bernadeta should stay at your apartment. Normal appearances. Marek, Jerzy and Henryk should disappear for a while."

"Not a problem," said Marek. "As soon as we get out of these uniforms and back into our civilian clothes, we'll make our way into the countryside. Stay with friends. Until we feel safe to return."

"I can't stay at the embassy long," said Thaddeus. "Nor do I want to."

"No," Jack agreed. "The faster we get you out of Poland the better."

"Can you ride a horse?" Thaddeus teased, sipping more of the scotch. "That's how I returned from Germany to Poland."

"I can fly an airplane but I won't ask you – or me – to jump from it." Laughter again filled the small room. "Actually, Ambassador Griffis has assured me he can get you onto a plane. We've already got Polish and U.S. passports for you, whichever is needed."

"Or whatever else you might need," said Griffis, now standing in the open doorway. "I'll help any way I can. Just tell me what you need. You have taught me some valuable lessons." He stepped inside and shook hands with the cow pen soldiers.

"Thank you," said Bernadeta. Then she spoke to Thaddeus. "You can ride in Ambassador Griffis' car – diplomatic immunity – to the airport. He will stay with you onto the plane." Griffis nodded.

"To where?" Thaddeus asked.

"West Berlin," said Jack, "where we can put you on an airlift plane to the West."

"The West?"

"I'm thinking the United States and a new life," said Jack.

"I am too," said Bernadeta.

Her quick decisive reply surprised Thaddeus. "You are prepared to leave our homeland?"

"I love Poland, love it dearly, but you will be a hunted man here. And anyone who protects us would be in jeopardy. So for us to have a long life together, yes," Bernadeta said firmly, "I am ready to go."

Thaddeus nodded thoughtfully. "You will want to say farewell to your father and sister."

"Ambassador, can you possibly arrange for a car and driver to take me to our farm? Please?"

"Is tomorrow soon enough? I'll have a car and driver ready early in the morning."

✝✝✝

Two days later at about 4:00 in the afternoon Mrs. Ostrowski was sitting at Bernadeta's table. She was sipping tea. "I am worried about Thaddeus," she said. "He has been in custody for so long." By now Bernadeta had told Mrs. Ostrowski about Thaddeus' arrest but nothing more. This afternoon Mrs. Ostrowski was intensely curious about the black sedan that had picked up Bernadeta yesterday morning and returned her late last night.

Bernadeta was tempted to confide to her neighbor that Thaddeus had been rescued and that they were about to leave for the United States. Indeed, she was yearning to tell someone besides Barbara, Kaz and her father. But as helpful as Mrs. Ostrowski had been, especially during and after the stillbirth, Bernadeta checked herself. She said only, "I am worried too and praying for him."

"Have you heard anything more, dear?"

"The police tell me nothing."

"Have you learned the charges?"

"The police turned me away."

"He must have done something-" Mrs. Ostrowski stopped herself. "Maybe one of his students informed on him."

"Perhaps." But not likely, Bernadeta thought, remembering Felix Glemp's reports. "Or someone else close to him."

Mrs. Ostrowski felt a chill of anxiety as her neck hairs straightened. Does she know? Or suspect? Mrs. Ostrowski's curiosity gave way to a strong and immediate desire to put distance between herself and Bernadeta's calculating mind. "Well, dear, this has been pleasant." She put her teacup on its saucer and rose. "Let's hope for good news soon."

✝✝✝

Two days later Dominik Szota turned right from Freta Street onto Mostowa Street. He was walking slowly, looking at building numbers. Dusk was giving way to darkness which experience told Szota was the best time for intimidating unsuspecting targets. Blackness increased their uncertainty. It was just the natural order of things. By the time I get her back to the station she should be thoroughly frightened. If she knows anything about her husband, she'll confess quickly. I won't waste time with the soft interrogation. I'll have my men begin roughing her up right away. It won't make any difference to them that she's a woman. If need be, I'll have them-

Szota's thoughts were interrupted when he saw another figure emerging from the lowering curtain of darkness. It was a man, and Szota could see his white shirt and thin necktie framed by a dark suit jacket. Szota stopped but the man kept approaching, slowly but unwaveringly straight toward him. Szota was surprised when he felt a twinge of anxiety. It's the darkness, he thought, the natural order of things. Then Szota felt relief. A familiar face, just a few feet away, and stopping. "Detective Glemp. What are you doing in this neighborhood? At this hour? Wait. I know. You've heard about what I'm doing. No offense, but this is my case. Metz is mine."

Glemp stood patiently and silently outside the entrance to 22 Mostowa Street.

"Is that clear?" Szota's voice took on a hard edge. "You may be my equal in rank but Metz – Metz and his wife-" Szota's left arm pointed to a second floor window where light was shining from Bernadeta and Thaddeus' apartment – "are in my portfolio."

Still, Glemp said nothing. Nor did he make any gesture of acquiescence. Calmly his right hand reached across his chest and slid beneath his suit jacket to his leather belt. When it emerged, it was holding a VIS. Glemp steadied the VIS with both hands. Szota's widening eyes reflected bafflement, and he had time enough only to take one halting step backward. Glemp squeezed the trigger and Szota's arms flew backward and away from his crumpling body.

The sharp report startled Mrs. Ostrowski. Timidly she edged to the corner of her living room window.

Glemp was in no hurry. He stepped beside Szota's supine body and squatted. A red stain was spreading from a hole in Szota's upper left chest. Szota coughed weakly, once, then a second time. He tried to say something but couldn't. Glemp could see puzzlement in Szota's fading eyes.

Up and down the street faces were appearing in windows. One visage was Bernadeta's. She had been packing her luggage. Thaddeus already was en route to the U.S., and she would be leaving in the morning, passport and travel arrangements courtesy of Ambassador Griffis.

Still, Glemp waited patiently. When Szota drew a final shallow breath and his empty eyes froze open in death, Detective Glemp stood. He replaced the gun beneath his belt. Then he glanced up at the window where Bernadeta was standing. He raised his right hand to the side of his forehead, held it there and nodded. Then he walked away.

The next morning Bernadeta was on the sidewalk in front of 22 Mostowa Street with her belongings. Szota's corpse had been removed but red stained the sidewalk. The previous night, neither Bernadeta nor anyone else within earshot, save Mrs. Ostrowski, had ventured into the street to learn the identity of the shooting victim. In Bernadeta's case it wouldn't have mattered since she'd never met Szota or heard his name. But Mrs. Ostrowski, she had come outside and she did know and recognize Szota. She had felt the unmistakable cold of permeating fear. This morning she still was shaken but had forced herself to venture outside to quiz Bernadeta.

But Bernadeta asked the first question. "Did you know him?"

"No," she lied.

An embassy driver, an American, was loading Bernadeta's luggage into a black sedan. Embassy staff had given her two suitcases and a trunk.

"Only one shot," Bernadeta mused. "It must have been planned. An execution." A pause. "Well, I must be going."

"I don't understand," said Mrs. Ostrowski. "Why didn't you tell me you were leaving?"

"I was instructed to tell no one."

"But we are friends."

"I am sorry." Bernadeta's loyalty to friends was beyond question, but this morning she wasn't feeling her usual warmth for Mrs. Ostrowski. She wasn't sure why. Perhaps because her mind was focusing so strongly on joining Thaddeus.

"And you can't tell me where?"

"Not now."

"Later?"

"Eventually. I will write you."

"I will miss you, dear. And Thaddeus." Mrs. Ostrowski, in her own warped way, meant what she was saying, even though her own sense of loyalty rose and fell like a malfunctioning elevator.

"I will miss you too." Bernadeta extended her right arm and gripped Mrs. Ostrowski's hand, then covered it affectionately with her left hand.

"Ready," said the driver, closing the car's trunk.

"I am ready," Bernadeta said, disengaging from Mrs. Ostrowski. As she stepped toward the car door being held open by the driver, Bernadeta saw three men come striding down the walk. Her throat thickened immediately and tears began filming her eyes.

"You didn't think you could escape us without a proper goodbye," Marek Krawczyk said, eyes twinkling.

Bernadeta dabbed at her eyes with the back of her hands. Her head shook, sadness engulfing her.

Marek held out his arms and Bernadeta stepped into his embrace. Then Jerzy Pinkowski and Henryk Wyzynski, flanking Bernadeta, wrapped their arms around her and Marek. Their groans of sadness had the driver averting his eyes and Mrs. Ostrowski looking on with envy.

Bernadeta pulled back just enough to look into their incredibly kind and caring eyes. "I love you," she whispered, voice quavering. "I love each of you."

"We do not own a camera," Marek murmured, his bass voice cracking. "But we do not need a picture to remember this moment. You will live forever in the memories of the cow pen soldiers."

CHAPTER 50

The vote was 180-16. That was the result of the parliamentary election that gave the presidency of South Korea – now officially the Republic of Korea – to Syngman Rhee. His defeated opponent was Kim Koo who had served as the last president of the provisional government. The date was August 15, 1948. The Republic of Korea was formally established as a sovereign nation.

Rhee was ecstatic but not entirely satisfied. He was determined to be president of Korea – South and North. He also was ruthless. Soon his army and police were detaining and torturing suspected communists and North Korean agents. Many were executed. Rhee's government oversaw several massacres of left-wing groups.

Rhee's fanatical anti-communism quickly made him a darling of U.S. officialdom and news media – for a time. Then his excesses gradually began to chip away at his popularity, and his handsome, erudite veneer failed to mask a penchant for cruelty. Rhee was too egotistical to foresee how losing U.S. support might undermine his otherwise laudable ambition for a united Korea.

The two horses were walking slowly. Thaddeus Metz and the gray-haired elder were riding side by side. It was mid-morning in August

1948 on the Tohono Reservation. The unblemished sky was a rich blue, the ground hard and the air dry. The former Polish lancer and the aging, distinguished-looking Indian leader were both erect on their saddles. They were meeting for the first time.

"Our land is not like your homeland," said the elder. "That is my understanding from Father Brecker."

Thaddeus smiled beneath his new broad-brimmed brown stetson. "Your understanding is good. My land is green and mostly flat. In our south we have mountains – Carpathians we call them – but they are lower than yours and they are covered by trees."

The elder chuckled. He was wearing a red headband knotted behind his head with a tail nearly as long as his shoulder-length hair. "Our mountains are like the man who has lost most of his hair. You can see his bare scalp."

Thaddeus smiled. "I want you to know that it is a privilege to be riding with you. Father Brecker has told me how much he respects your people and your history."

The two horses continued walking placidly along the base of a stark, steeply rising ridge.

The elder paused before replying. "He has told me much about your people and their bravery and your horsemanship. When he told me that you wanted to visit us, I knew we must ride together."

"Your horses are fine animals."

"Today we have few horses. Mostly to herd sheep. But horses are one with our heritage so we give them good care."

"Excellent care," said Thaddeus.

He and Bernadeta were now living in Ajo and both were working for Elgin Hunter's copper mining company. Hunter had offered Thaddeus a job driving a large ore truck used in the open pit mine. "A truck is not a horse," Thaddeus had joked with Jack who had joined him and Bernadeta in West Berlin for their journey to the U.S., "but I am learning to handle it. Sometimes when I shift gears, I hear the truck complaining. General never did." After landing in the U.S., Jack had wasted no time before contacting the Hunters who, as expected, reacted expeditiously and generously. Elgin Hunter told Thaddeus that, with time, he expected him to join his son Walt in a management job. First, though, Hunter wanted Thaddeus to learn the basics of mining. Meanwhile the senior Hunter, impressed by descriptions of Bernadeta's work at the Warsaw embassy, added her to his office clerical staff.

"You fought the Germans from horseback?" the elder asked.

"Yes."

"With a spear? Like my ancestors?"

"We carried a rifle across our back, but we charged the enemy with our long lances."

"Ah, better to frighten your enemy. And the lance was more accurate from your charging horse."

"Precisely."

"Your warhorses must have been magnificent creatures."

"They were a sight to behold. My regiment – one thousand men – all rode white horses."

That image, a thousand charging white horses, caused the elder's eyes to brighten. "And later you jumped out of airplanes, like Father Brecker."

"Yes."

"I have been in an airplane only twice. Both times with Father Brecker. In the air with him, I feel like a spirit. I can see everything – at the same time."

"Like God."

"Yes. When Father Brecker flew over Grand Canyon, I knew I was seeing God's creation, his perfect scar."

Thaddeus nodded his understanding. "I am looking forward to seeing that same scar. You know, my wife has a scar. On her face. I see the scar as adding to her beauty."

"Do you have a picture?"

Thaddeus smiled and reached back, extracting his wallet from the rear pocket of his blue jeans. He unfolded it and removed a photo of Bernadeta. He handed it to the coppery-skinned elder.

"She is a beautiful woman," the elder concurred, his eyes studying Bernadeta's visage. "You are right. The scar makes her more beautiful. Perhaps God has created a second perfect scar."

Thaddeus smiled as he took back the picture and inserted it in his wallet. "I think you might be right."

"You are a young man but you have lived a full life."

"Sometimes," Thaddeus grinned, "I think experiencing boredom might be a good thing."

The elder chuckled lowly, then observed seriously, "You have fought much against your enemies. You should live in peace now."

"This is peaceful country."

"Now, yes. But in the past we had many enemies. The Spanish. Other tribes. The American horse soldiers. There were days when these desert sands were running red."

"You persevered."

"Persevered. That word is strange to me."

"You didn't give up your way of life. You worked to preserve it."

"We have tried, but it is not the same." A pause. "A Polish lancer and an Indian. We should run our horses together."

"Now?"

"Can you think of a better time?" the elder asked, smiling wryly.

An acknowledging nod from Thaddeus and both men kicked against the horses' flanks, flicked their reins and shouted remarkably similar battle cries. Within seconds their mounts, manes and tails streaming wildly, went racing across the desertscape. Pounding hoofs were kicking up small clouds of dust and chunks of the hard ground.

Thaddeus removed his stetson, slapped it against his horse's right flank and then waved it above his head. The elder's gray hair and the tail of his red headband were flowing out behind him, parallel to the ground. They ran their horses hard for about two minutes and then pulled back forcefully on the reins, bringing them to a skidding stop.

"I can see you were a fine horse soldier," the elder said, breathing heavily. "God made you to be one with a horse."

"I think he made you for the same purpose. You would have made an excellent lancer."

The elder smiled and said, "I was"

✝✝✝

Min was riding Sejong into Munsan from the south. Ahead on the left on the town's main street, which also was the road north to his hometown of Kaesong, Min could see the Choi's butcher and cutlery shop. He smiled and spoke softly to his horse. "They have been so kind to us. They are not that much older than I am – just nineteen years – but they treat me like a son. I see them as my second parents." Both Choi Chun Kuen and his wife were born in 1910, the year the Japanese had occupied Korea. They had grown up under the heavy boot of the Japanese occupiers and like most Koreans were longing for lasting freedom.

Min reined in Sejong in front of the shop and hopped down. He looped the reins around a hitching rail and stepped inside. "I'm back," he announced happily.

Chun pivoted from a side of beef he was carving and Mrs. Choi looked up from plucking a newly decapitated chicken. Both wore faces of profound sadness.

"What is wrong?" Min asked. "Is it bad news from Kaesong? Is someone ill?"

Mrs. Choi wiped her hands on a cloth and picked up a single sheet of paper. She went walking toward Min and handed him the paper. He looked at Mrs. Choi's tortured features and then down at the paper. It was a governmental form. Park Min Shik was being notified that he had been drafted in the South Korean – Republic of Korea (ROK) – Army. He was being ordered to report for training at Suwon, a walled town some 30 miles south of Seoul.

CHAPTER 51

The autumn of 1948 and much of 1949 bore witness to many remarkable facets of the complex human condition – hope, love, treachery, disappointment, dismay and redemption and their innate propensity for shaping individual lives and altering world affairs. From cozy, quiet Belvidere, Illinois to burgeoning London to scheming Seoul to the sinister Kremlin to plotting Pyongyang to proud Sandhurst, those thickets of human existence and endeavor were complicating choices, influencing decisions and determining destinies.

"You really should," Theresa Hassler Morton said to her mother-in-law Jane. "You know you like serving in Congress, and you know you're good at it and getting better."

"Thank you, dear. Yes, I enjoy the work. But, Theresa, if I run, that means campaigning, and it means not getting to spend nearly as much time as I'd like with you and little Marilyn. If I win, well, she's already a year old, and for the next two years I wouldn't get to see her more than a weekend or two a month."

"I don't have a good answer to that. I wish I did. Marilyn adores you and loves to be with you. That's plain to see. I guess my only answer is that we all have our own lives to live, and I think you'd be happiest – most satisfied – if you were elected to Congress in your own right."

"You are a wise young woman. You've been through a lot and learned much. You have a lovely young daughter. But let me ask you, what do you see in your own future? What would make you happiest, satisfy you the most?"

Theresa sighed and shook her head. "I don't think I'm nearly as wise as you think," she smiled. "I don't have that figured out yet. It's only been..."

"I know, dear. It's only been a few months."

"Sometimes I wonder if there will be any place that I can really consider home again."

"Are we both dancing around the subject of men?"

"I think so."

"That's what I thought."

Theresa smiled. "You are a beautiful, intelligent woman, and I think you'll have Washington men seeking your company."

"A couple have." Jane shrugged. "Too early. That's what I told them. But what about you? You're so young and pretty."

"I know it's silly, but I feel star-crossed. Losing Dean – and Hal Walker." She didn't mention Jack Brecker. "I'm not sure I'm up to loving again. And besides, I'm a mother, so," she smiled ruefully, "it would have to be a man willing to take two females."

†††

Jane Morton did campaign, vigorously, and in November easily won election as a Republican to the House of Representatives. That night, after the tally was announced, Jane, elated and exhausted, found herself going to bed with her campaign manager. She was surprised it was happening, but if felt good to hold and be held once again.

Theresa slept alone, as she had each night since the plane crash, with Marilyn in the adjoining room. Theresa agreed to go to work in Jane's district office in nearby Rockford, taking the job Dean had held. In Belvidere, Theresa found a middle-age widow, Mrs. Cassandra Lawson, who happily took on babysitting Marilyn.

✝✝✝

"I'm a virgin," Lucy Crispin said softly.

Michael Cornelius' reply was slow in coming. He was surprised not by Lucy's virginity but by her declaration. Then he spoke equally softly. "It doesn't seem an altogether undesirable state."

"It's not entirely by desire. In Wellington, losing my virginity just wasn't the proper thing to do. Not for the daughter of a leading surgeon and a respected teacher. Not that I was pining to lose it." She looked up at Michael and smiled. He was home on holiday leave from Sandhurst, and he and Lucy were seeing each other evenings after her nurse training ended. "And here in London my life has been at St. Thomas, mostly with women and many of them nuns."

"Not conducive to frank talk about sex."

"Not at all."

"So why bring it up now?"

"It's Christmas season." Lucy and Michael were strolling along the Embankment adjacent the Thames. They were nearing Cleopatra's Needle, the 69-foot-high granite obelisk erected in Egypt between 23 and 12 B.C. and brought from Alexandria to London in 1877. Darkness had fallen and the light from occasional street lamps and passing cars was just enough for Lucy and Michael to see each other's eyes. "I was just thinking of Christ and the virgin birth. A biological challenge if ever there was one."

"A theological contrivance?"

"That too."

"Yes, well, now that you've brought it up – your virginity, I mean – and since we have been spending a lot of time together and, well, given our feelings for each other, I'm thinking-"

Lucy cut Michael off. "Your normally facile tongue seems more firmly tied than the Gordian Knot. Are you a virgin too?" Her blunt question met stoney silence. "We nurses-to-be learn the benefits of directness." Through the darkness Lucy could sense Michael blushing.

"Yes."

Lucy removed her right hand from Michael's left and wrapped it around his waist. "We should speak plainly, don't you think? A soldier-to-be and a nurse-to-be should be able to manage that, don't you agree?"

Michael could feel the heat in his reddened cheeks dissipating as he began recovering from his embarrassment. "You are spot on, nurse-to-be Crispin." He draped his left arm across her shoulders.

"Then tonight let's end our extant virginal state."

"Ahem. You just a moment ago spoke of speaking plainly."

"Screw?"

"That's plain enough."

✝✝✝

In March 1949, Jane Morton took the oath of office as a newly elected Congresswoman. It had felt good to be asked by the governor to complete Raymond's unexpired term. It felt better to be starting one after being elected by constituents free to accept or reject her candidacy.

In May 1949 Joseph Stalin lifted the blockade of Berlin that he had ordered on June 24, 1948. But the airlift would continue until September. At its peak cargo-laden planes landed in West Berlin at a rate of one every 45 seconds. In addition to necessities pilots had dropped tons of candy to appreciative, exuberantly waving children. Following the airlift, Germany was partitioned into east and west with West Berlin remaining an island of democracy in the repressed east.

In mid-1949 Syngman Rhee and Kim Il Sung both were preoccupied with thoughts of wars – ones each ruler wanted to start. The brothers Park, Min and Han, were both hoping war could be avoided. They dreaded the prospect of their nation being sundered – and of being on opposite sides of any armed conflict.

Rhee sought support from President Truman for a South Korean invasion of North Korea. Truman refused him; the United States would not send weapons or equipment or armed forces of consequence. It would, he told Rhee, continue to provide consultative assistance through KMAG – Korea Military Advisory Group. Rhee was disappointed and distressed and had good reason to be.

Kim Il Sung had better luck. He traveled to Moscow to meet with Stalin.

"I want to touch the South with the point of a bayonet," Kim told Stalin. "If I could strike preemptively with an armored assault, I could defeat Rhee and the South in a matter of days."

Stalin paused before replying, stroking his bushy mustache. He was remembering a March 12, 1949, speech delivered by United States Secretary of State Dean Acheson at the National Press Club in Washington, D.C. In describing America's Asian defense perimeter, Acheson had made no mention of South Korea. How significant was that omission? Did it mean that the U.S. wouldn't trouble itself to defend a South Korea under attack? Stalin wasn't sure.

"Invading the South now would be premature and excessively risky," Stalin told Kim. "We are not ready to fight the United States nor are you. Mao Tse Tung feels likewise. You can ask him. China will need time to recover from its long civil war. Neither of us wants to risk an atomic response from America." Stalin could see the disappointment in Kim's eyes. He wanted to keep Kim as an ally – an unstable one who would prove distracting to both America and China. "But I will not send you home empty-handed. I will supply you with new military muscle – tanks, artillery, automatic weapons and carbines. Soon I will do better; I will also send you Soviet-piloted planes."

Kim's spirits soared. Whereas moments before he had despaired unifying the Koreas, he now saw the way to fulfilling his dream. At some point he now felt, perhaps not too far into the future, he could win Stalin's approval to invade the South. And Mao's too.

After departing from Moscow, Kim journeyed to Beijing to see Mao. In the Chinese leader's office in the Forbidden City his reply echoed Stalin's. "As you know, we have just completed defeating Chiang Kai Shek's Nationalist Army. It took us years and cost millions of lives. We simply cannot go to war again, not with the U.S. Not yet." Privately, though, Mao felt an obligation to aid Kim who had been a valued ally in

Mao's defeat of Chiang's Nationalists. At some point Mao expected to repay his debt to Kim.

Despite the rejections of his proposals for preemptive strikes in Moscow and Beijing, Kim returned to Pyongyang ebullient. He was confident that both Stalin and Mao would eventually support him in a war with Rhee's South Korea. Kim's remaining concern was that Rhee might strike first, even without U.S. support. We are only sixty miles north of Seoul, Kim reflected, but I am confident my army could stop his, especially with the equipment Stalin has promised to deliver. My goal is within reach. The signs are favorable. This is an auspicious beginning.

✝✝✝

The Duke of Gloucester was there. He was decked out in colors that would have made a peacock proud. The Duke was the queen's uncle and King George VI's brother. It was customary for a royal family member to attend commencement at the Royal Military Academy at Sandhurst where the graduation ceremony was known as the Sovereign's Parade, so decreed by King George V during his 1910-1936 reign. Reason for the decree: graduating cadets receive the Sovereign's Commission as second lieutenants.

Michael Cornelius and Kendall Thorne were understandably excited. They had completed Sandhurst's rigorous curriculum, and they and fellow graduates were being feted amidst considerable ceremonial pomp. On this sun-splashed Sunday in late July 1949 they were standing ramrod straight in their ceremonial dress – navy blue tunics with a vertical red stripe on the matching blue trousers and peaked navy blue caps with a red band.

Spectators thronged three sides of the huge paved parade ground in front of the massive Old College. Scattered trees provided little shade. Both Michael and Kendall's parents were there, but Michael's eyes were locked on Lucy Crispin, resplendent in a pale yellow dress and a small yellow hat that seemed to struggle to remain in place atop her crown of curly brown hair. Her eyes were on Michael, and her slightly crooked smile, left side a smidgen higher than the right, was showing her brilliantly white teeth. She raised her right arm and waved, knowing that Michael couldn't break formation to return her greeting. From her slightly withered left arm hung a small white purse.

† † †

After the ceremony, at the parade ground's fringe Michael shook hands with his father Roger, warmly embraced his mother Florence, grasped Lucy's shoulders and decorously gave her an air kiss on her right cheek. "I'm so glad you could come," he said, verging on gushing his gratitude. "I'm sorry I couldn't be there for your graduation." He was referring to Lucy's having completed the St. Thomas nursing program.

"Not to worry. I received cabled congratulations from my parents and brother. One of the nuns even hugged me."

"Did you hug her back?"

"I was too startled."

"Are you staying at St. Thomas? I'm sure they would love to have you stay on."

"They would, but I'm not certain. Where will you be posted?"

"Germany."

"Oh." Lucy had been hoping it would be someplace in England. "How long?"

Michael was starting to feel awkward, discussing their plans in front of his parents and strangers, and everyone sensed his growing embarrassment. "I have leave before going to Germany. Let's talk more at tonight's ball and then in London."

The night following graduation, Sandhurst tradition included a ball that much resembled American proms. Newly commissioned second lieutenants wore their dress blues, their dates formal evening gowns, and Lucy had brought hers. The affair was held in the Sandhurst gym. That night an orchestra would play for dancing, and a cabaret performer would sing both traditional and contemporary favorites. Also providing entertainment that night would be a sextet of mustachioed singing waiters. Afterward the graduates and their dates would leave campus for dinner, then return to the gym for dancing till dawn followed by breakfast.

"Right," said Roger, relieved by Michael's suggestion. "Now let's find your friend Lieutenant Thorne and his parents and extend our congratulations."

Before they could do so, another newly commissioned officer approached Michael and, before extending his hand, snapped off a salute. It was Elton Leighton. "Thank you," he said to Michael who returned the salute. "You made all the difference."

They shook hands.

"You are most welcome, Lieutenant Leighton. Congratulations."

Elton then moved away to speak with other graduates and their families.

"Who was that and what did he mean by his comment?" Lucy asked.

"It's a long story," said Michael, shrugging. "Later, when we have more time."

† † †

Two nights later Michael and Lucy both were groaning. They were naked, and their sweat was mingling in Lucy's warm, small room above Ronald Turner's bicycle shop. Lucy's tongue flicked her upper lip. Michael was breathing heavily.

"Lieutenant Cornelius, I would think all of your military training would have you properly conditioned for strenuous exercise," Lucy teased.

"Quite right, Nurse Crispin, but our training somehow omitted the exertion required when taking the pleasure of a woman's close company."

"Well put, Lieutenant."

They laughed and Michael dismounted and rolled onto his back.

"How long will you be in Germany?"

"Three years."

"Oh."

"Seems like an eternity – or a long exile. And to think that before I fell in love with you I saw the army as a grand adventure."

"Fell in love?"

"No use denying it. Or obfuscating."

"No, indeed." Lucy inhaled and then reached for a sheet and pulled it over her.

"And?"

"And what?"

"Are you in love with me?"

"Do you think I'd let just any randy officer screw a New Zealand lass?"

"Might I take that as an affirmative?"

Lucy knew the truthful answer was yes. She also knew that saying yes could lead to complexities – a quick marriage, maybe an early pregnancy and perhaps it already was too late to prevent that, and a long separation depending on whether or when she could move to Germany. It might also mean closing the door to her putative nursing career. She decided against obfuscating. "Yes, I am in love with you. But…"

"But what?"

"But I don't want us to think of marriage. Not yet. There are too many uncertainties."

"My service in Germany."

"That's a big one. Michael, I'm thinking since you'll be away for so long that I'll go back to New Zealand for a bit. Start nursing in Wellington."

"I get leaves."

"I know."

"Whew. I…I never imagined you would be returning to New Zealand. Not to take a job. It sounds so permanent."

"Not necessarily. But I need to see my family."

"Of course."

"Your British upper lip is proving admirably stiff."

"Too stiff actually. Let me loosen it. I was hoping we could be married. Perhaps during my first leave. Could we at least become engaged now?"

Lucy sighed. "I really do feel a need to see my family, Michael. This seems like a good time. While you're away. A few months from now, a year perhaps, if we still feel the same way we do now, then I could come back to London and get engaged." She smiled. "We could make it a very short engagement."

✝✝✝

Theresa Hassler was returning to London and not alone. She had little Marilyn with her. They had taken a train from Southampton's port, and a taxi was bringing them from Waterloo Station to the Royal Horseguards Hotel on Whitehall Court. In Theresa's mind the hotel was conveniently located, only a block from Whitehall Street to the west and the Thames to the east. And just a short walk after crossing the river were St. Thomas Hospital, hulking, bustling Waterloo Station and Ronald Turner's bicycle shop in quiet Carlisle Lane.

✝✝✝

The next morning about 10:00, with two-year-old Marilyn cradled in her right arm, Theresa pushed open the shop's door.

Ronald Turner was talking with a male customer who was seeking advice on bicycle repairs. Barely looking in Theresa's direction, Turner said, "Be with you in a few minutes, Ma'am." He then returned to talking with his customer.

Moments later the customer turned away from the sales and service counter. He nodded to Theresa as he passed by. Theresa smiled and began stepping toward the counter. Mr. Turner looked up from his paperwork. "Now, Ma'am, how might I?" – and he stopped, mouth agape. Theresa said nothing, just stood there smiling. "Good heavens," Mr. Turner sputtered. "It is you! Oh, how witless of me. Of course it's you. I mean – and this darling child," he stammered as he stepped from behind his counter.

"Would you take her from me, please?"

"Of course." And Ronald Turner reached for Marilyn who didn't complain but showed no pleasure in being handed off to this stout man, balding, in his mid-50s.

Theresa reached out with both arms and embraced both Mr. Turner and Marilyn. Even as Mr. Turner, unaccustomed to being the object of affection in his shop, began to redden, Theresa kissed him firmly on his left cheek. "Should have done that years ago," she said pluckily.

"I'm glad Mrs. Turner wasn't here to see it," he said brightly. "She would be in shock, just as I am. But pleasantly so, let me add."

"Good!"

"Your lovely daughter…"

"Marilyn Carter Morton. Do you want me to take her back?"

"No. Unless the little lady wants you to take her back."

"We named her after Lieutenant Colonel Marilyn Carter."

"I remember…your commanding officer who was killed." Theresa nodded. "How very thoughtful. She would be pleased beyond words. And your husband?"

Theresa sucked in a deep breath and then let it out slowly. "I lost him earlier this year. A plane crash."

"Oh my Lord." Mr. Turner was visibly shaken. Theresa's loss of Hal Walker came crashing back into his memory.

Theresa inhaled and exhaled again. "A small plane. Piloted by Dean's father. They were returning from Washington and were hit by lightning and high winds."

Mr. Turner's head shook in sadness and dismay. "I am so sorry."

"Thank you. Dean had time to write me a short note in the logbook. They found it in the wreckage. It meant a lot to me."

Mr. Turner swallowed hard and caressed Marilyn's cheeks. "Are you here to stay?"

"I'd like to but no. Just visiting. Getting a change of scenery."

"A necessary diversion, I'm sure. You know, I've another nurse from abroad living in your old room. Young woman from New Zealand. Would you like to meet her while you are here?"

"Yes. That would be nice."

"She's working now. At St. Thomas."

"Perhaps this evening – or at the hospital."

"Where are you staying?"

"At the Royal Horseguards."

"I know it. Good location. A pretty pound?"

"Not to worry," which she guessed was precisely what Ronald Turner was doing. "Dean saw to it that we were well cared for by life insurance. Double indemnity in case of accidental death. And I've a job working for my mother-in-law. She succeeded her husband in our House of Representatives."

"Good." Mr. Turner's eyes reflected his relief. "You said you'd like to remain in London but can't."

"It still feels like my home. But I've got Marilyn to think of and my job."

"Would you consider extending your visit a bit if you had larger and less expensive accommodations?"

"I might."

"Well, you heard me say the young nurse is still occupying your old room. But my larger flat will be vacant in another few days. Would you like to see it?"

Theresa paused and reflected before replying. Her mind was beginning to sort out unintended consequences of a longer stay. They seemed manageable. "I just might. For another two or three weeks."

"Good. Come with me. The tenants – a couple – are at work. The flat has a nice living room, a bedroom, a private bath and a kitchen with a fridge and stove. Not merely a hotplate." They both chuckled at the thought of the small device that Theresa had used to warm soup and tea and that Lucy Crispin likely was using similarly.

"You make it sound very appealing. Perhaps I could stay on a while. It would help if I could find a babysitter."

"Perhaps I can help there too. Let me think about it."

"Where are your tenants moving?"

"New York. He's in banking and his wife is willing to give up her job – clerking at Fortnum and Mason – to make the move."

† † †

Tomasz Dolata was on the move as well. After Kaz Majos had left Warsaw for Zyrardow, Tomasz continued to use the long beer delivery drives for contemplation. Three years had passed since his arrival in Warsaw from Cracow. Although his business continued to flourish – he now owned three wagons and employed two drivers – prosperity wasn't bringing with it the anticipated contentment. In fact, a sense of disappointment – vague at first but sharpening – was taking hold. He never tried to dismiss it as idle daydreaming, and now it was consuming most of his self-described "think time" during the placid wagon rides. He also had done some investigating, and the results had given him a modicum of encouragement – not enough to fuel unbridled optimism but enough to nurture hope.

On a Friday morning in August 1949 Tomasz told his drivers they would cease operating for a few days. "Give yourselves and our animals a rest. I'm leaving for a while but should be back within a week. Perhaps within a few days." He would be traveling south.

† † †

Jacek Frantek was ready to fulfill the promise he had made to Marzena in autumn 1946 after Tomasz had departed with Kaz for Warsaw. It

270

was the same Friday night in August, the restaurant's last customers had departed, and the Frantek family had ascended to their apartment. Jacek asked Maria, Marzena and Edward to sit with him in their living room. Marzena was holding little Daniel, now past age two.

"I've been giving this a lot of thought," Jacek began. Immediately sensing their curiosity and wanting to head off alarm, he forced a smile. "I think it's time. I made a pledge and I must fulfill it." He sighed and smiled again, this time more easily. "I am going to look for Tomasz."

Silence followed, a long one during which Jacek was comfortable. Then Marzena shook her head, a movement that momentarily puzzled Jacek. "Oh, Father. I am so proud of you. Thank you." She placed Daniel on the floor, stood, stepped to Jacek, bent down and hugged him.

Maria was beaming, her pride in her husband equally evident.

"I might not find him. Perhaps I have waited too long. He might have left Warsaw. He might be married."

Edward bit his lip. "I'm thinking too." Three pairs of eyes shifted their focus to him. "I would like to do it. Go look for Tomasz."

"Edward-"

The son cut off his father. "You are needed here. To run the restaurant. You know that. I'm old enough. I can do it. I want to." What Edward was thinking was this: I, a Catholic, can go looking for a Jew and not be ashamed.

Now it was Jacek's eyes showing pride, tempered with a measure of concern. "If you go, if I let you go-"

"I am going."

"Yes. All right. When you go, you must take care. Be cautious. Poles asking questions about other Poles can have the secret police asking their own questions."

"I will say I am looking for a friend. I won't lie."

"Smart. But they would probe. Who is this friend? Where did you meet him? How long have you known him? What is his background? Why are you looking for him? Why now?"

Edward nodded. "I will stay with the truth."

"One more question," Jacek said. "What if they ask if your friend is a Jew? You could endanger him."

"In that case I will lie."

The next morning, a Saturday, Edward would be journeying north, by bus.

†††

Tomasz's train, a prewar steam-billowing relic, departed Warsaw on schedule, and he hoped that unexpected happening foretold success.

†††

The road north from Cracow paralleled railroad tracks, and from his seat on the right side of the wheezing, rattling bus Edward watched a passenger train cruising south. The bus and train were sliding past each other too rapidly for Edward to make out any faces among the train's passengers, not that he was expecting to see anyone he recognized.

†††

At his destination that evening Tomasz stepped onto the platform with his bag. His heart was beginning to race. It was a feeling he hadn't experienced in years but was nonetheless familiar. He remembered all too vividly his heart's reaction to uncertainty and the resulting stress. The daily mass murders at Auschwitz and disposal of corpses of fellow Jews and other victims. Planning the escape. With crucial help from Aline Gartner. The breakout. On the run from the Nazis. In hiding. Nerves taut and jangling so fiercely he half-expected people nearby could hear them. Today there was no danger of death, but uncertainty and its accompanying anxiety were threatening to overwhelm his resolve. Should I go through with this? Can I? What will I find? Am I being foolish? He had asked himself those questions dozens of times.

As Tomasz walked into the Rynek Glowny, the expansive central plaza, he paused to take in the bustling Saturday crowd and slowly sucked in a breath. Then summoning waning determination and feeling perspiration begin to leak from his armpits, he headed to the building on the plaza's far corner. At the door he breathed deeply again and pushed it open.

Polska Kopernika was busy. Tomasz stood still with his bag, and the scene before him seemed a blur. Calm down, he told himself. But his heart and nerves were proving as disobedient as a stalking house cat creeping closer to a caged bird. Then he heard it; slicing through the restaurant's normal din was a shriek. It silenced conversation, and some 30 pairs of eyes shifted first to the shriek's source and then to its target. There followed a third shift – to the sight of the shriek's source hurriedly placing two full plates on the nearest table and then scurrying among tables toward the man standing mute inside the entrance.

Before Tomasz could step forward, much less utter a word, he found himself locked in a tearful, crushing embrace. The young woman's sobs would have been heartrending were they not so obviously manifesting ecstasy.

Tomasz lowered his bag to the floor and wrapped his brawny arms around Marzena. He could feel his heart slowing and his nerves relaxing. Her exuberant I-won't-let-you-go hug was answering unasked questions and banishing uncertainty.

Marzena stepped back, wiped tears with the hem of her flowered apron, looked up and half-moaned, "I can't believe it. I stopped hoping."

In the next moment a second shriek pierced the smoky air. It was Maria's. She and Jacek went racing to greet Tomasz. Jacek grasped Tomasz's right hand with both of his hands, and Maria hugged him with motherly ferocity.

A blonde-haired little boy came toddling from the kitchen. In his first two years the scene before him was unprecedented. He had never seen adults behaving with such gleeful abandon. He hung back for several seconds then continued taking small, tentative steps, the knot of embracing arms drawing him forward as would a powerful magnet.

Marzena saw him approaching and beckoned with a small wave and warm smile. Jacek and Maria freed Tomasz's arms, and Marzena lightly grasped his left arm with her right and pointed to the little boy. Then she gazed rapturously into Tomasz's dark eyes and murmured, "Do you see the resemblance? He is your son. Our son."

Sensing the reunion's significance diners began applauding, tentatively then with mounting exuberance. Maria turned toward the customers. "He is our hero!" she exulted. "He has returned!"

Cheering began to accompany the applauding, and many diners rose to their feet.

Tomasz had yet to speak and wasn't sure what words would emerge first. He shook his head and smiled. Then he reached down and patted the little boy's head.

"Calm down, dear," Jacek said to Maria. "Come with us. To the kitchen."

Marzena picked up Daniel who was gazing curiously at Tomasz and the thick beard that rendered his face shadowy. Their unblinking eyes locked on each other's. As the fivesome moved through the tables, several customers reached out to pat them on their shoulders and backs.

"He is mine?" Tomasz murmured, knowing the question was stupid but unable to refrain from asking.

"You are his father," Marzena said, beaming. "Now he has his father."

Inside the kitchen Maria dabbed at her tears and asked, "Where is Edward?"

"What? What do you mean?" Tomasz replied.

"Isn't he with you?"

"No."

"Edward went looking for you. In Warsaw."

"Did he go by train?"

"By bus."

✝✝✝

That night, at Marzena's suggestion, Tomasz slept in Edward's bed. She was still sleeping with Daniel, and the bed wasn't nearly wide enough for a third body. She thought it would be too unnerving on this first night for Daniel to have this strange man in bed with them. Besides, though she and Tomasz were parents, they weren't husband and wife, and Marzena knew that she and her parents would be discomfited were she and Tomasz in bed together in their apartment.

The next morning in the restaurant kitchen Maria prepared a sumptuous breakfast featuring potato pancakes and blood sausage. At a dining room table with Maria, Jacek, Marzena and Daniel, Tomasz felt much more confident and relaxed. He had hardly slept – barely an hour or two – but this morning had no difficulty organizing his thoughts and speaking clearly. "With your permission, I would like to make your daughter my wife. It

274

seems I am a trifle late doing so," he said with amusing self-deprecation that was greeted by warm smiles.

Tomasz's words were thrilling Marzena, hands clasped in front of her chest.

"If you really need our formal blessing," Jacek said, "You have it."

"Thank you. I understand we can't be married in the Catholic church unless I convert, and I am willing to do that. I also know that a Jew, even a converted one, can't live comfortably in Poland with a Catholic wife and son." No one voiced disagreement with his assertion. They knew it to be true. Jews had been slaughtered and among gentiles a degree of sympathy had resulted. But anti-Semitism remained, virulent among some Poles. "There could be harassment. Persecution. My business has been succeeding. I have made much money and I've been saving it. I have also been making inquiries. I think we can qualify to emigrate to the United States."

✝✝✝

"Finally. If I can only take one step at a time, this is a huge step." Kim Il Sung was exultant. "This is my reward – my just reward – for fighting hard – hard and long – for communism. Now I have even a stronger foundation for pressing my case for a unified Korea with Stalin and Mao. I will be persistent. I am nothing if not persistent. I cannot let that rogue Rhee deliver the first blow."

It was September 9, 1949, in Pyongyang, and the North Korean communists, with Stalin's permission, formally announced establishment of the Democratic People's Republic of Korea. Along with South Korea, North Korea now was formally a sovereign nation.

Not everyone was celebrating. Many ordinary Koreans – South and North – including the Park brothers saw this development leading inexorably to indefinite tension and verbal hostilities if not all-out war. Neither Min nor Han expected to be wearing civilian clothes again anytime soon. Min's girlfriend, Ahn Kyong Ae, was despondent.

Elsewhere on the planet the formal creation of North Korea made few headlines, virtually none on front pages. After all, Kim Il Sung already had been handed control of the North; this new development was seen as a mere formality capping a fait accompli. If asked, few people outside Asia could locate the Korean peninsula on a globe. To them, The Land of the Morning Calm – the name attached to the peninsula by its residents for centuries – might as well have been an unnamed cartographic dot.

CHAPTER 52

The two women were approaching each other in the narrow hallway of the floor above the bicycle shop. They needed no third party to introduce them. Lucy Crispin took note immediately of Theresa Hassler Morton's limp, and Theresa's nurse's eye for detail could see Lucy's slightly deformed left arm and hand.   They reached out to shake hands.

"I know it sounds terribly trite," said Lucy, "but I've heard so much about you. They describe you as a legend. I am so very pleased to meet you."

"Likewise," said Theresa. "I have heard only the best about you – from both Mr. Turner and the nuns at St.Thomas. But a legend? That makes me sound positively ancient."

"A yankee and a kiwi, both nurses at St. Thomas. Perhaps we should inform Mr. Ripley. He might commission wax figures of us for his museum."

Theresa and Lucy both laughed.

"And he might photograph us for his next *Believe It Or Not*. Emphasizing my limp of course."

"And my shriveled limb."

"We do make an unlikely pair of Florence Nightingale protégés."

The two women were taking a quick liking to each other, and a bond was forming.

"I've heard that you are returning to staff at St. Thomas," Lucy said.

"Yes. I thought I'd try it for a year or so. See how my daughter adjusts to big city living. My mother-in-law – a very sweet woman – and my family back in Shelby – that's my hometown in Ohio – aren't thrilled, but I do so love London. And, Lucy, I hear you are leaving soon for New Zealand."

"I love it here too, but my family and I need to spend some time together."

"I understand. Well, before you depart, how do you feel about spending some off-duty hours together?"

"I'd love to. And to get to know your daughter."

"Do you play gin?"

"Not too shabbily."

"Good. How about we make Saturday night's entertainment a game of gin, a bottle of wine – my treat – and listening to the BBC?"

"Sounds delightful."

"Of course, before I put Marilyn to bed, she'll likely want to crawl onto your lap."

Lucy laughed. "I think I can hold her with one arm and my cards with this," she said, holding up her left arm.

"I've another thought," Theresa said, brown eyes shining brightly. "Since you'll be departing soon, let's ask Mr. Turner to take pictures of us together. As reminders of good times and of each other's pusses as the years go by."

"In our uniforms!"

"Even better!"

CHAPTER 53

It was early morning just before the onset of a gloomy dawn in the late autumn of 1949. Captain Kwon Oh Bum stood before his 200-man rifle company that included two mortar teams. They were positioned just north of the 38th Parallel atop one of the many high hills in the area east of Kaesong. The men were standing in the gray opaqueness of a low-hanging cloud that seemed intent on remaining as motionless as the hill beneath it.

Kwon lit a bitter, Chinese-made cigarette. He inhaled deeply, his lungs holding the acrid smoke for long seconds before beginning to slowly exhale. Sometimes, he reflected, his head shaking in quiet dismay, it is hard to believe how much things have changed. I remember the face of the first man I killed. A Japanese corporal. A young one. Younger than me. At close range. It happened so fast. In truth it wasn't so difficult.

Our training was excellent. I certainly didn't feel guilty. It was duty. The Japanese were evil. Pitiless. But I wasn't expecting that the killing would go on for…for so long. Or that it would lead to killing other Koreans. Or that I would come to find it so easy. Kwon inhaled again. Hatred. That is the key. It's something I have learned, mastered. In a way, I'm glad. That sounds strange, but it makes serving Kim easier. There's something else I'm glad about. My parents and sisters are safe in Pyongyang. They mean so much to me. Kwon took another long drag. Well, enough of this. There's no sense in looking back. The past is past. I can't change any of it. If I could I'm not sure I would. I have a mission, and if hating helps, so be it. I'm not afraid to let it rule me. Just the opposite. It can keep working for me. He looked down at the cigarette and flicked the lengthening ash. That's what I need to do, just keep flicking ashes.

Park Han was a member of Kwon's combat company and, unexpectedly, was experiencing a tinge of homesickness. His parents and brother Min's girlfriend Kyong were close by but felt as far from his touch as distant stars on a clear cold night.

✝✝✝

Park Min now was a corporal and leading an eight-man squad patrolling south of the 38th Parallel. Min was glad the boredom of repetitive training was behind him but was uneasy during these predawn hours. He had reason to be. What amounted to border warfare between South and North Korea had been intensifying, taking lives and inflaming tensions since back in November of 1948.

✝✝✝

Captain Kwon straightened his five feet eight inches. "Despite this cloud, our mission this morning is quite clear," he told his men. "We are to inflict punishment on soldiers loyal to that scurvy dog Syngman Rhee. He is corrupt and already is stealing from the pockets of our countrymen in the South. If he had his way, he would be doing the same thing here in the North."

Loyal? Han was listening cynically. Loyal to whom? What choice did I have? What choice does anyone have these days? I am serving in Kim Il Sung's army because I was conscripted. Not from any sense of duty. And the men we will be shooting at? They are in the South Korean Army because of accidents of birth and geography – and probably were conscripted like me. If what Kwon says about Rhee is true, I feel sorry for the people in the South. But I am wondering if Kim is just as corrupt.

"We will use mortars to draw their fire and fix their positions," Captain Kwon explained. "And then we will charge. We will kill the enemy. We will take no prisoners. If you see a wounded enemy, kill him. That is Rhee's way and it will be ours. Under no circumstance will you retreat. Anyone who retreats is a traitor to our Great Leader and deserves only instant death."

✝✝✝

Min and his squad mates were treading gingerly. The rocky ground was unstable. Loose stones and pebbles were freckling their path, and the area was laced with mines and peppered with unexploded shells. The next step could be my last, Min was thinking nervously. He paused and looked to the north. The cloud-crowned high hill opposite showed no sign of activity. He looked down at the pebble-strewn trail and took another step.

In the next instant a mortar shell exploded above and sent pine tree limbs and needles and shrapnel cascading down on Min and his men. They flattened themselves against the hard cold earth. A second detonation followed moments later. The third noise Min heard was human; it was a primal scream erupting from one of his men. Min pushed his helmet up and saw a friend with his right arm nearly severed at the elbow.

Min's men, some lying prone and others kneeling, pivoted and prepared to fire on the hill to the north. "Wait!" Min ordered. His training was kicking in. "Hold your fire. That's what they want. We can't see them and they can't see us. Those mortars. They want to see the fire from our rifles. Locate us. Zero in on us. Then send more mortars and open up with rifles and machine guns."

✝✝✝

Impatience and exasperation. That's what Captain Kwon was experiencing. There must be South Korean troops in that sector, he was

279

thinking. They are always patrolling that area. Rhee knows this would be a major invasion route. Come on; answer us with even just a few rounds.

†††

"You two," Min directed, "help him up. Get him back to our camp. Have him treated." He will no doubt lose an arm to amputation, Min knew. Our combat medical facilities are primitive. "Tell our CO what happened. We will stay here and wait for relief or reinforcements in case the North is planning an incursion."

†††

Han was relieved. He sighed and swallowed. With no return fire from the South, our company won't be crossing the 38th Parallel this morning. But maybe tonight or tomorrow morning. Kim Il Sung seems to be spoiling for war.

†††

Not quite. Warning and goading. That's what Kim Il Sung and Syngman Rhee were up to in the last months of 1949.

The United States Central Intelligence Agency concluded that Kim had an estimated 3,500 to 6,000 guerillas who already had penetrated south of the 38th Parallel. Rhee's roundups and executions of suspected North Korean guerillas and agents were not without foundation. For the most part the North Korean infiltrators were armed with U.S.- and Japanese-made rifles and also carried clubs and bamboo spears. They attacked – often at night – South Korean Army troops, police stations and civilians.

Rhee's South Korean forces aggressively hunted down the guerillas. During these months they captured, interrogated, tortured and killed an estimated 5,000. In one four-day battle, 400 North Korean guerillas, 225 South Korean troops and 100 civilians died. Another day-long fight included an exchange of artillery barrages. Koreans in that area could be forgiven for thinking a war already was underway.

Kim's underlying purpose for instigating these deadly engagements: undermine Rhee's regime and warn him that a strike north by his troops would meet with disaster. Rhee's chief reason for enthusiastically skirmishing Kim's southern guerillas and his troops along the 38th Parallel was to goad Kim into a war. President Truman had told Rhee that he would receive strong U.S. military support only if South Korea were attacked without provocation. So much the better, Rhee brazenly concluded, if he could provide the spark for a provocation. Rhee further calculated that strong U.S. support would lead to a quick victory over the North and the unification that he was lusting for.

At the time, the U.S. advisory contingent amounted only to 500 troops, hardly a major deterrent to northern aggression. Still, Rhee was mindful of the continuing need to balance his ego and ambition with another reality: in the late 1940s South Korea was receiving $100 million in aid yearly from the U.S. Most of it was in the form of outright, unrestricted grants that Rhee used to finance everything from manufacturing plants to libraries – and to fatten his personal bank accounts and hoards of gold bars. South Korea's entire annual budget was only about $120 million.

Inexplicably, as 1949 on the Korean peninsula ground to a cold and ugly end, the North-South fighting died down. Some distant observers saw the cessation as signaling a conclusion by Kim and Rhee that contenting themselves with presiding over their respective domains might be the wise course. Observers closer to the scene – Min and Han among them – judged the lull as the harbinger of a coming storm.

In Arizona a storm was forming over the mountains near Charco. Roiling black and gray clouds seemed to be chasing angrily one after another. The elder looked up at lightning bolts spearing the rugged peaks and smiled. The coming rain would be welcome as it almost always was on the Tohono. To the elder the roar of thunder rumbling down from the mountains was one of nature's welcome greetings.

During the last half of December, Tomasz and Marzena Dolata with little Daniel and Lucy Crispin were concentrating on a different sound. It included water, but instead of the sound of storm-driven rain tattooing dry ground, it was the hypnotic rhythm of seas slapping the steel hulls of ships carrying them to distant destinations.

Tomasz, Marzena and Daniel were crossing the North Atlantic on a liner bound for the United States. They were told that the vessel was nearing New York's harbor and, despite the raw cold, were standing on deck, straining for their first glimpse of the Statue of Liberty and all that she represented to those seeking precious freedoms.

Lucy's ship was steaming south through the Atlantic, bound for the Indian Ocean and then the Tasman Sea. She was still thousands of miles from New Zealand, but she was standing on deck, eyes closed against the breeze and imagining her homecoming celebration in Wellington. The sun and sea air were intoxicating and she couldn't help smiling. Even thoughts of Lucy's lover, Michael Cornelius, soldiering in Germany, couldn't diminish her anticipation. She stepped back from the rail and reached into her black leather purse. She extracted three pictures. One showed her and Michael perched on the back of one of the huge bronze lions at Trafalgar Square. The second showed her and Theresa, in their nurse uniforms, grinning like a pair of silly schoolgirls. The third touched Lucy and caused her to reflect. In it she was holding little Marilyn. Some day she hoped to be holding her own daughter. She replaced the photos and again closed her eyes, visualizing a loving embrace with her parents and brother. Had any members of the ship's dance band been playing on deck, Lucy would have been looking for a partner or broken into song.

✝✝✝

Barbara Majos was thrilled and her sister Bernadeta was thrilled for her. The population of the Gudek farm had just increased by one lusty-lunged son. With Bernadeta and Thaddeus now in the U.S., Barbara and Kaz were inspired to name their son Thaddeus, after both Bernadeta's husband and Thaddeus Koskiusko (1746-1817), the Polish general who had assisted America in its fight for independence from Great Britain.

In reading Barbara's letter Bernadeta could almost hear her sister laughing. In part, the letter read:

Father is doting on his first grandson. He holds him while strolling around the farm. He tells little Thaddeus about the animals and the crops. He also has taken him into Zyrardow to show him off at church. And I must confess, dear sister, that I have had little Thaddeus on General with me. I think he will become a fine horseman. Please tell your Thaddeus that our Thaddeus and General are both doing splendidly.

Kaz of course is a proud papa. And he has another reason for feeling good. His friend and business partner Tomasz Dolata visited us to tell Kaz that he had married the girl from Cracow and that they, like you, were emigrating to America. Can you believe that? America might end up with more Poles than Poland. Tomasz sold the beer delivery business for an excellent price, and he came to the farm to give Kaz a large bundle of zlotys. I had never seen so much money. Kas was touched but not surprised. I think he and Tomasz are as close and trusting as brothers. Now we can buy a camera so I can take pictures of your nephew and send them to Arizona.

I hope this letter reaches you in Arizona and finds you and your wonderful husband very happy.

Your loving sister,
Barbara

CHAPTER 54

The drizzle was steady and raw on a Friday morning in March 1950 at Buller Barracks in West Germany. The 29th British Brigade's base outside Munster was not far from the Netherlands border. Lieutenants Michael Cornelius and Kendall Thorne deemed Buller Barracks' accommodations "pretty good." Some of the brigade's men were housed in former Wehrmacht barracks that were three and four floors high, brick and built to last. Michael and K were housed in newer British-built barracks that were the equivalent of an architectural yawn; they were single-story nondescript structures lined up in a single row as straight as a rank of soldiers awaiting inspection.

On this morning, Michael and K were breakfasting together.

"Any plans for this weekend?" K asked Michael.

"Polish brass and shine boots," Michael grinned dispiritedly. "What about you? Anything special?"

"Actually I have a thought."

"No need to keep it to yourself," Michael said, forking scrambled eggs and taking a bite of toast heavily buttered.

"Secure a pass. Three days. Take a train south to Frankfurt. Find a nice hotel that's amenable to offering attractive rates to a pair of underpaid British junior officers."

"Sounds like a ripping good military strategy," Michael replied with vigor. "We could stand a change of scenery. Tell me more."

"Glad you approve, Lieutenant. Once there, then find a nice winstub or biergarten and perhaps a pair of ladies of the night. Affordably priced, of course."

Michael grinned with exaggerated lasciviousness. "When does the next train leave?"

† † †

"Lucy, have you heard?" One of her nurse colleagues had just arrived at Wellington Public Hospital on Adelaide Road in suburban Newtown to begin her shift. Lucy was standing at a nurse's duty station counter, completing a report.

"Heard what?"

"About the whales. Nineteen of them are beached south of Kapiti. It was on the radio."

Kapiti was a town of about 12,000 people some 30 miles north of Wellington.

"Poor things," Lucy replied. "Is anyone doing anything about it?"

"I don't know. The radio didn't say."

† † †

By noon on Saturday, Michael and K were approaching the stately Steigenberger Frankfurter Hotel on Kaizerplatz, a busy plaza in Frankfurt's central business district.

"This looks posh," said K.

"It docs."

It was. Built in 1873-74 the baroque hotel was designed by Swiss architect Alfred Bluntschli. It was damaged but not destroyed during World War II. Repairs had begun soon after V-E Day. The hotel's façade was beige stone. Its main entrance was expansive; a dozen pillars supported five wide arches topped by an ornate balustrade.

Michael and K carried their bags through the central archway, up the steps and into the richly marbled and paneled lobby.

"Too rich for our youthful British blood?" K murmured to Michael, looking at a small sign behind the front desk that showed room rates.

"These days posted rates are just that," Michael muttered through the narrowest crack between his lips, "posted."

†††

Lucy hurried down the long hallway to her father's hospital office and barged in. Dr. Morgan Crispin looked up. He had been writing post-surgery notes.

"May I borrow your car, please?"

"You seem in a rush."

"I am."

†††

Michael and K hefted their bags, turned away from the reception desk and headed toward the elevator at the rear of the lobby.

"You make a good negotiator, Michael," Kendall said admiringly as the elevator carried them to room 321.

"I simply accepted as fact what I observed about posted rates. Besides, we *are* underpaid British second lieutenants, and it didn't strike me as likely that a ritzy hotel in postwar Frankfurt would be overrun with guests on a wet and windy early spring weekend. Plus I had an extra incentive in my negotiating."

"That being?"

"We need to budget our meager funds should we find those ladies of the night."

K punched his friend on a shoulder and chortled. "Cheeky but clever fellow you are."

†††

An hour later Lucy stood in her nurse's whites atop a bluff overlooking the wide sands and the beached whales. They were lying forlornly in a gray ragged row, unmoving, huge heads pointing landward. Lucy's heart swelled with sympathy. She couldn't differentiate males from females, but she could see that the 19 leviathans – some as long as 60 feet – included two calfs, each about 20 feet long.

At least 100 people, including newspaper and radio reporters and photographers, were milling about. Their tongues were clucking sadly, but no one seemed intent on trying to aid the stranded animals.

Someone had to take charge, Lucy was thinking, and she began descending the bluff to the beach.

† † †

Michael and Kendall didn't have to walk far down the street to find a biergarten.

"Lunch?" said Michael.

"With good German lager first," K replied. "I'm famished but I'm even drier."

They stepped inside the dimly lit biergarten and sat on two high wooden chairs at the bar and ordered their first lagers.

Minutes later a tall man in a gray suit with blue tie entered and maneuvered onto a chair two empty seats to Michael's right.

"Like some company?" Michael asked, motioning to the empty chair beside him.

The man looked at Michael and K in their British uniforms and hesitated. "Thank you." And he moved to the chair adjacent Michael's.

† † †

Every spring thousands of whales, mostly humpbacks and rights, went swimming past New Zealand on their way north to summer feeding areas. By 1790 whales – and seals – in New Zealand's coastal waters were attracting whalers and hunters.

The beached whales were humpbacks that tend to swim nearer to land.

As Lucy came striding across the sand, she saw a few people gently stroking the stranded giants.

One middle-age man, standing idly, heard footfalls crunching the sand and turned to look. "What have we here?" he said snidely. "Why it's a nurse, a bloody nurse, all dolled up in white and ready to tend to these dopey creatures."

"Stand aside," Lucy replied cuttingly, "or pitch in and help."

Her rejoinder startled the man, a head taller than Lucy. "Be careful with that tone of voice, young lady," came the man's hardened reply.

"I am being quite careful with my tone of voice. It seems I've chosen just the right one."

"Why you uppity little do-gooder. I should-"

"I've no time for this," Lucy interrupted, brushing past him.

Lucy thrust her arms skyward and held them aloft. "Listen, please," she called out loudly. "If these whales are to have any chance of survival, we must help them. Beached whales cannot live long. Out of the water they overheat. Their own weight gradually crushes their vital organs. Or they will drown when high tide covers their blowholes. Splash them with water. Cover them with anything wet – towels, coats, blankets, throw rugs, draperies. Anything you are willing to sacrifice to spare these gentle creatures or ease their suffering."

Onlookers hesitated only moments and then began responding. Some men, women and children removed their shoes, waded into the sea and began scooping water with hands and buckets and tossing it on the whales' backs. Others went scrambling back across the sand and up the bluff to their homes and businesses to fetch the items Lucy had mentioned. The man who had mocked Lucy stood watching the reaction to her entreaty and then approached from behind. "Miss?"

Lucy recognized the voice and turned with a hardened stare. "Yes?"

"I apologize," the man swallowed, lowering his head. "Don't know what came over me. Is there anything I can do?"

Lucy's glare softened. "I think our best efforts should be directed to the calfs. As the tide comes in we might be able to float them and turn them back to sea. Could you organize two groups to care for them and try to turn them at the earliest opportunity?"

"Consider it done."

✝✝✝

"Lieutenant Cornelius," Michael introduced himself, extending his right hand.

"Gerhard Oberster." He shook Michael's hand.

Then K reached across in front of Michael and offered his hand. "Lieutenant Kendall Thorne."

Oberster took K's hand. "Thank you for inviting me to join you. It surprises me."

"Why?"

"Legendary British reserve. And not so long ago we were mortal enemies."

"But no longer," said Michael, sipping his lager. "And I guess we have been thoroughly exposed to Americans who assuredly possess little British reserve."

"Very tactfully put," said Oberster. He downed a swallow of his lager.

"Did you see action?"

"Some."

"Where?"

"For much of the war I was posted in a small French village. Ribeauville. Lovely place. Surrounded by vineyards and mountains. We had to deal with partisans. There was, uh, some violence. Nothing I am terribly proud of. Duty."

Michael and Kendall had heard enough about clashes between the French Resistance and the occupying Germans to be able to imagine Oberster's situation. They chose not to probe.

"And then?" Michael asked.

"After Paris was liberated and the Allies continued advancing east, we were ordered to leave Ribeauville and go north to Metz."

"Hard duty," Michael observed.

Oberster nodded. "It could have been worse."

"You survived," Michael murmured.

"I had my doubts. More than once. I was assigned to meet with General Patton's emissary to discuss surrender terms for our forts."

"Impressive," said K.

"Actually, I think of the experience more as memorable."

"Why?"

"Patton's emissary. He sent a chaplain." Oberster's head shook in wonder at the memory.

"A chaplain? Strange," Michael agreed.

"He had a German sounding name. Brecker. That's it. Captain Brecker."

"Do you remember his given name?" asked K.

"I never heard it. But I also remember vividly what he was holding. In his one hand a large white cloth. For a truce. In his other a small cross. He held them aloft – like this – as his jeep approached me on the road. Seemed a decent fellow. Not arrogant. Not armed and not afraid."

"Was he alone or did he have someone with him?" K asked.

"The driver. A sergeant. His name…Parma, I think." Oberster smiled and shrugged. "Funny the things you don't forget."

"What happened?" said K. The look on his face – and Michael's – reflected both their curiosity and amazement.

Oberster chuckled. "Captain Brecker was clear that General Patton had lost patience and would accept nothing other than unconditional surrender."

Michael and K both nodded. "Sounds like Patton," Michael said. "Then what?"

Oberster shrugged. "End of war for me. I was taken prisoner. It was a new experience in more ways than one. I was sent to a POW camp in Arizona."

"A long way from Germany," Michael observed.

"But not so bad," Oberster said genially, brightening at the memory. "We were treated well. Honest work and good food. I worked in a copper mine. And members of my family had emigrated to America before the war, and they came to visit me."

✝✝✝

Lucy went walking slowly past the whales, emitting pathetic groans of distress and despair. Occasionally one would exhale through its blowhole. The ensuing cloud or spout consisted chiefly of water vapor with traces of mucus as well as oil droplets. By now some 200 people were shrouding the whales with all manner of soaked cloth items. Lucy paused in front of one of the calfs and an adult lying only a few feet to its left. Its mother? Lucy thought she saw panic in the calf's eyes and resignation in the adult's. She felt tears beginning to well in her own. She heard other people sniffling and dabbing at their eyes. Touching and amazing, Lucy was thinking. In such a brief time, humans were bonding – warmly and sadly – with these imperiled giants that could strike fear when breaching at sea near small craft. We humans can be maddeningly complex, she reflected, but we respond to some very simple impulses.

✝✝✝

"What do you do now?" Michael asked Oberster.

"I write. For a newspaper. The *Frankfurter Allgemeine Zeitung.*"

"What do you write about?" Michael asked.

"Business. With the Marshall Plan helping to rebuild our economy, business is beginning to recover. The Americans are amazing. We were their worst enemies. Well, other than the Japanese. Millions hated us. The fighting barely ceases and they are helping us get back on our feet. Unbelievably generous people."

"You sound as though you like the job," Michael said.

"Oh yes. I am fortunate. The *FAZ* – that is what we call the paper – is well respected, and I like writing about positive developments that are helping our country."

"You've come a long way from being a POW in Arizona," said K. "I'd rather not be a POW anywhere."

"I don't think we have to worry about that," Michael said.

"No," Oberster said softly, "not here in Germany."

✝✝✝

I wonder if these remarkable creatures are in some way prisoners. Prisoners of some unseen force that drives them to suicide. Or of some virus that attacks their natural compass. It's my nurse's curiosity, Lucy mused. I wish I knew the source of their dilemma. Lucy was standing just a few feet from the huge, unblinking left eye of the adult she thought might be mother to the adjacent calf. I wonder if you can sense that we care about you and your survival. Are you injured? Do you feel pain? Which one of you led you here? Lucy surveyed the beach, watching the small army of New Zealanders working frantically to keep sopping wet the miscellaneous cloth items now draped over all 19 whales. Lucy returned her gaze to the huge eye. Do you understand we are trying to help you?

The tide was rolling in. Lucy moved away from the whale's head to its flank and walked into the surf. It soaked her nurse's whites to the waist, rendering her skirt virtually transparent. Her brown curls now were hanging down, looking like nothing so much as hopelessly tangled strings of Christmas tree lights. She cared not. She stepped back onto the beach and began walking past the whales, telling the rescuers, "You can remove the cloths now. The surf and splashing water will keep them wet enough. It's just a matter of time before we see if the tide can lift them." That is, she was pondering, if they want to be lifted.

Lucy walked to the second calf and began speaking softly. "How old are you? Is that your mother? Are you frightened? Who could blame you?" The nearby rescuers who had been working to keep the calf wet and cool listened intently. "Do you want to live, baby? Are you willing to try? You could have a long life. If we help you, will you please try? If you can?" Lucy's voice was thickening with emotion. "I hope you don't have internal injuries."

By now the tide was rising high on the calf's flanks.

"It's nearly time," Lucy told the people. "We'll let the water rise a little higher, but not too much or it will cover the baby's blowhole and she'll drown." Lucy smiled inwardly; girl or boy, I don't know which you are.

Several people shuddered, aghast at the thought of this calf drowning helplessly before them.

For another 30 minutes Lucy and the people stood watching. Clearly they were looking to her as their leader. A few minutes more and Lucy shouted, "Now! Now! Try to lift and turn her." Immediately 18 men and women drew in deep breaths, squatted below the water's surface and strained to lift the calf. Lucy didn't stay to watch. She went running down the beach to the first calf and repeated her instructions to another group of rescuers. This time she stepped into the water with them. She entertained a quick, rueful thought: I'll likely not be much good with an arm and a half, but – and she inhaled, squatted and strained to lift with the others. They could feel the calf rising in the water. Lucy and the others came up for air. "Turn her!" Lucy shouted, spitting seawater and brushing tangled curls from her face. "Turn her out to sea."

The rescuers, Lucy laboring with them, awkwardly, half-stumbling, slowly pivoted the calf. "Swim, baby, swim," Lucy urged the calf. "Come on, I know you can do it."

It was late afternoon when Michael and Kendall were returning to the Steigenberger Frankfurter.

"Interesting chap, that Oberster," K observed.

"He's been around," said Michael, "and I think he's taken time to think about what he's seen and experienced."

They stopped at the base of the hotel's steps.

"Well," K said, leaning close to Michael and whispering in his right ear, "it appears as though our search for ladies of the night will be a brief one."

Leaning – not erotically but artfully – against the arch supports and railings on the steps leading up to the hotel's entrance were nine women. All were young and pretty. Seven were blondes and two had coal black tresses. Their dresses were tasteful and to Michael and K appeared expensive. They were wearing little makeup; their fresh-faced youth required little. Some were smiling demurely, almost shyly, others not at all. They appeared poised to begin their night's work.

Michael and K stopped to consider their choices.

✝✝✝

Tears were coursing down Lucy's face, and she made no effort to stem them. Most of the other rescuers were sobbing loudly or weeping quietly, men and women alike. A few children were distraught.

High tide was washing over the blowholes of the adult whales that made no effort to avoid drowning. Worse, heart wrenching actually, the two calfs, after swimming a short distance out to sea, had returned and settled in close to the same two adults. Children and their mothers, Lucy thought sadly. *They are perishing together.*

✝✝✝

"Am I not proving satisfactory?" The young woman's English was stilted and teutonically accented but easily understandable. She was lying on her right side, left hand resting on Michael's bare chest. "Is there more I can do? Is there more you want? I can do more." Her concern seemed genuine and perhaps, thought Michael, well practiced. Ah, but don't be a cynic, he scolded himself.

In his hotel room's darkness, relieved only by the dim glow of street lamps peeking around the edges of draperies, Michael studied the woman's face. He had chosen her for her black hair because he liked the way it framed and contrasted with her creamy complexion. The overall effect was an appealing if false innocence.

"No."

"You are the first British soldier I am with. British businessmen, yes, many. Americans too. Businessmen and GIs. They like me."

"I like you too."

"Then why do you not love me? I make you ready."

She had indeed demonstrated ample foreplay expertise, and Michael was aroused. But unexpectedly, melancholia had invaded and shaded his intentions. At first he wasn't sure why. But then images of a young woman with a slightly crooked smile and curly brown hair began to crowd his conscience. Michael leaned closer and lightly kissed the woman's lips. "You are very nice and very skilled." He reached across with his right arm, grasped her shoulder and pulled her closer. "Just lie with me here for a bit. No talking. Just rest your face against my chest."

"That is all?"

"For now."

"Maybe we love later?"

"Maybe."

CHAPTER 55

Kim Il Sung was in Moscow again. The swaggering young leader was at his charming and diplomatically savvy best. Dictator-in-the-making playing to an audience of one – the world's longest-ruling and foremost tyrant. Three times between April 10 and 25, 1950, Kim walked from his hotel suite to the Kremlin to meet with Joseph Stalin, who was showing far more patience with the North Korean leader than he customarily did with his fellow countrymen.

During their discussions Kim repeatedly assured "Uncle Joe" that President Truman wouldn't intervene to halt a North Korean invasion of South Korea. He had too much to lose and not nearly enough to gain. How much, Kim asked rhetorically, did the U.S. citizenry care about goings on in Korea? There would be no public outcry, no congressional pressure on Truman to thrust the U.S. into another war, much less in some little known corner of Asia.

Gradually Kim's doggedness caused Stalin to swing toward Kim's position. On April 25 Stalin sat at his desk across from Kim. He struck a match to his pipe tobacco and puffed. "I am in agreement with your proposal. You have my approval for a preemptive strike against Rhee's South Korea. You have my political support, and we will continue to provide materiel. But no men."

Kim was elated but believed he needed one more particular endorsement and pledge of support. He left Moscow and rushed to Beijing to make his case again with Mao Tse Tung. Kim, emphasizing that he now had Stalin's backing, quickly won the approval he was seeking. Why? Mao had become convinced that Kim could win – with Soviet and Chinese support that would include Mao's surreptitiously positioning thousands of Chinese Army "volunteers" north of the Yalu River. They would be held in readiness, just across the border from North Korea.

CHAPTER 56

Sunday, June 25, 1950.

The Korean War. Day one.

It was 4 a.m. in Korea – 3 p.m. Saturday, June 24 in Washington, D.C. and noon on the Tohono reservation.

"Open the doors. It is almost time to get onboard." In the predawn darkness Captain Kwon was walking briskly among some 1,000 North Korean troops standing alongside the train in Pyongyang's station. Park Han was one of them. Kwon was addressing his men prior to boarding 25 boxcars that soon would be rolling south to Kaesong.

In the locomotive's cab the engineer and his fireman were busily building up steam pressure.

"You have your instructions," Kwon was telling his men. He had become skilled at projecting his voice. "You know what to do when the train reaches Kaesong. The town is filled with Rhee sympathizers, and we must use them as an example of what happens when they give their loyalty to that accursed yankee lapdog. Show no pity at the station. Now let's get moving."

Most of Kwon's troops, including Han, had little stomach for the hell they soon would be unleashing. Kwon himself? He was eager to get underway to help his Great Leader unify the two Koreas.

✝✝✝

At that same hour the first North Korean artillery batteries commenced firing. They were based on the country's Ongjin Peninsula that juts into the Yellow Sea on a straight line west of Kaesong. Those batteries began lobbing shells on South Korean Army positions just south of Kaesong across the 38th Parallel. Simultaneously, North Korean armored and infantry units began advancing southeastward along the border. The Korean War was on.

✝✝✝

Just south of Kaesong was the only point along the frontier where an American KMAG (Korea Military Advisory Group) officer – Joseph

Darrigo – was posted that morning. He had been advising the ROK (Republic of Korea) 12th Army Regiment. At 5 a.m., booming artillery jolted Darrigo awake. "What in the world?" he mumbled to himself inside his tent. He flicked on a flashlight and looked at his watch. "Who the hell is firing at this hour?"

Within minutes the shelling volume was telling him plenty. This was no mere border skirmish. A full-scale attack was getting underway.

✝✝✝

The shelling was wakening everyone within earshot of exploding shells along the 151-mile length of the 38th Parallel.

"I don't think this is a military exercise or a minor border flareup," Park Bong Suk said drowsily to his wife, Park Soon Im. "We should get out of bed. Now."

"And then what?" She bit off a yawn.

Mr. Park shook his head to clear his morning-fogged mind. "Get dressed. Pack a few things. Then let's get to the station and get on the first train south. I think Kaesong is going to be caught in the middle of this."

Mrs. Park propped herself up on her left elbow. "Our shop?"

"Our sons. Living to see them is more important than our shop."

"Much more."

✝✝✝

The baby was squirming and squalling. The elder was chuckling. Jack Brecker was praying – and smiling. On the Tohono Reservation they were gathered in the chapel at Charco with about 120 other villagers. The chapel was a handsome, gleaming white stucco structure with a red tile roof and a hammered copper crucifix mounted atop the small bell tower.

Jack always enjoyed performing baptisms. He saw each one marking the beginning of a new spiritual life. He wasn't convinced that babies were born with the stain of original sin, as the church taught, but he could see in the faces of those attending baptisms that they too saw the ceremony as a religious birthing.

All those in the chapel for today's ceremony were in a festive mood, and Jack encouraged attendees to crowd close to the baptismal font. Two of the Indians had box cameras, and Jack invited them to take pictures while he performed the sacrament.

Today's baptism was special for Jack; it was the first time he had performed one for a member of the elder's family, in this instance a grandnephew. It was special too, because the elder had invited Thaddeus and Bernadeta Metz to attend. They were thrilled by the invitation and had brought a gift for the baby and his parents – a black and white photo of Thaddeus taken during his training as a lancer. It wasn't the original; Thaddeus wanted to keep that for his progeny. But it was a clear, sharp print showing Thaddeus seated on his white warhorse, his right hand holding upright his long lance. The elder took great pleasure in explaining the picture's significance to his nephew and niece and in describing how, as a youngster in the late 1890s, he too had once carried a lance.

At the conclusion of the ceremony Jack stepped outside into bright sunshine with the elder and his family and Thaddeus and Bernadeta. He looked toward the brilliant blue sky. "This is a good life, isn't it?" he said to the group. "We are fortunate to be here together."

Park Min swung his legs off a cot and rubbed sleep from his eyes. His unit was stationed to the east of Munsan. Artillery, he thought, it must be North Korea's. We have so little. And mostly small howitzers. Min stood and began buckling on a webbed belt to which were attached a sidearm, ammunition and canteen. If this is a major invasion…My parents. Han. Kyong. What will this mean for them? When will I see them again? If-" He stopped himself and began rousing his men.

Min and his troops were at the south end of a corridor in western Korea that KMAG advisors called the bowling alley. It had been used by invaders of the peninsula since Genghis Kahn in the 1200s. The north-to-south route is a valley running through the mountainous terrain. This morning Min and his lightly armed men would be bowling pins standing in the path of six reinforced divisions of North Korean infantry, more than 60,000 men who were driving down the historic invasion route to Seoul. Supporting them were the best that Russia had to offer from its extensive arsenal – yak fighter aircraft, heavy artillery and Soviet-built T-34 heavy tanks.

Elsewhere along the 38th Parallel eight more divisions – roughly 10,000 men each – were crossing into South Korea. In all, that morning the 140,000 North Korean infantry enjoyed Soviet-supplied support from 1,600 artillery pieces, 150 T-34 tanks (out of a total of 242 that Kim Il Sung had at his disposal) and 40 yak fighters and 70 attack bombers (out of a total of 180 aircraft).

Within hours, Min's men were feeling the brunt of the bowling alley onslaught. His troops were falling, some torn to unrecognizable shreds. Many more were panicking. Nearby, Min saw a fellow trooper's head sliced off by shrapnel. When some of the decapitated soldier's spouting blood splattered Min's uniform, he dropped to his knees and retched.

Moments later he raised his head and saw a T-34 hungrily coming at him. It was no more than 100 yards away. Min got to his feet. Though he stood five feet ten inches, he felt Lilliputian. *A few ineffectual howitzers, that's all we have to try to slow them down. And with their tanks and troops getting tactical close air support, we have no chance. We might as well be armed with sabers and muskets.*

Around him Min saw men fleeing south in terror. Many were throwing down weapons and equipment that might slow their flight. *I should be running with them,* Min thought. *Why don't I? Fool's courage?* He holstered his sidearm, laid down his carbine and picked up a discarded submachine gun. Min could see the T-34's turret pivoting slowly, searching for prey. He leveled his gun, squeezed the trigger and fired a long burst. Over the roar of the tank's engine and the clanking of its treads, Min could barely hear his rounds pinging harmlessly off the monster's thick plating. Then a flash erupted from the tank's big gun.

"Where is the train?" Mrs. Park asked.

"Late. Or maybe not coming at all," her husband replied, listening to the thunder of artillery. "Nothing might be running on time this morning."

They were standing at Kaesong's station with a crowd that already numbered in the hundreds and was growing larger by the minute. All were carrying luggage of various sorts – leather and cardboard suitcases, large cloth bags, baskets – and some were holding prized possessions, including hens. All were desperate to escape south, not knowing what might be awaiting them but frantic to put distance between them and the advancing tide of destruction and death.

Captain Kwon was riding with the engineer and fireman in the locomotive's cab. He   could see the train was approaching the northern outskirts of Kaesong. Behind him, sitting cross-legged on top of each boxcar was one of his men. Han was perched atop the third car. In a few minutes when the train braked at Kaesong's station, Kwon would signal the first man who would begin relaying the signal to the men on the following cars.

"Here it comes now," Mr. Park said, relieved.

"It's not our train," Mrs. Park replied. "It's a freight train."

"It must be taking priority over the passenger train. Maybe it will just pass through."

"I don't think so," said Mrs. Park. "It seems to be slowing."

Friction. Steel wheels were screeching as they ground to a stop on steel rails. Captain Kwon turned and waved to the soldier atop the first boxcar and then jumped down from the locomotive to the station platform. Within moments the soldiers were scurrying down boxcar ladders from the roofs to the platform. Each then gripped the handle on a boxcar door.

"Strange," said Mr. Park. "I wonder what they are doing."

Mrs. Park grabbed and pulled on his left arm. "Look," she said excitedly. "Isn't that Han?"

"Where?"

"Standing beside the third boxcar." Mrs. Park raised her arms above her head. Simultaneously she began crisscrossing them and shouting, "Han! Han!"

Han heard his mother's voice and strained to see her. A surge of anxiety chilled him. Before he could locate his mother, he heard another shout. This one came from Captain Kwon. "Open the doors!" he bellowed. "Open them now!"

In unison 25 boxcar doors slid open, and 1,000 North Korean soldiers in their mustard-colored uniforms started pouring from the cars onto the platform. They began fanning out and leveling their machine guns and carbines.

Mr. Park digested the situation immediately. "Run!" he commanded his wife. "Drop your bag and run. Now."

Mrs. Park, as with many Kaesong residents that morning, was bewildered. "Why? What is happening?"

"Do as I say," her husband said sharply. "Move." He knocked the suitcase from her right hand, grabbed her shoulders, spun her away from the platform, grasped her right arm and began pulling her roughly back through the puzzled throng.

"Open fire!" Kwon ordered. "Open fire!"

In the next split instant rounds from 1,000 guns began tearing into and ripping apart fellow Koreans. Long, piercing cries were erupting from shattered bodies. Sharp wails of anguish and low groans were creating a symphony of misery. Other Koreans were screaming their terror and scrambling to join Mr. and Mrs. Park in a desperate attempt to escape the carnage.

Han made a choice. Knowing that his parents were somewhere in the panicked crowd, he purposely fired high.

As ammunition clips were emptied, soldiers quickly reloaded and continued firing. Mrs. Park felt her husband's grip loosen. She saw him falling to the earthen street outside the station. She started to turn and squat.

"No," he said through clenched teeth. "Keep going."

She saw blood staining his chest where the bullet had exited after penetrating his back. "Bong!" she cried.

"Keep running," he coughed. "Do not go home. Go south." His head drooped to the earth.

"Bong."

He tried to raise his head but couldn't. "Go. Please," he mumbled.

CHAPTER 57

Joseph Stalin was livid. Andrey Vyshinsky often had seen the boss in high dudgeon but never had seen his face more explosively crimson than it was at this moment. He almost expected Stalin to begin spewing volcanic lava instead of words.

"How could this be? Do you know just how disastrous this could be?" Stalin barked at his new foreign minister.

In 1949 Vyshinsky had replaced Molotov who retained his position as deputy prime minister and remained a member of the Politburo, the Soviet Union's policy-making tribunal. Molotov, probably because of his growing renown and Stalin's unbounded paranoia, had lost the boss's favor. Indeed in 1948 Stalin had ordered Molotov's Jewish wife arrested. Only quiet interceding by Molotov's colleague, Laurenti Beria, himself widely feared as head of the secret police, had saved his wife's life. Molotov knew that Beria had risked his own life in intervening and was deeply grateful.

Vyshinsky flinched visibly. He thought he might wet his trousers. What he wanted to say but dared not was, "This is entirely your doing. You are responsible." Speak those words, Vyshinsky knew, and he might not leave the Kremlin alive that day. Instead, he forced himself to find his carefully modulated voice and put to work his unsurpassed obsequiousness. "I am so sorry, Comrade Leader. Your wisdom, as always, is unmatched. I will do everything possible to prevent this error from being compounded."

Stalin wasn't placated. His right hand slammed his desk pad so hard that his pipe bounced out of the ashtray. "Perhaps," he hissed, "you have reached the limits of your usefulness. Maybe I made a mistake when I removed Molotov."

At this moment Vyshinsky was wishing Stalin had never tapped him for this position. He would have much preferred to remain a midlevel functionary and out of Stalin's line of sight.

Vyshinsky knew there was no acceptable reply other than to continue toadying. "I am sorry. Abjectly and profoundly so."

But Vyshinsky was right. What had transpired at the United Nations in the hours after North Korea launched its assault was squarely Stalin's fault.

The fighting in Korea had been raging for nine hours before Harry Truman was informed. Stunned though he was, almost immediately he directed his UN ambassador, Warren Austin, to convene a meeting of the United Nations Security Council. After brief formalities Austin introduced a resolution calling for a united defense of South Korea.

Russia was a permanent member of the Security Council and as such possessed the right to exercise the lone veto necessary to thwart any binding resolution. But Soviet Russia, at Stalin's order, was boycotting Security Council meetings to protest Nationalist China's council membership. Thus the Soviet delegate was absent when the resolution vote was taken. It passed.

Meanwhile, Kim Il Sung was claiming that the "bandit traitor" Syngman Rhee had initiated hostilities by sending his troops into North Korea. Though Rhee had longed to strike first, Kim's assertion was a lie and widely seen as such.

Before long, 16 UN member nations would send combat forces to aid South Korea. Five more nations would send medical staff and supplies. In all, 41 nations would contribute. By August 47,000 U.S. troops would join South Korean soldiers. In addition there would be 12,000 British, 8,500 Canadian, 5,000 Turkish, 5,000 Philippinos and 11 other contingents of 1,000 troops or fewer. The U.S. would pay most bills for the Allied forces.

As the war kept escalating 480,000 U.S. soldiers and 39,000 from other nations would join 590,000 South Korean troops.

CHAPTER 58

On the morning of June 25 Ahn Kyong Ae, now 20, was fortunate in two respects. She had not gone to Kaesong's train station where hundreds of innocents had been gunned down, and Mrs. Park had disobeyed her dying husband. As instructed, she had kept running but not south. Instead she had gone hurrying to tell Kyong and her parents about the massacre and to warn them to stay inside until the maelstrom had passed.

Kyong and her mother and Mrs. Park then dispensed with cultural restraints and embraced warmly. Mr. Ahn stood mutely, his chagrin obvious.

"Han was there," Mrs. Park said.

"You saw him?" Kyong replied in disbelief.

Mrs. Park nodded. "Only for a few moments, but I know it was him."

"And he was shooting?"

"Not when I saw him. He was getting ready to open a boxcar. After the shooting started, I didn't see him again."

"I am going to Munsan."

"What?" Kyong's mother said, alarmed.

"I am going to see Min. Father, Mother, please do not try to stop me." She bowed to her father and hugged her mother. "We have been apart too long. This war could kill him. It already has killed Mr. Park. It could kill all of us."

Within 30 minutes Kyong had filled a cloth bag with a change of clothes, toothbrush and comb, tied it off at the top, and was peddling a borrowed bicycle south toward Munsan. She was hardly alone. Refugees of all ages were beginning to clog the narrow dirt road. Some were on bikes, a few on carts drawn by lumbering oxen, most on foot, with many of them trudging under heavy loads strapped to their backs or balanced on their heads.

Kyong was about three miles south of Kaesong when artillery shells began bursting around and above the refugees. It was clear that the North Korean Army was not differentiating between military and civilian targets or between North and South Koreans. Their only goal was to clear the road south to Munsan and Seoul beyond. Panic erupted as jagged shrapnel began exacting a punishing toll. Within seconds blood was staining clothing and seeping onto the dirt road. People were screaming, scrambling for protection in the ditches. Kyong looked around for cover and decided to scurry into a patch of forest. She took only a few steps when a tree limb sheared off by a shell blast went crashing down, striking the back of her skull. Kyong felt herself blacking out and crumbling.

An hour later Kyong was regaining consciousness. Slowly she pushed herself to her knees. Beside her was the large limb that had struck her.

She examined her clothes; there was no sign of blood but they were filthy. Her head was throbbing. She reached behind it and fingered sticky blood matting her long black hair. On the road she saw numerous corpses – at least 20 she thought – and three dead oxen.

She rose to her feet and a moment later heard shouts of protest and screams of terror. They seemed to be coming from the far side of the woods. For a moment Kyong was torn between investigating their source and continuing to Munsan. She chose the former and began edging farther into and through the leafy copse.

A few minutes later the scene before Kyong froze her in midstep. Across a rice paddy about 100 feet to the east, a Korean farm family – father, mother, son and two daughters – were standing, backs against their home's front wall. The older daughter appeared to be about 16, the younger perhaps 10. The boy looked about 12 or 13.

In front of them, weapons leveled, were a dozen North Korean troops. A moment later an officer, Captain Kwon Oh Bum, emerged from the house and stepped in front of the farmer.

"They have nothing valuable," Kwon said to his sergeant. "Nothing of any use to us."

"Should we get back to the road?"

Kwon started to say yes but then noticed a look of disdain in the hardened farmer's narrowed eyes. "You do not respect us, do you?"

"Should I? For starting a war against your own countrymen?"

"It is the-" Kwon began to explain and stopped. "You cannot be trusted."

"I? It is you who are betraying the trust of fellow Koreans. You bring shame, shame on yourself."

Kwon gritted his teeth. His men looked on uncertainly. Han and others were feeling shame for their actions back at Kaesong's station. Calmly, Kwon unholstered his sidearm and from six feet shot the farmer, the bullet entering his left eye. His body slammed against the house and crumpled, blood pouring down his face and onto the ground. His wife and children screamed shrilly. Kwon's men looked on in stunned silence. They had fired into the crowd at Kaesong, but this was murder committed intimately.

Kwon hesitated only a moment before stepping in front of the quivering boy and shooting him, the bullet tearing into his forehead, splattering bits of bone and brain.

The 10-year-old girl, cowering, screamed again and clutched her older sister's left arm. Both were trembling as was their mother who was slipping into shock.

"His hate could have made him our enemy," Kwon muttered darkly to the sergeant who nodded dumbly.

Kwon then stepped before the mother. She averted her eyes, expecting her life to end in the next instant. Kwon studied her shocked countenance. He now was devoid of any sense of pity. "Take her and the girls inside. I will take the youngest first. Then all of you," Kwon said, grimly addressing his men, "can have a turn. Take your pick. But do not take long. We need to keep moving south."

"When we're done?" the sergeant asked.

"I will leave that to you."

From inside the house the younger girl's hysterical, unceasing, high-pitched screams of pain brought Kyong to tears. She tried to avoid imagining the scene – the little girl on her back, arms pinned to the earthen floor, legs spread, soldier's engorged penises tearing at her genitals. Mother and older daughter lying beside her, long skirts covering their anguished faces, enduring similar agony and shame, knowing execution was nearing. In the coming weeks and months it was a scene that would be replayed frequently as North Korean forces cruelly bulled their way south.

Kyong knew what the mother was thinking. If she could, she would will her death. To be raped was the most profound of shames. In Korea's 5,000-year-old culture, even if her husband was alive, she couldn't expect him to touch her or even look at her. With her husband dead, no other man would acknowledge her existence. The shame would be too great.

When Kwon finished raping the younger daughter, he stepped outside. He searched his pockets for cigarettes, slipped one between his lips and lit it.

Kyong was watching him. She wanted to leave but couldn't. Not until the screaming stopped. When at last it did, she carefully retraced her steps, found her bicycle intact and resumed peddling south, no longer sure she would reach Munsan but determined to keep trying. She knew that witnessing this monstrous tragedy would forever scar her heart.

Inside, the sergeant looked down at the three bedraggled victims, long full skirts still masking their faces, blood dripping onto the ground between the girls' legs. He buttoned his fly and buckled his belt. Then he picked up his submachine gun and pointed it at the mother.

"Don't." It was the voice of one his men, speaking softly, barely above a whisper. "They are no threat to us," Park Han murmured. He was among those who had raped the older daughter, knowing that if he hadn't his own sergeant likely would have executed him for disobedience. The morning's massacre at Kaesong's rail station had taught him that and other lessons he wished fervently he could have skipped. Han already was feeling remorse that he expected to linger eternally – if his sergeant didn't turn on him and end his life. At that moment Han didn't much care.

The sergeant hesitated, then nodded to his men, gesturing to them to leave. Perhaps it was Han's disregard for his own life that spared him and the mother and her daughters.

✝✝✝

Late that afternoon Mrs. Park, accompanied by Kyong's parents, returned to Kaesong's train station. They were pulling a small, rickety two-wheeled cart. Many other townspeople were there as well. The scene before them was unutterably sad. Before them lay the torn and twisted corpses of hundreds of innocents, including friends and neighbors. Blood had congealed in dark pools. Most of the searchers were in tears, consumed by grieving. Within minutes they found Mr. Park's body, lifted it and gently placed it in the cart.

During the next three years of fierce combat many bloody engagements – Pork Chop Hill, Chosin Reservoir, Imjin River – would receive extensive news media coverage and become the subject of articles, books and movies. The emphasis virtually always was on heroism. But in none of those battles would as much blood be spilled during the first fleeting minutes as that which poured onto the ground that first morning of the war in Kaesong.

CHAPTER 59

Monday, June 26.

The Korean War. Day two.

Syngman Rhee was on the radio early. "My fellow citizens. This is our darkest hour. The communist dictator Kim Il Sung has ordered his forces to invade our democratic nation. He has violated our sovereignty without any provocation. Now I urge you, beseech you, to remain in Seoul. I implore you to stand and fight. Our nation's future depends on your courage. Together we can defeat Kim and unify all of Korea in one democratic nation. I know that I can depend on your loyalty and I am deeply grateful."

✝✝✝

Munsan's main street, a snaking dirt ribbon, also was the road north to Kaesong and south to Seoul. This morning it was thronging with refugees from the north joining Munsan-area residents beginning their flight south and away from approaching danger. Most expected the South Korean capital, Seoul, ringed by mountains, to be a haven from the fast advancing North Korean troops, already earning a deserved reputation for wanton depredation.

Kyong was walking slowly beside her bicycle. She was looking for Mr. and Mrs. Choi's butcher and cutlery shop. When she spotted it on the west, or right, side of the road, she lowered the bike's kickstand and stepped tentatively inside – where she was thunderstruck.

"Min!" she screamed shrilly and went lunging into his arms, crushing herself against his chest. A torrent of tears quickly stained his army tunic.

He wrapped his arms around Kyong and for a long moment said nothing. Then he murmured, "Kyong...Kyong."

Mr. and Mrs. Choi needed no introduction. The unplanned reunion was misting their eyes and thickening their throats. Mr. Choi hugged his wife, and she leaned her head against his chest.

"I-I didn't expect to see you," Min stammered. "I was only hoping to find Mr. and Mrs. Choi." Still holding Kyong, he sighed. "And to urge them to leave. Take Sejong and leave. Go to Seoul."

Kyong sniffed and brushed tears from beneath her eyes. "Yes, Min is right. You must leave. The North Koreans are coming fast. They are – they are killing civilians, not only South Korean soldiers. I can hardly believe what I have seen."

Min released his grip on Kyong and stepped back. "What have you seen?"

"I have seen too much. I don't want to talk about it now. It hurts too much."

Min placed his hands on Kyong's shoulders. "You and Mr. and Mrs. Choi can travel together. With Sejong. But you must leave now," Min said firmly.

"No," Kyong protested. "We deserve some time together. Even a little. After all this time, I…"

Mr. Choi spoke. "You two stay here for a while and talk. We will wait out front." Mrs. Choi smiled understandingly and exited the shop with her husband.

"At a time like this, I know it sounds strange to say it, but this is so wonderful," Min smiled. "I was fearing we might never see each other again."

"This might be the last time."

"Why? What do you mean?"

"I have seen what the North Koreans are doing. Slaughtering innocent people…"

"You have seen them do that?"

"Yes. They are murdering and raping. I saw a family-" She buried her face against his chest. "It was awful."

Min pursed his lips and sighed. "You and the Chois must leave. Our army will try to stop the invaders."

"Can you?"

"Truthfully, I don't think so. They have more men and better weapons. Much better – and more modern."

"You will be killed. Come with us, please." She made no effort to mask her desperation.

Min shook his head. "I am sorry. But too many of our soldiers have fled already. The rest of us need to stay. Try to slow down the enemy. If we don't, they will overrun everyone."

"They might anyway."

Min nodded his agreement. "You have to go now."

"No. Not yet," Kyong said with resolve, her voice regaining its normal timbre. "There is something I want." Her tears had stopped flowing and she was struggling to smile.

"What is it?"

"I want you to make love to me."

"What?"

"Yes. And then kill me."

Min's eyes widened in shock. He knew she was serious. She simply would never say such a thing if she wasn't. He didn't want to say something witless or demeaning, so for a long moment he said nothing. He gazed into her unblinking black eyes that once again were sparkling like a pair of polished onyx. Polished and determined onyx. "I cannot kill you. I won't."

Kyong sniffed and cleared her throat. "I do not want my life to end like so many other women today. In unspeakable shame. And I don't want to live after being violated." She was speaking with clear-minded grit. "You might be a modern Korean man, but could you live with me after I've been raped? Raped by who knows how many heartless soldiers? Could you love me like that?" Kyong knew that, figuratively, she was forcing Min into a corner and she was continuing to press. "What if I became pregnant?" Min blushed. "It could happen. If they didn't kill me after raping me, I could have a bastard child. It would be impossible to know the father. Could you be its father? Treat it like our child? What future would there be for that child? Or me? Make love to me, Min."

In one day, actually less than a day, Min's world was turning upside down. Things previously unspeakable had happened and were happening with incredible speed. He nodded. "When?"

"Now. There is very little time. You know that."

Min stepped away from her and walked to the shop's front door. "We need a little more time. Don't wait for us," he said to the Chois who were standing in the street. "Continue your preparations and then leave quickly. Take Sejong."

"What about you and Kyong?" Mrs. Choi asked worriedly.

"We need to be alone for a while. Discuss some things. We will go out back. Kyong and…we will catch up with you soon." And then he took Kyong by her left arm and led her through the rear door.

"We will wait," Mrs. Choi whispered to her husband with a certainty that left no room for debate. "We will get ready to leave, but we will wait for them."

A bit warily, Mr. Choi nodded his assent.

Min guided Kyong inside a small, cramped storage shed that had been serving as his quarters. The sides were vertical boards, unpainted. Min motioned toward a small cot and Kyong didn't hesitate. She lay on her back and said, "I know…Do this for me, please."

Min lay beside her. He couldn't help thinking that this never would be happening if the war hadn't changed everything in a matter of mere hours. Kyong pulled back her long skirt and maneuvered to remove her underwear. She could see Min was embarrassed and smiled. "It would be easier if you helped."

"I don't-"

"I know." She raised her hips. "Just reach over and pull them off my legs. Then touch me."

A welter of emotions was assaulting Min. Excitement. Awkwardness. Desire. Awe. Disbelief. He did as Kyong instructed. When he touched her, she shivered.

"Now you," she said, "Unbutton your pants. Free your organ."

The narrow cot left little room for maneuvering. Min smiled self-consciously. "I think I'd better stand."

"So stand," she said spunkily.

He did and as he finished unbuttoning, his hardened penis made its appearance. He looked down and hesitated.

Kyong spread her legs. "I am a virgin," she smiled, "but I know how this is supposed to work."

† † †

The two of them lay panting. Their coupling had lasted only a few minutes, but it left them breathless. Min rose up on his elbows and kissed

Kyong. With their lips touching, she mumbled, "Make it last." He pressed his lips tighter to hers and the tips of their tongues met.

After a long minute, Min pulled back. "That was nice."

"Yes." Kyong's eyes were glittering.

"You are beautiful."

"I know," she said guilelessly.

"We could be so happy together."

"I know."

"But-"

"But I meant what I said. I want you to kill me. Now."

"I can't. I – I am still inside you."

Kyong pushed hard against Min's shoulders and he disengaged.

"Now do it."

Min's head shook. "You are young. Too young. You have…you can't let North Koreans determine your destiny. You have to live – for us."

"Not if I am raped. You might be modern but not that modern."

Tears sprang from Min's eyes. He was surprised. He hadn't wept in so long he couldn't remember the last time. He wanted to deny her assertion but couldn't bring himself to lie. Using his knees he brought Kyong's legs together. Then he rocked up and back so that he was sitting on her thighs. He reached down with his hands and grasped her neck.

Tears were beginning to mist Kyong's eyes, but she also was smiling her gratitude. She blinked twice, and Min began squeezing. Then he jerked his hands back. "I can't."

Kyong was still smiling. "I didn't think you could. Get up."

Min eased off her and rose from the cot. He pulled up his uniform pants.

Kyong pushed her skirt back down but left her underwear at the foot of the cot. She swung her legs and stood. She rose up on her toes and kissed Min. Then she stepped around him, exited the shed with purpose and walked the few feet to the shop's rear doorway and entered. Min, re-buttoning his fly, was slow to follow.

"Is everything all right, dear?" Mrs. Choi asked.

Kyong smiled enigmatically at the Chois but didn't reply. Instead she walked serenely to the shop's sales and service counter. She eyed an array of knives and selected one with a slightly curved blade eight inches long. Then she stepped away from the counter.

Min entered the shop. He looked at Kyong holding the knife, at the Chois and back at Kyong. In horror, he watched Kyong point the blade toward herself. "No!" Min shouted.

She gripped the haft with both hands and plunged the first four inches of the blade through her skirt and into her abdomen. She cried out piteously, "Min!" Her face twisted grotesquely and, groaning, she dropped gracelessly to her knees. Her head drooped and then she toppled sideways, her hands falling away from the haft.

✝✝✝

In Ajo Thaddeus Metz was sitting with Jack Brecker in the Immaculate Conception parish rectory living room. They were smoking White Owls, sipping scotch and listening to a radio report on the outbreak of hostilities in Korea.

"This Kim Il Sung," Thaddeus observed, "he seems like another Hitler. Invading another country. On a flimsy provocation or none at all."

"And," Jack said, "it seems like he has Stalin's backing. The reports say he is using Russian planes and tanks. Probably artillery and small arms too. And I don't need to tell you how heartless Stalin is. If ever there was a prime candidate for everlasting hell."

"The South Korean Army seems much like our Polish Army in 1939. Outmanned and outgunned."

"But you Poles had strong leadership. I'm not so sure about Syngman Rhee."

✝✝✝

Others were listening to similar radio accounts of the new war.

In Wellington Public Hospital Lucy Crispin and several other nurses as well as doctors and orderlies were gathered around a radio in the staff lounge. If New Zealand sends troops, she was thinking, I'll volunteer. They'll need nurses, lots of them. Mother and Father will be opposed. At least I think they will. We'll see.

Theresa Hassler Morton, holding Marilyn on her lap in their London flat, was listening to the BBC. Not even five years since the last war ended, she was reflecting. Just what the world needs, another civil war. How can man – men – be so insane? So careless with other people's lives?

In Shelby Tom and Bridgett Hassler Brecker were saddened. Bridgett shook her head. "The United Nations is pledging to help South Korea and you know what that means," she said to her husband. "More young men will die."

"Or," Tom added somberly, "lose their limbs."

Bridgett looked at their twins Jack and Theresa playing with wooden Tinker Toys and Lincoln Logs on the living room floor. "I pray that when Jack is a young man there is no war."

Tom said nothing more. His missing foot was a daily if silent reminder of war's tolls, and he saw no point in voicing his doubt that another generation – another 20 years – would pass without United States troops fighting and dying somewhere. In Asia, in Europe, in Africa. Or maybe some country he hadn't heard of. He eased off the couch and joined the twins with their toys. Little Theresa was playing with Tinker Toys and was making what looked vaguely like a ferris wheel or perhaps a model of the solar system. Tom wasn't sure which. Little Jack was building a cabin with the Lincoln Logs. "Hmm," said Tom to Theresa, "maybe you'll grow up and become an engineer. Not many women engineers. You'd be in demand. And you," he said to Jack, "maybe you'll be an architect – or a home builder." He chuckled and his comments delighted the kids and Bridgett.

But as to Bridgett's wish that there be no war when little Jack reached manhood, Tom was ambivalent, privately so. Oh, he was thinking, I wouldn't wish combat on my son or anybody else's. But military service? That's something else. I think military service has its benefits. All of a sudden young men have to work to someone else's high standards and expectations and there are no excuses. You have to get the job done. You have to work for the greater good, not just the individual. It speeds up maturing. I'd say the same thing applies to young women if there was some form of national civilian service. I also think military service makes for more effective U.S. presidents. Truman is a World War I vet. He knows what it's like to sacrifice. And I don't just mean losing life or limb or watching friends killed or maimed. I mean knowing what it's like to work under intense pressure, to experience long separations from loved ones. I think it helps a president make more informed decisions. Choices that are better for our nation. Roosevelt was too old for duty during World War I, but even so he toured European battlefields and came away with a perspective he never would have had otherwise.

In Zyrardow Kaz Majos heard the news on a radio in a small food store where he was buying wheat and sausage. Outside the store he mounted General for the quick ride back to the farm. Barbara was holding little Thaddeus outside the house.

"It didn't take you long," she said. "No one to chat with?"

"Where is your father?"

"In the barn. Why?"

"I heard news in town."

Minutes later Kaz, Jszef and Barbara holding Thaddeus on her lap were sitting around the kitchen table.

"Have you ever heard of Korea?" Kaz asked.

"No," said Barbara. "What is it?"

"A country, I think," said Jszef.

"That's right," said Kaz. "A country in Asia. Squeezed between China and Japan. A war broke out there yesterday."

"Who attacked it?" Barbara asked.

"Apparently it's a civil war," Kaz said. "At least that's what I'm understanding. The northern part of the country attacked the south."

"That's what happened in the United States," Jszef observed. "In the last century. At least, if I am remembering correctly, then it was the south attacking the north. Strange, isn't it? I now have a daughter living there. I feel sad for the people of Korea. But at least no other countries are involved."

✝✝✝

The Chois and Min rushed to Kyong and knelt beside her. Min, more frightened than he could ever remember, cradled her head. Mr. Choi held her right hand. "She needs surgery," he said.

"The nearest surgeons are in Kaesong and Seoul," said Mrs. Choi, her head shaking. "You know that."

The furrows in Mr. Choi's forehead suddenly seemed much deeper. "We must get the knife out," he murmured urgently. "Carefully."

Kyong's eyes opened, closed and opened again. Color was draining from her face. "Let me die," she whispered. Then her face contorted anew as though the blade was twisting.

"I am sorry, dear," said Mrs. Choi, "I cannot do that." She turned to her husband. "Get me a clean cloth. Any cloth. And bring your bottle of soju."

Chun, unaccustomed to being addressed so abruptly by his wife, merely stared for a moment. This was the second time in recent minutes that she had spoken so assertively. In Korea male dominance flourished. Wives treated husbands with utmost deference. Their ancient culture dictated that wives insisted on nothing at any time. Even their suggestions and requests were generally circuitous. Now Chun's wife was commanding him. It is the war, Chun realized, it is changing everything. He sprang to his feet to fetch the soju and the cloth.

Scant seconds later he was back. "Give me the cloth." She wrapped it around the blade and pushed down hard, creating pressure, trying to staunch the bleeding. Then to her husband, "Get her to drink some of the soju. Now."

Mr. Choi put the bottle to Kyong's lips. "Drink it, dear. Please."

With his left hand Mr. Choi helped Kyong part her lips. He poured some of the fiery spirits into her mouth. She gagged and swallowed and then coughed. "More," Mr. Choi urged her. "It will help with the pain." She swallowed again. Soju is as clear as vodka and, some would say, even more potent.

"Min," said Mrs. Choi, "can you pull the blade out? Slowly. Carefully."

Min felt faint. He looked at his hands. "I don't know."

"I understand," she said. "Hold her arms down. You can do that. Chun, put the bottle down. Take my place holding the cloth in place." She removed her hands from the cloth, Kyong's blood reddening it. "Keep pushing down firmly."

Mrs. Choi inhaled deeply and rubbed her hands on her skirt to dry and steady them. She gripped the haft and began easing the blade out. Kyong screamed. Mrs. Choi blanched but kept pulling, sweat beading on her forehead and above her upper lip. The blade came out and she tossed it behind her. She drew a deep breath. "Remove the cloth," she told her husband. She picked up the bottle of soju and handed it to him. "I am going to spread the wound. When I do, pour some in."

315

As Mrs. Choi positioned her fingers around the wound, Kyong tensed. So did Min, still pinning her arms to the clay floor. Firmly Mrs. Choi forced the sides of the wound apart. "Pour." Chun did so and Kyong shrieked primally – and then her eyes rolled up and she lost consciousness. Mrs. Choi removed her fingers and let the wound close. "Pour some more on the wound." Chun obeyed.

"Do you think she will die?" Min asked, color drained from his face. He let go of Kyong's arms. The ordeal had exhausted him.

"I don't know." And to be honest, she was thinking, I don't even know if we did the right things. I did only what seemed best. Again Mrs. Choi wiped her hands on her skirt. She breathed deeply, closed her eyes and said, "Bring me my sewing kit."

CHAPTER 60

Tuesday, June 27.

The Korean War. Day three.

North Korean troops advanced to Seoul's northern outskirts.

Syngman Rhee was broadcasting again, still urging Seoul residents to remain and join South Korean troops in resisting the North's forces. Once off the air, he and his wife, Francisca Donner, and his cronies scurried from the president's residence two miles south to Seoul Station where two trains awaited, their stacks belching gray clouds. Already loaded aboard were most of Rhee's bodyguards and the nation's gold reserves, emptied from the treasury during the night. As soon as Rhee and his party were aboard, the trains moved out to the south, leaving Seoul residents to their own devices.

Immediately after the trains crossed the Han River, South Korean troops, at Rhee's direction, dynamited the bridges. Destroying those spans would prove disastrous for Seoul's fleeing civilians as well as South Korean soldiers, retreating but still resisting the northern onslaught.

† † †

"He is a coward. I knew it," Kim Il Sung said to his senior staff. His words were less boasting than confirming a long-held suspicion. "Rhee has never seen combat. He has no taste for drawing blood – or," he sneered, "seeing his own. Bridges or not, our soldiers will make quick work of crossing the Han." Kim would soon be proved correct.

Remaining behind in Seoul were the nearly 200 members of South Korea's parliament. They were hoping to negotiate a peace with North Korea. Rhee didn't discourage them from doing so.

"Do you know where Korea is?" Kendall Thorne asked Michael Cornelius.

"No, but President Truman does."

K and Michael were listening to a radio update on the war in the Officers Club at their Bullock Barracks army base in Germany.

"Then I presume Atlee does as well."

Clement Atlee, Britain's prime minister since succeeding Winston Churchill in 1945, already had conferred with King George VI who was nearing the end of his reign begun in 1936. He had been crowned following the abdication of Edward II who had vacated the throne to marry commoner Wallace Simpson. Atlee and King George had agreed quickly to dispatch British troops to join United Nations forces in Korea.

"I think our posting here in Germany might be foreshortened," Michael observed. Another thought occurred to him; he was wondering where Korea was relative to New Zealand. "Let's get educated," he said.

"What lesson do you have in mind?"

"Geography. Let's find a globe."

Captain Kwon's company was in the vanguard of North Korea's 6th Division. At his signal the men paused at the northern fringe of the grounds of South Korea's capitol. There was no fire coming from the imposing white granite domed structure that the Japanese had built to house its colonial government during its 35-year occupation of Korea. Instead a large white sheet was hanging from a fourth floor window. Kwon motioned to his men to continue their advance. They proceeded cautiously, weapons at the ready, alert for an ambush. As they neared the building, parliament members, dressed in western suits with neckties, emerged from the capitol. Kwon raised his left arm, signaling his men to halt. Then he turned to his radioman. "Get us patched through to our Great Leader's headquarters."

The corporal manning the radio knelt and went to work.

The parliamentarians began walking slowly toward Kwon. One, Yi Kwang Hee, said, "We have come to negotiate. To end this fighting."

"Stop," Kwon replied. "Do not come any closer."

Yi and his legislative colleagues complied, waiting patiently.

A couple minutes more and Kwon was holding the radio handset, speaking with Kim Il Sung. Their conversation was brief. They enjoyed a trust and communication intimacy born from years of fighting together as guerillas. Kwon returned the handset to his radioman and stepped forward. "Go back inside. All of you. We will talk there."

"Very good," Yi replied, encouraged. Perhaps a military disaster could be averted. He turned and his fellow lawmakers did likewise. Kwon motioned his men to follow.

The parliamentarians passed through a portal into a courtyard. Kwon and his men, about 150 soldiers, filed in.

"This is good," Kwon said.

"Our chamber would be better for discussions," said Yi.

"This will do," Kwon said. He turned to his three lieutenants, one for each platoon, and conferred quietly. They nodded their understanding, then turned, stepped away and spoke lowly to their men, including Park Han. In the next few moments the men fanned out, forming an arc across the front of the lawmakers' assemblage. Then Kwon unholstered his sidearm.

"Wait!" Yi cried, sensing tragedy. Alarm was spreading quickly through his fellow lawmakers.

"You made a choice," Kwon replied, jaws set grimly, "an unwise one. You chose to support Rhee, an enemy of all Koreans."

Yi threw up both hands, palms held outward signaling appeasement. "Let's talk. We are all Koreans. We all want the same thing – one peaceful nation."

Kwon's head shook slightly. "You are enemies of the new Korea and cannot be trusted to support our Great Leader." He gripped his gun with both hands and squeezed off the first shot. It struck Yi in his abdomen and he bent double, hands pressed against the wound. Kwon's men then opened fire with submachine guns and carbines. Han was one of several soldiers who purposely fired high or low, but enough were firing into the helpless legislators to send bodies sprawling on the paving stones. Amid the gunfire and screams some lawmakers turned and started scurrying to the far end of the courtyard. Kwon's men followed and cut them down.

The massacre required only a few minutes. Kwon called out to his men. "Finish off the wounded. All of them." Kwon walked back to Yi, lying in a fetal position, moaning, still clutching his abdomen. Kwon inserted a fresh ammunition clip in his sidearm, placed it at the rear of Yi's head and squeezed the trigger.

Han hung back.

✝✝✝

By afternoon Min and his men were pushed back to the north bank of the Han, a fast-moving river that was continuously rising and falling with the incoming and outgoing tides of the nearby Yellow Sea. During these last three days Min had witnessed more destruction, cruelty and death than he had thought imaginable. Below him in the water were floating some 800 bodies, mostly civilians, caught on the bridge when it was blown. The span's twisted remains were serving as a grotesque grave marker. More unsettling was seeing thousands of stranded South Koreans crowding the beach, panicking, trying to pack into small boats and onto hurriedly constructed and flimsy rafts. It was clear that most would not cross the Han before North Korean troops arrived. Their fate was predictable.

Min checked his ammunition. He had only the clip in his rifle and a few spare rounds in a bandolier he'd removed from one of his fallen men.

Kwon's hardened troops were no more than 200 yards from the river. They had ample ammunition. The men, including Park Han, were advancing rapidly as South Korean resistance was toppling as easily as a spindly tower constructed from playing cards. By now

Kwon's men needed no additional operating orders from their captain. Their mission was clear: kill all soldiers and civilians in their path.

✝✝✝

Standing above the river in his sweat-stained grimy uniform Min was disgusted by the craven behavior of some South Korean soldiers. Panicking as profoundly as civilians, they were shooting their way into and onto any evacuation craft. Defenseless citizens, killed or wounded, were falling into the swift current. Those still alive were crying out for help while being swept down river and out to sea. The Han isn't all that long – some 300 miles – but is nearly two-thirds of a mile wide as it flows south of central Seoul.

Min half-scrambled, half-slid down the steep bank to the beach. "Protect these people," he bellowed to his men, "or I will shoot you." They knew he meant it, and he knew he was risking being shot by his own soldiers. "Get back up the bank and provide covering fire."

Min then began looking to see if he could help launch a boat for escaping civilians. The din and chaos notwithstanding, Min's thoughts turned briefly to Kyong. I hope you live through this. The Chois too. I hope you're hiding. If you and Mrs. Choi are seized..." Min tried not to finish that thought.

✝✝✝

Kwon and his men were closing on the north bank. They began firing on Min's men who flopped onto their bellies and scooted down below the lip of the bank. They then raised their guns above the lip and fired blindly and ineffectually at Kwon's advancing company.

From below, Min quickly digested the coming disaster and began clambering up the bank. He knew his men needed leadership at the top if they were going to buy additional time for refugees trying to cross the river. Min had barely begun climbing when a shower of grenades began exploding among his men. Several were blown off the bank, dead or mortally wounded before they landed on the beach. The rest came sliding down the bank, spun and prepared to fire on the first North Koreans to appear at the top.

Within seconds North Korean troops were looming above them and firing effectively from the advantage of high ground. Min returned fire with a carefully aimed shot that sent an enemy trooper staggering back from the bank's lip. When Min pivoted to target again, he saw a North Korean aiming a rifle at him. Why is he hesitating? Min wondered. Then came mutual recognition. Min started to hail Han but refrained when he found his mind functioning with remarkable speed, calm and precision. Nodding ever so slightly Min took aim at his brother and fired. Han's rifle flew from his hands as he crumpled and went careening down the bank. Min wanted to rush to Han, writhing and groaning just a few feet away, but restrained himself. Instead he glanced up, saw a North Korean officer targeting him and went zigging and zagging toward the near end of the collapsed bridge. Bullets from Kwon's sidearm were kicking up sand around Min's flying feet. One of Min's men, not certain of his leader's intention, was following.

Moments later Min slung his rifle across his back and scrambled onto one of the collapsed bridge's long girders. I can't swim the river, he knew, not in boots and with my rifle. Too wide. But if I can get part way across on the wreckage, maybe I've got a chance. Min began making his way gingerly along the treacherously angled girders and beams and sections of partially submerged rails and roadbed. He was calling on a combination of strength, concentration, balance and athleticism. Min was nearing the river's midpoint. Glancing back he saw one of his men not far behind.

"You!"

Min swung his head, looking to see who was calling to him.

"You!" This time a beckoning wave accompanied the hail. It was an elderly woman sitting near the prow of a crowded 12-foot-long rowboat. "Come with us," she called loudly above the din.

"You are already overloaded," Min shouted his reply.

The woman spoke to the pair of rowers. "Get closer to the wreckage." They eased the small boat carrying 14 terrified refugees as closely as they felt prudent without risking a gash from the jagged end of a submerged steel beam. "Now," the woman called to Min, "jump in and swim to the boat. You can hang onto the side for the rest of the crossing."

Min hesitated, then gently tossed his rifle toward the boat. An elderly man reached up, tried to catch the gun, failed, but broke its fall and kept it

321

from injuring a passenger. Min then leaped into the river and swam a few strokes to the boat's starboard side. His man leaped in after him and swam to the boat. Both grasped the top of the boat's gunwale.

"I'll move around to the other side," Min said. "For balance."

"Good," said the woman.

After Min edged his way around the stern to the other side, he eyed the woman. "Why me? Why help me?"

"Back at the beach I saw you trying to protect our people." She brushed black hair away from her forehead. "I have a son in uniform. I'm not sure where he is. If he is alive, I hope he is as gallant as you."

Min, still holding on with his right hand, reached out with his left to touch the woman's hand. She took and held it. "Thank you," Min said. "I'm not sure if it was gallantry or simply duty."

"Is there a difference?"

✝✝✝

Kwon, now on the beach, reached down and jerked Han to his feet. His hands were blood-covered from applying pressure to his calf wound.

Kwon jabbed his sidearm's snout into Han's midsection and he doubled over, groaning. "Why did you hesitate?"

"I don't know," Han lied.

"You could have killed him easily. Instead he escapes." Kwon then slammed his gun's butt against Han's left temple, and he fell hard on the packed sand. "And now you are wounded and useless to me." Kwon briefly considered executing Han, but soldierly discipline told him to hold off, knowing that Han would recover and fight again and knowing that his other men could mutiny against him for killing the popular Han for no obvious reason.

As darkness was lowering its curtain on June 27, with Seoul now controlled by Kim Il Sung's conquering troops, some 34,000 South Korean soldiers already were killed, missing or captured. No one knew with exactitude how many civilians had been killed or wounded. No one ever would.

CHAPTER 61

Friday, June 30.

The Korean War. Day six.

President Truman authorized General Douglas MacArthur to use American ground forces in Korea. The order was vastly more impressive than the facts warranted. The troops would come from Japan where MacArthur still presided as viceroy and the U.S. had four divisions that were manned at less than 70 percent of their authorized strength. Most of their men were young untested soldiers who had been living softly as occupation troops and who were about to receive some humiliating on-the-job training.

As with the early days of World War II when many Americans mistakenly assumed that the Japanese, smaller in stature than westerners, would prove to be inferior fighters, arrogance again had many Americans – military and civilians alike – assuming that the North Koreans would fold like typhoon-blown tents when confronted by studly GIs. Slant-eyed, nearsighted and bucktoothed, North Koreans were spineless, unintelligent half-humans – or so the conventional wisdom held. Considering that the Japanese had routed MacArthur from the Philippines at the outset of World War II, it was surprising that the general didn't act to quash such thinking about the North Koreans. The answer likely lay with an ego massive enough to fill every cranny in the Pentagon.

The first American contingent flown from Korea was dubbed Task Force Smith. Lieutenant Colonel Brad Smith and 540 hastily assembled men were flown in C-54 transports from Itasuki, Japan to Pusan on South Korea's southeastern coast. Immediately they were shuttled from the planes to a train and moved to a location just north of Osan, a town about 45 miles south of Seoul. By 3 a.m. they were deployed on three hills overlooking the road. It seemed a good defensive position. The men were confident. They were equipped with small arms and five howitzers, only one of which was supplied with armor-piercing anti-tank shells – a scant six rounds.

This confidence soon melted faster than a hailstone on a southern fried afternoon. Standing on the middle hilltop Colonel Smith surveyed the countryside. Through his binoculars he caught his first glimpse of the enemy. It was unnerving. Coming at his men were 33 T-34 tanks and 10,000 crack North Korean troops. Rain was falling steadily. Smith lowered the binoculars and, peering through the watery curtain, shook his head.

The encounter started at 8:16 a.m. on July 5. Smith had his men well spaced, but they presented a front just 400 feet long. As North Korean troops in their mustard-hued uniforms began fanning out over rice paddies, Smith knew it wouldn't be long before his men were flanked.

He was right. In seven hours Task Force Smith was out of ammunition and on the run. Some men, in their haste to flee, threw away their weapons. Some removed their boots because it was easier to run through the water-soaked rice paddies barefoot. Their behavior disgusted the proud Smith. Later, about 150 of his men were reported killed, missing or wounded.

The North Koreans continued slugging away to the south. The U.S. 24th Infantry Division soon arrived in South Korea, and their arrogance soon was replaced by fear and respect for the North Korean troops. The 24th resisted feebly and failed to check the communist drive.

✝✝✝

Kim Il Sung was elated by his troops' easy victories and the speed with which they were capturing ground. But one development surprised him – stunned him actually – the United States entry into the war.

Joseph Stalin and Mao Tse Tung had a different reaction to this turn of events. They were livid. Both had relied on Kim's assessment that the U.S. would let him have his way in Korea, and both were soon placing calls to Kim's office. For the first couple days Kim made himself "unavailable." Better to let their rage cool, he concluded, before speaking with them. By then my troops should be well on their way to pushing the Americans into the East Sea. I will reap lasting glory, and Stalin and Mao can use my victory to strengthen their holds over their dominions in Europe and Asia. My success might even embolden them to expand their communist empires. Perhaps Stalin will try to spread his influence to Latin America. There are millions of disaffected people there. And Mao, he might decide to throw his weight into Vietnam.

† † †

"Are you sure about this?" Jack asked, his concern obvious in his furrowed brow and tone of voice.

"Quite sure," Thaddeus replied.

"Yes, he is sure," Bernadeta echoed with visible dubiousness. "Even though I have told him he has done enough. But," she added with loving exasperation, "he is a man. A Polish man."

Thaddeus blushed. "It is more than that. I feel I owe a debt of gratitude to my adopted country. It helped save my Polish homeland and it – you – helped me escape death at the hands of the secret police."

"Well, perhaps," Jack replied modestly. "We can't be sure."

"Thankfully," Bernadeta smiled wryly.

"Do you mind if we smoke?" Jack asked Bernadeta.

"Outside, no."

"Good." Jack stood and stepped to the end table in his rectory living room. He opened a decorative cardboard box of White Owls and removed two. "Let's go out on the porch."

"Perhaps I could make some iced tea," Bernadeta suggested.

"Great idea," Jack said enthusiastically. "With lemon. It'll go great with the cigars. I'll show you where everything is in the kitchen."

"Iced tea is something we didn't drink in Poland," Bernadeta smiled. "You are Americanizing us."

Jack laughed. "I've no doubt you will hang on to some of your Polish culture, even here in this summer oven called Arizona."

On the porch the three friends sat on wooden rocking chairs. Jack and Thaddeus lit their cigars and puffed contentedly. All three sipped tea. They were rocking leisurely.

"Does Mr. Hunter know about your plan?" Jack asked.

Thaddeus nodded. "I think he questions my sanity – like the elder – but he said he will hold my job for me."

"What branch of our military are you thinking of joining?" Jack asked.

"Do they have lancers?" Thaddeus was chuckling almost before he finished posing his question. "Air Force, no. I have been in planes enough. Navy? Voyages too long away from home."

"Is he not so very thoughtful?" Bernadeta asked with mock sweetness, and Jack and Thaddeus both laughed.

"Army, perhaps. But I think I would prefer the Marines. They fight on land, sea and air, and I think they give me a better opportunity to help."

Jack puffed again and watched the circle of smoke spirally ascend. "What about training?"

Thaddeus nodded pensively. "That is something that does not appeal to me. Not basic training."

"Didn't think it would. Lancer training. Airborne training. You've had more than enough."

"You are thinking of something?"

"Yes," said Jack, "a way around it. Training, that is."

Congresswoman Jane Morton was listening attentively to Jack's words. "I think I can help," she replied.

"I was hoping you could."

"I admire your friend's motive. That makes it easier. Even though I'm a first-term representative, my colleagues elected me to my late husband's seat on the Appropriations Committee."

"That gives you influence."

"Quite a bit, actually," said Congresswoman Morton, chuckling. "Some might even call it power."

It was precisely that.

"A Marine captain?" Thaddeus' widened eyes and tonal pitch evidenced his surprise.

"It's true," Jack said, "that most new officers are commissioned second lieutenants. Ensigns in the Navy. But Mrs. Morton explained to her contact at the Pentagon that you had served as a Polish Army captain, and at the moment our armed services are woefully short of experienced combat officers. He knew she was right."

"So," said Thaddeus, "she was clear to her contact that I do not desire a desk job."

"Oh yes, very clear."

Thaddeus grinned knowingly. "I see that good contacts are as valuable in America as they are in Poland."

Jack cleared his throat. "You realize I can't let you go alone."

"Oh? I thought you made a point to emphasize my experience," Thaddeus said playfully.

"True enough. But I'm thinking our Lord could use a pair of terrestrial eyes to look over you from time to time in a strange land."

"Marines too?"

"Army."

"Mrs. Morton?"

"Yes, she made a second phone call. She put in a word for me with the chief of chaplains in Washington. Seems he also can use an experienced man."

"Your bishop?"

Jack chuckled. "Believe me, Bishop Metzger is very used to hearing me make special requests."

"Your friend, the elder, he might think we both are a little crazy. Or loco as he says."

"He has told me often that white people are confusing."

CHAPTER 62

"You look troubled," said Marzena Dolata to her husband as she came walking into the living room from little Tomasz Michal's bedroom. Their apartment was on Ridge Street in Manhattan's lower east side in the shadow of the Williamsburg Bridge.

Tomasz was sitting in his favorite chair, a padded rocker, smoking a Camel and reading the most recent edition of *Zagoda*, an English-language Polish newspaper published in Chicago and mailed to New York. The Dolatas subscribed because it was a way to keep up with happenings – too often depressing – in their homeland and to sharpen their English reading ability.

Tomasz laid the paper on his lap. "It is an article about atrocities committed by North Korean soldiers. It brings back memories I can't seem to erase." He was alluding to his work as a sonderkommando at Auschwitz. His head shook and he sighed. "North Korean soldiers massacred hundreds of civilians – their own countrymen – at a train station, and they executed all of South Korea's legislators. Two hundred of them. In cold blood inside their own capitol building." Marzena was sensing the depth of her husband's lingering torment. Tomasz continued. "I can't believe all the North Korean soldiers involved in those atrocities really wanted to be part of the slaughter. To be murderers. I am sure some must have done it because not to do it would have meant their own deaths at the hands of their superiors. Still..." his voice trailed off.

"I think I know what you are thinking," Marzena said sympathetically.

"It was still wrong. So wrong. And they know it. They will have to live with their sins, and it will never be easy."

"After the war," Marzena said softly, "perhaps they will be able to forgive themselves."

"Perhaps."

"You did."

Tomasz peered into Marzena's caring blue eyes. "Only with the help of a loving wife. An understanding and forgiving wife." A pause. Forgive myself? Not entirely, Tomasz reflected, but that was a lie he didn't mind living because it made life easier for Marzena who continued to regard him as a hero who had saved her life and those of her family, and at least that wasn't a lie. Tomasz was glad that he hadn't had to lie on his immigration application. He had merely indicated that he had been a prisoner at Auschwitz; neither the forms nor the embassy officials had queried him about whether he had been a sonderkommando. Trying to come to grips with his past was hard enough without having had to lie about it. "Living with a secret isn't easy," he murmured. He had escaped Auschwitz, but his sadness had proved inescapable. "I will never be able to talk openly about my past. Not with our children. Certainly not with our friends. I don't think they could ever get beyond the shock of knowing; they could never understand or forgive. I couldn't blame them. It is something to take to my grave."

"Our graves." Marzena, as she had done so often, reached out and patted his hand.

✝✝✝

Park Han lay on his back on the ground with only a blanket beneath him. His hands were clasped behind his head, staring up at the stars. The late-August night was pleasantly cool. It should have been a night when sleep came easily. It didn't. Yes, Captain Kwon's vanguard company and the rest of North Korea's 6th Division were still advancing relentlessly southward, shoving back South Korean and Allied units. The 6th Division's ultimate goal was taking Pusan, the major port on Korea's southeast coast, and forcing Allied troops out of the city, onto the beaches and back onto their ships. Success seemed inevitable.

Han knew, though, that when sleep did at last overtake him it would likely be plagued by nightmares. They struck frequently and kept fresh in his mind the slaughters he had witnessed. The rape he had committed. The men he had slain in combat. The remorse that was swamping him. He could have killed Kwon at almost any time. He could kill him tomorrow. That others could do so too did nothing to assuage his guilt.

What of the future? Han asked himself. What will it hold for me? My leg wound has healed but not my conscience, and I doubt that it ever will. I will bear scars of the flesh and the spirit. If I survive the war, I will have secrets – awful ones – to keep. Forever. That thought alone was deeply troubling. He and Min had shared virtually all their deeds, thoughts, hopes, aspirations and shortcomings. Never again would he and Min enjoy that elevated level of brotherly intimacy. There are nights, Han reflected dejectedly, when I wish morning would never come.

CHAPTER 63

Pusan Perimeter had become a haunting term. During the summer of 1950 it was being seen daily in newspapers and heard hourly on radio reports. It often was the lead story on the 15-minute television networks' nightly newscasts.

The usual reaction was hand wringing. The term called to mind images that Americans found deeply disturbing: United States troops overrun and falling back in inglorious retreat. Asian soldiers kicking the bejesus out of American fighting men. Could North Koreans actually push American and South Korean forces off the peninsula and into the East Sea? Would a second Dunkirk be needed to rescue trapped soldiers? There were days when North Korean success made such a disaster seem a too real possibility.

The Pusan Perimeter had become a haven, albeit a painfully embarrassing one, for American and South Korean units. It stretched some 50 miles east to west and 100 miles north to south in an irregular rectangle around the port city of Pusan. The Nakdong River formed much of the Pusan Perimeter's western boundary. After North Korean assaults, its waters often flowed red. The East Sea formed the perimeter's southern and eastern boundaries. The northern boundary weaved across rugged mountain terrain.

In the Pusan Perimeter's early days the South Korean Army and the U.S. 24th Infantry Division were struggling frantically to hold the line. Park Min found himself in firefights daily. Later, the U.S. 25th Infantry Division and the 1st Cavalry Division arrived and bolstered perimeter defenses.

Keeping the determined North Korean forces at bay, especially along the Nakdong, required both mental agility and physical mobility. American and South Korean commanders continually had to redeploy troops to fend off determined North Korean probes.

Complicating and slowing Allied movements was a mammoth influx of refugees. During the middle two weeks of July some 380,000 scared, hungry and exhausted civilians crossed into Allied-held territory. By the end of July, 58 refugee camps had sprung up inside the perimeter.

✝✝✝

September 15 changed everything. That was the day General MacArthur orchestrated a landing at Inchon, inland Seoul's port city at the mouth of the Han River about 15 miles southwest of the capital. Although North Korean intelligence had warned Kim Il Sung of potential danger there, the Great Leader was euphoric over his army's astonishing string of successes and dismissed as preposterous the possibility of a large-scale Inchon landing.

His disregard was understandable. Inchon's tide is the world's second highest – after the Bay of Fundy's in Nova Scotia – rising 35 feet in three hours. When the tide is out, broad mud flats extend 6,000 yards – nearly three and half miles – from the shoreline and convert the harbor into a gummy quagmire. Who would be so utterly foolish as to attempt an invasion at Inchon?

That combination of danger and improbability was exactly why MacArthur selected Inchon. He had assembled a fleet of 230 ships from seven navies plus swarms of landing craft. His surprise landing was exquisitely daring but well-conceived. His timing in those treacherous waters demanded precision that would have been the envy of Swiss watchmakers. Confusion or delay would have spelled disaster for amphibious troops and equipment. Bogged down in deep mud, they would have made inviting targets for North Korean artillery shells, bombs and machine gun fire.

At dawn on the 15th a reinforced battalion of the 1st Marine Division brushed aside light resistance and captured Wolmi-do, an island at the harbor entrance. Not a single Marine was killed and only 17 were wounded. At the next high tide an armada of LCVPs – Landing Craft Vehicles & Personnel – was plowing determinedly toward shore. In the rear of one, a disgruntled Marine, Private First Class Edmund Brown, grumbled, "That accent. What the fuck did we do to get stuck with a Polack captain?"

His buddy, PFC Galen Richards, was like-minded. "Word is, somebody pulled strings to get him a commission. What the hell are the Marines coming to? We that hard up?"

"The Krauts ran right over the Polacks," Brown sneered. "Plus everybody knows they're dumb as posts."

A third trooper, Quentin Fensch, spoke up. "I heard some stuff too."

"Yeah? Like what?" said Brown.

"The captain fought the Germans on horseback in Poland. Escaped to France. Fought for the Frogs. Then made it to England and volunteered airborne. Got hit somewhere along the way."

"Sounds like comic book crap to me," Brown muttered.

"Yeah, Super Polack," Richards cracked. "Where's his fucking cape?"

Moments later their LCVP drove onto the beach and slammed into the 14-foot seawall with its engine running wide open.

"Here we go," Brown said, subdued. "Buckle up."

On the beach North Korean machine gun fire and carbine rounds were beginning to kick up sand.

The LCVP's roaring engine was holding the craft in place against the seawall.

"Bring the ladders forward," the captain shouted. "The cargo nets too."

He and his men were staring at the seawall, wondering what lay on the other side. Then the LCVP pilot cut the engine, letting the craft drift back slightly. In the next moment, winches spun, chains uncoiled in a metallic clatter, and the bow gate dropped. "Out! Out!" came the captain's command.

Immediately Marines were jamming and steadying wooden ladders against the stone barrier and throwing the nets over too.

"Well, I'll be," Brown sputtered with a mix of surprise and awe. "Look at that. Shit on me."

The first man up and over the wall was Captain Thaddeus Metz.

"Well?" said Fensch.

"Don't need to worry about his Polack accent," Brown conceded. "Maybe your shit was straight."

✝✝✝

Once over the seawall Thaddeus' men were among those who went storming into Inchon. Again they overwhelmed light resistance, took the city and swung north toward Kimpo Airport. MacArthur's losses: 20 men killed and fewer than 200 wounded. None of Thaddeus' men were among them.

On September 18 the Army's 7th Infantry Division waded ashore at Inchon and wheeled south. As was his custom, Father Jack Brecker was with the front-line troops. His fatigue uniform bore the 7th Division's distinctive arm patch, an orange circle with the points of two black triangles meeting in the center. The result was a spreading military fan that soon had the North Koreans falling back in disarray. The operation threatened to break their back 150 miles behind their front lines near Pusan.

In Pyongyang the Great Leader was aghast. He could foresee his own capital threatened if MacArthur's forces started penetrating north. This time when the inevitable phone calls came in from Moscow and Beijing, he felt obligated to listen to and accept the blisterings from Stalin and Mao.

Along the Pusan Perimeter in the south, MacArthur's stunning assault signaled the freshly muscled 8th Army to begin slugging North Korean positions. Captain Kwon and his men, including Park Han, soon were feeling the brunt of the fierce counterattack.

Several American units quickly pierced communist lines and Kwon's company knew retreat was unavoidable. They were battle hardened and initially warded off panic but rapidly began making their way back north. The reversal of fortunes galled Kwon and deepened his hatred for the United States. He made a pledge to himself: eventually defeat the imperialists and celebrate a united Korea with the Great Leader.

This was Han's first experience at being on the defensive, and he was ambivalent. He knew his chances of being killed were increasing, but he also sensed that the Allies' success was decreasing the likelihood that more civilians would be dying. He found himself giving thought to defecting to the Allies. *Would they kill me, thinking I am an infiltrator? If Kwon catches me trying, he would shoot me on the spot.*

On the second day some of Han's 6th Division mates began panicking and clandestinely discarding their uniforms, pulling on civilian clothing and trying to blend in with villagers. Some succeeded in their ruse, but most were being fingered by vengeful villagers to advancing Allies who killed or caught the majority of the deserters.

Parts of the motorized U.S. 1st Cavalry Division rapidly sped more than 100 miles to link up with the advancing men of the 7th Infantry Division. Along their route the 1st Cavalry was cutting off and capturing entire North Korean units.

The Allies' offensive was further complicating the situation for the North Koreans. Their supply lines, perilously long and stretched thin before the Inchon landing, snapped. By contrast, U.S. logistics were smoothly orchestrated. Reinforcements and supplies flown from American units neatly supplemented troops and equipment already hauled ashore from ships standing off the coast and stockpiled behind U.S. lines.

✝✝✝

Later that month as death continued to claim thousands of victims throughout Korea, lives were taking shape both in the Land of the Morning Calm and elsewhere.

Kyong was puzzled and concerned. She had not menstruated. This, she was thinking, is the second month my blood has not flowed. Did the knife wound do damage to my womanly organs? Or could I be pregnant? Min and I loved only once. Was that enough? I am so ignorant of these matters. I wish I could ask Mother. Given the chaos that reigned up and down the peninsula and capricious visits by sudden death, Kyong knew trying to journey north to see her parents – if they remained alive – in Kaesong was out of the question. Moreover she still felt occasional twinges of pain from physical exertion. Kyong made a decision: I will ask the woman who saved my life.

✝✝✝

Bernadeta had been missing her period, and she knew it meant motherhood was coming. She smiled. Farm girls learn early the rhythms of life: mating, pregnancy, birth. They saw it often among the livestock.

Bernadeta also was worried. Having delivered a stillborn baby in Warsaw, would this baby emerge breathing and full of life? She tried to shrug off her concern and think positively. In America she knew she could consult a doctor for prenatal care and soon would do so.

I should sit down and begin writing letters, she told herself. To Thaddeus. To Barbara and Father. They will be so excited. To Mrs.

334

Ostrowski? Occasionally, when Bernadeta's thoughts turned to her former neighbor, questions arose. She had been a kind, caring friend. She had been a Godsend during and after the stillbirth. But who else might have tattled on Thaddeus? There was no evidence, was there? This distracting brew troubled Bernadeta, and she tried to expunge it. It wasn't easy.

The next morning Bernadeta had a thought that cheered her and it had to do with work – or more accurately her co-workers. After having written and mailed letters to Thaddeus and Barbara and her father, she got into her car and drove to the mining company offices where she confided her situation to the Hunters – Elgin and Walt. They were thrilled – because a young woman they greatly admired was carrying Thaddeus' child and because she had told them directly. Excitedly, Elgin and Walt asked Bernadeta if they could continue spreading her good news. She said yes.

After work that day Bernadeta acted on another impulse. She drove through the desert to Charco.

"I am surprised to see you here," said the elder, brushing desert dust from his blue jeans. "But pleased."

"I have news."

"About Thaddeus? I worry about him and Father Brecker."

Bernadeta smiled wryly. "Sort of."

The elder's black eyes narrowed. They peered deeply into Bernadeta's. A flat grin began creasing his leathery countenance. "I am 64 years on this land," he said somberly. "That is many. Now that I am close to the end, new life has special meaning. I see it bringing new spirit and new hope. I hope your baby brings much joy and hope to you and Thaddeus and all your friends. I am privileged that you have come to tell me."

In fact, Bernadeta was astonished. "How did you know?"

The elder smiled kindly. "My eyes have seen much. In your eyes I see great happiness – a happiness special to women who know they are bearing new life."

Bernadeta sniffled. Tears were beginning to film her eyes. She brushed away the first drops. "I am so happy – for Thaddeus and me. But I am also worried."

"I know."

"You do?"

"Thaddeus once told me about your stillbirth."

335

"Oh."

"Do not worry."

"I wish-"

He interrupted gently. "You need not worry." He reached out and lightly touched Bernadeta's scar. Yes, he was thinking, it is perfect, just like Grand Canyon. "Your baby will be born and he will be healthy." His words were spoken gravely and with a quiet, comforting certainty.

"How can you be so sure?" Bernadeta was more quizzical than skeptical.

"It is difficult to explain – to put into English words. But you need not worry any longer."

CHAPTER 64

Park Han was dirty – he hadn't bathed in more than two weeks – hungry – rations were depleted and he was reduced to living off the land – and drained – physically and mentally. So were his fellow soldiers, including Captain Kwon Oh Bum. They had been on the run, retreating continuously since MacArthur's Inchon landing and the Allied breakout from the Pusan Perimeter. Twice Kwon's company had come perilously close to being surrounded and captured – a fate that had befallen thousands of North Korean troops. Still, more than half of his 150-man company had been killed, wounded, captured or deserted. Troop morale had plummeted, and maintaining control was becoming increasingly difficult. Kwon's company had run out of medicines. When men were wounded, their injuries often became infected, with death a virtual certainty.

Still, Kwon remained doggedly determined. This evening after darkness had fallen near a tiny fishing village on the Han River's south bank, Kwon assembled his men. "We have no choice. From what I am seeing and hearing, we have to get back north of the 38th Parallel. And soon. If we don't we will be cut off and surrounded. That could happen at any moment with little or no warning. We could all be killed or captured. I will not let it happen to me. The imperialist yankees have entered our country through the back door to rescue Rhee and his criminal cronies.

They should be lined up and shot, every one of them." Kwon's fatigue notwithstanding, he was pacing and fuming, using his dwindling reserves of energy to again show his disdain for Syngman Rhee and all things American. "We came south to liberate our fellow Koreans from Rhee's corrupt regime. Now mercenaries from America and other countries are doing his fighting."

Han rolled his eyes. Kwon's words carried not a shred of credibility. Han didn't know the extent or depth of American intentions. Do they mean to rescue Korea from the grip of Kim Il Sung? Or to occupy Korea as the Japanese did? But he had seen Kwon in action often and long enough to know that his moral compass was smashed. Kwon, Han had learned, seemingly found it easier to lie than speak the truth. Repeatedly he had shown a readiness – an eagerness – to inflict suffering – torturing, raping and murdering wantonly.

"American and South Korean units are closing in on us from the south," Kwon continued. "They are also moving west to east and might cut the entire peninsula in half. We have to stay clear of Seoul and Kimpo. The Americans control both. And we need to cross the Han without being detected. Tonight."

Kwon's assessment was accurate. American and South Korean forces were continuing to seal off and capture North Koreans. Within days after Seoul was finally retaken, more than 100,000 North Korean soldiers had become prisoners of war.

In Kaesong, Min and Han's mother and Mr. and Mrs. Ahn were largely unaware of recent developments. The same was true for Mr. and Mrs. Choi and Kyong in Munsan. They had heard only scraps of information that they regarded as unreliable unless confirmed in some credible way. As yet no radio news was being transmitted from Seoul, and the broadcasts from Pyongyang still spoke only of smashing North Korean conquests. No newspapers were being published in either Kaesong or Munsan. Mrs. Park, Mr. and Mrs. Ahn, the Chois and Kyong knew only that the North Korean

Army's brutalizing of civilians seemed to have ended after Kim Il Sung's swaggering forces had swept through on their way south.

Now Mrs. Park tried to go about her daily life as routinely as possible, anxiously awaiting word – any word – about Min and Han.

Kyong had confided in Mrs. Choi who had told her, "Let me examine your wound, dear." Adjacent the butcher and cutlery shop, in the cramped living quarters she shared with the Chois, Kyong pulled her blouse up from her skirt. Mrs. Choi scrutinized the knife wound. She probed gently. "I don't see any sign of infection. I think the last discomfort should end any day now. But you will soon be experiencing another kind of discomfort."

"Oh?"

Mrs. Choi smiled as a mother might smile at a daughter. "Morning sickness."

✝✝✝

Kwon and his company's remnants – now down to 70 desperate men – had been forced by escalating American air attacks to travel only at night. Now, Kwon led his men into the sleeping riverside village. He issued instructions to two groups of four men each. They went barging into two small thatched-roof houses, rousted the terrified occupants from their sleeping mats and roughly pulled and pushed them outside. Two families – a total of four adults and five young children – were quivering, expecting to be executed for no explicable reason or perhaps for no reason at all except for being in the wrong place at the wrong time. Instead, Kwon uttered only one word: "hostages."

Kwon led the assemblage to the river's edge. There in the moonlight he saw three small fishing boats, each about 12 feet long. "Put three hostages in each boat. If they resist, do not shoot them. No gunfire. Strangle them. Children too if they resist or call out. Dump their bodies in the river. The Americans are too close for us to make any noise. Understood? We'll put ten of our men in each boat."

Han decided he would not be among them. He could not abide the thought that hostages – innocents – would be used to shield him from harm. No more, he thought. I have seen enough deaths of women and children.

Of men who have committed no wrongs. He eased his way back from the water's edge.

"Get them into the water and shove off," Kwon ordered. "The rest of you," Kwon said as he stepped into one of the boats, "are on your own. I fully expect you to find a way across and to make your way north to rejoin us."

✝✝✝

For Han and the 40 others the night was a long one. They remained awake and alert. He and several others spent hours silently roaming the river's south shore, looking for more boats or an unguarded pontoon bridge. No luck.

At daybreak in the fishing village, Han and the other soldiers heard ominous rumbling and clanking. "Tanks," Han said. "American tanks." He knew they couldn't be North Korean tanks that had been destroyed or captured during the retreat up the peninsula. "They are behind us."

"What do we do?" nervously asked one of the men, Private Lee.

"Take cover behind the houses," Han replied. "But no hostages as shields. Tell the villagers to stay inside and stay low."

Private Lee and other soldiers carried out Han's instructions. During the night and this morning he had become de facto leader and he knew it.

Eight minutes later the first tank came rumbling into view. Walking cautiously on either side and in front of it were 1st Cavalry Division troops. The village was quiet and the Americans were wary, their submachine guns and M-1s at the ready.

Han shook his head slightly in resignation. Then he signaled the men nearest him to prepare to fire. This is suicidal, Han knew. We have only small arms and not many of those. Ammunition is short. I wonder how many tanks are behind the first one. Certainly this one isn't alone. We have no avenue of escape. How many more of us have to die? And for what? How many of us deserve to live? After what we have done? I can't believe Kim Il Sung would ever permit democracy, not after fighting so long to gain power. And these villagers? Poor things. They probably have no idea why this war is being fought. Not really. And the two families Kwon took as hostages. Will they survive? Only if they are lucky.

Han, kneeling, took aim with his rifle and then paused. He stared hard at the oncoming tank and troops, still unaware of the North Koreans' presence. The tank stopped. A South Korean soldier emerged from among the Americans and walked several paces in front of the tank. He slung his submachine gun over his left soldier, cupped his hands around his mouth and called out loudly: "People of this village. We have come to liberate you. Do you understand? Do not be afraid. Come out of your homes. I am with the Americans. You are safe now."

As the first villagers began to trickle timidly from their small homes, Han slowly stood.

Villagers continued to step into the open, shuffling and fearful. Han watched them, looked at some of his fellow soldiers and then bent down, carefully laying his rifle on the ground. Then, heart racing, he stepped from behind the house, cupped his hands around his mouth and shouted, "Min!" Then, hands raised above his head, he moved forward among the villagers. Other soldiers began following his lead, laying down their weapons, stepping from concealment and raising their arms. To a man, they were sensing an opportunity to end their war.

††††

The next night north of Seoul, Captain Kwon's confidence was growing. For the first time since before escaping across the Han, he liked his chances of reaching sanctuary north of the 38th Parallel. I can move faster and attract less attention if I'm alone, he thought. He waited until after midnight, then slipped away, deserting his men and their hostages.

Kwon's plan: I'll hide in Munsan during the day and make my way across the border tonight. But first get some food. Before sunrise, at Munsan's southern fringe, Kwon unholstered and checked his sidearm. Satisfied that it was loaded and clean, he reholstered it. Then he unslung his submachine gun, stepped to the road's right side and entered town.

In the predawn grayness, a few townspeople had ventured outside, getting an early start on sundry tasks. Those who saw Kwon paid him scant notice; after all that they had endured during the previous four months, a lone soldier sparked little curiosity or alarm, whatever color his uniform.

Near the town center Kwon saw the butcher shop on his left. Meat, he thought hungrily. A hearty breakfast of meat and rice will give me the strength to keep going. This far north I might even chance moving during daylight. American air attacks are still centered around Seoul and south of the Han. And if pilots do see me, they won't waste time, fuel and ammunition on a single soldier.

✝✝✝

"Ahem. Your arm. I must say that nursing requirements in a war zone can be quite demanding." The physician at the New Zealand Army recruitment center in Wellington was addressing Lucy Crispin starchily but with a measure of deference, chiefly because of her father Morgan's reputation as a surgeon.

The inspecting physician's attitude wasn't surprising Lucy nor was it daunting her. "I am fully qualified," she replied confidently, "and experienced. This arm is smaller than the other but far from useless. I can do my bit. Shall I demonstrate?"

The army physician, a major, rubbed his chin and shook his head. "Miss, I must tell you, I am tempted to refuse you." The starch in his voice was losing its stiffness. "But I admire your pluck, and our med unit can use experienced nurses. We've too few volunteers. It would seem Korea holds little appeal for our doctors and nurses."

Actually, Korea offered little attraction to New Zealanders in general. New Zealand was sending troops – an artillery regiment in the main – because it was a British Commonwealth member and Great Britain was supporting the United Nations resolution to come to South Korea's assistance. The artillery unit's men were mostly volunteers who had fought in North Africa and Italy during World War II.

"When do we depart?" Lucy's eyes were glittering. She reached across the major's desk, and he took her right hand and shook it.

"Our supplies are being loaded aboard a ship as we speak. How soon can you be dockside?"

Lucy grinned a trifle sheepishly. "I made an assumption. My bag and kit are on the floor outside your office. I need only phone my parents and brother so they can see me off."

† † †

The door to the butcher and cutlery shop bore no lock. In prewar Munsan the level of trust among residents meant the town had no locksmith. Anyone wanting a simple padlock could buy one at the local hardware shop. Few were sold.

Kwon pushed open the door. Faint shafts of daylight were beginning to shove aside darkness. Kwon considered briefly the early hour, then began pounding on the counter to rouse the shop owners in their adjacent living quarters.

Choi Chun Kuen soon entered the shop. He was irritated, muttering and rubbing sleep from his eyes. He buttoned his brown vest. The mustard-hued army uniform surprised but didn't intimidate him. He stopped, hands on hips. "What do you want?" His question sounded more like the challenge that it was.

"Breakfast" was the brusque reply.

"We are not a restaurant or an inn." Mr. Choi was glaring. "You are rude. We do not serve rude customers."

"You will serve me. I need to eat meat, lots of it. You have it, and this morning you will cook it for me." At which point, Kwon leveled his submachine gun at Mr. Choi.

"This will take time," he said, his voice's hard edge softening slightly.

"Who else lives here?"

"My wife" – the briefest of pauses – "and our daughter." In the narrowest sliver of time, Mr. Choi concluded it wise to acknowledge Kyong as more than a young friend.

"They can help. Get them."

With Kwon's gun muzzle following him, Mr.Choi went to rouse his wife and Kyong – and to tell Kyong of his deception. Minutes later the three of them entered the shop.

One look at Kyong and Kwon's appetite expanded to include more than breakfast. The Chois both saw the lust in his eyes. Kyong didn't miss it either and felt a shiver of dread so intense she was wishing to become a ghost.

"We have some pork already butchered and a couple chickens," said Mrs. Choi, wanting to divert Kwon's attention from Kyong. "What do you prefer?"

"Chicken."

"With rice and kimchi. I will begin preparing it. Come with me, Kyong. I can use your help."

In the interest of further diverting Kwon's attention from Kyong, Mr. Choi decided to chance a question. "We have heard so little about the war. Why are you alone?"

In this situation Kwon saw no reason to lie. "The Americans are pushing north hard. You've heard their artillery."

Mr. Choi shrugged. "We have heard artillery. We didn't know whose it was."

"Not ours. I need to get back north of the 38th Parallel. I can move faster alone." Kwon's dour expression softened and he appeared to relax.

"It will take a while for my wife and daughter to cook the chicken." Gesturing toward the counter, he said, "Why not put your gun there? Your helmet too. Sit down," Mr. Choi added, pointing to stacked sacks of rice.

"I will."

✝✝✝

With the Inchon landing an unqualified success and the liberation of Seoul completed, Thaddeus Metz was daily learning more about American military needs. He was giving serious thought to volunteering to undertake a mission that was both necessary and hazardous. First things first, though. This morning he was striding to Namdaemun or South Gate. It was one of four great city gates constructed in the early 1400s during the first years of the Yi Dynasty that endured from 1392 until Japan's 1910 conquest. South Gate, about two miles due south of the capitol, was an imposing structure that had survived centuries of warfare. Framing and flanking a thick central archway were large rectangular stones of varying hues that extended straight in each direction for some 40 feet. At each end of this expanse were two stone wings that angled slightly forward for another

15 feet each. Atop the long center section and rising about 20 feet was a wooden two-story, tile-roofed guardhouse.

Jack Brecker had asked a 7th Division radioman to contact Thaddeus and recommended that they meet at the great gate. The early autumn morning was clear with the temperature 50 degrees Fahrenheit.

From a distance of about 75 yards Thaddeus spotted his friend standing by the archway and smoking a White Owl. "Jack!" he shouted.

"Thaddeus!" Jack replied, waving the cigar.

Moments later the two men were shaking hands warmly. "We have become close friends, but in public, should I address you as Father Brecker? Or Captain?" Thaddeus' eyes were twinkling merrily.

"After all we've been through together," Jack grinned, "you can call me anything you like." They laughed. Then Jack gestured with his cigar. "Want one?"

"It is early," said Thaddeus, "but yes."

Jack removed another White Owl from his jacket pocket, produced an army issue Ronson lighter and put the flame to the cigar while Thaddeus puffed. Thaddeus ran his tongue around the inside of his mouth. "Tastes good."

The two men moved to one end of the gate and leaned back against it.

"Heard from Bernadeta?"

Thaddeus' eyes widened gleefully. "When we return to Ajo, how would you like to perform a baptism?"

"She is with child?"

"Very much so," Thaddeus confirmed excitedly. "Arizona's Polish colony will be growing."

"Well, my fine Polish friend, congratulations! I'm glad we have these cigars to celebrate. Too bad we don't have some scotch."

Thaddeus flicked ashes and said, "Hah! One of my Marines no doubt could get some. I have learned an important lesson; Marine scrounging skills are a match for the Polish airborne troops."

Jack laughed heartily. "That's quite a concession. Let's finish these cigars and then meet again later for scotch and smokes."

"Done."

"And when you write to Bernadeta, please tell her how happy I am for both of you."

"Done."

"So what's next for your Marines?"

"I suppose I should tell you what I have in mind."

Captain Kwon was sitting on a stool at the end of the counter nearest the shop's front door. Mr. and Mrs. Choi and Kyong were standing at the other end, chatting and avoiding staring at Kwon. With his chopsticks Kwon was hungrily consuming the chicken, rice and kimchi. His stomach was filling with hot food for the first time since the Inchon invasion and Pusan Perimeter breakout. Now he was nearly finished with his breakfast which he found tasty and plentiful. He looked up and nodded his appreciation.

"I have no money to pay you," he said. "Sorry."

"We did not expect payment," Mr. Choi said, not unpleasantly and truthfully.

At that moment an elderly customer entered the shop. He paused at the unusual sight – a soldier eating at the shop's counter. But then, he thought, these are unusual times.

Mr. Choi, recognizing the customer, stepped toward him and bowed. "Good morning, Mr. Kang. How may I help you?"

Kang, glancing at Kwon, returned the bow. "I was hoping you would have some beef to slice so my wife can make pulgogi."

"If you can wait, I will slice some for you." Pulgogi is thin strips of beef, usually marinated and cooked on a tableside brazier with vegetables.

"That will be fine," said Kang. "My wife was hoping to prepare some tonight." He looked again – this time curiously – at Kwon. "Haven't I seen you before?"

Kwon placed the chopsticks inside the nearly empty large wooden bowl. He shrugged. "You don't look familiar."

Kang's lips pursed and he scratched his forehead. Kwon slid off the stool and stood, preparing to depart. Kang's eyes narrowed and began showing glints of recognition as he wrestled with his memory. "I remember now. Yes. The massacre at Kaesong. It's you." Both his eyes and voice were betraying mounting contempt. "You commanded the troops on the train. You directed the slaughter."

345

Mr. Kang's words seemed to quick-freeze everyone in the shop. They stood stock still in awkward positions. Mouths were agape at the accusation.

Kwon looked at Mr. Kang and sighed. At the moment, his stomach full and his objective of reaching North Korea foremost in his thinking, he preferred to let Kang's assertion pass. "You are mistaken."

"No," Mr. Kang said pensively, "it's you. I would never forget the face of the man who ordered those murders."

The allegation shook the Chois and Kyong. The massacre had taken hundreds of lives and was regarded as the war's largest-scale and most shocking atrocity. "Is that true?" Mr. Choi asked, voice barely audible.

Kwon looked scornfully at the shop's other four occupants. "What do you know about war?"

Before Mr. Choi could reply, Kang spoke bluntly. "I know you are an ugly blot on the history of Korea. I know you are guilty of mass murder." Mr. Kang's disdain was bottomless. "Mass murder of unsuspecting innocent civilians. You are beyond shame."

Kwon bristled. "And just how innocent are you, old man? Did you collaborate with the Japanese? I fought them. Did you side with Rhee?"

Mr. Kang walked to within two feet of Kwon, standing with arms crossed. Kang cocked his right arm behind his ear and lashed out, slapping Kwon's left cheek.

The Chois and Kyong shuddered, eyes riveted on the rapidly escalating drama.

Kwon unfolded his arms and shoved Kang, sending him stumbling backward across the shop. Then he reached on the counter for his submachine gun.

Mr. Choi put his hand on top of Kwon's. "Don't. Please. No more violence."

Kwon hesitated only briefly before swatting Mr. Choi's hand aside. Gun in hand, Kwon wheeled to face Kang. "What do you have to say now, old man? Is your brain cramping your tongue? You are a worthless piece of shit."

Mr. Kang had regained his balance and began stepping calmly toward Kwon. "I can see now why you directed the massacre. You fought the Japanese, but your spirit has been corrupted. It has rotted. Korea would be a better place without you. Who would mourn your death? Who would miss you?"

Christianity had been making small inroads into Korea's culture but often it was said that Koreans practiced no religion. In truth, most Koreans made no pretense of observing formal religious rites or attending services. Still, native beliefs, the ethics of Confucius, the precepts of Buddha and Christian ideals all were set firmly in the thinking and behavior of the people of the Land of the Morning Calm. Mr. Kang was among the justifiably righteous.

"Your rantings are pathetic," Kwon said, utterly dismissive. "You are an ingrate. It sickens me to think that I lost men fighting the Japanese for the likes of you."

The Chois and Kyong were watching, transfixed.

"The Japanese were cruel masters," Mr. Kang replied. "But you are lower than the snakes that slither across the forest floor. You murder your own countrymen and call it patriotic. You are evil and delusional."

"And you are a dead man standing," Kwon hissed. He squeezed and held his gun's trigger. A hail of bullets tore into and through Mr. Kang, lifting his feet from the clay floor and splattering body parts and blood as he went sprawling toward the front door. He landed on his back, eyes open in death.

Kwon turned toward Mr. Choi. "You are a butcher," he said bitingly. "Blood and dead bodies are your specialty."

"I am a butcher of animals," Mr. Choi said hotly, "but you are an evil butcher."

Mrs. Choi and Kyong were in shock and cringing. The gunfire had Munsan residents scurrying inside shops and homes. Those already inside were peeking from windows.

"Shut up, shopkeeper," Kwon snapped, "or your wife and daughter will have two bodies on their hands." Kwon walked to the front door and looked outside to see whether the shots had created any threats. As he did so, Mr. Choi reached for a sturdy paring knife with a four-inch blade. Protection, he was thinking, just in case. He hid the knife in his palm and inside his wrist and shirtsleeve.

Kwon returned and laid his submachine gun on the counter next to his helmet. "Prepare some food that I can take with me," he ordered Mrs.

Choi. "And hurry." She turned to leave the shop, Kyong following. "No," Kwon said sharply. "Your daughter stays here. I'm taking her with me. A hostage."

Mrs. Choi and Kyong braked but didn't look back. Mr. Choi's jaws clenched. "A hostage?" He could feel his anger-fueled blood pressure rising.

"That's right. I will let her go when I cross the Imjin and get close to the 38th Parallel. She will guarantee my safe passage."

Mr. Choi knew the army captain was lying; he had no intention of freeing Kyong, not before raping her and maybe not then. Kwon was a killing machine, and it was easy for Choi to visualize Kwon ravishing Kyong and then casually executing her. Mr. Choi wasn't sure he could prevent such a tragedy, but he knew he had to check his temper.

Then came Mrs. Choi's voice, clear and composed. "Leave our daughter. Take me."

On hearing her words, a wave of affection went surging through Kyong.

Kwon snickered derisively. "You would make a less valuable bargaining tool."

"I will do whatever you want," said Mrs. Choi, remaining outwardly calm while her insides were screaming their disgust at what she was offering.

Kwon's laughter was mirthless. "You would do anything I want, but I want nothing you have." He faced Kyong. "Come with me."

"No," Mr. Choi said evenly. "She stays here."

"That's enough!" Kwon barked. "I've had enough – more than enough – disrespect."

"I can't let you take her," Mr.Choi said.

"You can't let me?" Smirking, Kwon reached for his helmet and put it on. Then he reached for his gun – and roared his pain. Mr. Choi's paring knife, propelled by his brawny right arm, had plunged into and through the back of Kwon's left hand, the blade point penetrating the counter and immobilizing Kwon. Bellowing, he flattened his face and right hand against the countertop.

Mr. Choi reached for another knife, newly sharpened with an eight-inch blade, and slashed the back of Kwon's thighs, blood quickly reddening his trousers. Again Kwon roared.

With his left hand Mr. Choi picked up the submachine gun and without a word handed it to his wife. Then he opened Kwon's holster and removed his sidearm. He shoved the gun into his waistband and then, using his left hand to press down on Kwon's left arm, his right hand gripped the paring knife's haft. He loosened the blade point from the counter and pulled the blade up and through Kwon's hand.

The captain's scream was long and primal. Kwon felt he might faint.

"You were correct," Mr. Choi said, voice hard and unforgiving. "I have slaughtered many animals. I have done it to provide food for my fellow residents. But you, you are not the equal of those animals. You enjoy killing. Leave! Leave now."

Kwon, half-snarling, half-moaning, thinking he might vomit, stepped around Mr. Kang's corpse and staggered from the shop. He looked back, hatred's venom pouring from his eyes. Then he began shuffling north, blood staining his trouser legs and dripping from his hand to the dirt street.

✝✝✝

"Semper Fidelis. It is a good motto," Thaddeus said thoughtfully. "It would have been appropriate for our lancers."

He and Jack were sitting in Jack's tent, sipping Johnnie Walker Black Label and puffing White Owls. The scotch tasted particularly good on this chilly autumn evening.

"Is that why you volunteered for this mission?"

"I suppose. But it's more than being faithful to the Marines. It's also being faithful to my adopted homeland. And to myself."

"Still, my friend, are you really sure about this?"

"How many American soldiers have experience operating behind enemy lines? Most are green. They didn't join the Marines or Army until after World War II."

"I see your point," Jack smiled. "Where will you be?"

"On a tiny island. In the Yellow Sea off the coast of North Korea. There are three thousand of them. Uninhabited. Most have no name."

"Yours?"

Thaddeus grinned slyly. "Mine had no name."

"It does now?"

"Polska."

Jack threw his head back and laughed. He then raised his mug of Johnnie Walker. "A toast. To Polska."

They clinked mugs.

"To Polska," Thaddeus smiled and sighed. "I have no choice but to survive, you know. A child should grow up with his father. So as you said, perhaps you can help keep God's busy eyes looking over me."

"You won't be alone."

"No. I will have a squad with me. Some good men. Three of them were with me on the landing craft at Inchon. Brown, Richards, Fensch. When they learned I was volunteering, they did too. Good men."

Captain Metz's mission would comprise two jobs. He and his small band of Marine volunteers would conduct reconnaissance behind enemy lines, and they would jump from helicopters into the Yellow Sea to rescue downed American pilots.

† † †

Park Han was relieved – glad, actually – to be a POW. He was being fed adequately if not abundantly, got to visit with Min and was immeasurably safer. He also would not have to do any more killing. The temporary camp was adjacent Kimpo Air Base – a dusty, sprawling complex of runways, Quonset huts, corrugated metal hangars and sheds, fuel storage tanks, vehicles, stacks of gas cans, one large water tank perched on a platform crowning a superstructure of metal beams and girders, and the flags of the nations fighting as allies. There also was a baseball field – Han could not begin to divine what young men were trying to accomplish when scampering around on that dusty patch of ground – and an outdoor basketball court – although he'd never seen basketball played, it didn't take long to figure out the game's simple objective.

The near round-the-clock takeoffs and landings of roaring planes was a continuous reminder of the death raining down on North Korean forces. Han had no doubt that falling bombs and strafing runs were ripping apart many of his friends. What the future held for him was of little moment. At a young age – 20 – he was learning the meaning of living in the present. Soon, he had been told, POWs would be moved to a permanent camp on

Koje-do, an island off the south coast some 25 miles from Pusan. It would, Han knew, mean an end to his war.

✝✝✝

"Letter from Lucy?" Kendall Thorne asked Michael Cornelius who was stretched out on his cot.

"Just arrived. Already read it twice."

My Dearest Michael,
This must be brief. I am scribbling it madly – can you read it? – because momentarily I will be running to board a ship for Korea. Yes, I have volunteered my nursing experience to the cause. I am certain it is the right thing to do.
Must run, darling. I hope this finds you safe in Germany and remaining that way.
With much affection,
Lucy

Michael carefully refolded the letter and inserted it in the envelope.

"What are you thinking?" K asked.

"That unless we get sent to Korea I'll not be seeing Lucy again. And that if we do get sent there I still might not see her again."

✝✝✝

"Do you think he will come back?" Mrs. Choi had waited to pose the question until Kyong was beyond hearing range.

"I don't know," Mr. Choi said somberly. "But if he does, he will be seeking revenge. I should have killed him."

"You are too good a man to lower yourself to murder."

"I am not so sure that killing him would have been murder. He deserves an early death. It might have been justice."

Mrs. Choi pursed her lips. "Maybe we should saddle Sejong. Put Kyong on him. Then lead them to Seoul. It would be safer there."

"That's what we were prepared to do earlier. But now with the Americans advancing, the danger seems to be subsiding. Do you really want to do that?"

"No."

"I thought not. Nor do I. This is our home." A pause. "Let's share our worries with our friends and neighbors. Ask them to watch for Kwon. He will have a nasty scar on his hand. Maybe still bandaged. And might be walking with a limp."

"Kyong?"

"You are right. She would be safer in Seoul. In case Kwon does return – without warning. We should ask her what she wants to do. We know what Kwon would do. And she has her baby to think about."

Mrs. Choi eyes softened. "It's Min's baby too."

Mr. Choi smiled. "Perhaps we can be the baby's honorary grandparents."

CHAPTER 65

Michael Cornelius was getting his wish. Soon he would find himself closer to Lucy Crispin. On July 24, 1950, Prime Minister Atlee told his Defense Committee that Britain needed to contribute a strong brigade group – an armored regiment, three infantry brigades, an artillery regiment and New Zealand's medium artillery regiment – to the Allies' cause.

Before it could be deployed, though, soldiers were needed. Britain's post-World War II military forces were badly depleted. Atlee knew it would be necessary to call up at least 2,000 reservists and to ask for volunteers. Michael and Kendall were among the first to answer the call.

In October 1950 Britain's 29th Brigade – 2,000 men including Michael and Kendall and organized into three infantry regiments – was ordered to Korea. Commanding would be Brigadier Tom Brodie. Michael and Kendall each would lead a platoon. Preceding the 29th was Britain's 27th Brigade that had been dispatched from Hong Kong and arrived at Pusan on August 28. Greeting the 27th was a U.S. Army band comprised of black soldiers playing the *St. Louis Blues March* and Korean school children singing *God Save The King*.

Also deployed to Korea were Canada's 25th Brigade and Britain's Commonwealth Brigade that included troops from other British Commonwealth nations, including India, South Africa and Australia.

The British units were made part of the United States 1st Corps, better known as I Corp.

Michael and K's sea passage to Korea aboard the Empire Orwell was a lengthy one, five weeks. The vessel had begun life as a Nazi cruise ship and in 1945 was taken as a war prize. Now it was making its way east across the Mediterranean, south through the Suez Canal, east across the Indian Ocean to Singapore for refueling and replenishing food stocks, and finally north through the South China Sea to the Yellow Sea and Korea.

During that last leg of the journey Michael and K were standing at the rail, taking in the seemingly endless expanse of sea and sky.

"Did you ever imagine seeing so much blue?" K asked. "Keeping in mind our gray British origins."

"Virtually impossible to see where the sky meets the horizon. I'm not sure whether we should be enchanted or bored silly."

"After this voyage we might as well request transfers to the Royal Navy," K said drolly. "On land, I think my legs likely will have the consistency of unprocessed rubber."

"And," added Michael, jiggling his hips, "we might never be able to sleep in a bed that doesn't sway."

"Swaying beds," K mused. "They could jolly well lead to some particularly thrilling amorous adventures."

"A true test of balance."

"Not to mention aim."

The two young lieutenants permitted themselves cathartic guffaws.

† † †

Darkness had descended in London. Theresa Morton in her flat was holding a letter from her sister Bridgett in Shelby. In part it read:

The big news here is that Jack has volunteered to serve in Korea. From what I hear, it's because his friend Thaddeus Metz volunteered. Isn't that just like him? I'm praying for their safety every night. Korea seems like such a dangerous place.

Theresa stood and walked to the bedroom door. She opened it just wide enough to slip through. She looked at Marilyn sleeping angelically and smiled. She tiptoed across the room to where a small cross was hanging on the wall above Marilyn's bed. She removed it and retraced her steps to the living room.

It was the same cross that the Polish airborne troops had given Jack as a token of gratitude for celebrating Easter Mass for them in 1944.

Jack, she was thinking that drizzly night in London, you're a priest. You counsel troubled souls all the time. Tell me, why must life be so complicated? And let's not talk Adam and Eve. Okay? Just tell me why I didn't leave this cross with Mother? Or send it to you in Ajo? Or give it to Bridgett to donate to St. Mary's in Shelby? Why is it here with me in London? I'm almost afraid of the answer. Okay, it's because we humans just can't let go of the past. Not entirely anyway. Part of me really wants to. Just open my hands, spread my fingers and let go. Move on. And then there's the part of me that says, wait, don't do that. Hold on to the memories you cherish. Let them be threads in the fabric of your life. Guess which part is winning, Jack? All those years ago you got a grip on my heart and you won't let go. Now, Jack, is that proper priestly behavior? Theresa smiled wistfully. She ran her palm over the cross and sat in the rose-hued overstuffed chair. Stay safe, Jack Brecker. May you live to see this cross again.

✝✝✝

Major Tom Williams knew he was in trouble. His World War II-vintage Mustang fighter could reach 437 miles per hour. The Russian-built MiG-15 jet on his tail was some 230 mph faster and armed with three cannons and 200 rounds to his Mustang's six Browning .50-caliber machine guns. The name MiG derived from the plane's developers, Artem Mikoyan and Mikhail Gurevich. Tom could see his flying ability was superior to his adversary's, but in the next sliver of time realized that his skill wouldn't suffice to elude the predator's speed and firepower. A cannon round tore off part of his Mustang's tail assembly, and Tom knew his only chance of survival was bailing out. But not here, not over terrain controlled by enemy troops bent on executing Allied pilots whose planes had been raining death, maiming and destruction. Lord, Tom prayed briefly, let me make it over water. Just another minute or more.

Moments later with the MiG still hotly pursuing his mortally wounded craft, Tom wasn't sure whether God had heard his plea. But he could see welcome blue water below and he was grateful. At about 800 feet, his crippled plane scant seconds from ditching, Tom pried open the latch on his thermoplastic canopy and parachuted. Even from the low altitude, the parachute slowed Tom's descent enough so that he could see his plummeting Mustang meet a fiery end as it went cartwheeling three times across the Yellow Sea's sparkling surface.

Seconds later he was in the water but knew his troubles weren't over. *I'll be lucky to see another sunrise or even a sunset.* He shivered and spit saltwater. *If that MiG doesn't return to strafe me, how long can I last in this water? Geez, it's cold. The Yellow Sea up here sure isn't the South Pacific. I hope that MiG is low on fuel.*

He had little time to ruminate when the ungainliest of guardian angels materialized above. Its wings were fluttering as madly as a hummingbird's, rendering them virtually invisible. But the ungodly racket – this angel was as noisy as a sheet metal stamping plant pounding out quarter panels for new jeeps. And then the angel gave birth, dropping a baby from its womb. Tom's angel was an HO3S-1 Sikorsky four-seat helicopter, one of a growing fleet based on aircraft carriers with a few stationed on small islands off North Korea's coasts. The baby was life-jacketed Captain Thaddeus Metz, splashing into the sea just a few swim strokes from the downed pilot.

Thaddeus spit a mouthful of seawater and smiled broadly. "Nice to meet you, Major."

"Very nice to meet you, Captain."

"Let's get you harnessed and a little closer to heaven."

Tom spat again, the briny taste lingering. "They say you Marines fight in the air and sea as well as on land, and now I'm a believer. But your accent. I don't think I've heard it before."

Thaddeus, continuing to affix the harness, permitted himself a wide smile as he readied Major Williams for the lift. "I'm Polish. And there was a time when I was far more comfortable on land. On a horse actually."

"Where are you based?"

"Polska."

"Where's that?"

"It is near – and far."

Back on June 25, Russian-built, propeller-driven Yak fighters had supported invading North Korean ground troops. The subsequent arrival of MiG jets quickly added to North Korea's air superiority. Ironically the Russian MiGs were powered by Rolls-Royce engines sold to the Soviets by the British government in 1946 as an ill-advised favor. MiGs rapidly showed themselves superior not only to Mustangs but also to the United States Air Force's Shooting Star jets, outpacing them by 120 mph. Thankfully for the Allies, the MiGs' rule didn't last long.

Enter the swept-wing F-86 Sabre. At sea level it could hit 687 mph and at 35,000 feet 599 mph. The sleek fighter arrived in Korea in November and downed its first MiG opponent on December 17. At first, MiGs outnumbered Sabres 450 to fewer than 100. And the Sabre's machine gun armaments were less destructive than the MiGs' cannons. But the Sabre's speed and maneuverability in the hands of well-trained American pilots soon were inflicting heavy losses on MiGs.

Their duels would keep HO3S-1 angels alert for rescues, an exercise Thaddeus found a welcome diversion from his reconnaissance missions.

CHAPTER 66

If ever battle lines resembled an oscillating fan, sweeping back and forth, those in the Korean War qualified. First it was well trained and equipped North Korean troops advancing virtually at will, much like playground bullies, shoving outnumbered South Korean and U.S. soldiers south to near Pusan. Then it was MacArthur's Inchon invasion force slicing in from the east and Allied troops hammering their way north, pushing North Koreans back through Seoul and toward the 38th Parallel. More such oscillating was to follow.

Meanwhile an intermission occurred on October 15, 1950, when President Truman and General MacArthur finally met – not in the White House Oval Office – but on remote Wake Island in the Pacific. Twice MacArthur had received and turned down what amounted to presidential commands to journey to Washington. Truman understood MacArthur's true "message;" while flying to Wake Island for their meeting, the president wrote a note to his cousin Nellie Noland: *Have to talk to God's right hand tomorrow.* The following April 11 Truman would fire MacArthur.

Leading up to that historic sacking, MacArthur ordered his forces to drive to the Yalu River, North Korea's border with China's Manchuria province. His thinking: invade China where Kim Il Sung had rushed seeking refuge, forever crushing his dream of unification by force.

Meanwhile just north of the Yalu, from as early as October 10, Mao Tse Tung had been massing hundreds of thousands of troops. Many were conscripted "volunteers" while others were veterans hardened by combat during China's civil war. As MacArthur's Allied forces neared the Yalu, Mao's field commanders were awaiting orders to attack. Shortly before midnight on November 25, Mao's troops pounced across a 15-mile-wide front, hurling themselves at the U.S. 2nd Infantry Division and South Korea's II Corps. Soon those surprised men were reeling, retreating southward as Chinese troops bravely and skillfully penetrated gaps between Allied units, overrunning them and inflicting heavy casualties. Once again, arrogant Americans learned a military lesson the hard way.

China's success had Truman and MacArthur pondering using nuclear bombs to halt Mao's invasion – which in fact was more an attempt by the Chinese leader to save face after having pledged support to Kim Il Sung than it was a desire to grab the Korean peninsula. Various Allied units, including Turks in the west and Marines in the east at Chosin Reservoir, fought hard to stem the Chinese tide.

By now Michael Cornelius and Kendall Thorne had joined the fray north of Pyongyang. Their first taste of combat would prove a bruising baptism for the young lieutenants. Intense Chinese pressure proved unstoppable, and on December 10 Allied troops abandoned Pyongyang, retreating south and leaving Britain's 29th Brigade to serve as rear guard. Remnants of the tattered U.S. 2nd Division, Turkish Brigade survivors and battered elements of South Korea's II Corps regrouped along the Imjin River just north of Munsan. They couldn't hold.

Stalin was relieved, Mao was pleased, and Kim Il Sung was again euphoric. With massive Chinese manpower now engaged he foresaw his dream of a unified Korea coming soon to fruition.

Retreating farther, Allied forces prepared to retire south of the Han River, again all but handing Seoul to Kim.

"We're in trouble," Michael said to K. "Here we are again, serving as stopgaps with the emphasis on gaps. How we are supposed to halt or even slow down the Reds is rather beyond me. They seem to have more men than we have bullets."

"Geniuses at work," K replied caustically. "We're a brigade group, but they've got us spread out to positions designed for a complete division."

Michael and K were huddled in a shallow slit trench in K's platoon's sector of responsibility.

"Did you ever imagine it could be so cold?" Michael asked, shivering and rubbing his gloved hands together. "Sort of makes me wish for a dip in wintry Wish Stream."

"My piss streams are freezing before they hit the ground."

"I've never felt so far from Sandhurst – or home."

"Or Lucy?"

Michael nodded and smiled tightly. "She's here somewhere. I just hope she stays safe. Damn, well, I've got to get back to my men. Hope it stays quiet tonight."

Michael was alluding to the unnerving bugles and whistles that the North Koreans and Chinese used to communicate during their nighttime attacks.

"One more determined assault by the Reds," K said, grimacing, "and they could be planning memorials for us back at Sandhurst."

Michael shrugged, eased from the trench and, crouching low, scooted back to his sector. Fleetingly he wondered whether he would survive the night.

†††

Backing Brigadier Brodie's 29th Brigade was the Royal Thai infantry battalion. They were willing but undone by the brutal weather. Although outfitted with American winter clothing, the Thais were numbed by cold debilitating to the south Asians.

Facing the 29th from across the Han River? China's entire 39th and 50th Armies. Brodie had a straightforward choice: stand and be slaughtered or bug out. He chose the latter. Under cover of darkness Brodie's men began slipping southward. This withdrawal wounded Michael and K's pride, but they knew it was prolonging their lives.

Brodie's final act during this inglorious retreat: ordering a squadron of British sappers to blow the Han's recently rebuilt bridges. They succeeded.

On January 4, 1951, Seoul changed hands for the third time. By February 10 the Chinese retook Kimpo Air Base and Inchon.

CHAPTER 67

The night sky was moonlit and Thaddeus was nervous. He had reason to be. Despite treading as softly as possible, every footfall on the snow-crusted ground seemed to herald the presence of him and his seven men as resoundingly as a flourish of trumpets. They were behind enemy lines, and their mission was clear: scout the size and disposition of advancing Chinese and North Korean forces, determine the strength of their armor and artillery and assess their supply situation.

Thaddeus and his men had blackened their faces and rowed ashore from Polska in two black rubber rafts that they tried to conceal among rocks. Were they discovered before returning, the men knew their chances of survival would plunge as precipitously as nighttime temperatures in what would be recorded as the coldest Korean winter during the last 100 years. The men, like Thaddeus, were volunteers.

† † †

Captain Kwon Oh Bum was leading a platoon-strength patrol in the same sector, and his men also were nervous. They were accustomed to launching mass assaults on enemy positions at night to limit the ability of American planes to provide air cover for Allied ground troops. But night patrols were different and more threatening. They were, for example, vulnerable to friendly fire if mistaken for Allied patrols. Or they could stumble into Allied positions where they were outnumbered and outgunned.

Kwon was determined to survive. The slash wounds on the rear of his thighs had scabbed over. They still itched but he was relieved that no infection had set in. The wounds to his left hand – back and palm

– had closed, but they had cost him dexterity. He intended to return to Munsan, but his agenda included more than exacting revenge on Choi Chun Kuen. Kwon's ultimate ambition was to rise in the North Korean Army's hierarchy to a senior level and again become a trusted aide to Kim Il Sung when he presided over a unified Korea.

From time to time Kwon wondered why he hadn't already been promoted to major or lieutenant colonel. He had carried out all orders with dispatch and thoroughness. Had he somehow lost favor with the Great Leader? Had he been in the field so long that he had become victim to the out-of-sight-out-of-mind syndrome? Had word of his deserting his troops during the retreat north somehow reached Kim? He didn't think so but couldn't fathom why he hadn't been accorded more recognition for his successful leadership. The absence of a definitive explanation and the seeming slight nagged at him.

✝✝✝

Thaddeus and his men were edging their way across the summit of a ridgeline, pausing often to peer into the valley below. He heard footsteps nearing and raised his left arm, signaling his men to halt. Using hand signals, he motioned them to split into two groups and conceal themselves behind the nearest cover on the boulder-strewn ridge.

✝✝✝

Kwon's platoon was walking the same ridgeline. Occasionally Kwon would halt the platoon, and he and his sergeants would peer south into the moonlight through binoculars, straining to see even the faintest signs of movement among the Allies.

✝✝✝

Thaddeus' mind quickly digested the situation. His squad could ambush Kwon's patrol and kill a goodly number of his men before they could recover and return fire. Then what? Thaddeus knew the answer. His mission would be compromised. The North Koreans would rapidly outflank and overrun his men. He likely would not live to radio his findings. And inconsequential ones at that. Word of engaging a patrolling enemy platoon would receive scant attention at Allied headquarters which was chiefly interested in major North Korean and Chinese concentrations and movements. Thaddeus and his men remained silent and hidden while 50 pairs of black North Korean canvas sneakers went crunching by on the hardened snow.

✝✝✝

Inside the operating tent Lucy Crispin pulled off the bloody surgical gloves and dropped them into a waste bin. She reached up to a coat hook and removed and pulled on a long U.S.-supplied parka with a fur-lined hood. She then stepped outside into the frigid night and slowly drew in a breath of knife-like air. Lucy rocked her head back and peered up at the inky sky sprinkled with countless distant suns and one looming white moon that seemed to be peering down curiously. The man in the moon, Lucy reflected, you probably think we are bonkers for enduring this. And to think I volunteered. She lowered her head, cupped her hands and blew into them. How many hours was I in there? How many men did we operate on? How many lives did we save? How many did we lose? Just one, and he had no chance when they brought him in. Too many shards of shrapnel had sliced too many veins that leaked too much blood.

A black-haired, dark-complexioned man emerged from the operating tent and stood beside her.

"Is it just me," Lucy asked, "or do the stars shine more brightly in frigid air?"

"I believe you're right," said the man. "Of course, in Delhi we've been known to have desert dust obscuring the sky. That doesn't seem a problem here." Lucy smiled at his understated reply. The man was Dr. Sanjay Desari, and he was alluding to the Thar, or Great Indian, Desert that lay just west of the city.

Doctor Desari was a member of the 60th Indian Parachute Field Ambulance Service. Commanded by Lieutenant Colonel A.G. Rangaraj, the unit's members were admired by all United Nations forces in Korea for their surgical and nursing skills as well as their warm hospitality. Routinely they offered visitors a mug of superbly made tea and, if available, their legendary curries. When word had reached Lucy that the Indians were busily treating members of Britain's 29th Brigade and could use another pair of experienced hands, she quickly got herself transferred from New Zealand's artillery unit that had remained mercifully free of casualties. She was intending to stay with the Indians as long as needed.

"Tea, Lucy?"

"It would taste scrumptchy but likely keep me awake," she smiled tiredly.

"Frankly," said Doctor Desari, "I need something stronger to help me sleep after a long round in there."

"I'm not much of an imbiber. But if you've got something that will settle my insides and weigh down my eyelids, I'm game." She shivered and crossed her arms to pull the parka closer to her torso.

The doctor was amused. "Your fatigue hasn't dulled your wit. We've just the proper stuff, as it were. Sort of a medicinal relaxant. Follow me." Doctor Desari led Lucy to his tent.

Inside he lit both a kerosene lamp and a 50-gallon perforated drum that was serving adequately as a stove. Taking note, Lucy observed, "I see your surgical skills extend to operating on metal carcasses, as it were."

The doctor chuckled. "I have the proper incentive," he replied dryly. "It's a bit chillier here than in Delhi."

"Wellington, too."

"An Indian and a kiwi in Korea. Who ever would have guessed?"

"This can't be what the British colonizers had in mind."

"Actually, as you know, our British colonizers had in mind riches and empire," observed Doctor Desari without rancor. "They would have blanched at the notion of a United Nations all but demanding that they join other countries in a war with no resulting financial wealth."

"You are correct. They would have been sniffily aghast at the entire concept. Ironically, though, in a way we are building wealth – if you regard a nation's independence and freedom as wealth."

"And as Indians we assuredly do." India had gained independence from Great Britain just three years earlier in 1947. Doctor Desari smiled, bent to open his footlocker and removed a bottle and two glasses. "We Indians have gained our independence but we remain fond of if not dependent on some of Britain's finest." He showed her the label on the Johnnie Walker scotch and poured two generous measures. "To warmth and sleep," the doctor toasted.

"And to survival," said Lucy, clinking glasses with Doctor Desari. As she sipped, her thoughts turned to Michael Cornelius. She had not yet received the letter he had posted before his departure from England. Her mind slipped into reverie, dreamy images of her and Michael in London coming into focus.

"A game of chess?" Doctor Desari asked, disrupting her memories. "Before we call it a night?"

"I'd like that. It's a game but nothing is left to chance. No dice. No cards. No spinning wheels. Just skill. Of course," Lucy added self-deprecatingly, "one can still make silly moves."

"I rather doubt you've made many of those," Doctor Desari said, arranging pieces on the board that sat on a wooden shipping crate-as-table. He picked up two pawns, white and black, and put his hands behind his back. Then he brought them forward, fists closed, and extended them toward Lucy. She tapped the right fist that opened, showing the black pawn.

"A black pawn on a black night in a black war." Lucy shook her head. "Not that I'm superstitious," she grinned, "but an omen if ever there was one."

CHAPTER 68

Kyong screamed. For long seconds her contorted face reflected her agony. Then, sweating, black hair matted against her forehead, she whimpered. "Am I dying?"

Given the frequency of death in her circumstance in wartime Korea, the question was understandable.

"You are a strong young woman. You will live," Mrs. Choi assured her. "And so will your baby."

It was the evening of March 11, 1951. Mrs. Choi, childless herself, was serving as midwife, very ably and not for the first time. The birth was taking place on Mr. and Mrs. Choi's bed. Kyong had first felt labor pains late that morning, and she was shocked and frightened when her water broke. Prenatal counsel in war-ravaged Korea was virtually nonexistent, and Mrs. Choi had apologized for not alerting Kyong to this crucial juncture in the birthing process.

"Try to relax. Take a deep breath. I am going to spread your legs and push them back against that big tummy."

"Ohhh," Kyong groaned piteously. "I don't know how much longer I can endure this." Then much to her surprise she found a reservoir of good humor. "Is this what women have always had to go through? If it is, I am surprised the human race still exists."

Mrs. Choi chortled. "We might be extinct, dear, if it were not for the pleasure that precedes the pain. You do remember the pleasure, don't you?"

Kyong's half-smile, half-grimace provided the answer. She remembered vividly the pervasive warmth and intense excitement that had accompanied her coupling with Min. "Ohhh," she groaned again. "I think it is almost time."

"I think you are right. I can see the top of the baby's head. That's good. That is what we want to see first. Now I want you to push, push as hard as you can."

Moments later tiny Ahn Min Han, covered with nature's lubricant, greeted the grim, grimy world that was Korea in that troubled spring. Mrs. Choi's sharp slap on his bottom had Min noisily announcing his arrival.

"I think you have picked a wonderful name," Mrs. Choi cooed lovingly. "Min would be pleased and proud and so would his brother."

The squalling baby was nuzzling against Kyong's chest, and the new mother was experiencing both unprecedented joy and nagging guilt. "My baby is beautiful – and he is a bastard," she sniffled.

"Shush, child," Mrs. Choi replied, placing the fingers of her right hand against Kyong's lips. "He is no such thing. If his father were not caught up in this deplorable war, you two would be married. No matter what happens, never think of your little boy that way." Mrs. Choi was speaking kindly but firmly and not for the first time wishing she herself could have undergone what she had helped Kyong and other young women experience. "Never use that word again."

"All right," Kyong replied meekly.

"Now, let me cut the cord and clean him up. He is hungry and you will bare your breast and give him the milk of life."

✝✝✝

Lieutenant Kendall Thorne screamed. It was the scream of the newly wounded, the scream that magnified and underscored the horrors of combat.

K's platoon was patrolling along the north bank of the Imjin River. He stepped on a mine. The thunderous explosion lifted him from the ground, spun him around, severed his left leg at the calf and sent hot shrapnel ripping into his torso and slicing virtually every vital organ.

The war's oscillating fan this time had freshly supplied and reinforced Allied forces again pushing north, retaking ground lost during the December-February retreat.

Within moments a medic was by K's side.

"Not good," K groaned, eyes watering and blood rapidly soaking his uniform. "Need morphine."

The medic quickly opened his pack and removed a morphine vial. He jammed a needle through K's fatigue pants and into his thigh. He then set about tying off his stump. Urgently, K's radioman called for a helicopter.

"Glad you know what you're doing, Doc," K said, coughing up blood.

✝✝✝

An ocean away, thousands of miles to the southeast in Ajo, Bernadeta screamed. Twice. She too was giving birth. And she was praying, pleading that her second baby not be another stillborn.

✝✝✝

An orderly with the 60th Indian Parachute Field Ambulance Service was the first to hear the helicopter's rumbling approach and shouted, "Casualties! Incoming! Everyone to their stations!"

A team of surgeons, nurses and orderlies went racing from the compound to the helicopter's landing site. Two jeeps accompanied them. Both plastic-canopied side pods contained a wounded soldier from Britain's 29th Brigade. Working urgently the team removed the canopies, transferred the wounded to stretchers and away from the swirling dust. Then they placed the stretchers on the ground where two surgeons hurriedly began assessing the wounds' severity. Lucy, peering down over Doctor Desari's right shoulder, was stunned.

"Kendall," she whispered so softly that sound barely escaped her lips. "Oh, my God."

Doctor Desari glanced up. "You know him?"

365

Lucy nodded.

Kendall, his wits dulled by the morphine, opened his eyes and tried to smile.

Orderlies lifted the two stretchers and gently laid them across the jeeps' rears. They then walked beside the jeeps, steadying the stretchers for the short ride back to the compound.

On the way Doctor Desari spoke with a crisp calm. "We need to get this one into surgery immediately."

Kendall Thorne was semiconscious, and Doctor Desari didn't want his voice to betray his deep concern. Four orderlies, one at each end of the stretcher and one on each side, carried K into the operating tent.

Before K was anesthetized, Lucy desperately wanted to ask him about Michael, but professionalism restrained her. All attention now had to be focused on the grievously wounded young soldier.

✝✝✝

"I am Polish. I am in America. In Arizona. My husband is in Korea. I am so grateful you have come here."

The elder's lips were turned downward, but it was a frown born not of disgust or frustration. Instead it was a quiet acknowledgement of Bernadeta's sentiments. "It is good you sent word to me." His eyelids lowered, an attempt to hold in tears. "I - I am proud to be here with you." Bernadeta sensed that his rugged bass voice was verging on cracking. He paused, regaining composure. "To see your beautiful daughter. What is her name?"

"Tosia Marie. After my mother."

"A beautiful choice." The elder sniffled briefly then grinned, twinkling eyes peering from his face with lines that resembled canyons. "Sounds almost Indian."

"Would you like to hold her?"

✝✝✝

"We've done everything we can. I wish we could do more." Doctor Desari, assisted by Lucy, another nurse and an anesthesiologist, had labored

366

strenuously for three hours trying to save Kendall. "Now it's up to a higher power."

✝✝✝

"I hope it doesn't embarrass you," Bernadeta smiled, her left breast exposed, tiny Tosia Marie sucking hungrily.

"Ho, ho, ho," chortled the elder. "In my many years I believe I have seen all that nature has to show. Did you know that I am a father? And a grandfather?"

"I didn't know...you were married."

"I was. She died years ago. In an accident. Before I met Father Brecker."

✝✝✝

Kendall Thorne was lying on a cot in the post-op tent. He opened his eyes to find Lucy standing at the foot of the cot, holding a chart.

She smiled. "Can I get you anything?"

"I'm cold."

Lucy hung the chart on a hook suspended from the cot's steel frame, went hustling and returned within moments with another blanket. She spread it over K and patted it down around him. "Better?"

K's nod was an inaudible lie. He breathed in shallowly and exhaled. "Get word to Michael. Please. I want him to write my parents." His words were barely more than mumbles.

"You can write them yourself," Lucy said softly, blinking back tears. She now was sitting on a low stool at K's right side. "You'll make it."

K smiled wearily. Lucy was lying and he knew it. The look in his fading eyes said as much. "You're a good one," he whispered. "A keeper. Tell Michael I told you that."

Lucy tried semi-futilely to smile through the tears springing from her eyes. She brushed them with the back of her slightly clawed left hand. "I will. I promise." A pause. "Can I do anything else?"

"Go ahead and ask," K replied, his lips barely moving.

"What?"

"About Michael."

"Oh."

367

"He's fine. Desperately in need of a shower." He smiled faintly. "He could use hot food. Could use a look at you too."

"Thank you." She sniffed and again brushed at tears. "Anything more?"

"Water." K's tongue flicked his dry lips. "And a chaplain. Can I see one?"

"Would a Catholic do?"

K sipped water from a cup that Lucy was holding. "If he'll see one of Henry the Eighth's Church of England progeny." K coughed a small laugh. "Might be time for ecumenism."

"He's American."

"A true test."

"Just a moment," Lucy said, rising from the stool and scurrying from the tent. In another minute she returned with a chaplain. Lucy stood at the foot of the cot while the chaplain seated himself on the low stool. He took K's right hand and squeezed gently.

"I'll leave you two alone," Lucy said, wanting to afford them privacy and starting to turn away.

"No," K whispered, eyes closed. "Stay. Please."

"Of course."

K opened his eyes. He tried smiling again. "What are you doing with this Indian unit?"

"They serve all races and religions," the chaplain replied. "So do I."

"I'm not Catholic."

"Are you a believer?"

"I am now."

"Good enough."

"Favor?"

"By all means. Anything."

"I have a friend." K's breathing was flattening, becoming ever shallower.

"Lieutenant Michael Cornelius," Lucy interjected, trying to help K conserve effort.

"Get word to him," K whispered. "Ask him to write to my parents. Lucy refuses." K managed a wink and Lucy's eyes, her chest heaving, let loose a torrent. "And tell him he must wade again in Wish Stream."

He coughed. "He'll understand. And tell God – ask God – to look at the scales. He should see more good than bad."

"He knows that."

"Tell him for me."

"I will."

"My eyes. I'm having trouble seeing. What is your name?"

"Father Brecker."

"Captain?"

"Yes." Jack leaned in over K and then raised K's right hand so he could feel Jack's two silver bars.

"Thank you." A pause. "Nurse Crispin?"

"Yes, I'm here."

"One more thing."

"Yes."

"Don't let me die with my eyes open. Bad Sandhurst form."

CHAPTER 69

The dangers confronting Thaddeus weren't confined to reconnaissance patrols and sea rescues. The North Koreans and Chinese had deduced that his little band of Marine volunteers was based on one of the small coastal islands. They weren't certain which one so when not otherwise engaged would lob artillery and mortar shells in Thaddeus' direction.

He and his seven fellow Marines stayed mobile, shifting among three locations on the island. At each they were living in small tents, covered with camouflage netting to conceal them from aircraft reconnaissance. They also had constructed nearby dugouts where they went to ground whenever shells were coming their way. Occasionally, though, incoming rounds afforded precious little warning. The result: some uncomfortably close brushes with zinging shrapnel. One jagged piece sliced through Thaddeus' tent top and knifed his canteen – when it was attached to his webbed belt. He decided to keep it as a souvenir.

Today, at least for the moment, those dangers seemed remote. Thaddeus was elated. Bernadeta's letter bearing word of Tosia Marie's birth had reached little Polska – a name Thaddeus' volunteers had proudly adopted, though none was of Polish ancestry. Upon learning the news, in short order PFC Brown secured scotch and White Owls – they knew their leader's tastes – and roundly saluted the new parent – who at age 32 his young troopers saw as a respected father figure.

"I have been blessed often," Thaddeus told them, "but never more than now. I am a very fortunate man. I think God and Jack Brecker are keeping watch over me." He grinned. "May they continue to be on guard duty."

✝✝✝

Michael Cornelius seldom thought to pray. His parents were believers but far from religiously zealous, and formal religion only sporadically had been part of his upbringing. But in grieving for K, yearning to see Lucy and assessing his current predicament, he recognized that divine intercession would be advantageous.

It was April 1951 and once again Brigadier Brodie's 29th Brigade was oscillating northward, this time supplemented by the Belgian battalion. As was beginning to seem customary, his force had been assigned a crucial defensive position on the historic invasion route to Seoul. And once more the brigade was assigned an impossibly long sector, one that extended for nearly 10 miles along the south bank of the Imjin River. Every day during April's first three weeks Michael led grueling daylight patrols north of the river. The unrelenting tension and physical exertion were draining. Typically, he and his men would spend the day continuously alert for enemy threats, then return to their camp at dusk with little to report. That all changed soon after dark on April 22.

Earlier that day a Belgian light reconnaissance plane and a Turkish foot patrol both reported increased enemy activity not far north of the Imjin. The Turks managed to capture a small Chinese survey party whose commander, under sharp questioning, confirmed that a large-scale attack was being readied. He expected it to come that night.

It did. The Imjin was running low and could be waded easily at several points. One of those fronted Michael's platoon. His men had prepared well; the spring thaw meant there was no frozen earth to impede digging slit trenches and foxholes. As dusk was settling, Michael made a point of visiting all 50 of his men. They – and he – were filthy and badly in need of showers, shaves and laundered uniforms. Many would never again enjoy any of those niceties.

"We've been through this before," Michael calmly told his men. "Check your weapons one last time. Be sure they are clean. Have extra ammunition at the ready. Fix your bayonets. If they come at us, wait for me to fire the first shot. We should hold off until the Reds are in the water. If I'm incapacitated, Sergeant Rossiter will assume command. God be with you."

✝✝✝

Across the river Captain Kwon was issuing similar instructions. "Watch for enemy muzzle flashes. Work to get yourselves between enemy firing positions. We will close on them with grenades and bayonets."

Darkness had barely descended when Kwon and other company commanders blew their whistles and masses of North Korean and Chinese infantry went plunging into the river at several fordable crossings.

Allied artillery already had zeroed in on the fords and radio calls from front-line units quickly had shells combining with small arms fire to begin cutting down charging North Koreans and Chinese. More kept coming. They were so determined that soon they were gaining footholds on the river's south shore.

Outside the 29th Brigade's sector, the Turks, fearsome fighters, were among the first Allied troops forced to give ground. The South Korean 6th Division, despite efforts by Park Min and other gallant individuals, soon was collapsing. The Philippino battalion also was backing off.

Before long the 29th Brigade was dueling the entire 63rd Chinese Army – three reinforced divisions or more than 40,000 men. The situation for Michael's platoon was worsening by the minute.

Captain Kwon's company had followed his instructions meticulously. His experienced men, outnumbering Michael's platoon three to one at the outset, patiently and relentlessly had flanked the British and were steadily inflicting casualties as they closed in. Michael pulled his platoon into a tighter defensive circle, bringing with them the dead – 11 – and wounded – 15.

Then piercing the darkness came the cacophonous shrilling of bugles. Michael's experience told him what they signaled: a bayonet charge.

"Brace yourselves!" he shouted. "Here they come!" *If I weren't on the verge of absolute exhaustion,* he reflected fleetingly, *I might panic. Terrible* thought, I know. Forgive me, K. "Kill as many of them as possible with grenades and fire." What Michael wanted desperately to avoid was hand-to-hand combat against superior numbers who also had shown themselves to be seasoned, tough warriors. Michael ordered his radioman to call for flares.

✝✝✝

Nearby in Munsan the Chois and Kyong with her baby were huddling in their living quarters. They had heard the sounds of war seemingly nonstop for nearly two years. Mr. and Mrs. Choi and Kyong were thinking the same things: When will it end? Will Munsan be leveled? Will we survive again? Will there be more rapes? They considered – discussed – fleeing south but given frequently shifting front lines again decided to remain in their home.

Then Mr. Choi made another decision. He left and walked briskly to the stable. Then he led Sejong back to their shop and inside. Ironic, Mr. Choi was thinking, I am bringing a horse to a butcher shop for safekeeping. I will stay with you, boy. Do not worry.

✝✝✝

At the first sounds of battle that night the 60th Indian Parachute Field Ambulance team began prepping to receive casualties. Nurses, Lucy among them, were busily equipping the operating tent. Motor pool personnel were topping off vehicles' fuel tanks in case a bug-out proved necessary.

Jack Brecker moved among men recovering in the post-op tent, offering assurances and joining in prayer men who requested it.

✝✝✝

Captain Kwon, jaws clenched, led the final assault against Michael's left flank. He tossed aside his submachine gun and picked up a bayonet-fixed rifle from one of his fallen men. Kwon then bellowed a blood-icing battle cry as age-old as close combat itself. He went scrambling forward among and over rocks, intent on slaying hated foes.

Michael's remaining men responded with resolve. They maintained discipline, lobbing grenades, firing calmly at the oncoming troops and imposing a brutal toll on Kwon's men. Michael was proud of them – and grateful for his Sandhurst training. Then amidst the din, under a canopy

372

of exploding flares, Michael sensed a presence. He whirled, jerking his gun's trigger and a North Korean screamed and fell at his feet. He still was breathing, and Michael was preparing to bayonet him. In the next sliver of time Michael felt cold steel penetrating his back. He groaned and writhed as the breath of life went rushing from his lungs. Kwon pulled back on the bayonet, freeing it. Behind him he heard a menacing growl. Before Kwon could confront the danger, Sergeant Rossiter delivered a sharp blow to the rear of the North Korean's helmet. The impact buckled Kwon's knees and sent him slipping into blackness.

✝✝✝

Michael's platoon and other units in the 29th did as they were told; they held up the enemy's drive long enough for the Allies to regroup and stop the Chinese and North Korean advance before it could again overrun Seoul – or what was left of it.

How closely contested was the Imjin drama? At one juncture shells fired by Allied artillery units covering the retreat were detonating within 50 yards of the rear guard. In the maelstrom, American tanks fired briefly on British troops before they could be identified. There was no time to remove or bury the dead. Heavy ground fire precluded helicopter evacuation of the wounded; some were abandoned where they fell. In addition to Allied soldiers killed and wounded, 600 were taken prisoner. Thirty of those would perish in captivity. A British commander, once the escape was complete, broke down and wept. The proud 29th now was but a splintered shadow of its original profile.

✝✝✝

Michael Cornelius blinked in disbelief. Twice. Following surgery, as he regained consciousness, an unexpected visage was hovering mere inches above him. He saw it as nothing short of heavenly – bright brown eyes, a slightly crooked smile, a crown of curly hair.

"Lucy." He forced a swallow and his tongue flicked dry lips.

She placed her right hand on his left shoulder. "No need to talk." She bent lower and brushed her lips against his forehead.

He shook his head weakly and cleared his throat. "Where am I?"

"Near Yeoungdeungpo, a suburb south of Seoul."

373

"How did I get here?"

"Your Sergeant Rossiter carried you out. Like a sack of potatoes, he said, over his shoulder." She smiled. "Got you a ride on an American tank and held you there."

"How is he doing?"

"Except for your blood on his uniform, just fine."

"My men…"

"The ones who made it to us, we saved them. All of them."

"How many did I lose?"

"Shush. I don't know. I'm sure your commander will be by soon to check on you and debrief."

Lying on the cot next to Michael was a young South Korean soldier. Park Min's head was swathed in white. Chinese mortar shrapnel had creased his left temple and nicked the top of his left ear. He didn't lose consciousness but his head still ached.

Lucy moved to his side and squatted. "I know you don't understand me," she murmured, "but you are going to be all right. You lost blood. Head wounds, even superficial ones, tend to bleed profusely."

Min surprised her. Forcing a smile he reached for Lucy's hand and squeezed gently. "Kamsahamnida."

She didn't understand his word – Korean for thank you – but his meaning was clear. Lucy returned Min's squeeze of gratitude.

✝✝✝

Jack Brecker was grateful. Today brought no need to view newly scorched skin, hear the anguish of the freshly maimed, comfort the dying, administer last rites. Instead he spent time talking with the recovering wounded, writing letters home for some of them. He offered Michael Cornelius solace for the loss of his friend K. Through a KATUSA (Korean soldier attached to U.S. Army) interpreter, Jack learned that Min's brother Han was a POW on Koje-do, that his father had been murdered at Kaesong's train station, and that he was worried deeply about his mother and the Chois and Kyong in Munsan.

Jack was moved profoundly as this lone soldier put an intensely personal face on the tragedy sundering the peninsula and its people. Jack wanted to help but not over-promise. He also knew that Min's wound wouldn't take him out of the war and that soon he would be returning to his 6th Division unit. So he told him only that he would begin asking about his loved ones and try to contact him with anything he learned.

✝✝✝

The next morning Lucy helped Michael up from the cot.

"Oh, oh." With his first step his legs began wobbling like a pair of licorice sticks.

Lucy, following closely, grabbed his arms. "Slowly now."

"Help me outside. Fresh air would be grand."

"Please?" she teased.

"By all means, please – although the extra word means expending extra energy." He winked.

Min, sitting on his cot, bare feet resting on the plank floor, smiled. As a young man in love, he could sense the bond linking Lucy and Michael. It was, he was sure, more than professional.

Outside the tent both of Lucy's hands were grasping Michael's right arm. "Can you stand on your own?"

Michael leered. "I'm not sure I want to."

Lucy blushed. "There are lots of ears on this compound," she smiled. "Your wound could get you sent home."

"I'll stay with my men."

"I knew you'd say that. Manly thing to do and all that rot."

"Mind reading, another of your talents."

"With this," she grinned, raising her polio-afflicted left arm, "I've had to sharpen other skills."

"Touche. You've done so rather admirably." A pause. "This war will end. What then?"

"I suppose I'll return to Wellington. That's where our New Zealand artillery regiment will be mustered out."

Michael nodded. Then he faced her. "Would you consider returning to London?"

✝✝✝

Michael and other surviving members of the 29th Brigade had their spirits lifted when Lieutenant General James Van Fleet, commanding the

U.S. 8th Army, had this to say about the British stand at the Imjin. "The loss of this gallant fighting unit will continue to be felt with deep regret by myself and members of this command. Its magnificent stand in the face of overwhelming odds contributed immeasurably to the maintenance of the tactical integrity of the entire U.S. I Corps."

CHAPTER 70

Captain Kwon was alone. At the moment, he neither needed nor wanted assistance. He was walking briskly south from the Imjin River. Dawn hadn't yet raised the shades of night. Darkness, he knew, was best for his solitary mission. It shouldn't take long, he was thinking, and I should be back at camp before being missed.

†††

This time Michael didn't get his wish. He wasn't cleared to return to his men. His wounds were deemed sufficiently severe to make him unfit for duty in a combat zone. That was Doctor Desari's verdict. Michael protested but futilely. Instead he was told that soon he and two other badly wounded British soldiers would be loaded into an ambulance, marked on its top and sides with large red crosses. They then would be driven to an evacuation hospital, preparatory to being transported back to England. Another long sea voyage.

His was the kind of wound some soldiers longed for – severe enough to be sent home but not permanently debilitating. Would Michael remain in the army? Occupying administrative or training positions? He wasn't sure. Perhaps he would seek counsel from his father or staff at Sandhurst.

†††

With the Chinese and North Koreans stalled south of the Imjin, resting and waiting for supplies, the radio message wasn't unexpected. Thaddeus and his band of Marines were once again to inflate their rafts and row at night from Polska to the mainland. They had earned respect from senior military leaders for their scouting prowess.

✝✝✝

Inside the post-op tent the lighting was dim enough to help induce sleep for patients and just bright enough for nurses to read charts and check IV drips. Michael, lying on his cot, handed his orders to Lucy.

She sat beside him. "Noon today," she whispered, looking at her watch. "Seven hours."

"They've decided I'm well enough for travel if not fit enough for duty."

"Doctor Desari has made the correct decision, Michael." A pause. "You were lucky. That bayonet didn't miss your heart or arteries by more than a smidgen."

He nodded. "I wish my luck was holding a bit longer. Leaving you…" His voice caught. "This homecoming, I wish I could delay it. Perhaps indefinitely."

Lucy surveyed the ward. The other patients were sleeping. "This is entirely against regulations," she whispered. "Most unprofessional. Move over."

Michael edged to the side of the narrow cot. Lucy lay beside him. He looked at her questioningly.

"How quiet can you be?" she whispered.

"Very."

On the adjacent cot, Min, in that fog befuddling a person between sleeping and awakening, couldn't be sure whether he was hearing faint rustling or dreaming. He chose not to open his eyes and drifted back to sleep.

✝✝✝

Kwon pushed open the door to the butcher and cutlery shop. He moved stealthily to the entrance to the adjacent living quarters and slipped inside. First, with his gun's cold muzzle, he prodded Mr. Choi and then his wife.

"Get up," he said roughly.

Mrs. Choi went icy with panic. Even in the murky predawn, she knew the intruder's identity. Mr. Choi struggled to suppress surging fear.

Keeping his submachine gun trained on them, Kwon stepped toward the narrow bed where Kyong lay with little Ahn Min Han. "Get up," Kwon ordered her with chilling calm. "Make sure the baby doesn't cry."

✝✝✝

Lucy's left hand was holding the top of her fatigue pants together while her right buttoned the fly. "That wasn't on your chart," she whispered, smiling, "but it seemed a fitting prescription."

"Can't say I ever imagined your fatigue pants at your ankles. I'm glad my wounds were confined to my torso"

"I don't think we slowed your healing."

"Quite the opposite. You know, you are quite capable of surprising me."

"Myself too."

"I wish there was something I could leave you."

"Besides your seed?"

Michael struggled to suppress a chuckle. "Something you can see. Something to remind you of our time together. That might be all we'll have."

✝✝✝

Kwon shoved the Chois and Kyong with her baby through the shop's door. "Move." He preferred to execute them then and there. Practicalities were restraining him. Shoot them in Munsan and he might not escape vengeful townspeople. And word of his crime could reach the very people whose support he needed to ascend to the senior government post he was lusting for. He might be able to satisfactorily explain killing the Chois, concocting some sort of bogus allegation, but trying to defend murdering the girl and her infant – a boy baby in a culture that prized males – could strain credibility. Kwon began herding his four captives from the town.

✝✝✝

Thaddeus and his men were carefully skulking inland. They intended to patrol until first light and then go into hiding during the daytime hours.

That night they would resume reconnaissance and begin making their way back to the coast and the rafts.

✝✝✝

Lucy was excited. The hazy gray predawn was accompanied by the aroma of coffee percolating in the mess tent. Real coffee. It was, she reflected, enough to cause a Commonwealth girl to forsake tea. She re-entered the post-op tent and walked briskly to Michael's side. She reached down and poked him with her left hand. "Wake up, sleepy head," she said, barely above a whisper.

Michael shuddered as he was jolted from sleep. "What?"

"Get up, you sluggard. See what a natural sedative can do? Dulls your senses."

Michael rubbed his eyes. "I'll take nature every time, thank you ever so much." Michael swung his legs over the cot's side and stood.

"A lover of nature. What more could I want? Here." Lucy handed him a ratty beige robe that had been worn by who knew how many wounded soldiers. Michael slipped it on over his flimsy hospital gown. "Now come with me to the mess tent."

✝✝✝

Kwon directed the Chois and Lucy into a copse a mile west of Munsan. The thick stand of trees and underbrush should muffle the sound, he thought. *First the Chois, then the baby. Then after I have the girl, her too. Out here there will be no need for graves.*

✝✝✝

"A trifle early for breakfast, no?" Michael said. "Whoa, what's this?"

"It – he – is a photographer, silly. Meet Sergeant Vince Tanner."

The camera was aimed at Michael, Lucy behind him peering gleefully over his left shoulder.

"Nice to meet you, Lieutenant," Tanner greeted him. "Hold still." A loud pop and a bright flash assaulted Michael's senses.

379

"Pictures before breakfast? And me in this robe? How dreadfully un-British." He chortled, Lucy laughed, and Tanner removed the used bulb and inserted a fresh one.

"You said you wanted to leave me something," she said. "At first I was thinking perhaps an insignia from your uniform. And then I thought, what better than a picture of the two of us, don't you agree?"

"How did-"

"Connections, kind sir. I have them. And I've friends who have them." She smiled prettily. "And voila! We have here a sterling representative of the illustrious *Stars & Stripes*."

"Ahem." Tanner cleared his throat. "Let me get a proper shot of you two. Well, as proper as possible given your natty attire."

"Natty, indeed," grumbled Michael, cinching tighter the much-worn robe. "Hope this never finds its way back to Sandhurst. Or to my parents for that matter."

Lucy rolled her eyes upward, choosing to ignore the stuffy jab.

"Side by side, shoulder to shoulder," Tanner instructed them. "Look like you like each other which I presume is the case." Tanner moved in closer. "I'll shoot from your shoulders up. There now. Ready? Smiles."

Another pop and another flash.

"Thank you," Lucy said.

"No problem. I should have prints to you in a week or so."

"That will be fine," Lucy said. "Really, thank you very much. I can mail a set to Michael."

"Thank you," Michael muttered grumpily, still uncertain about the propriety of this photo session.

"Right," said Tanner. "Well, I'm off." He turned to exit the mess tent.

"Wait," Lucy said. "I want one more picture. It will only take a few more minutes."

"What now?" Michael asked unenthusiastically.

✝✝✝

Moving gingerly through the trees and brush Thaddeus signaled his men to halt. Faint rays were pushing aside predawn dullness, but visibility remained limited. Thaddeus squinted. He continued to be amazed at how his eyes had acclimated to seeing in darkness. He marveled, too, at how acute his hearing had become. Funny how the body reacts to different situations and demands, he was musing. What he was hearing now was chilling and troubling. Scuffling. Whimpering? Pleading?

He signaled his men to halt and then gestured to them to fan out and continue advancing – very cautiously.

Lucy led Tanner into the post-op tent. She walked to Min's cot. He was awake now. Motioning with her hands she invited him to stand.

"Just a minute," Lucy said to Tanner. "Stay here," she instructed him.

She rushed outside the tent, saw Michael approaching cautiously, a mug of steaming coffee in his right hand. She threw him a half-wave but went running to the office tent of the commander, Lieutenant Colonel Rangaraj. In another moment she was hustling back across the compound, half-dragging a dubious KATUSA.

Inside the tent she told Tanner, "I saw this KATUSA driving you here." Then pointing to Min, she said to the KATUSA, "Please tell him that if we take his picture and give it to Chaplain Brecker and others, it might make it easier to connect him with his fiancée and friends."

The KATUSA smiled and translated and Min, surprised and touched, said "Kamsahamnida."

The *Stars & Stripes* photographer took both a full-body picture and a head-and-shoulders shot. "Will that do?"

"Very nicely," she smiled.

"Maybe I can get our editor to run one," said Tanner. "You know, tell him the reason for the shot. Couldn't hurt to have his picture in the paper."

"That would be wonderful!" Lucy saw Michael easing into the tent, taking a sip of coffee. A pause. "Wait. One more. Michael, come here, please." Lucy then positioned Michael and herself flanking Min. "A keepsake." To Tanner she asked, "Can you get prints for all of us?"

"Not a problem."

"We have a problem," Thaddeus said as he stepped from the forest into the small clearing, his men entering at other points on the perimeter.

Their appearance startled Kwon. Likewise the Chois and Kyong. They were as speechless as little Ahn Min Han, his face nuzzling against his mother's left shoulder.

"What do you think, Captain?" PFC Edmund Brown asked Thaddeus.

Kwon was watching warily, not sure what his next move should be. He counted eight American soldiers, all armed, all well spaced.

Thaddeus paused before replying thoughtfully. "It could be that these people" – he gestured toward the Chois and Kyong – "have committed a crime and this North Korean soldier – a captain I see – has been authorized to execute them."

"But you don't think so," said Brown.

"No. Not before dawn. Not alone. He would have enlisted men with him to carry out the execution. And not in these woods. The nearest town is Munsan. Probably there and in public where they think it might serve to deter other crimes. And not the baby."

"Then what?"

Thaddeus grinned. "I think probably that they do not speak Polish." His men chuckled lowly. "English?" Thaddeus asked. No reply from Kwon, the Chois or Kyong.

"If you don't mind, sir?" Brown asked.

"Go ahead. Speak freely," said Thaddeus. His men respected and valued Thaddeus' leadership style. He recognized that they all had volunteered for hazardous work, and he welcomed their thinking even though he was the far more experienced warrior.

"I'm thinking this North Korean is a bad guy. A really bad guy. You can see these people are scared shitless. If we don't do something, I think they are dead."

"I share your perception. If we proceed calmly, maybe we can prevent disaster. And make him our prisoner." Thaddeus surveyed his men, looking into the eyes of each. "I don't want to do something that jeopardizes our mission and our lives. But I do not think we should leave these people to be shot. Agreed?"

"Agreed," said PFC Galen Richards. "Let's let the North Korean know we want him to put his gun down."

Kwon's mind was racing now. Stunned though he had been, he found his brain processing the situation with remarkable speed and clarity. They are Americans. Where did they come from? We have once again pushed the Allies well south of Munsan. Did they parachute in? Were they trapped behind our lines as we advanced? I am in trouble. If I fire first, I could kill one of them, perhaps two. But they would kill me. Or I could get off a burst and kill the Chois and the girl. But the Americans would no doubt kill me before I could shoot even one of them. If I am taken prisoner, I would be disgraced. Unless I can escape. They are behind our lines. If I surrender and then escape, I would need only a few seconds head start, and I should be able to elude them and find my own men. I could say that I resisted bravely but was overwhelmed. Dying here would serve no purpose. None.

Kwon made his choice. Keeping his eyes focused on Thaddeus, he lowered his weapon's muzzle, squatted slowly and laid the gun on the ground.

"Wise choice, Captain," Thaddeus said. Then to PFC Richards, "Pick up his gun." Then to PFC Fensch, "Put his hands behind his head."

"Will do, sir."

Thaddeus stepped toward the Chois and Kyong who was cowering in the presence of the round-eyed giants. "Don't be afraid," he smiled warmly. "We are Americans. You can go, return to your home." Motioning with his hands Thaddeus indicated that they were free to leave.

Kyong was beginning to weep, tears of relief dropping onto her baby's head. Mrs. Choi placed her left arm around Kyong's shoulders and squeezed.

Now it was Mr. Choi's mind that was functioning with unexpected speed and precision. He decided to speak his thoughts, knowing that the American couldn't understand his words but hoping that his tone of voice and gestures might communicate at least some of his thinking. "Do you know what you have here? With this man? A monster. He has murdered – I have seen him kill – and raped and has no remorse. None." Mr. Choi was sneering and his forefinger was pointing at Kwon.

"Quiet, you traitor," Kwon snapped.

"You call me a traitor. But who has been killing his fellow countrymen? Raping women? Given an opportunity you will do so again." Mr.Choi turned to face Thaddeus and used his hands to simulate firing a gun at an innocent – in this instance Kyong who winced. "What will you do with him? Question him? Imprison him? For how long? What if he escapes from you? Either way, one day he will be free, and his evil will be felt again. Perhaps by us." Pointing at Kyong – "Probably by her and her baby. That should not happen. Not in our culture. I do not know your culture, but I am thinking it would not be acceptable to free a killer."

Thaddeus' right thumb and forefinger rubbed his chin. He looked at Mr. Choi and nodded.

PFC Brown spoke. "Sir, I think I get the gist of what he's saying."

"So do I. But it would be an atrocity to execute a POW. And that's what this man is. He probably has done some terrible things, but he is a POW and we will treat him accordingly." Thaddeus faced Mr. Choi. "I am sorry. We will take him with us. Perhaps after the war there will be justice." A slim possibility, Thaddeus was thinking. He shrugged. "We have to hide during the daylight, but by tonight we will have him on Polska. From there he will be moved to a POW camp."

Thaddeus thought of one more cultural gap to bridge. He stepped closer to Mr. Choi and bowed. Mr. Choi bowed in return. Thaddeus then extended his right hand and, after hesitating, Mr. Choi accepted it. They shook hands solemnly. Thaddeus nodded to Mrs. Choi and Kyong and then turned away. He motioned to his men to follow with Kwon.

Mr. Choi watched for several moments as the Marines began moving away, then stepped toward the last Marine, PFC Fensch. Mr.Choi reached out and touched Fensch's bayonet scabbard. With his eyes and right hand he conveyed his request. Mr. Choi held up his right forefinger, indicating he wanted only to borrow, not keep, the bayonet.

Puzzled, Fensch removed the bayonet from its scabbard hanging from his webbed belt and handed it clip first to Mr. Choi who bowed in gratitude. He then went striding toward the departing patrol, moving past three Americans. When he was beside Kwon, Mr. Choi tapped him on the left shoulder. Kwon stopped. He looked utterly smug. Mr. Choi's eyes locked on Kwon's. Without altering his expression or averting his gaze, Mr.Choi brought his right arm, a limb made powerful by years of butchering and carving, forward and up. Kwon screamed. The long blade had penetrated just above his navel. Kwon's eyes blazed hatred, then faded to doubt and shock. Reflexively, searching for the source of his agony, Kwon's hands closed on Mr. Choi's right hand, still gripping the bayonet and bleeding where the blade was creasing his palm. Mr. Choi, not blinking, thrust upward again and Kwon slumped, moaning.

The others – Thaddeus and his men, Mrs. Choi and Kyong – looked on, stupefied for long seconds.

Mr. Choi then jerked the bloody bayonet free and with his left arm shoved Kwon who stumbled backward to a sitting position.

"You traitorous peasant," Kwon mumbled, groaning. Then slowly, Kwon toppled.

Mr. Choi stooped and deliberately wiped the blade on Kwon's pants. Once, twice, a third time until it was clean. Then he stood, his palm dripping blood, and returned the bayonet to PFC Fensch.

Stupefaction among the observers now was giving way to a range of other emotions.

"I'm sorry, sir," said Fensch. "I – should we arrest him?"

Thaddeus sighed heavily. Mr. Choi was standing expressionlessly. Mrs. Choi and Kyong both were holding their breaths. Thaddeus was recalling the first death he had witnessed – a German infantryman he had lanced on the morning Hitler's blitzkrieg smashed into Poland. Mr. Choi looked more tired than proud or satisfied. "Fensch, I think we have witnessed justice administered. Not our way but justice. Let him be." Again, Thaddeus bowed to Mr. Choi who solemnly reciprocated.

"Let's go," said Thaddeus.

There would be no burial for Kwon.

CHAPTER 71

"You are a man of many surprises."

"Is that faint praise?" Jack asked, eyes twinkling merrily.

"Hah! You once told me it would not hurt for earthly eyes to be watching over me," Thaddeus grinned, eyes narrowing. "But I did not expect the earthly eyes to descend from the sky."

"Well," Jack said, poker-faced, "the first time I flew to your men it was in a plane. You were with me. I thought it was high time to fly to them in a helicopter."

Thaddeus laughed. "Tell me, Captain Jack Brecker, how did you find your maiden helicopter flight?"

"A night flight to your little island has little to recommend it," Jack observed dryly. "Black heavens above, black waters below. Thank the Lord for an experienced pilot, not to mention your flashing light."

"We do much of our work at night, you know," Thaddeus smiled. "It's certainly the safest time for us devil dogs to land and take off in choppers. That is what we have taken to calling ourselves – devil dogs."

Jack grinned. "If God has a sense of humor, you have no doubt given him frequent reasons to chuckle."

Two days before, Jack had radioed Thaddeus, suggesting a rendezvous on Polska.

"What brings you here now?"

"Let me answer with a question."

"Please do."

"How long has it been since you've heard Mass?"

"Too long."

"Thought so. It's too late for Easter" – Jack was alluding to the Easter Mass he had said for the Polish Airborne Brigade in 1944 – "but the circumstances don't seem all that different."

Thaddeus nodded. "Yes, I am still jumping, just out of choppers. And into water instead of on the ground."

"Precisely. Besides, I needed someone to share my goodies with – scotch – Johnnie Walker Black Label of course – and White Owls."

"A care package from home?"

"From my parents."

"Bless them."

"They sent enough for us and your men."

"You're a good man, Captain Jack Brecker."

"As are you, Captain Thaddeus Metz."

"The desert priest and the Polish lancer. No desert here and no horses. But bonds that keep getting stronger."

"May they be forever strong and blessed by our Lord."

"Before we sip and smoke with my men, would you honor us with a Mass?"

"Of course. After celebrating Mass, we can celebrate with these treats." Jack didn't have his large missal or wine and water cruets, but he would, as chaplains often did, make do.

"All my men aren't Catholic."

Jack shrugged. "I'll conduct a service that I hope will be meaningful for all."

"They will be delighted – and privileged." Thaddeus cleared his throat. "You see, I have told them a few things about the desert priest. The warrior priest."

"Oh no," Jack groaned in mock distress. "Let's hope I don't disappoint them."

✝✝✝

The next morning the eastern sun's first rays were ricocheting off the Yellow Sea onto Polska. Inside Thaddeus' tent Jack heard his friend stirring and looked back over his shoulder. "I'm sorry. I didn't mean to disturb you." Jack had been kneeling on his sleeping bag, murmuring a devotional.

"You didn't. Good morning." Thaddeus yawned and stretched.

"Good morning."

Thaddeus looked at his watch. "I am usually up earlier. The scotch-"

"Sir," said Thaddeus' radioman, announcing his presence outside the tent and an instant later pulling back the flap. "Sabre down. We just got word. Pilot in the water close to shore. We've called a chopper."

"Thank you, Corporal."

"Since I no longer have General – or your friend the elder to ride with – riding a chopper is the next best mount. We fly low and I have the wind in my face."

"I'm going with you."

Thaddeus' eyes narrowed dubiously. "I have heard you say that before. 1944. Still not a good idea."

"Oh? I thought you might want my eyes watching out for you in the air – like on land. And, of course, the Sikorsky is a four-seater."

"Clever, but not clever enough."

"Hold on, Thaddeus. During Market Garden you told me that crossing the Rhine with your men wasn't a good idea because I didn't speak Polish. That doesn't seem an impediment here."

✝✝✝

In Ajo Bernadeta was nursing Tosia Marie and reading Thaddeus' latest letter:

> *My Dearest Bernadeta,*
> *When I write to you, I try to imagine what you are doing. I look at the picture of you and Tosia Marie. It makes me feel closer.*
> *We are actually quite comfortable here on Polska. It is a cozy little island. We are well supplied. And, yes, I am careful. No unnecessary chances.*
> *My men are the best. You would like them. They are the equal of Marek, Henryk, Jerzy and the other cow pen soldiers. I would like to see them again. After I return, perhaps we can plan a visit to Poland and show off our beautiful daughter. And Mrs. Ostrowski, she would gush over our little girl. Your father needs to see his granddaughter, and your sister her niece.*
> *Why don't you write letters to everyone? Tell them our intention. Tell them it will be a high priority – our highest – when I return.*
> *I love you, Bernadeta. We have come so far together. From those first moments in 1939. A dozen years. My love for you grows stronger each day.*
> *Kiss our daughter for me.*
> *Love,*
> *Thaddeus*
>
> *P.S. Jack Brecker is coming to visit me here on Polska the day after tomorrow. It will be good to see him.*

✝✝✝

Kyong was nursing Ahn Min Han at the Choi's. She had no letter to write. She still didn't know Min's whereabouts – or whether he was alive. She hadn't seen his picture in *Stars & Stripes* nor had anyone else in Munsan or Kaesong. At that time in or near those cities, there were no U.S. troops to be discarding copies of the newspaper. Kyong could only hope – and there were days when hope proved elusive. She longed to show her son to her mother in Kaesong – just 18 miles north of Munsan – but a visit was out of the question. Trying to get through lines of rapacious North Korean and Chinese soldiers would invite the kind of disaster she twice had narrowly averted. She was thankful beyond words to the American captain for rescuing her and her baby from certain death. And to Choi Chun Kuen for freeing her from Captain Kwon's menace.

✝✝✝

"Come on, Marilyn," Theresa smiled. "Let's go for a walk. It's a lovely afternoon. A stroll by the Thames would be just the ticket. Or I wonder if Mr. Turner could rig a basket so I could take you on a bike ride? Wouldn't that be special? You'd love it. I'll ask him."

"Okay, Mama. I go get my baby." The little four-year-old went running for her favorite doll, a 15-inch tall cherry-cheeked moppet topped with blonde hair.

Theresa followed her daughter into the bedroom where she saw the small brass cross Jack Brecker had given her in 1946 hanging on a wall. Five years ago. So much had happened, Theresa reflected, and yet the years seemingly had flown by faster than one of those Sabre jets she was reading about in *The Daily Telegraph*. To her surprise, her throat began thickening. Her head shook. This is no time for tears, Theresa scolded herself half-heartedly. Marilyn didn't need to hear her crying over something the little tot couldn't see or understand. She walked across the room, removed the cross and caressed it.

"Is the cross going with us, Mama?"

Theresa pondered. "You know, Marilyn, I think that's a good idea. We'll both have something to hold."

✝✝✝

The gray-maned elder was standing near his home on the Tohono Reservation. The cloudless evening sky still was ablaze with sunshine, and a gentle breeze was stirring the dry desert air. A good time for a ride, he thought, and went walking to the small shed where he stabled his horse. "Wake up, my old friend. You have had your siesta. Now it is time for your aging back to carry your aging master."

The elder tossed a red wool blanket trimmed in blue on the animal and positioned and cinched the saddle, then the bridle. "And to think in my youth I rode bareback. That was in another lifetime – before yours." He led the horse outside. "You have been a reliable companion. A friend. For twenty years now, I think."

With an agility and grace that belied his age, the elder swung up and onto the saddle. He gently patted his horse's neck. "This is an evening for thinking about friends – old ones and new ones. Yes, I am thinking about Father Brecker and Thaddeus Metz. I think in Korea the sun has barely begun its daily journey. May it shine brightly and show them the way to safety."

✝✝✝

"Whee! Isn't this fun?"

"Make the bike go faster, Mama." Marilyn was beaming, the breeze blowing in her face. She was holding her doll against her chest.

Delightedly, Ronald Turner had affixed a deep basket in front of the handlebars on a sturdy blue bicycle. Now, Theresa was peddling west on Birdcage Walk toward Buckingham Palace.

"Oh, I think this is fast enough, darling. We wouldn't want to bump into any of these people walking. No accidents needed today."

✝✝✝

With the school year ended, Tom and Bridgett Brecker's twins, now 7, were outside playing. Dusk was beginning to settle in, but little Jack still was playing catch in the front yard of their Mansfield Avenue home with his nextdoor neighbor, Billy Alston. Little Theresa and three of her friends were using a stick of white chalk to draw hopscotch squares on the sidewalk. Twisted on the grass beside the sidewalk was a jump rope. Bridgett was watching, smiling and recalling fondly her own childhood summer pursuits. In just a little while, when falling darkness had crushed dusk, all the neighborhood kids would be joining together for a spirited game of hide-and-seek. Squeals and shouts would fill the neighborhood – and parents would regard them as sounds of security. They knew their children were nearby, that they were having fun and that they were safe from life's ambiguities and dangers.

Then inspiration struck Bridgett. She walked outside and toward the girls. "Can I play too?"

Moments later she was hopscotching giddily, and the girls were giggling their wonderment and delight. *If only Tom could see me now,* she reflected. *Too bad he's presiding over a City Council meeting. The mayor's wife trying to recapture a slice of her girlhood. What a hoot! Too bad there isn't a* Daily Globe *photographer here to get a picture for the paper. And Theresa and Jack, wouldn't it be cool if we all were able to hopscotch together again? Or go dancing? Where have the years gone?*

✝✝✝

How many people can say they have no regrets? Not many. Hasn't everyone made at least one or two choices they would like to change? Tomasz Dolata was watching Marzena read to their five-year-old son. She was pregnant. If the baby was a boy, he would be named Kazimir. If a girl, Maria. That was settled to their mutual satisfaction. *I have heard people say they have no regrets,* Tomasz was musing. *They are in denial. Or they are thinking shallowly – no deeper than a puddle after a summer shower. How many people are given a chance for redemption? A second chance. If that chance is given and taken, does it erase the first choice and its consequences? Not in my case. I have tried to atone for my bad choices, my terrible transgressions. But they will stain my soul forever. Marzena, she forgave me years ago. Actually, she never condemned me. She wants to believe I have forgiven myself and I let her believe that. But deep down, I think she knows better. We just don't talk about it anymore. When I draw my last breath, I will die a lucky man. Terribly flawed but oh so lucky. Do I deserve that? I want to say yes. But I don't know. I just don't know.*

✝✝✝

Thaddeus was seated next to the chopper pilot. Jack, life-jacketed, was sitting behind them. Briefly, he fingered the Saint Christopher medal that Theresa Hassler Morton had given him back in 1932. It always gave him peace of mind to know it was there. The pilot pointed downward, waggling his left forefinger.

Thaddeus nodded, then swiveled his neck. "We have found him," he shouted to Jack over the helicopter's roar. "Down there," – and he pointed.

391

"Your radioman was right," Jack observed, "he's not very far from shore."

"When our pilots are hit over land, they try to get to the sea. This one barely made it. Lucky man."

Jack nodded. "Be careful." Thaddeus shrugged and wrinkled his brow dubiously and, yes, Jack thought, those are among the most witless words I've spoken in a while. "Good luck," he added, his embarrassment obvious.

Thaddeus nodded and patted Jack's left shoulder.

The helicopter pilot lowered his craft and maneuvered it over the downed jet pilot. Captain Roger Burgher saw the metallic angel and tossed up a smiling wave of relief.

Thaddeus positioned himself at the side opening, checked his equipment and jumped. He splashed close to Burgher and began swimming toward him. Then he saw Burgher, alarmed, urgently pointing up toward the chopper. Jack was crouched in the side opening. Over the din of the chopper's engine and whirling rotor, Thaddeus could hear faintly and see the evidence of what was unnerving Burgher. Enemy ground fire from the mainland, less than a half-mile distant, was pinging the helicopter's fuselage, denting and holing the metal skin.

Thaddeus reacted instantly. His training and experience kicked in. Vigorously he motioned to his pilot to ascend and back away. Better to risk two lives – his and Burgher's – than four plus a helicopter. Burgher understood and so indicated with a confirming wave. The helicopter began climbing and retreating.

"I'll stay with you," Thaddeus shouted to Burgher.

In the next sliver of time, Thaddeus twisted in the water to look up again at the departing chopper. Jack was looking down, waving. Then he saw Jack's right hand grab at his midsection and his left reach out for the side opening's frame. Thaddeus felt a shiver of dread; he could see red seeping between the fingers of Jack's right hand. He teetered backward and then slumped forward. His left hand lost its grip and Jack, now bent double, went plunging into the sea.

"Jack!" Thaddeus cried out.

CHAPTER 72

July 4, 1951, Shelby, Ohio.

10 a.m.

Theresa and Marilyn were among hundreds gathered in Most Pure Heart of Mary church for the memorial service. The morning was sultry, holding out little hope for a reprieve from scorching heat and strangling humidity. Presiding were Bishop Wilhelm Metzger who had flown from Tucson and Father Michael McFadden who years before had arranged for Jack Brecker's transfer from St. Joseph's Seminary in Vincennes, Indiana to the Josephinum in Worthington, Ohio. Father McFadden also had been present in Shelby when Jack said his first Solemn High Mass after his ordination. Marilyn was holding her doll, and Theresa was clutching the small brass cross. This time she didn't try to hide tears from her daughter. And Marilyn understood, not the depth of her mother's affection for Jack Brecker, but death and what it meant.

Dabbing at her reddened eyes with a tissue, Theresa found herself reflecting: Jack, I hope they left that Saint Christopher medal on you. I'd like to think you still were wearing it for the final journey.

He was.

✝✝✝

Simultaneously in Charco, the elder was conducting a memorial service for Jack's legion of Indian admirers on the Tohono – and Bernadeta Gudek Metz. The elder thought she would want to be there, even though her husband still was in Korea. Also present were Elgin and Walt Hunter and their family.

The service was not being held in the reservation's chapel. It was not nearly spacious enough to hold all the people who wanted to attend. The elder had made a decision. The service would be held at the base of the ridge where Jack and the elder liked to meet to smoke cigarettes and sip coffee. The elder was using the ridge as his pulpit, standing high enough on it to be seen and heard by his people. He was holding the letter, describing how Jack had died, that Thaddeus had sent to Bernadeta.

"You have been a good and loyal friend," the elder began – and wondered for a moment whether he possessed the strength to continue. He breathed as deeply as his aging lungs would allow. "You always looked out for others. Is there anyone here today who can be surprised that you died on a rescue mission? You were new here, did not know us, and yet you protected our sheep from the mountain lion. You said Christmas morning Mass for us. I drank your coffee and you smoked my cigarettes. We had many good talks. We laughed. You took me into the heavens so I could see God's scar, his perfect scar. We can do all those things again, Father Jack Brecker, in the next life. More than ten years ago we christened you the desert priest. I know we can count on you to keep watching our flocks – our sheep and our people.

Epilogue 1

Erwin Kressler had been living a life of ambiguity in Buenos Aires. As the Third Reich was crumbling in early 1945, he had made his way from Auschwitz north to Gdansk, Poland's major Baltic Sea port. From there, disguised with mustache and glasses and bearing forged documents, he had shipped out for Argentina. There he had prospered, becoming a wine exporter.

Seldom, though, did he enjoy a night of sleep uninterrupted. Nocturnal images of Aline Gartner regularly invaded his dreams. Aline. Working in the I.G. Farben plant. Thinning from malnutrition. Protecting her girls. Smuggling black powder and lengths of fuses. Surrendering to him in the plant's washroom for guards. Walking with dignity to the gallows. Shouting her last words of warning to Nazis. In a way, Kressler knew, Aline Gartner still lived. She would live as long as he, and perhaps longer. Certainly she deserved to.

On an August afternoon in 1951 Kressler left his office. Arriving at home, he slowly descended the steps to his wine cellar. There is but one appropriate way, he was thinking. He unknotted his solid blue necktie. Then he picked up a stool and positioned it beneath an overhead water pipe. Standing on the stool, he looped one end of the tie around the pipe and knotted it. Hard. Will it be long enough? he wondered. Then he cinched the tie's other end around his neck. She could never forgive me, Kressler was certain. That would be asking too much of any woman. If only I had her resolve, her courage, her serenity.

Kressler kicked the stool from under his feet.

EPILOGUE 2

The October 1951 night sky over little Polska and the surrounding sea was inky black. Thaddeus was sitting on a gray rock near his small tent. He was puffing on a White Owl. Jack is gone, he was reflecting sadly, but I can try to keep his spirit alive by doing what he did best – helping others.

Thaddeus was remembering what Jack had told him about the reunion between Lucy Crispin and Michael Cornelius at the Indian Parachute Field Ambulance hospital as well as the tragic story of the Korean soldier who had suffered so much and had been separated from his bride-to-be. Before finishing the cigar, Thaddeus made a decision. First he wangled a helicopter ride to the hospital unit. After questioning staff, he asked for a jeep ride to Munsan. Request granted. Once there he found Ahn Kyong Ae and little Ahn Min Han with the Chois. He also learned about Sejong. In short order Thaddeus was swinging onto the saddle and riding south. He was feeling better than at any moment since Jack's death and sensed – accurately – that Sejong was happy to be carrying an experienced rider on the open road. The mount seemed to be straining to run faster than Thaddeus was asking.

Late in the afternoon Thaddeus and Sejong arrived at the gate to Yongsan Compound, just east of Seoul and headquarters for United Nations forces. There he found personnel records for Korean troops in disarray. But word spread quickly through the compound about the mounted Polish marine and his mission, and soon Thaddeus and Sejong were riding south toward Suwon.

Nearing the ancient walled town Thaddeus and Sejong heard a whoop that commingled disbelief and joy. In reply Sejong threw his head up and back. Park Min came running to the horse that he first had exercised for Colonel Fukunaga.

EPILOGUE 3

Thaddeus returned from Korea to Ajo in June 1952. In 1953, soon after Joseph Stalin's death on March 5, Thaddeus and Bernadeta and little Tosia Marie were on their way to Poland. The U.S. State Department, at Bernadeta's request, endorsed by Congresswoman Jane Morton, had issued fresh diplomatic passports, assuring safe travels for the family.

The reunion was held on the family farm near Zyrardow. Attending were Jszef, Barbara, Kaz, their son Thaddeus, Danuta Ostrowski and cow pen soldiers Marek Krawczyk, Henryk Wyzynski and Jerzy Pinkowski. Marek and Jerzy were married now, and their wives accompanied them.

Barbara, Bernadeta and Mrs. Ostrowski prepared a lavish dinner that included farm-fresh sausages and magnificent breads.

Afterward, while all still were squeezed shoulder-to-shoulder around the crowded kitchen table, Thaddeus said, "We should do something for Jack Brecker."

"Yes," Marek concurred gravely, "we must never forget the American chaplain who said Easter Mass for us Poles. It is only fitting that we have a Mass said for him – our warrior priest."

All voiced their support for Marek's idea.

"But I think we should do more," Thaddeus said pensively. "Something permanent."

"A plaque perhaps?" Henryk said.

"Yes," said Thaddeus, "a commemorative plaque."

"Where to put it?" Bernadeta asked. "Not inWarsaw. The communist government would not allow it. Even if we put it up secretly, the authorities would learn of it and destroy it."

"At the American embassy," Jerzy suggested.

"It should be public," Marek said.

"Steps," Thaddeus said. "Perhaps we should do this in steps. First, choose the words on the plaque. Then get it made."

"I can arrange that," Marek said. "No problem," he grinned and all laughed.

"Good," said Thaddeus. "Then we can mount it here at the farm. On the barn wall. Later, after Poland has regained her freedom – and she will regain her freedom – we can proudly display the plaque in Warsaw."

"At St. Ann's," Bernadeta said excitedly. "It survived the war, and I think Father Brecker would approve."

"Bravo!" cried Marek. "Perfect!"

"Now for the words," Thaddeus said.

"You should craft them," Kaz said. "You met him first and knew him best."

"He would want it simple," Thaddeus observed. "I think he would like to be remembered but not with great fuss. Do we have paper and a pencil?"

Barbara rose, eased away from the table and returned in moments with a lined pad and knife-sharpened blue pencil.

Thaddeus positioned the pencil, then closed his eyes. The kitchen was quiet and expectant. Then Thaddeus wrote these words: *Father Jack Brecker, U.S. Army chaplain and captain, man of honor, forever loyal to his friends. 1917-1951.*

EPILOGUE 4

"This is where we tried to rescue the whales," Lucy Crispin said, pointing toward the foaming surf. "I can still see their eyes. Forlorn. That was the mother's look. Her calf was frightened. Just like a child in strange surroundings. Not able to understand."

It was August 1953, north of Wellington. Lucy was standing, in nurse's whites, on the damp, packed sand.

"You were meant to be a nurse," Michael Cornelius observed. He was wearing brown corduroys and a green wool pullover sweater. "That's never been clearer, not even at the Indian hospital."

"How did you track me down?"

"I didn't. Not really. I just took a chance that you would be here."

"So you journeyed from Korea home to England and then to New Zealand."

"No choice, if you'll recall, Nurse Crispin. My wound was my ticket back to Mother England."

"And," Lucy teased gently, "you just couldn't get the nurse with an arm and a half out of your mind."

"Not for a second."

EPILOGUE 5

Tomasz Dolata continued prospering. After the war, with funds borrowed from Dime Bank in Manhattan, he founded a microbrewery near Huntington on Long Island. He branded his beer Polska, and the robust brew quickly won a following throughout New York and New England.

In 1958 he and Marzena and sons Tomasz Michal and Kazimir moved from their Manhattan apartment to Montauk, near the eastern tip of Long Island. Tomasz still suffered occasional nightmares from his years at Auschwitz and hoped that the sea air would help ease his torment. It did. But neither ocean breezes nor passing time entirely erased the stain on his soul. Not to his satisfaction.

EPILOGUE 6

Edward Frantek, the lanky 15-year-old from 1944, gradually took over management at Polska Kopernika at his parents' urging. By age 25 he was married and the father of a daughter and son. He proved to be an able, energetic restaurant manager.

By 1959 – Jacek then was 55 and Maria 54 – Edward had decided to take on a second job. He would dedicate his remaining years to helping Poland win back its freedom from Soviet-mandated repression. Edward, a clear-minded and clear-eyed man, had clear goals: he wanted to be able to vote in free elections untainted by fraud, and he wanted to practice his religion openly. He had never forgotten Michal Olenik and Tomasz Dolata and their sacrifices, and he wanted the same freedom for Jews, the few who had returned to Cracow and the remnants of once-vibrant Jewish communities elsewhere in Poland.

Edward wasn't at all certain how many years would be needed to achieve his goals, nor was he sure what sacrifices might be required. But as he told Jacek and Maria, he would begin searching out like-minded individuals and start down the road toward liberty.

EPILOGUE 7

On Christmas Eve in 1961 on the Tohono Reservation, the elder leaned against the front fender of his aging pickup truck. It rattles and wheezes, he mused, just like me. The elder was wearing brown boots, blue jeans, a blue flannel shirt, beige sheepskin jacket with wool lining and thick leather gloves. He poured coffee from a thermos into the metal top that served as mug. Then he lit a Camel. He drew deeply and held the smoke in his lungs for long seconds before exhaling. He shivered and began sipping coffee. Then he looked up at the star-sprinkled sky and let his mind drift back through time. I have my aches and pains, especially in my chest. And my eyes are dimming, Jack Brecker. The points on the stars are blurry. But my hair, I still have all of it. And I am letting it grow longer. Almost to my waist. Like so many young people. Red and white. What do they call them? Hippies? The ancient hippie, that's me. The elder laughed and shivered again.

You have been gone for ten years, Jack Brecker. You were a good man, the best white man I ever knew. You could have been one of us. In many ways you were.

The next morning, the elder died. He was 74.

EPILOGUE 8

Today in 2008 the plaque that Thaddeus designed to honor the memory of Jack Brecker resides in the vestibule of St. Ann's on Krakowskie Przedmiescie Street in Warsaw, completely rebuilt and prospering. Every Sunday an aged Marek Krawczyk, face etched deeply but back still unbent, shoulders still square, pauses before the plaque and smiles. Then he salutes smartly. The words are shown in both Polish and English. Father Jack Brecker, he muses, you were born in America and you are buried in America, but I still can feel your spirit with us in Polska.

ACKNOWLEDGEMENTS

Marzena Witek was born in 1977 and lives in Bedzin, a village near the southern Polish city of Katowice. She helped with research on my first book, *Warrior Priest*. At the time, she said she would gladly help with a future book. As I was mapping out *God's Perfect Scar*, I asked if she would serve as guide/interpreter while I visited certain areas of Warsaw, specifically Old Town, the University of Warsaw, and the neighborhoods where the U.S. established its first embassy two months after V-E Day and where Thaddeus Metz and Bernadeta Gudek took an apartment after their marriage. Before my arrival, Marzena already had done thorough research. Then over two days, the first in a steady, wind-driven rain, we walked the city. I took notes and photos, with Marzena holding an umbrella over me and my camera. While we were scouting the university campus, she spotted a sign indicating that a building was home to the department of history. In we went. We learned that the building was one that had survived the Nazi's systematic dynamiting of 85% of Warsaw after the 1944 Uprising. While there we also learned that the university has a museum dedicated to the school's history. That led to more discoveries. To say that Marzena's work added to the book's authenticity qualifies as a sizable understatement, and I will be ever grateful.

Peter Bloomfield and I met in 1979, and friendship took root quickly. Born and raised in London and now living near Petworth, a village of 3,000 about a 90-minute drive south of the city, he provided immense assistance as I was researching *Warrior Priest*. As *God's Perfect Scar* was taking shape, I decided to use the Royal Military Academy at Sandhurst as a locale. After reading its history and viewing photos online, I queried Peter about life as a cadet - which he was in the early 1950s. He answered all my questions – and then offered to arrange a visit for me. On arriving at Peter's home on December 5, 2007, he showed me a terrific collection of black-and-white photos taken during his cadet days. One shows him in midair, leaping from a high horizontal beam in the "confidence area" – the equivalent of the U.S. Army's obstacle course. The next afternoon, we arrived at the academy's main gate, there greeted by **Captain Louisa Clarke** who graciously led us on a wonderful tour of the grounds and several buildings, including the marvelous chapel where a Sandhurst chaplain happened to be speaking with prospective cadets. His uniform name patch read simply "Padre." He generously spent time with us, answering many questions. Afterward, with our visitors' badges clipped to our raincoats, Captain Clarke turned us loose on campus. Peter then took me into the library and gymnasium and pointed out the dormitory – Victory College – where he had roomed. By the time we departed, darkness had descended. But the visit had shone delightful light on this deservedly renowned institution.

While serving in the Army in Korea in 1968-69, I passed through Kimpo Airport several times. By today's standards, it was a primitive facility. Subsequently, on return visits to Korea, I arrived at and departed from an ever expanding and more modern Kimpo. As I began working on *God's Perfect Scar*, knowing that Korea and Kimpo would figure in the book, I wanted a clearer image of what Kimpo looked like in its earlier incarnation. For help I turned to **Ken Berger** of Mansfield, Ohio. Ken and I first met as American Legion baseball teammates in Shelby, Ohio in 1960. We played two seasons together before Ken, two years my senior, graduated from Ontario High School and matriculated at Miami University in Oxford, Ohio.

We lost touch. Then 45 years later in May 2006, I was doing a book signing in Ashland, Ohio. As I finished inscribing a copy of *Warrior Priest* for a customer, I looked up and – bingo! – there stood Ken, silver-haired but otherwise youthful and holding a copy of *Warrior Priest*. The passing years notwithstanding, I recognized him immediately. During the ensuing conversation, I learned that, after graduating from Miami, Ken had served in the Air Force in Korea for 13 months in 1966-67 – at Kimpo. In July 2007 I emailed Ken, asking if he had any photos from his time at Kimpo that I might borrow in the interest of adding to *God's Perfect Scar's* historical authenticity. A week later, my mail included a treasure – a package containing two picture books. One consisted of photos taken at Kimpo during Ken's tour of duty. The second shows images of the Joint Security Advance Camp on the southern fringe of the DMZ. The package also included a collection of snapshots, including one of Ken playing softball in Korea. The caption on the reverse of that photo reads: "Berger going 'deep' – just like at Shelby Legion Field."

When I needed details on a 1939 Chevrolet, I phoned longtime friend and former business colleague **Bob Leibensperger** who is a car enthusiast and collector in Canton, Ohio. In a next-day response, Bob emailed a sheet from the Lester-Steele Handbook of Automotive Specifications (1915-1942 – First Edition) that included the purchase price, weight and wheelbase for all versions of the 1939 Chevy. In addition to cars, Bob has an extensive collection of toy trains. He also is active in his community, in particular supporting charitable causes.

Annette Offenberger is a New Zealander and was one of my classmates at Stanford. In structuring *God's Perfect Scar*, I emailed Annette, asking whether she could provide the name and street location of a Wellington hospital that existed in the 1940s. Within 24 hours, she emailed the information – along with helpful commentary.

Jocelyn Armstrong McAuley, Nick Johantgen and **Pat Shedenhelm Papenbrock** provided insight on how polio could affect arms and hands. Jocelyn is a registered nurse who lives in Shelby, Ohio. Nick lives in Portland, Oregon, and his late father was an internist with a specialty in cardiology whose left arm had been withered by Polio. Pat, who lives in Novelty, Ohio, is one of my high school classmates. She too is a registered nurse – her specialty was hospice care – and provided details on requisite nursing responsibilities and skills. Pat also recommended that I read *We Band of Angels* for more insight into nursing during wartime. As you can see in the list of this book's Sources, I accepted her recommendation which proved particularly insightful.

Dick Parrish lives in Shelby and has an impressive collection of military weaponry and memorabilia along with extensive knowledge of who used which weapons. He is my brother-in-law. I queried Dick as to guns Russians and Poles used during World War II, and he responded promptly with indepth information. For example, in discussing the Russian submachine gun, the PPsh, Dick observed: "That was one mean weapon. It held 71 rounds and fired at a rate of 800 rounds per minute! That's fast. By contrast, the British Sten gun fired 500 rpm, and our 'grease' gun fired 450 rpm."

My good friend **Laura Ramaschi** speaks Italian, French, Russian and English. She lives in a house built in 1513 with her husband Kristoff and son Frederic in the Alsacian village of Ribeauville. She helped with research for *Warrior Priest,* and for *God's Perfect Scar* provided the translation for the dialogue between the soccer-playing Roman boys and Jack Brecker. Laura, thorough woman that she is, provided both formal and informal versions of what I wanted the boys to be saying.

Bryan Neff, superintendent of schools in Shelby, Ohio, filled in the last remaining research gap by providing the name of the man who was superintendent back in 1945.

To **Lynne Haley Johnson**, my loving wife of 38 years, I owe another huge debt of gratitude. She provided magnificent support and assistance with both *Warrior Priest* and *Fate of the Warriors* that is co-dedicated to her. She encouraged me to proceed with developing *God's Perfect Scar*, reviewed and critiqued the outline, and proofed and prepared the manuscript for publication.

As *God's Perfect Scar* was nearing completion, I was considering the question of a book title. As with *Warrior Priest* and *Fate of the Warriors*, I decided to explore title possibilities with a diverse group of people who enjoy reading and whom I know to be thoughtful. They then became members of what I call an email focus group. Each member reviewed a synopsis of the book, sample chapters and candidate titles. They replied with thoughtful opinions, and I am very grateful for their thinking. They are: Toni Martinez Anspach, Shelby, Ohio; Dave Bowes, Keedysville, Maryland; Deb Broka Coulson, Weatherford, Texas; Jane Foreman, Charlotte, North Carolina; David Funk, Ithaca, New York; Nancy Gravatt, Washington, D.C.; Francesca Femia Hahn, Marlton, New Jersey; Julia Vots Hatfield, Douglasville, Georgia; Bill Henson, Tucson, Arizona; Jim Hunt, Bay Village, Ohio; Jodi Hutchison, Madison, New Jersey; Trudy Cox Jacobs, Shelby, Ohio; Andrea Johnson, Columbus, Ohio; Helen Kalorides, Indianapolis, Indiana; Joachim Kramer, Saint Jean Troliman, France; Judy Misek, Solon, Ohio; Marie Kime Nelson, Moses Lake, Washington; Donna Noblick, Columbus, Ohio; Paul Pasternak, Coral Springs, Florida; Russ Pfahler, Sun Lakes, Arizona; Laura Ramaschi, Ribeauville, France; Jason Saragian, Perrysburg, Ohio; Alan Swank, Athens, Ohio; Carrie Thompson, Waynesville, Ohio; John Travers, Gaffney, South Carolina; Bob Tull, Lincolnton, North Carolina; Celia Turner, London, England; Carl Vandy, The Villages, Florida; Michele Yezzo, West Jefferson, Ohio; Miriam Yosick, Scottsdale, Arizona; Xiaoli Yuan, Taipei, Taiwan.

SOURCES

- The Coldest Winter. David Halberstam
- Facts about Korea. 1977. Korea Overseas Information Service
- A History of Poland. O.A. Halecki
- A History of Modern Poland. Hans Roes
- Interview with Tomascz (Tom) Wyszynksi – January 18, 2007
- The Kingdom of Auschwitz. Otto Friedrich
- Korea – Freedom's Frontier. United States Forces Public Affairs Office, 1967
- The Korean War. Michael Hickey
- Lester-Steele Handbook of Automotive Specifications (1915-1942 – First Edition)
- Marine Helicopters And The Korean War. Dissertation by Major Rodney Propst, USMC, 1989
- Marine Helicopters. Online photos and description by Jim Givens
- Online biography of Adam Mickiewicz
- Online biography of Vyacheslav Molotov
- Online biography of Syngman Rhee
- Online biography of Joseph Stalin
- Poland – The Threat to National Renewal – Richard Worth
- Poland: Eagle in the East. William Woods
- Poland in the 20th Century. M.K.Dziewanowski
- The Polish Officer. Alan Furst
- Poland's Politics: Idealism vs Realism. Adam Bromke
- Royal Military Academy at Sandhurst (visit)
- The Scariest Place in the World. James Brady
- The Secrets of Inchon. Commander Eugene Franklin Clark, USN
- The Story of Sandhurst. Online history
- The Twelve Little Cakes. Dominika Dery
- TIME magazine. February 16, 1948
- TIME magazine. January 8, 1951
- University of Warsaw (visit)
- U.S. Embassy in Warsaw, Poland
- We Band of Angels. Elizabeth M. Norman
- Whales, Dolphins And Man. Jacqueline Nayman
- World Book Encyclopedia

ROSTER OF REAL-LIFE PEOPLE

- Secretary of State Dean Acheson
- United Nations Ambassador Warren Austin
- Richard Baer
- Laurenti Beria
- Jakub Berman
- Ambassador Anthony Drexell Biddle
- Colonel Charles Bonesteel
- Brigadier Tom Brodie
- Bruno Brodniewicz
- Secretary of State James Byrne
- Chiang Kai Shek
- Winston Churchill
- General Lucius Clay
- Joseph Darrigo
- Eden Galinski
- Aline Gartner
- C.G. Keck
- Ambassador Stanton Griffis
- Rudolf Hoess
- Lieutenant Colonel Stanislaw Jachnik
- Josef Kramer
- Ambassador Arthur Bliss Lane
- General Curtis LeMay
- Arthur Liebehenschel
- General Douglas MacArthur
- Father Michael McFadden
- Mao Tse Tung
- Josef Mengele
- Hilary Mine
- Vyacheslav Molotov
- Judith Sternberg Newman
- Lieutenant Colonel A.G. Rangaraj
- Ernst Reuter
- Franklin Roosevelt
- Colonel Dean Rusk
- Lieutenant Colonel Brad Smith
- Brigadier General Joseph Smith

- General Stanislaw Sosabowski
- Joseph Stalin
- Dora Summer
- Kim Il Sung
- Harry S. Truman
- Andrey Vyshinksy
- Tadeusz Wiejowski
- Mala Zimetbaum

Printed in the United States
115952LV00006B/73-330/P